Suzanne Wright lives in England with her husband and two children. When she's not spending time with her family, she's writing, reading or doing her version of housework – sweeping the house with a look.

She's worked in a pharmaceutical company, at a Disney Store, at a primary school as a voluntary teaching assistant, at the RSPCA and has a First Class Honours degree in Psychology and Identity Studies.

As to her interests, she enjoys reading, writing, reading, writing (sort of eat, sleep, write, repeat), spending time with her family, movie nights with her sisters and playing with her two Bengal kittens.

To connect with Suzanne online:

Website: www.suzannewright.co.uk
Facebook: www.facebook.com/suzannewrightfanpage
Twitter: @suz_wright
Blog: www.suzannewrightsblog.blogspot.co.uk

THE DARK IN YOU SERIES

Burn
Blaze
Ashes
Embers

EMBERS

Suzanne Wright

piatkus

PIATKUS

First published in Great Britain in 2018 by Piatkus

3 5 7 9 10 8 6 4 2

A CIP catalogue record for this book
is available from the British Library.

ISBN 978-0-349-41629-8

Typeset in Goudy by Rules
Printed and bound in Great Britain by
Clays Ltd, Elcograf S.p.A.

Papers used by Piatkus are from well-managed forests
and other responsible sources.

Piatkus
An imprint of
Little, Brown Book Group
Carmelite House
50 Victoria Embankment
London EC4Y 0DZ

An Hachette UK Company
www.hachette.co.uk

www.littlebrown.co.uk

For the cake-making masters at the Hummingbird Bakery. Your Cookies and Cream cupcake helped me through writer's block—I'm not even kidding.

CHAPTER ONE

There was really nothing quite like having a stare-out with one of the most formidable beings in all existence. But as Harper's mate was also exceedingly powerful and she was used to this sort of thing, she wasn't quite as daunted as she probably should have been. "I'm not changing my mind, Lou."

The devil threw up his hands. "Why do you have to be so stubborn?"

"Why do you have to be so psychotic? You know what, don't answer that."

"You claim to love your son, yet you frequently expose him to one of the cruelest demons I've ever had the displeasure to come across."

Exasperated, Harper let her head fall back against the half-moon sofa. "My grandmother is not cruel. She is, however, an imp. So it baffles me that you expect her to do anything other than drive you insane. That's kind of what imps do."

Lou was easy to irritate because of his OCD streak. Simple

things like giving him an odd number of cookies, slicing his bread at an unsymmetrical angle, or adjusting the strings on his sleeveless hoodie so that one was longer than the other could send his blood pressure soaring—and Jolene Wallis did such things regularly.

To look at him in a ratty-assed Black Sabbath tee, washed-out jeans, a baseball cap, and old sneakers, no one would suspect he was so particular about, well, anything.

Despite that the mercurial male was the most antisocial being Harper had ever met, he loved spending time with her son, Asher. Then again, Lou was childlike in his own way—especially with his bratty sense of entitlement. Asher seemed to think of him as a playmate, which didn't say a lot for Lou's IQ really.

Looking down at Asher, who was sitting on the blue Persian rug playing with toy bricks, Harper had to smile. Honestly, the little sphinx was the most adorable thing *ever*. With his deep-set ebony eyes that were like dark velvet and his coal-black wisps of silky-smooth hair, he was essentially a mini version of Knox. The only features he seemed to have inherited from Harper were her long lashes and the reflective catlike quality to her eyes.

Demonic babies developed fast and were much stronger than human babies, so the six-month-old looked more like a ten-month-old. Asher could sit up, crawl, stand, say several words, and even walk if someone was holding his little hand.

As a rule, demons didn't need much sleep and could even go days without it. Thankfully, demonic babies slept as much as human babies or she'd be permanently on her feet and absolutely drained, because her boy was a handful. Obviously, as his mother, she was extremely biased and considered him to be the most perfect child that had ever graced the Earth. But he truly was bright and loveable. He had so many people wrapped around his little finger, it wasn't even funny. Seriously, one dimply smile and you were done for. He could win over anyone—even the devil himself.

"Come on, Harper," Lou whined, flinging himself on the sofa opposite hers. "Exposing the poor kid to Jolene borders on child abuse. Am I right, Tanner?" Lou asked her bodyguard, who was sprawled on the rug in his hellhound-form.

Large and fierce, the hound was heavily muscled with thick black fur. Not even the blood-red eyes or scent of burning brimstone could ruin its inherent majestic air. In response to Lou's question, it merely chuffed out an impatient breath.

"She's Asher's great-grandmother, Lou," said Harper. "She loves him, and he adores her right back."

Lou snorted. "Oh, *please*. Nobody 'adores' Jolene Wallis. Asher laughs *at* her, not *with* her."

Harper's inner demon rolled its eyes. The entity that lived within each demon was, to put it bluntly, a pitiless and somewhat psychopathic predator that possessed zero patience.

Rubbing her temple, Harper telepathically reached out to Knox and said, *Wish you were here.*

As Knox's mind brushed against hers, his psychic "taste" flooded her brain—almonds, red wine, and dark chocolate. *What's wrong, baby?* he asked in that rumbly, velvety voice that danced over her skin, making it prickle in sexual awareness.

One word—Lou. The vibe of male amusement that touched her mind wasn't unexpected. *How's the meeting going?*

So far, productive.

Roughly translated, he was getting his own way with his human associates. Knox blended in effortlessly with humans, hiding in plain sight just like the rest of their kind. The billionaire also owned a chain of restaurants, hotels, casinos, bars, and security firms.

Demons often held high positions that provided them with the power and control that they instinctively craved. CEOs, politicians, bankers, celebrities, lawyers, surgeons, journalists, police officers—the list went on.

Looks like the meeting will run late, he added, *so I'll have to meet you at Jolene's house in a few hours.*

You don't need to come; it's not like it's anyone's birthday. Imps didn't need an excuse to throw a party.

Nonetheless, I'll be there. On another note, how's your ass?

She almost flushed at the memory of him spanking it earlier as he'd fucked her from behind. *A little tingly.* Sensing his smugness, she felt her lips thin. *You shouldn't like the idea.*

I'm just remembering what a pretty shade of pink your ass turned.

To describe Knox as "highly sexual" would be an understatement. Dominant and demanding with psychic hands that could deliver phenomenal orgasms, he was a total rock star in the bedroom. He was also as sensually lethal as he was physically lethal.

"*You* go to the party," said Lou. "I'll babysit Asher."

Harper held up her finger. "Okay, first of all, you will *never* babysit Asher; we've gone over this before—"

"How can you not trust me with him?"

"Was that a trick question?"

"It's not like I'm stoned today or—" He jerked as flames engulfed his cap, which then abruptly disappeared. A millisecond later, fire erupted out of Asher's hand . . . and there was Lou's cap, completely intact.

Giggling, Asher dropped the hat and clapped his little hands as his mind touched hers, buzzing with mischief and pride. His giggle was the purest, infectious, heart-melting sound, and she couldn't help but laugh along with him.

Although she'd yet to see him pyroport like Knox, she'd often seen objects pyroport *to* Asher—mostly her knickknacks that lined the mantel of the fireplace. Since he was so young, the ability didn't always "answer" him. Plenty of times she'd seen him glaring at his hand, as if annoyed that it was empty.

Lou grinned at him. "Such a clever boy! Ah, did it bug you that I wasn't paying you any attention? You know your Uncle Lou is your biggest fan." Standing, Lou crossed to him. "Time to hand over the cap."

A shower of ashes, embers, and sparks surrounded Asher—a tough-as-shit shield he'd first raised when in her womb. He'd also released a blast of disabling energy whilst in her womb, but he hadn't done it again since being born.

Lou laughed. "Damn, Harper, I *totally* dig this kid." With a mock sigh of reprimand at Asher, he placed his hands on his hips. "Don't you smirk at me. I want that cap."

Inside the shield, Asher instead dumped a brick in the cap.

"It's not a toy, mister."

But Asher apparently thought differently, because he plopped another brick in it.

Lou tried pushing his hand through the shield. Sparks buzzed, hissed, and popped. Lou jerked back with a harsh curse, blowing on his blistered palm.

"Why do you do that every time?" Harper asked him, sighing. "You know you can't get through the shield." The only person she'd seen do it was Knox's demon when it was in its full, body-of-flames glory. There were far worse things in hell than Lucifer, including archdemons—cold and brutal creatures that were born from the flames. And, unknown to most, Knox just happened to be one.

"I'm trying to work out what it's made of," said Lou. "It's hard as steel and burns worse than hellfire. I've never come across anything like it." And that seemed to excite him.

"I thought you'd lose your fascination with Asher once you

saw that he isn't some soulless being that was born with the sole purpose of obliterating the universe."

"I never thought he'd be *soulless*."

"Pure evil, then."

"He may not be evil, but he could still decimate life as you know it. Don't give me that look, is it *my* fault you can't handle the truth? I think not." Lou grimaced as his cap returned to his head in a small spurt of fire ... which wouldn't have hurt him if the cap wasn't bulging with bricks. Lou emptied them onto the rug. "He might be a Thorne, but there's a lot of Wallis in him."

Lowering his shield, Asher clapped again. "Ma!"

Harper smiled. "I saw you, little man. Very good." He didn't call her Mama, as if too lazy to finish the word. Similarly, he called Knox "Da".

A familiar mind touched hers as a voice said, *I'm here. You ready?* It was Keenan, Asher's personal bodyguard who, like Tanner, was also one of Knox's sentinels.

We'll be two minutes, Harper told him. "Tanner, time to go. I just need to quickly pack Asher's bag." She headed into the kitchen to find Meg, the housekeeper, sticking a bottle of formula in Asher's bag.

Meg put the bag into Harper's hands. "Diapers, formula, wet wipes, his blanket—it's all there."

Honestly, Harper didn't know what she'd do without the woman. "Thanks, Meg, you're a star."

Meg flushed, pleased. "Have a good time at the party!"

"Will do," said Harper. Honestly, though, taking Asher off the estate always made her nervous. For the first four months of his life, they'd kept him there for his own protection. Awful as it was, there were people who would use him for their own ends. After all, anyone who had him in their possession could effectively control Knox, who'd do anything to keep his son safe.

And since Knox was believed to be the most powerful demon in existence and was also rumored to have the ability to call on the flames of hell, their kind feared him in a *major* way.

When Harper was heavily pregnant, a she-demon had kidnapped her with the intent of taking Asher, hence why the bitch had died an excruciating death. Nora was part of a group, the Four Horsemen, who wanted rid of Knox. They viewed him as an obstacle to their goal of causing the US Primes to fall. So far, three of the Horsemen had been eradicated, but the fourth was still out there. And no one seemed to know who it was.

Walking back into the living area, Harper saw Tanner in his human form, gently bopping Asher's nose with the plush hellhound he'd bought him—Asher took it everywhere, even to bed.

Just as Tanner handed him the soft toy, Harper took Asher into her arms. "We gotta go see Grams now. Say bye to Lou."

Dimples flashing, Asher waved at him. "Bye."

"Bye, little guy." Lou slipped on his jacket. "And good luck with Jolene. You're going to need it." In a blink, he was gone.

Letting Tanner carry the bag, she followed the broad shouldered, dark-haired male along the wide hallway, through the marble foyer, and then out into the warm air.

Keenan's tall, defined form was leaning against Tanner's Audi. The incubus flashed his boyish grin at Asher and said, "Hey, little mister." Asher babbled at him, making the incubus chuckle. "You got everything you need, Harper?"

"Yep, thanks to Meg." Once she'd strapped Asher into his car seat, she slid into the Audi. The tires crunched as Tanner then began a slow drive along the lengthy driveway.

At one time, Harper had been intimidated by the estate with its heavy metal gates, long manicured lawn, neatly-trimmed hedges, and the high-brick walls. Then there was the house itself. Well, "house" wasn't the right word. Not for such an expansive, magnificent piece of custom-built architecture. It was way ahead of its time and possessed the same allure and charm as its owner.

Before Knox, she'd lived in a dingy apartment in North Las Vegas. She'd never known this kind of luxury. Never thought she'd be able to feel that she "fit" amongst high vaulted ceilings, winding staircases, upscale furnishings, and walk-in cedar closets. But the estate had become her private little oasis.

Riding shotgun, Keenan glanced over his shoulder. "Is Knox meeting you at Jolene's house?"

"Yes. I don't think he's disappointed that he's running late. An afternoon with my family is never relaxing." Wild and rowdy, Wallis imps would test even a nun's patience, especially with their penchant for lying, stealing, and cheating, amongst many other things.

"It's a kids' tea party," said Keenan, facing forward. "How bad can it be?"

When they pulled up outside Jolene's house a short while later, "I Don't Fuck With You" by Big Sean filtered out of the open windows. The front of the house was virtually covered in balloons and paper lanterns. Yard cards were strewn across the lawn—some were clocks, some were tea pots, others were playing cards. All of them surrounded a huge cardboard cutout of the Mad Hatter.

As Harper carried Asher up the path and to the porch, he pointed at the decorations, oohing and awing. She rang the doorbell, rubbing her cheek against his plump, petal-soft one. His hands gently slapped her cheeks, squishing her face.

"Ow," she mumbled. He just giggled.

Just then, the door swung open. Jolene Wallis didn't look like a grandmother. Not with her chic blouse, sleek skirt, high heels, perfectly coiled hair, and veneer of sheer elegance. She also didn't look bat-shit crazy, but she *totally* was.

"Finally, you're here." Jolene stepped back and gestured for them to enter. "Harper, I've missed you." She gave her a one-armed hug. "And where's my little guy?" Jolene plucked Asher out of her arms. "Come to Grams. I love this little outfit you're rocking."

"You should, since you bought it," said Harper. Well, Jolene bought the jeans and checked shirt. The boots came from Raini, Harper's friend and business partner.

Jolene kissed his cheek. "Come see what's in the backyard."

Harper and the sentinels followed her down the hallway. Passing the living room, Harper peeked inside. Male imps were crowded on the couches, chairs, and floor, drinking beer and eating chips while watching a basketball game on TV. She was pretty sure the one curled around the beer keg, clinging to the funnel, had passed out. Typical.

She heard laughter, squealing, and the whir of an air compressor before she even stepped into the backyard, so the bouncy castle came as no surprise.

People waved and shouted out welcomes. Some sat on lawn furniture and floor pillows while others stood around the long patio table, filling paper plates with snack foods. A bunch of female relatives swarmed Jolene to fuss over Asher, who giggled at the kids that were jumping in the bouncy castle like demented kangaroos.

Frilly three-tiered cake stands sat on kid-sized tables among plastic teacups, saucers, and spoons. There were dozens upon dozens of cupcakes—all were covered in different colored swirly frosting topped with either edible sprinkles, pearls, glitter, flowers, or chocolate chips. Harper would nab a few when she got a chance.

Her aunt, Martina, left the outdoor bar and approached with a tray of Jell-O shots. "Drink, anyone? We also have iced tea, lemonade, mojitos, margaritas, and beer."

Keenan's brow furrowed. "This *is* a kids' tea party, right?"

"Uh-huh." Martina downed a shot like a pro. "No Knox?"

"He's meeting me here later," Harper told her. Hearing the snap of flip-flops, she looked to see Raini approaching. "Hey, how are you?"

"Good, thanks," replied the succubus, flicking her white-blonde, pink-streaked hair over her shoulder. "Ooh, I'll have one of those." Raini grabbed a neon-blue shot and chugged it down. Even in her casual clothing, she exuded sex with her wicked curves, flawless skin, and sharp amber eyes. "Where's my honorary nephew?"

"With Grams." Harper frowned when she saw Jolene coming toward them, empty handed. "Or, at least, I thought he was. Where's Asher, Grams?"

"On the bouncy castle. Khloë has him," Jolene replied.

Keenan's frown deepened. "*Khloë's* in there?" He sighed, adding dryly, "Well of course she is. Where else would she be?"

Yeah, Harper's cousin wasn't exactly the most mature person in the world, so it often surprised people that she was incredibly well-organized. It was that very quality that made Harper and Raini hire her as the receptionist at their tattoo studio in the Underground—a subterranean demonic paradise owned by Knox.

Chuckling, Harper watched as Khloë gently bounced Asher, who tried stomping his little feet on the inflatable castle.

Tanner's own chuckle cut off as he looked over Harper's shoulder and grinned, golden eyes lighting up. "Here kitty, kitty."

Devon, an apprentice at their studio, glared at the hellhound. "Eat shit, pooch."

Tanner put a hand to his chest. "Is that any way to speak to someone who bought you a present?"

Devon snarled. "If it's more cat litter, I'm going to punch you right in the muzzle." The hellcat turned to Harper. "Where's my gorgeous little dude?"

Harper snickered. "Well, hello to you, too. I'm great, thanks."

Devon rolled her eyes. "Look who I brought with me."

Harper felt her brows rise at the sight of the lean, tattooed male heading their way. "Drew. I had no idea you were in Vegas." It shouldn't have been awkward. She'd known him since they were kids, he was Devon's older brother, and Harper hadn't seen him in three years. Maybe if their last meeting hadn't ended in a drunken make-out session, she wouldn't have found herself fighting a blush.

Like his sister, he had cat-green eyes and dark ultraviolet hair. Whereas Devon's hair fell in ringlets down her back, his was short and tousled. He was indeed incredibly hot and had a powerful magnetic energy about him. Like most females of Jolene's lair, Harper once had a mad crush on Drew—he'd broken many hearts when he moved to Cuba six years ago, only paying their lair the occasional visit.

If there was one person she might have broken her no-dating-demons rule for back before Knox came into her life, it was Drew. But he'd shown no interest in her. As an adrenalin junkie who lived for finding the next high, he focused all his energy into his own life. Their make-out session had been nothing more than a farewell kiss that went too far. He'd returned to Cuba the next day, and she hadn't heard from him since.

"Only got here last night." Grinning, he pulled her into a hug. "It's good to see you."

As a menacing growl rumbled out of Tanner, Harper stepped back to see that both sentinels were glaring at Drew. She forced a smile. "Guys, this is Devon's brother, Drew." But the glaring continued. Not that it seemed to bother Drew. But then, he *lived* for the thrill of danger and wasn't easily intimidated.

Having gratefully accepted a beer from Jolene, Drew gestured at Harper with his bottle. "I heard you're mated," he said, tone strangely flat. "That was ... a surprise. And then I heard you're a mom, too. That was even more surprising."

"That's my little guy right there with Khloë."

Drew's mouth curled. "He's cute. Like his mom." Ignoring Tanner's growl, Drew asked, "What's it like to be a Prime? You always said you didn't want to be one."

That was true. It had never been her dream to rule a lair, but she'd become a co-Prime on mating with Knox. Running a lair that spanned most of Nevada and much of California was no easy thing, but ... "It's not as bad as I'd expected it would be, since I have Knox to share the burden."

"I'll bet the Primes are mortified that he claimed a Wallis."

"They've gone from 'mortified' to 'disapproving'. They've accepted I'm a permanent fixture, though. It's surprising what a difference it made that I've taken Knox's surname."

Drew's brows lifted and he swallowed. "You've taken his surname?"

"*And* she's wearing his rings," Keenan interrupted, still glaring at Drew. "One of which is a *black diamond*," he added meaningfully. As it was a sign of the ultimate commitment, demons only gave a black diamond to the person they intended to take permanently as their mate.

Drew gave her a wan smile. "Congratulations. But I gotta wonder what happened to your 'no-dating-demons' rule."

Harper shrugged. "I guess I broke it." A hard weight slammed into her leg. She looked down to see her younger cousin. "Hey, Heidi-ho." Harper stroked a hand over the little girl's bright blonde hair. "What you up to?"

"Helping Ciaran set up the dining room for the clown," she said.

"There's a clown?" Harper turned to see Ciaran, Khloë's twin, heading their way . . . with *the freakiest*-looking clown she'd ever seen in her life.

Raini gasped. "Oh, my God. He'll *terrify* the kids."

He skipped past them and planted himself in front of the bouncy castle. "Hey little people, ready for your magic show?"

"Yeah!" they shouted in delight. They then followed the creepy clown into the house like he was the damn Pied Piper.

Ciaran was at the back of the line with Asher in his arms, who was chewing his thumb. "I'll take him inside, so he can watch the show."

Tanner's brows drew together. "You don't find that clown even *the slightest* bit creepy?"

Ciaran blinked. "In what sense?"

Tanner shook his head. "Never mind."

Mouth twitching, Harper followed Ciaran into the house, who then headed into the dining room and sat on the floor with Asher between his legs. Standing just outside the doorway, Harper spoke quietly to Jolene. "About Heidi . . . Any news on who hired the demon to snatch her?" It had happened when Harper was pregnant, but they'd had no luck tracking the culprit.

Jolene's lips tightened. "No. If anyone knows anything, they're not talking."

"Devon told me what happened," began Drew, face sober. "Do you think the person behind it will send someone else after Heidi?"

"I'd like to think that if that was their intention, they would have tried it by now," said Jolene.

"Nora could have been lying when she said that it wasn't her," said Harper.

Keenan nodded. "I agree. Nora hired the hunters who went

after you, Harper. She contacted them anonymously using an encrypted, self-deleting email. Heidi's kidnapper was contacted in the exact same way. It seems too much of a coincidence that two different people would use the same technique to hire demons in such a short space of time."

"Unless this person is somehow linked to Nora," said Raini. "I doubt I'm alone in thinking it was the fourth Horseman."

"But Nora said that they weren't working together at the time because he/she wanted to keep a low profile for a while," Harper pointed out. "Sending someone after Heidi isn't maintaining a low profile."

"So maybe it wasn't that they cared about keeping a low profile; maybe it was that they simply didn't want to work with Nora anymore," Drew suggested.

There was a distinct pop followed by the hiss of air. Harper popped her head into the dining room and glanced out of the window that overlooked the backyard. "Oh, shit, the bouncy castle's deflating." And Khloë and Martina were struggling to get off it.

They all hurried outside. Keenan grabbed Khloë's wrist and literally hauled her out of the collapsing castle while Tanner did the same to Martina.

Jolene sighed. "Khloë, what did you do?"

"It wasn't me!" the small, olive-skinned imp insisted. "We were just lying there, relaxing."

Martina nodded. "It was weird, the thing just . . . popped. Then it was caving in, and we were scrambling like idiots to get—"

The air compressor spluttered loudly, and then there was an ominous rattle. The guys all moved to switch it off, but they didn't appear to be having much luck with it at all.

"Everything all right out here?"

Hearing Ciaran's voice, Harper twisted to see him peeking

out of the back door. "Not really," she replied. "It burst, and now the air compressor's having a nervous breakdown."

Jolene threw up her arms. "I can't understand what's wrong with it."

Feeling Asher's mind touch hers to get her attention, Harper said, "I'll just be a sec." As she headed back into the house, Ciaran went out into the yard to help.

She walked into the dining room. And skidded to a halt, heart jumping into her throat. The kids were still watching the clown, rapt, aside from Asher. He was surrounded by his shield of embers, sparks, and ashes ... staring curiously up at the woman a few feet away from him, who was cooing and telling him it was time to go home—a woman who was a carbon copy of Harper.

"What the *fuck?*" Harper burst out.

Her replica stilled. A surge of glacial energy abruptly whipped across the space, freezing everything and everyone that it touched. Except for Harper. The biting chill only slid over her skin, leaving goosebumps in its wake.

Snarling, she charged at the bitch, but a bitterly cold wind swept up Harper and flung her out of the room like she was no more than a ragdoll. The breath gusted out of her lungs in a heavy rush as she hit the hallway wall, slamming her head hard.

Coughing and grimacing at the ringing sound in her ears, Harper righted herself. With a grating, crackly sound, the sheet of frost that was spreading along the living room walls began to form a barrier across the doorway. Her heart leaped with horror. *Fuck, no.*

She quickly squeezed through the slight gap before it could close, scraping her skin along the sharp ice as it tore through her shirt and side. She ignored the pain. Ignored the taste of her fear. Ignored the arctic chill in the room. She only cared about getting to the bitch who was currently probing Asher's shield, trying to get to him.

Harper was on her in a flash. Fury ripping through her bloodstream, she gripped the other demon by the throat and slammed her into the wall. The protective power that lived inside Harper sprang to her hands and sent soul-deep agony blasting through the bitch—burning every nerve ending, severing every organ, axing every bone, and flaying her soul. The she-demon's back arched and her mouth opened in a silent scream.

It wasn't enough for Harper. Not even close. Tightening her hold on the bitch's throat, Harper slammed her head into the wall over and over and over, relishing the crack of her skull, the look of sheer agony on her face, and the way she struggled for breath as Harper squeezed her throat *hard*.

There was no mercy in Harper. No reason. No rationality. Only a blinding rage. It had engulfed Harper just the same as soul-deep pain had engulfed the motherfucking bitch in front of her.

Harper's vision was a haze of red. Her heartbeat thrashed in her ears. Her inner demon roared and hissed, livid and murderous. The agony in the bitch's expression didn't appease the entity any more than watching awareness dim from her eyes. No, Harper's demon wanted to watch the *life* leave her eyes.

Needing no urging from the entity, Harper whipped her stiletto blade out of her boot, infused hellfire into it, and rammed it into the she-demon's heart. The bitch sucked in a sharp breath, eyes wide and swirling with pain. But then the throat in Harper's grip suddenly started to slim. Fade. Grew faint until it became totally insubstantial.

With her vaporous face set into a mask of rage, the she-demon exploded into particles and then disappeared in a whirl of icy smoke.

Panting, Harper stood there, staring at the empty space in front of her. "Fuck."

Hearing a distinct pounding, she turned to see that Tanner was charging at the frosted sheet blocking the doorway while others hurled balls of hellfire at it. But Harper didn't spare a thought for the people struggling to enter the room, or even for the kids around her who were heart-wrenchingly still frozen in place. Her only thought was for her son.

Unable to still the tremors of rage running through her, Harper crossed to Asher, who instantly lowered his shield. "Hey, my gorgeous boy," she said, voice shaky, fighting to sound gentle when it was the last thing she felt. Picking him up, she pressed a long kiss to his temple. Remarkably, he wasn't crying. Didn't even seem the slightest bit distressed. "I'm sorry, baby, I shouldn't have left you."

Ciaran abruptly appeared in front of her, teleporting into the room. "*Finally* it worked. I didn't think I'd ever get through, it's like the ice is some kind of energy shield—" He cut off as his gaze skimmed over the frozen children. "Fuck me. Is Asher okay?"

Harper nodded. "Ciaran, you need to get us out of here *now*." They needed to be home, where Asher was safe and no one could reach him. Home, where it was safe for Knox to lose his everloving mind ... because that was *exactly* what he was going to do.

CHAPTER TWO

Arriving in the living area of the mansion with Asher still in her arms, Harper turned to Ciaran. "Did she enter the room while you were still in there, fooling you into thinking she was me? No, of course she didn't, or you'd have been shocked to see me in the yard," Harper reasoned. It was hard to think clearly when her world was in utter chaos.

Ciaran frowned. "Was *who* in there? We couldn't see shit through the frost blocking the doorway. We just heard slamming and pounding and knew something bad was going down."

Nerves raw, she gave him a quick rundown of what had occurred, finding it utterly surreal. It had all happened so damn fast. One moment, she'd been enjoying the party. The next moment, she'd been terrified for her son's safety. Would the demon have hurt him? Or had she only meant to take him? Neither bore thinking about.

Harper tightened her hold on Asher, trying not to squeeze

him too hard. He didn't writhe or fuss. He just babbled to Hound, tugging at its ear.

Paling, Ciaran rubbed a hand down his face. "Shit, Harper, I should have stayed with him."

"No, I should have stayed with him." She was his mother; she was supposed to protect him.

"You hurt? You have blood dripping down your temple."

Becoming suddenly aware of the wet trickle, Harper wiped it with the back of her hand. "Hit my head on the wall." Until right then, the throbbing ache of the wound hadn't registered. "I'm fine. But the other kids are, and they need help. Maybe if you teleport them out of the room they'll unfreeze or something—I don't know. I need you to go back, do what you can, and make sure that everyone knows that me and Asher are okay. We can't afford for Jolene or the sentinels to go off the deep end."

Ciaran nodded and then gently shook Asher's hand. "Take care, kid." With that, he teleported away.

She pressed a kiss to Asher's head, inhaling his sweet scent. Tears stung her eyes, but she held them back. "You okay, baby boy?" she asked softly, doing her best to mask her fear. He was here, safe and warm and unhurt. "I think it's time to call your father. But not while you're in the room, just in case his demon blows a gasket." *Meg, I need you.*

Meg entered the room moments later, brow furrowing. "Harper, what's wrong?"

"I need you to take Asher up to his room and just watch him for a little while. Can you do that, please?"

"Of course." Meg carefully took him. "But you haven't yet told me what's wrong."

Harper flexed her fingers. It had hurt to let him go when all she wanted was to cling tightly to him. "I will; I just need to speak with Knox first."

"All right. Call me when you're done here."

Once they left the room, Harper closed her eyes and took a long, steadying breath. She wanted to cry. Lash out. Scream until her throat hurt. Instead, she desperately sought calm. If she didn't, she'd only feed Knox's anger. But it was hard while the panic and terror were still so fresh and the adrenalin crash had left her edgy and restless.

She found herself pacing, footsteps stiff and jerky. She simply couldn't settle. Couldn't shake off the anger or fear. Especially while her inner demon was raging, demanding vengeance. Demanding that someone pay and pay *dearly*. Knox's demon would no doubt demand the same thing.

The first time she'd met Knox, he'd rattled her typically dauntless inner demon. He didn't just exude blatant danger, he embodied it. He was as brutal, merciless, and ruthless as the demonic population believed him to be. Still, Knox never spewed venom or yelled. Never exploded or foamed at the mouth. But he didn't always contain the rage either. And when he let it out, well, people tended to die. Especially if his demon—an entity that was cold, malevolent, and hard as stone—took the reins.

Knox had a better hold on his inner demon than most did. There was no way for anyone to fully control the entities. Work *with* them? Yes. But that meant ceding control to them at times while still maintaining the position of dominant figure. The constant power struggle led some to turn rogue, go insane, or commit suicide. As such, most demons were eager to find their psi-mates.

Demons came in pairs, which meant each had a predestined psi-mate, or "anchor", that would make them stronger and enable them to maintain the dominant position over their inner demon. The bond was purely psychic, not sexual or emotional. Still, anchors were often very close. Even the pairs who didn't get along very well would still be supportive, loyal, and defend each other against any threat. Who wouldn't want such absolute loyalty? Someone they could always count on, no matter what?

It wasn't all stars and rainbows, though. Anchors could be possessive, overprotective, and highly meddlesome. It was also psychically uncomfortable for the pairs to be apart for long periods of time. Moreover, the death of an anchor was painful and draining for a demon. So, yeah, there were good points and bad points.

In addition to being Harper's mate, Knox was her anchor, so he'd been annoyingly protective and intrusive from the beginning. It had surprised her that he wanted the anchor bond. He was powerful enough all on his own and maintained dominance over his inner demon just fine. Of course, he still relinquished control to it when necessary, but never for long. But it didn't need "long" to cause utter destruction, and she knew it would be tempted to cause exactly that when she told him—

Her head snapped up as Ciaran reappeared with the sentinels.

"What the fuck just happened?" demanded Keenan, eyes manic, as he slung Asher's bag on the floor near the sofa.

"Who was attacked—you or Asher?" Tanner asked, muscles rigid.

"Me, but it was Asher they wanted," said Harper, grim. "I was just about to call Knox. Thanks for bringing them here, Ciaran."

Her cousin nodded. "No problem. Good luck dealing with your mate."

Yeah, she was pretty sure she'd need it.

"The only reason *I* didn't call out to Knox was because I figured you already had," said Keenan when Ciaran was gone.

"Same here," Tanner told her. "I couldn't see anything through the frost. I thought he was already in there with you."

Harper shoved a hand through her hair. "I was too busy

panicking about Asher to think of anything or anyone other than him." But now it was time to reach out to Knox.

She took a deep breath. *Knox?* She tried to sound casual and failed by a long, long mile. Her telepathic voice fairly shook with the fear that still clogged her lungs so that it hurt to breathe.

His mind touched hers, vibrating with concern. *Harper, what's wrong?*

I'm at home. Could you please—

Fire erupted out of the ground in front of her, snapping and crackling. The flames died away, revealing a tall, solid, imposing figure in a tailored Armani suit. Shimmering pools of black roamed over her, taking in everything.

"What is it, Harper?" Brows drawn, Knox stalked toward her with an animal grace that usually made her stomach flip. Right then, her stomach was rock hard. "Baby, you're shaking. What is it?"

She licked her lips. "Someone tried to take him. Someone tried to take Asher."

For a moment, Knox simply stared at her. Then his face tightened into a mask of savage fury and flames flickered from his fingertips. His rage crashed into her as it swept through the room like a tidal wave. The furniture shook, the ceiling spotlights buzzed, and tremors rattled the walls. Then it stopped, but she wasn't mistaking that for the danger passing.

"Where is he?" clipped Knox, body unnaturally still.

"Upstairs with Meg. He's fine, Knox," she assured him, even though she suspected he'd already touched Asher's mind to see that much for himself. "Really, he's okay."

Knox's eyes bled to black as his demon rose to the fore, and the room temperature dropped so low she shivered. "He wasn't harmed?" asked the demon in a flat, chilling, disembodied voice.

She swallowed. "No. They didn't even touch him. They couldn't; he'd raised his shield."

"I want to know everything." The demon prowled toward her, every inch the lethal predator. "I want—" It cut off, nostrils flaring, and its obsidian eyes glittered with renewed fury. "I smell your blood."

Shit. The air suddenly turned muggy and oppressive, like just before a storm. The demon's rage was so live and electric, it was almost tangible. Meeting its unblinking stare, Harper forced herself not to tense. It didn't matter that she knew the demon wouldn't harm her. Only a total idiot wouldn't find something that old, dangerous, and pitiless to be unnerving.

Neither she nor Knox had expected his demon to form such a powerful attachment to her that it wanted to claim her as its own. Knox would have been forced to give her up if things had turned out differently, because a person couldn't take someone as their mate unless their inner demon accepted them too.

Even though joining their psyches had made Harper more powerful, Knox and his demon were still just as overprotective as ever. It didn't even matter that, thanks to his power flooding her mind, she could also call on the flames of hell—Knox still wished he could tuck her away somewhere safe.

Now that she had Asher, Harper finally understood why. She worried for Knox just as he worried about her, sure, but she had the comfort of knowing that he was a supreme badass. Knox, however, didn't have that same comfort, because she was nowhere near as powerful as he was. To Knox, she was vulnerable in ways he would never be. Likewise, Asher—though powerful—was vulnerable to harm in ways that neither she nor Knox were. It made her want to hide him away, where no one could ever touch him. And maybe that was exactly what she should have done.

Feeling like an utter failure, Harper licked her lips. "Please don't go postal. I need Knox. I can't do this by myself."

*

It was the shake in her voice that reached the demon through the red hazing its vision. Its mate was strong. Brave. Resilient. Incredibly self-reliant. To admit to needing anyone, to being unable to bear the situation alone, meant she was in genuine distress. The demon's fury receded slightly. "I don't like the taint of fear in your scent, little sphinx." When Knox fiercely reached for the surface, wanting to reassure their mate, the demon retreated.

In control once more, Knox cricked his neck. His chest expanded with a full breath that he slowly blew out. Anger simmered low in his core—an anger that had moments ago inflated inside his chest until there was no way to breathe without tasting red-hot rage. It had flooded his body, poured into his extremities, and made his blood boil and smolder like lava. His demon had gone into a volcanic rage, roaring so loudly it had made Knox's head throb.

Only one thing had stopped both him and the entity from losing control—on touching Asher's mind, they'd sensed no anguish or fear in him. Only calm and contentment.

Focusing on his mate, Knox saw just how terribly shaken she was. He knew Harper. Knew she'd be blaming herself. Knew that she'd be hurting right down to the deepest part of her soul. He also sensed that she was keeping a chokehold on her anger so that she didn't exacerbate his own. He could do no less for her. She needed comfort. Support. Reassurance. Not the rage sitting in his gut like lead.

Locking down the dark emotions threatening to send him into a frenzy, Knox crossed to her. "Come here, baby." He curved his hand around her nape and pulled her close. At first, she remained stiff and unresponsive, as if she thought she deserved no comfort. He smoothed his hand up and down her back until the stiffness leached out of her. "Tell me everything."

Pulling back, Harper licked her lower lip. "We were at Jolene's tea party. The kids were all sitting in the dining room with Ciaran, watching the clown that Jolene hired." She gestured at the sentinels, adding, "The three of us were stood in the hallway just outside the room—we could see Asher clearly. We heard the bouncy castle burst outside, so we ran out into the yard. Thinking back, it seems likely that someone burst it to distract us. Asher's mind touched mine. I knew he wanted me for something, so I went to him. And there was this woman."

"A woman?"

"She looked like me. *Exactly* like me. Either it was a shape-shifting demon or my fucking doppelgänger. She was cooing to him and saying it was time to go home, probably hoping he'd think it was me and then lower the shield he'd wrapped round himself."

Knox's demon snorted. Their son would never be so gullible, infant or not.

"When she saw me, she let out this weird surge of ice cold energy that froze everything and everyone in the room. Asher's shield must have protected him from it. It didn't work on me either, so she conjured a wind that flung me into the hall. I managed to get inside the room before a sheet of frost built across the doorway. But the frost blocked the others from getting inside to help."

"I bashed it with every bit of strength in my body while others hurled orbs of hellfire at it," Tanner cut in. "It didn't even weaken."

Harper plucked at her clothes. She felt so hot and edgy that the cotton chafed her skin and made her feel smothered. "I flew at her, dealt her some soul-deep pain, stabbed her with my blade and . . . I don't know if I killed her. She just faded right in front of me and then disappeared."

A familiar mind slid against Knox's. *Is everything all right?* asked Levi, his sentinel and personal bodyguard. Knox had left him outside the conference room at the hotel where he'd held his business meeting.

No, it's not. Knox quickly explained what had happened, pausing only when Levi bit out several curses. *Relay the situation to Larkin*, Knox continued, referring to his fourth sentinel. *I'll meet you in my office within the hotel soon.* Knox couldn't ask Levi to leave without him. It was important that Knox was seen to be both coming *and* going from places or it would raise questions.

Breaking his connection with Levi, Knox smoothed his hand over Harper's shoulder and down her arm. "Where are you hurt?"

"I whacked my head on the wall and scraped my side on the frost." She shrugged, as if it were nothing.

"Let me see." He peeled up her T-shirt, finding an ugly slash on her side, and ground his teeth. "Looks more like someone slashed at you with a razor blade." The she-demon would die for that alone—but not until he was done "punishing" her, if he ever *would* be done.

"It doesn't matter. What matters is that someone tried to snatch Asher."

"Firstly, you very much *do* matter—never say that again." Probing her head gently, Knox found a lump, but she barely winced. "Secondly, you should have called me."

"I wasn't thinking of anything other than getting to Asher. I fucked up, I know—"

"You didn't fuck up. It was only natural that your thoughts were only of Asher." He squeezed her nape. "You did good."

Her shoulders slumped a little. "No, I didn't, and we both know it."

He could see that she was awaiting judgment. "You think I should blame you?"

"I left him."

"*I* left him," said Keenan glumly.

"We *all* left him," clipped Tanner. "The bitch who tried to take him fucked with the bouncy castle to distract us. We fell for it."

Knox dug into Asher's bag and pulled out a wet wipe. He gently cleaned the blood from her temple and then carefully dabbed the cut on her side. Later, they'd shower together, and he would properly clean the wounds and baby her until it drove her so crazy that her needless guilt was drowned out by irritation. First . . . "I need to see Jolene's dining room. I might pick something up."

Harper lifted her chin. "I'm coming with you." She didn't want to leave Asher, but she needed to see for herself that the other children were okay.

"Me, too," said Tanner. "If I can detect the bitch's scent, I may be able to track her. And I need to get the car anyway."

"We'll all go," declared Knox. What he wanted most was to see Asher. To touch him. Hold him. Assure himself that he was okay. But Knox didn't want to go to his son while in this state. Anger was riding him hard, taunting him with the cutting impulse to hurt and mangle and avenge. Making it worse, his demon continued to seethe, demanding vengeance, pushing at Knox to hunt the bitch who'd tried to take Asher and had made Harper bleed.

The only thing currently keeping it from surging to the surface and taking control was, quite simply, Harper's nearness. She was an anchor to both Knox and his demon in every way that counted. In that sense, she had more control over the demon than Knox did. It was calmer and much better behaved when Harper was close by. It detested parting from her, and it quickly became bored and restless without her.

Knox couldn't claim to need her any less than the entity did. Control was important to him. Essential. Not just due to the scars his childhood left on him, but because he had to keep a tight hold on his abilities and his inner demon. If Harper was taken from him, that control would eviscerate, and all hell would quite literally break loose.

He wouldn't simply hunt and destroy those responsible for her death. That wouldn't satisfy him. Vengeance wouldn't be enough for him or his demon. The entity would want the freedom to do exactly what it was born to do—wreak havoc and chaos. Knox would give it that freedom, and an immense amount of destruction and death would follow.

In that sense, Knox's emotional stability rested on her. He hated that she had to bear the weight of it, but there was no changing it. She'd been his one vulnerability until Asher came along. Now Knox had two, and both had been threatened today.

Brushing a kiss over Harper's now clean temple, Knox squeezed her wrist gently. "Call Ciaran, baby. He can teleport us all there." Knox didn't pyroport in front of many people, liking to keep their kind guessing about what he could and couldn't do.

Moments later, Ciaran appeared, looking somewhat frazzled.

"Any luck unfreezing the kids?" she asked him.

"No," her cousin replied. "I can't melt the frost barring the doorway either. Hell, I can't even teleport anyone into the room. It's hard enough to teleport myself in there."

"Why is it such a struggle?" Knox asked.

Ciaran shrugged. "I don't know. It's like the frost on the door and walls of the room acts as an energy barrier or something. I can't explain it. Please tell me you can do something."

"Take me to Jolene's house," said Knox. "Let's find out what we're dealing with."

Ciaran teleported Knox, Harper, and the sentinels to Jolene's hallway. It was crowded with people who were obviously anxious to get to the children. They parted at the sight of Harper and Knox, letting them through.

Jolene turned to them, looking harried. "How's Asher?"

"He's okay, Grams," Harper assured her. "No one hurt him. I just needed to get him out of here fast." To a place Harper knew beyond any doubt that he was safe. She lightly touched his mind and felt only contentment.

"Ciaran told us everything," said Jolene. "He also said you were bleeding."

"I'm fine. Really." The wounds stung like a bitch, now that the adrenalin had faded, but Harper had had *way* worse. She didn't say that aloud though as it would have riled Knox. Right then, he looked unnaturally calm in a way she found plain terrifying. Harper figured that if it weren't for the way his rage thickened the air, people could think him completely unmoved by what had happened.

Devon gave her a quick hug. "Did she really look exactly like you?"

At Harper's nod, Raini spoke, "Must be a demon with the power to shapeshift."

"It's not an unusual gift," began Khloë, "so that won't help us work out who it was."

Jolene's face hardened. "They'll pay for this. Nobody tries to harm me or mine—especially in my own home."

"Yes, they will pay," agreed Knox, voice low, steady.

Drew reached around his sister and lightly touched Harper's shoulder. "You all right?"

Knox's eyes slammed on the unfamiliar male that touched his

mate. A hellcat, Knox sensed. The demon's psychic shields were weak, so Knox caught some of his thoughts. The male thought Knox to be cold and uncaring and without mercy. Believed he was as emotionally stunted as Harper's father. Didn't understand why Harper had committed herself to such a creature or believe that she belonged with someone who could never truly care for her.

Envy spiced the internal rant, which would have made Knox smile if there wasn't also a possessive edge to the hellcat's thoughts. Knox didn't fucking like that at all. In fact, he felt the grip on his anger loosen just a little, which was very, very dangerous. His inner demon snarled, deciding the hellcat needed a ball of hellfire lodged up his rectum.

As Knox possessively shackled Harper's wrist, the male boldly met his gaze and said, "We haven't met before. I'm Drew Clarke."

"Devon's brother," Keenan added, shifting in front of the male so that he effectively cut Drew out of the main circle of people. Apparently, thought Knox, the sentinel didn't like him either.

"Do you think you can help?" Martina asked Knox, gesturing at the frosted doorway. "We've been hitting it with orbs of hellfire for what feels like hours. It's not melting."

Knox examined it closely. "This isn't real ice. It won't melt."

"But it can be destroyed, right?" asked Harper. She watched as he lifted his hand and released a wave of raw, undiluted power that buzzed in the air like a swarm of bees. The frost didn't crack. It dissipated, becoming pure mist. Going by the boom of silence, people were too awed by his show of strength to be relieved that the barrier was gone.

She kept pace with Knox as he prowled into the room—each step was slow, deliberate, casual. Again, a wave of raw power swept out of his hand, making the air buzz and shimmer. The frost on the walls dissolved, and the kids and creepy clown immediately resumed what they were doing, as if nothing had occurred. While some imps rushed inside to fuss over the kids, others followed Harper and Knox to the rear of the room.

Studying the wall, Knox felt the waves of violence and the residue of his mate's rage. She'd been blinded by it. So blinded that she hadn't even thought to call for help, and he wondered if her attacker had counted on that. "You fought her here."

Even though it wasn't a question, she nodded. "I kind of slammed her against the wall a few times before I stabbed her with my knife after I infused it with hellfire. She faded until she was like vapor, and then she was just . . . gone." Feeling the prick of her nails in her palms, Harper realized she'd clenched her fists so tight that her knuckles turned white. "I should have bitten her fucking face off."

Knox gave her nape a gentle squeeze. "I'd say she walked out of that fight in more pain than you did. Tanner, do you have her scent?"

The hellhound turned to them, jaw hard. "No. There's not even a *hint* of one that doesn't fit the people already in the room."

Harper's lips parted. "How can she not have a scent?"

Tanner shrugged. "There's no scent of death either."

Harper swore. "Not only is she still alive, you can't track her." Groaning, she rubbed a hand down her face. "None of this makes sense. All I can be sure of is that she's pretty powerful. Most people are so overwhelmed by the soul-deep pain that they can't think through it, let alone find the will to defend themselves or try to escape. They just turn into a ball of misery. The pain distracted and weakened her, but it didn't disable her." And that was frightening, because Harper relied on that power to protect her.

Keenan held out her stiletto blade. "This is yours, right? Found it on the floor."

"Thanks. I must have dropped it." Harper frowned. "There's no blood on it. I stabbed her with this right in the heart, but there's no blood."

A baffled silence met that statement.

"It was probably an ice demon," said Drew, glancing around.

"No," said Knox. "None of it was real ice."

Drew jutted out his chin. "So, what was it?"

"Glacial energy that immobilized whatever it touched," Knox said simply. "If it had been molten energy, it would have presented itself as fire. But it wouldn't have been real fire, just like that wasn't real ice."

Drew stuffed his hands in his pockets. "Does that help work out what she is?"

"No," replied Knox.

"Then I don't see that it matters."

"It matters. Every piece of the puzzle matters."

Harper nodded. "She's able to shapeshift, leave no trace of herself behind, transform into vapor, and emit glacial energy to form ice or wind. Knowing these things may not lead us to her, but they do help us know how to combat her if she makes a reappearance. Asher was sitting over there," she added, pointing to the center of the room. "He'd popped up his shield. She didn't seem able to get past it. He didn't even cry."

"Of course he didn't," said Jolene. "He's a Wallis."

Knox's jaw clenched. "He's a Thorne."

Jolene waved that away. "You know what I mean."

Drew folded his arms across his chest. "Do you think one of the Primes could be behind it?"

Harper's nose wrinkled. "I doubt it."

Drew frowned. "You're the only mated Primes in the world. You're both powerful, and so is your kid—I could sense it. That has to make the other Primes nervous."

"It probably does, but you haven't seen them with Asher. I really don't think they'd hurt him." Before Asher was born, Harper wouldn't have thought she'd *ever* say those words. Demonkind had feared that the baby would be the same breed as Knox—they might not know *what* Knox was, but they sure didn't want another hanging around.

The Primes had been especially nervous so, when Asher was five months old, Harper and Knox had done the unexpected: They'd taken him into a meeting with the other US Primes. All of them had fallen head over heels for the little guy.

The move had not only demonstrated that Knox and Harper believed in their ability to protect him, it had forced the Primes to view Asher as a person, not an abstract potentially soulless baby who might be too powerful to exist. They'd seen how playful, inquisitive, and happy he was. Seen that he was just like any other baby. Sensed that he had the air of a sphinx, like Harper, which they seemed to have found particularly comforting. The only gift Asher used during the meeting was his shield. It had impressed people but, as a defensive ability, hadn't made the Primes in the least bit nervous. They'd found it cute.

Honestly, Harper often wondered if there was something preternatural about Asher's ability to win people over. Like maybe he'd been gifted with strong charisma or something. She was sure he would even have won over Knox's bitchy ex-bed buddy, Alethea . . . if the she-demon wasn't missing. No one had seen Alethea since just after Asher was born. Her brother, Jonas, was worried, despite that he could still feel her psychically and, as such, knew she was alive.

"I agree that the Primes wouldn't hurt him—Asher has them wrapped around his little finger," said Jolene. "But that's not to say they wouldn't hire someone to kidnap him so that they could use him for one reason or another."

"I'm more inclined to think it was the fourth Horseman," said Raini. "I actually thought he or she might abandon the group's goal, since the other three are dead. But maybe not."

Knox would put his money on the fourth Horseman being *behind* the attack, but he wasn't so sure that the demon who tried to snatch Asher was in fact the Horseman. Striking while Asher was at the home of a strong Prime like Jolene Wallis was extremely bold. The fourth Horseman had never appeared on the scene to help defend Isla, Roan, or Nora when they were up against Knox and Harper. That suggested the remaining Horseman was happy to sit back and let others not only take the risks but deal with any consequences alone.

Turning to Ciaran, Knox said, "I'd be grateful if you could return us to our home."

Tanner gestured outside with his thumb. "I'll drive the car back."

"I'll come with you," Keenan said to the other sentinel.

Knox turned to Jolene. "I doubt that the she-demon will return here, but if she does, call me." The female Prime didn't respond. He arched a brow. "I know you're angry, Jolene, but this she-demon made my mate bleed and tried to take our son. It happened in your house, true, but Harper and Asher are my family and part of my lair. As Primes, Harper and I deal with anyone who threatens it."

"I can't promise I won't kill her if she returns here," said Jolene. "I don't have that kind of restraint. Won't it be enough for you to know she's dead?"

"I don't want her dead. I intend to find out who she is. I will seize and detain her, but I won't kill her. I will mentally destroy her. Completely. Utterly. I will break her. Crush her spirit. Torture her until there's no fight left in her. And she will live in fear that I'll return to her prison to do it again and again. And I will."

Jolene looked at him for a few moments. "I can get behind that."

With an amused snort, Devon squeezed Harper's hand. "Take care."

"And give Asher a kiss for us," added Khloë.

Knox curled his arm around Harper's shoulders, who leaned into him and slipped an arm around his waist. Just like that, more of Clarke's thoughts split the air like gunshots. No one else heard them, of course. Only Knox. This time, it wasn't just thoughts that leaked through Clarke's shields. It was memories. Memories of Harper. Her taste spiced with mojitos. The softness of her skin. The weight of her breasts. The feel of her pussy, hot and tight, around his fingers. The raspy sigh she let out when she came.

Knox's rage mingled with that of his demon, who lunged for the surface, making the room temperature plummet. It spoke to the hellcat mind-to-mind, effectively crashing into the male's thoughts. *I could steal those memories from you so very, very easily.*

Drew's eyes widened.

Perhaps I should share some of my own with you. The demon thrust past Drew's weak shields, forcing its own memories to replay in the hellcat's brain. Harper screaming as she came. Her telling Knox she loved him. His flesh burning as her demon branded him. Her face all soft and warm as she slid his rings on her finger. Her laughing as they both played with Asher, happy and relaxed.

Clenching his fists, Drew scowled. "Get out of my head."

Harper belongs to me. Belongs with me. If you wish to challenge my claim on her, do so now. I will enjoy watching you die. When Drew remained quiet instead of disputing its claim to Harper, the demon retreated.

"What going on?" asked Harper, wary, as she fisted the back of his shirt.

Knox stroked his thumb over Harper's jaw. "Nothing, baby. Ciaran?"

With a nod, the imp teleported them back to the living area of the mansion.

CHAPTER THREE

As soon as Ciaran left, Knox gently pulled Harper flush against him and kissed her forehead. That gentle side of him hadn't shown itself until she came along. Or maybe it hadn't developed until then. "Stop feeling like you failed Asher." Her shame was so strong that it brushed the edges of his consciousness. Even if their psyches weren't joined, the emotion would have been easy enough to sense just by the look on her face.

Harper closed her eyes. "I shouldn't have left his side."

"It's not as if you left him in a room all by himself. Others were with him. And you weren't gone for long, were you? No. Because you thought he was safe. He *should* have been safe. No one could have predicted that someone would be so bold as to try to get to Asher while he was in a house full of people. The important thing is that he's fine, which he is."

Intellectually, Harper knew he was right. Knew she'd had every reason to believe that Asher would be safe at her grandmother's house. Especially since Jolene was a strong Prime who was well-known for retaliating *hard*. But that had obviously been what the mystery she-demon had counted on, hadn't it? And Harper couldn't help feeling like she should have been prepared for that, just as she couldn't help feeling like she should have seen even *halfway* through Nora's act.

Harper hadn't suspected her half-brother, Roan, or Knox's ex-bed buddy, Isla, of being part of some fucked-up group intending to see the fall of the Primes, but she *had* been repelled by both of them. Not Nora, though. No, Harper had actually *liked* the woman.

Stroking a hand down her hair, Knox pulled back to meet her eyes. So much torment there, he thought. It caused a twinge in his chest. "What are you thinking that makes you look like you want to slap yourself?"

"I'm thinking that it's not even the first time I let Asher down. Yes, I know it's illogical to feel guilty for not suspecting Nora of being a Horseman, but the guilt's there all the same."

"I can't help feeling guilty that I didn't escort you to the restroom the day she took you. If I had, you wouldn't have been forced into early labor and you wouldn't have gone through so much of it alone."

Harper's face scrunched up. "Why would you have escorted me to the restroom?"

"Why would you have suspected Nora?" he shot back. "If I'm not to blame, you're not to blame." But Knox understood why she struggled with the guilt. He knew it wasn't his fault that he hadn't been at her side during every second of the labor, but that didn't stop the guilt from creeping in. There was a truck load of anger there, too. It gutted him that he hadn't been able to live up to his promise to be with her every step of the way; that he hadn't experienced every single moment of the labor right along with her.

She absently rubbed at her upper arm. "I just can't help feeling like I neglected Asher by leaving him with Ciaran."

His demon pushed his way to the surface and spoke, "Your shame and guilt are senseless, little sphinx. You did all you could do. The child is unharmed. He is not in distress."

"Which is the only reason I'm halfway rational right now."

Knox seized control, forcing the demon to retreat and said, "You didn't neglect Asher at any point. You protected him. No one could ever describe you as a neglectful parent, Harper."

Knox knew why she was so hard on herself. She'd needlessly worried from the start that she wouldn't be a good mother, considering her own parents were completely useless as not just parents but as living beings.

Her mother, Carla, was a twisted bitch who'd sold Harper to Jolene after aborting her hadn't worked. Harper's father, Lucian, was a self-centered nomad with the emotional age of a child. Knox had known that Harper would never be anything like either of them. She was everything a mother should be—caring, protective, nurturing, admiringly patient, and she loved Asher unconditionally.

Knox curled her hair around her ear. "We knew someone would try to get to Asher eventually."

"I guess I was hoping that just maybe he'd be left alone."

"They won't get to him, Harper. No one will touch him. I'll destroy demonkind before I let it happen."

"I know. And I'll be right at your side while you do it," Harper vowed, meaning every word. And then he kissed her. As always, his potent sex appeal and alpha energy wrapped around her. Really, there was no escaping the effects of his raw sexual magnetism. No stopping her nerve endings from sparking to life or goosebumps sweeping across her flesh, making it hypersensitive.

Knox drew back and swiped his tongue along her lower lip. "You taste good."

She smoothed a hand down his chest. "You look good. Far too good. It scrambles my thoughts."

"Kind of like your scent scrambles mine." He sipped from her mouth again. Inside him, his demon settled a little. It had missed her. Always did.

From minute one, she'd intrigued both Knox and his demon. Complex, guarded, elusive, and almost pathologically stubborn, his pretty and shiny little sphinx was a walking, talking challenge for any male. Barely five and a half feet tall, she was all carnal sensuality, innate grace, and iron strength. Her mouth, lush and erotic, was as tempting as her delicate yet sinfully curved body.

He loved knowing she was his. Loved knotting his fingers in her sleek dark hair as he fucked in and out of her. Loved watching her unusually glassy eyes, which were presently a soft violet shade, change color—it was something they did randomly yet often.

She was unique. Singular. There was literally no one like her ... and she was all his. No one got to harm her and live, which meant the demon who made her bleed was on borrowed time. "Let me take another look at the scrape on your side," said Knox.

She waved a dismissive hand. "It's fine."

"I want to see. Lift your shirt."

"No, because you'll fuss. I'm done with the fussing."

His demon smiled at her snippy tone. People tended to do their best to please Knox, whether out of fear, respect, or a wish to win his favor. Not Harper. She'd never had a problem telling him "no". Never bowed down to him. Never allowed him to intimidate her. Never sought his company or approval. Hell, she hadn't even flirted with him.

Even now, she persistently defied him. Teased him. Frustrated him. Amused him. Constantly tested his patience. Pushed back if he pushed too far. Called him on his bullshit.

She also had a wicked temper and absolutely no problem unleashing it on him, just as she had no issue at all with standing up to his demon. Few people would dare to do the latter.

"You know I won't drop it, Harper. Not when you're hurt."

She snorted. "And you know your tyrannical shit is absolutely wasted on me. You learned this on day one, and yet you keep on pushing. I'm confused."

Knox wasn't going to lie, he had initially *tried* to control her; it was instinct for him to control the things around him. It had been a pointless attempt in this case. His mate had her own mind—one he found supremely fascinating—and she knew how to use it. In truth, he didn't want to control her. He liked that he couldn't. Admired that she demanded that he respect her insistence on being heard and counted. But that didn't mean he wouldn't always push to get his way.

Using his psychic hands, Knox shackled her wrists and pinned them behind her back. Ignoring her string of curses, he kept her plastered against him with one hand while peeling up her shirt with his other. "It's healing well," he said. "The wound's closed." He probed the cut on her head. "It seems to also be healing nicely."

"I *told* you I was fine," she clipped.

"You did," he said, pressing a soothing kiss to the sensitive skin of her neck. Not wanting to get her all riled up, he released her hands. She splayed her hands on his chest and probably would have tried shoving him away if he hadn't scraped his teeth over her pulse. He smiled at her little gasp. She was incredibly responsive, and he relished and took advantage of that. Had done since they very first met. It still shocked him just how hard and fast he'd fallen for her. What had shocked him more was that his demon did the same. It hadn't been long before it pushed to collect and claim her.

If the entity could have felt love for anyone, it would have been her. Although it lacked the capacity to love, it treasured her. Respected her. Was exceedingly possessive and protective of her. She charmed, amused, and fulfilled it—something Knox wouldn't have believed anyone would ever be able to do.

Even if Harper wasn't their psi-mate, she still would have anchored the entity in her way. It trusted her, which said everything, since the demon trusted no one. She'd given it total acceptance, just as she had Knox. In doing so, she'd sealed her fate. It was firmly and irrevocably attached to her. Once a demon fully committed itself to someone in such a way, it *never* let them go.

Knox rubbed his nose against hers. "Love you, baby." Like that, she lost the stiffness in her spine. Probably because he didn't say the words often. It wasn't just because they didn't come easy to him, it was also because they felt *wrong*. Weak. Soft. Unlike the love he'd sensed in others, there was nothing soppy or tender about what he felt for Harper. No, it was a dark, intense, hissing, spitting emotion that consumed and clawed at him.

She went pliant against him. "Love you."

It amazed Knox that she did, given the darkness that stained his soul. And, he suddenly remembered, it similarly amazed a certain male hellcat. "Tell me about Drew."

She blinked at the abrupt change of subject. "He's Devon's older brother. He lives in Cuba, but he came home for a visit." She tilted her head. "Why was your demon in his head?"

Knox's feet moved soundlessly along the light pine flooring as he walked to the small bar. "Drew's shields are very weak. I picked up some of his thoughts. I didn't like what I heard." He gestured at the bottles. "Drink?"

Shaking her head, she folded her arms. "What thoughts did you hear?"

"Like your father, he has a lot of distaste for me due to the rumors he's heard over the years about my versions of punishment. Such as the time I subjected a vampire to horrific torture, confined her to a solid brass coffin, and then set a fire beneath said coffin. Of course, she'd kidnapped and caused much harm to one of my demons, but people tend to leave out that part."

Pausing, Knox poured himself a gin and tonic. "He thinks I'm bad for you. Too dangerous. Too cold. He believes I couldn't possibly care for you the way I should, so he has absolutely no idea why you have committed yourself to me. Although ... he does wonder if you feel comfortable with me because I'm like Lucian."

Harper's eyes widened. "What? You're *nothing* like my father."

"I know that. But to Drew, I'm as emotionally unavailable as Lucian. Therefore, Drew wonders if it's a case of you having daddy issues." Knox took a swig from his tumbler. "Baby, he just wants there to be a reason you're with me that doesn't mean you care for me. He's jealous that I have you, and he despises me for tying you to me."

"Jealous?" Harper's arms slipped to her sides. She shook her head, unconvinced. "I'm sure he finds it surprising that I'm mated and have a kid, considering the last time he saw me I was still intent on not getting involved with a demon—"

"A rule you broke for him one night," Knox reminded her, voice carefully controlled. "He projected his memories quite loud."

Harper felt her cheeks heat, though she wasn't sure why she was embarrassed. His voice hadn't raised even a single octave, but cold menace was stamped into every line of his perfectly sculpted face. "I was hammered."

"Yes, you were so hammered, in fact, that he got to . . . what's the term? Third base."

The taunt there made Harper narrow her eyes. She had a vague memory of Drew making her come with his fingers in her old apartment. She remembered pushing him away after that. He hadn't pressured her for more. He'd just kissed her forehead and left.

Knox took another swig of his drink. "As you can imagine, I don't like having all that in my head. My demon was kind enough to share some of its own memories of you with the hell-cat. Memories that would drive home *exactly* who you belong to. If the hellcat has any sense, he will stay away from you."

"Knox, I really don't think Drew has any designs on me. Even if he did, he's hardly going to think he has a chance with me. You and I don't just live together, we exchanged rings, we have a son, and I took your surname. If all that doesn't scream 'commitment' I don't know what will. Even the skanks from your past have given up trying their luck with you." And, really, she just didn't believe that Drew cared enough to bother.

Crossing to her, Knox curved his hand around her chin. "Harper, do you really think that if you'd been in a relationship with someone when I met you, it would have stopped me from pursuing you? I've told you before, I would have taken you from them—no matter what it took. Not even the sight of a black diamond on your finger would have discouraged me."

"Yeah, well, Drew never cared for me the way you do. That fumble in my old apartment wouldn't have happened if we hadn't both been smashed."

"I doubt that he's never cared for you. He's certainly possessive of you. I felt it." Knox knocked back the last of his drink and then placed the glass on the table. "In any case, I don't want him near you, whispering words in your ear that might make you doubt me."

"Even if he does think you're bad for me, he wouldn't try to cause problems if for no other reason than we have Asher. Drew isn't a bad person. He wouldn't try to break up a family."

"I'm not so sure of that." Knox combed his fingers through her dark hair and then rubbed the silky gold ends between the pads of his fingers. "I don't like that he's known you longer than I have. I don't like that he knows what you taste like." Knox cupped her pussy. "Or that he knows what it feels like to have this, hot and slick, rippling around his fingers. It's mine."

Gripping his arms, Harper swallowed. "He's known me longer, but he doesn't know me better than you do. Nobody does."

"No, they don't," Knox agreed. He breezed his thumb over the tattoo-like brand his demon had left on the V between her thighs. It was an intricate swirl of thorns that he often made a point of tracing with his tongue. "Just like nobody knows me better than you do. Which means you know *exactly* what I'm capable of. You know just how dangerous I can be and just how far I'd go to keep and protect you. It would be better for Clarke if he never has to learn that."

Knox kissed her. Hard. Deep. Wet. Punctuating his words. Taking everything because it was his to take. She was essential to him. Indispensable. Something he *needed*. He'd never let her go. Never. Not even if she begged him.

He could admit that he'd railroaded her the entire time they'd been together, and he didn't feel the least bit guilty about that. He was as ruthless and calculated as he was rumored to be. He did what it took to get what he wanted—lied, hurt, manipulated, exploited, destroyed. What he'd wanted most was Harper, and he'd done whatever he had to do to have her. He had no limits when it came to her.

He'd pushed her to give herself to him and form the anchor bond, and it still amused him that while he'd spent time using various manipulation tactics to lure her to him, he'd been unknowingly falling for her. In a short time, he'd pushed for more. Pushed her to accept him as her mate, to move in with him, to wear his rings, and to take his surname.

He'd been elated to hear she was pregnant, and a darkly possessive part of him had thought ... *Now she's tied even further to me.*

She bit his lip and pulled back. "Ease up, you made your point." She pushed his hand away from her pussy, not liking when he used his sexuality against her that way. "Wait a minute, your demon didn't share the memory of *branding* me down there, did it?" Because she'd never be able to look Drew in the eye ever again.

Knox raised a brow. "Would it bother you if it had?"

"Uh ... *yeah*. Don't play with me, Thorne. Did the weird motherfucker share it or not?"

Knox felt his lips twitch. He was quite sure that *no one* would ever dare call his demon a weird motherfucker—or any other offensive name, for that matter. He was also quite sure that his demon wouldn't find such an insult amusing if it had come from anyone other than her. It was such a simple thing, but it brought him pleasure because it proved she trusted both him and his demon.

"No," replied Knox. "But now that you've put the idea in its head, I can't say it *won't* ever share said memory with him." She gaped in horror, and he chuckled. "Really, Harper, do you think my demon would ever give Clarke or anyone else a glimpse of that pussy?" Grabbing her hips, Knox pulled her flush against him. "You should know better than that."

"Like I said, your demon can be weird. I mean, the fact that I have a brand down there only goes to prove that."

Knox smiled against her mouth. "There are much worse brands it would like to leave on your body. Well, *you* would define them as 'worse'. I'd call them ... interesting."

She stilled. "That's not funny."

"Nor is it a joke." But the sheer panic on her face was priceless. Teasing wasn't something he'd done with others. He hadn't thought it was in his nature *to* tease, but she brought that out in him.

Before Harper, he'd been solitary for a very long time. He'd had everything he could ever have wanted—success, power, luxury, decadence. Nothing had been off-bounds to him. And yet, he hadn't been satisfied. Not by the money or the fame or the women who constantly sought him out.

He hadn't once committed himself to a female, despite the loneliness that had plagued both him and his demon. The entity hadn't ever pushed Knox to claim one. It had occasionally fixated on women but had tired of them quickly. Females were always interchangeable to the demon; none had stood out more than the other. Once the thrill of the hunt had been satisfied, the entity had lost interest.

"Then you'd better have a good long talk with your damn demon," she told him, "because three brands are quite enough. Especially since one of them is a freaking *choker* that pretty much screams 'property of Knox Thorne'."

"Hmm, it really does say that, doesn't it?" Knox feathered his fingertip over the thorny choker.

"You don't have to sound so happy about that," she grumbled.

How could he not be happy about it? He wanted everyone to know she was his. After centuries of dealing with users, manipulators, and gold diggers, Knox had become jaded. Lonely. Even empty. A numbness had started to creep in, and the things and people around him gradually lost their importance. Harper pierced right through that numbness. She'd not only showed him how empty his life was, she'd filled and lit it up.

Just looking at her made him want to cosset her. Shield her. Spoil her. Protect her. Tuck her away somewhere safe. Take care of her however he could. And he was very aware that she *let* him take care of her. She *let* herself rely on him because she knew it was what he needed, despite that her instincts would be to handle everything herself.

It angered him that she'd been forced to become self-sufficient at an early age and was used to taking care of herself. She'd never had anyone she could truly rely or depend on. No one she could turn to when times were tough. No one, more importantly, who would put her first. He'd become that person for her, determined that she'd never feel alone or second-best to anyone ever again.

It had taken time, but she'd come to trust that—unlike others in her life—he wouldn't leave her. Not ever. She was now secure in their mating. As she'd warned him, though, there was a little part of her that would likely always worry that he'd leave her. He hated that. It meant he didn't have every single piece of her, and he wanted it all. Also, he didn't want her living with such a worry. He knew how it felt because before he'd told her he was an archdemon, he'd lived with it too.

"Baby, I don't think you're in any position to judge my demon on this," said Knox. "*Your* demon left two brands on me."

"Yeah, but not a damn choker. Seriously, why not just collar me?"

"Not a choker, no, but one of the brands *is* on my nape, so it's highly visible. It even melds with the one it left on my back, making each brand look larger. Not exactly inconspicuous." Which was part of what made the brands so hot. They were a statement to both Knox and the world that he was off-limits. "Admit it, you *like* that I'm marked."

She sniffed but didn't deny it. He loved that her demon was so possessive that it had branded him. It was enough that it and Harper *accepted* him. Who could have blamed her or her inner demon for turning away from him, given that archdemons were malignant, callous creatures that belonged in the depths of hell? But they hadn't turned away. Instead, Harper had told him "big motherfucking deal".

It wasn't that she didn't fear what he was. She did—and rightfully so. But she also didn't care that he was part of the fabric of hell. She still loved and trusted him, still believed she was utterly safe with him. Although she'd struggled with the truth of what he was when Knox finally told her, it had only been for mere moments. She'd never backed away from him or the demon. Never rejected them, not even for a second.

He brushed his mouth over hers. "You're a miracle to me, you know." She frowned, so he bit her lip before she could argue. "It's true." It couldn't be in any way whatsoever easy to be mated to someone as dominant, demanding, and possessive as Knox. Especially when he was overprotective to the point of making her crazy and not always entirely rational in his possessiveness. He was also extremely controlling—he knew that. Owned it. And he had his reasons for it.

When he was a child, a cult-like leader had snatched the control right out from under Knox. Every waking and sleeping moment of his life had been dictated by others—not just when he woke and when he slept, but when he ate, what he wore, and where he slept. He'd had no say over his own life. Any form of rebellion was punished severely.

His parents had eventually stood up to the leader only to have their throats slit. That was when, for the first time in his life, Knox lost control of his inner demon. It hadn't been about defending himself. It had been about vengeance, pure and simple.

On joining the outside world, he'd vowed that he'd never again be under another person's control. As an adult, he'd sought and seized everything he'd earlier been denied—knowledge, money, independence, success, possessions, and power. He'd become someone who lived life by his own set of rules, who moved at his own pace on his own schedule, and who took exactly what he wanted whenever he wanted it.

Any female would find all that hard to deal with. But Harper let him be, for the most part. Accepted him. Didn't judge. In truth, she fucking owned him—mind, body, and soul. But he was okay with that, because he owned her just the same.

He was just about to ravish that fantasy mouth of hers once more when a small mind brushed against his—it held a question. Knox smiled. "Asher's wondering where we are."

Harper's mouth curled. "Then let's go see our boy."

Knox's fury still festered inside him like an open, infected wound. But the anger was no longer hot and blinding. It was cold and calculating. More importantly, it was contained and wouldn't leak out onto Asher.

Locking his arms around Harper, Knox pyroported them to the nursery. He loved the room. Bright and airy with lemon walls, smooth pine furnishings, and woodland murals decorating walls and closet doors, it had a warm and serene atmosphere that invited a person inside.

As the flames died down, there was a heart-lifting giggle of excitement. Asher's face lit up. "Da!" He dropped his truck on the plush carpet and raised his arms, flexing his little fists.

Knox scooped him up and pressed a light kiss to his cheek. "Just how crazy have you driven Meg?"

Asher blew bubbles at him.

"Thought so," said Knox.

Harper smiled at the cute sight her guys made. If people had expected Knox to soften now that he was a father, they had thought wrong. If anything, having a child to protect had made him even more intense than before. Harper figured it was partly because his own parents had failed him—he was determined to do better by his son.

Lounging in the rocking chair, Meg gave Harper a stern look. "This is where you tell me what happened."

Standing beside the chair, their butler, Dan, said, "Meg's mind has been running away with itself."

While Knox held Asher up high so the kid's little finger could trace the white tree mural that spanned from floor to ceiling, Harper relayed the incident to Meg and Dan. "She didn't fool him, though," Harper said, looking at Asher. "No, she went to him in the form of someone he trusted, but he didn't fall for it. The other kids didn't sense that she wasn't me, but he did."

"Asher knows you by scent as well as by sight. She might have looked like you, but she won't have had your scent," Meg pointed out.

"She didn't have *any* scent. Plus, she was saying, 'Come to Mama. Time to go home.' He doesn't call me that." Harper rubbed her nape. "He wasn't scared. When his mind brushed mine to call for me, there was no alarm there. No impression of him needing help. It was more like a, 'Hey, Mom, check this out.' The same kind of touch as when he sees something he finds intriguing."

Knox cast him a smile that glinted with pride. "He knew you'd protect him; that's why he wasn't scared."

Harper snorted. "Or he's a cocksure little bugger who was certain he was safe right inside that shield."

Dan's mouth quirked. "It was probably a bit of both."

A flutter of wings was followed by a hoarse, grating "caw".

Asher's face split into a huge grin as he noticed the crow

perched on a tree branch near his closed window. He even waved at the damn thing.

In an almost haughty movement, Dan flicked his hand. There was a slight *push* of power in the air, and the crow flew away.

"You can control animals?" Harper asked him.

"No, but I can communicate with them," said Dan. "I merely told it to leave."

"I need to go back to the hotel so I can be seen leaving it with Levi." Knox handed Asher to Harper and then kissed her temple. "When I'm back, I'll check over your wounds again."

She rolled her eyes. "I think we can safely say that they'll be fully healed soon."

"I still want to check them out." He wouldn't be satisfied until they were completely gone. Knox ruffled Asher's hair. "Be good for your mom." Again, Asher blew raspberries at him. With a chuckle, Knox pyroported to his office within the hotel he'd earlier held his meeting.

Gun-metal eyes hard, Levi pushed out of the leather chair, brow cocked in question.

"Asher's fine," Knox assured the reaper. "The only person who was physically hurt was Harper, and her wounds were healing nicely last time I checked. We're not sure who tried to take Asher, but we know that they're not dead."

Levi nodded, rolling back his wide shoulders. "Tanner filled me in on everything. It's odd that the she-demon left no scent behind. Everyone has a scent."

"Everyone bleeds, too, but there was no blood on Harper's knife."

Levi twisted his mouth. "What that she-demon did today was cocky. It's likely that she followed Harper to Jolene's house. She somehow kept a close eye on what was happening, ensured there was a distraction that would keep people occupied, and then pounced on what she felt was the right moment to enter the house. That kind of thing takes patience, smarts, and balls. That means we're not dealing with a near-rogue, which is always good news." He folded his arms across his broad chest. "Any theories on what kind of demon she could be?"

With a sigh, Knox scraped his hand over his jaw. "No. Although I suppose we should consider that it wasn't necessarily a 'she'. They took on Harper's form in order to get close to Asher, but that doesn't make them female. They could just as easily be male."

Levi swore. "Never thought of that. So we can't even be sure what gender they are, let alone what breed of demon they could be?"

"No, we can't," confirmed Knox. "But we know one thing for sure."

"What?"

"They may not bleed—or, at least, they may not leave behind any blood—but they can feel pain." Knox's tone deepened. Darkened. "That brings me a lot of comfort, because I intend to put them through a world of endless, unendurable, soul-destroying torment. I'll revel in every cry and scream and plea for mercy. Lap up their fear and terror and hopelessness."

"And when it's over?"

"It'll never be over." Even before she'd gotten pregnant, Knox and Harper both vowed that if anyone dared to come after their child, they would subject that fucker to an unimaginable suffering and relay a strong message that targeting their child would be a *grave* mistake.

Levi's grin was somewhat bloodthirsty. "It's been a while since we really partied like that. I'm looking forward to it. I'll bring the popcorn. And the chainsaw. The rusty one with the duller blade. The fucker won't be needing their limbs for what we have in mind."

Knox returned his grin. "Just don't forget the hot iron so we can cauterize the stumps. You always forget the hot iron."

"I know. Who forgets to bring a hot iron to a party, for God's sake?"

CHAPTER FOUR

A few days later, Knox looked up from the computer monitors within his home office when there was a knock at the door. "Come in," he called out. As Levi strode inside wearing a sober expression, Knox's muscles went rigid. "What is it?"

The sentinel let out a long breath. "There's something you need to see." He held up his iPhone. "This footage was aired on YouTube last night, but it took a while for anyone to really notice it."

Knox took the cell phone and tapped "play" with his thumb. The camera provided a close-up view of a woman bound to a chair with thick rope, her lips and chin trembling. The only light in the dark room seemed to be the one above her head, and that light illuminated the sheer terror in her familiar eyes. *Fuck.*

"Smile for the camera, Alethea," a voice in the background said. Oddly, that voice belonged to Alethea herself.

Another figure appeared then and moved to stand behind her.

It was impossible to be sure of their height, since only a slight portion of their body was visible.

"As you can tell," the voice went on, "I've stolen Alethea's voice for a little while. Can't have her shouting anything incriminating, can I?"

Alethea mouthed something, but no words came out.

"I think most of you will know who I am," the person behind her continued. "Well, maybe not who I am exactly. But you'll know *what* I am. You'll know you're looking at the fourth Horseman."

Knox swore through gritted teeth, but he didn't move his eyes from the screen.

After a pause for what was clearly dramatic effect, the voice went on, "Yes, to all those who doubted my group's existence, we are real. Although my compatriots—Isla, Nora, and Roan—are dead, the goal remains the same. The US Primes *have* to fall. But, really, must there be deaths? I don't see why. If each of the US Primes step down, this will end here. If not, many will die. And you, Mr. Thorne, will be the first to do so. It's nothing personal. You're simply in my way, much like Alethea is in my way."

She snapped something at the Horseman, but her words were once again silent.

He rested his hand on her head. "Now you get to see what I do to those who stand in my way." Hellfire streamed out of his palm and engulfed her body in a rush. Her screams would have no doubt overridden the sounds of fire hissing and popping if the Horseman hadn't stolen her voice. Her skin blistered and melted as the hellfire ate at it. Finally, her charred, blackened, steaming corpse slumped in her seat. Then the video came to an end.

Knox rubbed a hand down his face. "Jesus."

Grim, Levi nodded. "I never liked her, but death-by-hellfire . . . I wouldn't have wished that on her."

If he were normal, Knox probably would have felt some ele-
ment of grief over her death. He'd known her for centuries, and
they'd shared a bed many times. But she'd also done her best to
hurt Harper ever since Knox claimed the little sphinx as his
mate. As such, he'd come to feel little for the she-demon other
than utter contempt.

Like the other women from his past, Alethea had been
elegant, cultured, sophisticated, and well-groomed. Since she'd
viewed Harper as somewhat beneath her, Alethea had taken
his claim on Harper as, in Levi's words, a "personal insult". But
that wasn't the only reason Alethea had been an absolute bitch
to her. She—like many others—was intimidated by Harper.
Moreover, Alethea had been unable to work out what made his
mate "tick". Unable to pierce Harper's aloof "you're not worth my
time" air or hit her where it truly hurt, no matter what Alethea
did or how far she went.

Harper was indeed a hard nut to crack. She was difficult to
predict. Hard to offend. Impossible to manipulate. Rare for their
kind, she also had no aspirations for power whatsoever. Nor was
she driven by greed, addictions, or a craving for adrenalin rushes.
Unlike other Primes, she didn't demand respect or submission.
Didn't flaunt her status or act like she was above others. Alethea
had just never been able to understand her.

She'd no doubt also been jealous that Harper was incredibly
powerful—so powerful, in fact, that she'd fought off a death
hex. Demons respected strength and, as such, the other Primes
had grudgingly come to not only respect her but accept her as
Knox's mate. Alethea, however, had never treated Harper with
anything less than hostility. For that reason, he couldn't find it
in him to feel any grief over her death. But, since he didn't have
a lot of good in him, that wasn't at all shocking.

Snapping out of his thoughts, Knox handed the iPhone

back to his sentinel. "I'm surprised the clip even made it onto the website."

"Some viewers have commented on it, slating the 'special effects' and calling Alethea a bad actor. I doubt the people at YouTube thought it was real. Why would they?"

Knox inclined his head, conceding Levi's point. "I'll need to call Jonas. I'm sure he's seen the clip by now and isn't in the mood for conversation, but I need to speak with him. The Horseman said he wanted me to die first. And although he also said he'd only kill me if the Primes didn't agree to step down, I don't think it means he's not behind what happened to Asher."

"Neither do I. It doesn't make sense that he'd give you advanced warning that he meant to attack—he'd need whatever advantage he could get. I think he sent someone after Asher. I think he waited a while, hoping you'd lower your guard, and then struck out of nowhere. Probably believed that an abrupt attack would be effective."

"But it wasn't. All it did was alert us to his plans, so he had nothing to lose by making this video and spouting dire warnings."

"You should make a public statement," Levi recommended. "Disclose that someone was sent for Asher. It will enrage a whole lot of people, especially our lair and even some of the Primes. We need demonkind to be angry, not afraid."

"Once I've spoken with Jonas and I have the facts about his sister, I'll make a statement." Knox twisted his mouth as he considered the footage. "The Horseman said she was in his way. It seems likely that he knew her personally."

Levi nodded. "She was sleeping with Thatcher, but it didn't last long. Alethea's relationships never did."

True enough. "I need to tell Harper about this before someone else does." *Baby, you got a minute?*

Her psychic taste of honey, coffee, and truffles poured into his mind, filling every empty space. *Sure*, she responded. *I'm just making a snack while Asher has his afternoon nap.*

Knox pyroported to their kitchen to find her standing at the counter, spreading soft cheese on a bagel. "Where's Meg?" he asked. The housekeeper often prepared their meals before they got the chance.

"Visiting her sister." Harper frowned at whatever she saw on his face. "What happened? Please tell me you found out who tried to take Asher."

"I wish I could." Knox took her hands and drew her to him. "There's no tactful way to say this. Alethea's dead."

For a long moment, Harper said nothing. "Dead?"

"Dead. Her murder was posted on YouTube." He told her about the footage and that the killer claimed to be the remaining Horseman. "I advise you not to watch the clip—it's ugly. You don't want that in your head."

Harper shoved a hand through her hair, shocked. She couldn't pretend to feel any upset over the she-demon's death. In truth, she hadn't felt even the most basic respect for Alethea, hence why she'd found great joy in toying with the woman, calling her "dolphin" due to her kind's random ability to shift into such a mammal. Still, Harper experienced no sense of satisfaction over her death. "That's a hell of a way to go. I wouldn't have wished it on her. Wouldn't wish it on anyone. Except maybe for the person who tried to take Asher. *Them* I would wish never-ending torture on."

The culprit would suffer a fuck of a lot worse than what Alethea did—Knox would make sure of it. Many might have been surprised by Harper's merciful response to Alethea's death, but that was because they didn't see the marshmallow center that lay beneath her hard exterior. Knox loved that she had such compassion and mercy in her. Some might view those qualities as weaknesses. But the fact that she was as kindhearted as she was bloodthirsty made her strong, in his opinion. She had many facets, and that gave her an edge.

"I intend to speak with Jonas and find out who Alethea was associating with before she disappeared," said Knox. "It might be insensitive not to give him space and time to grieve first, but the Horseman is making their move—we don't *have* time."

"Jonas will want the fucker caught. If you make it clear that you intend to make that happen, he'll be more cooperative. Damn, I feel bad for him. I don't trust him—not knowing he wanted to make a deal with Lou in the hope of getting his hands on an archdemon—but it must be hard to lose a sibling." Harper winced, because she remembered that she herself *had* lost a sibling. She'd also been the one to kill him.

"You're thinking of Roan. Stop." Knox rested his hands on her shoulders. "As you've said before, it was him or you. You chose you. He was never a brother to you. Never. And let's not forget that he was working with whoever killed Alethea. Her murderer even named Roan as one of the Horsemen on the video."

"Carla won't take that well," Harper said. Her estranged mother was not only adamant that Roan would never have been involved in a conspiracy to see the US Primes fall, she didn't believe that the Four Horsemen were even real. Now, she'd have to face the truth. More, she'd have to face that she'd been wrong. Harper was pretty sure that Carla would hate both those things.

As Carla, her mate, Bray, and their youngest son had switched to a lair in Washington, she and Harper hadn't spoken since before Asher was born. Maybe that should have saddened Harper. It didn't. Who wanted an attention junkie in their life who'd not only once tried to abort them, but had sold them to their paternal family when trapping their soul in a container hadn't worked? Harper certainly didn't.

As an adult, Harper had discovered little things that had suggested a very small part of Carla wished things had been different between them, but the woman really was too twisted to have a healthy mother-child relationship with any of her kids. It was textbook of narcissists, really, so Harper didn't take it personally.

Initially, it had seemed that Carla had eventually come to terms with Harper being her co-Prime, but Harper had recently discovered that she'd been looking to switch lairs even *before* Roan's death. A never-ending victim who thrived on drama, Carla had milked whatever sympathy and attention she could get for his death. She'd also hoped it would turn the lair against Harper. It hadn't. Carla's rage had intensified when Harper's pregnancy earned her the limelight that Carla perpetually craved. So, yeah, there was no hope for them.

"No, she won't like it," agreed Knox. "But as she's in Washington, you won't have to hear about it."

"Unless she ventures to the Underground," Harper pointed out. The demonic playground could be best described as a hyped-up version of the Las Vegas strip, and it attracted demons worldwide.

"The doormen of the club above the entrance to the Underground are under strict orders from me not to allow her, Bray, or Kellen inside. I know you were hoping to have some sort of relationship with Kellen, baby, but I won't allow him to mess with your head anymore."

"Neither will I," said Harper. The teenager had reached out to her initially, but he dropped her like a bad habit each time there was conflict between her and his family. He'd sent her a congratulatory text when Asher was born, but she hadn't heard

from him since. Considering she was responsible for his older
brother's death, she didn't see how they could have a relationship
at all anyway. It would just have to be enough that she'd gotten
to know him a little.

"Back to the subject of what happened to Alethea," said
Harper. "I know that, as your co-Prime, I should go with you to see
Jonas. But there was so much animosity between me and Alethea
that I'm the very last person he will want to see right now."

"You're right. And I don't trust that he won't take out his grief
on you, so it would be best all round if you stayed here." Which
suited Knox's overprotective streak just fine.

"Are you going to tell him what almost happened to Asher?"

"Yes." Knox slid his hands over her shoulders, down her arms,
and then cupped her hips. "I'll be making a public statement
about it, but I need some information from Jonas first."

"Do you really think the Horseman made that clip just so that
he could tell the Primes they must step down?"

"No. He wants people to be scared. To fear him. That would
give him power. Alethea was the sister of a Prime. Other Primes
will soon wonder if one of their own relatives will be targeted.
Her killer said that I'd be next, but that won't make anyone feel
at all reassured. They'll be worried, off-balance, and won't know
what to think."

"Which he'll *love*."

"Yes, I think he will." Knox traced her hipbones with his
thumbs. "The Primes will likely want a meeting to discuss
the issue. I doubt any of them will be prepared to step down,
no matter how worried they are, but they'll want to address
the matter."

"We should call the meeting ourselves. If it's in Vegas, we
won't have to travel." She didn't want to leave Asher behind,
but she'd be unwilling to take him along.

"I'll have Levi arrange it." Knox dabbed a light, lingering kiss on her mouth. "We'll talk more later. Enjoy your bagel."

Returning to his office, Knox gave Levi orders to arrange a meeting for the Primes and then pulled up the YouTube footage on his computer. His monitor was large, so Knox had a much better view than he'd had on Levi's cell.

He watched the recording again, this time with a critical eye. Watched the way the Horseman moved, observed their body language, and noted their clothing. He also examined the background, looking for clues as to their location.

They didn't move like a woman, he thought. There was a male swagger there, a masculine confidence in each step. Although it was difficult to be sure of their build, they didn't appear to have any feminine curves. Their clothes were dark and plain, from what he could tell.

As he reached the part where the Horseman placed their hand on Alethea's head, Knox paused the footage and zoomed in on the hand. Thick, masculine fingers. No long nails. In fact, they were cut to the quick. Their skin was white, but not pale. Caucasian male, Knox decided.

No matter how close Knox zoomed into the footage, he couldn't discern any objects in the background. If he had to guess, he'd say the wall paint was dark, as no color at all lightened the shadows. It appeared to be an empty, drab room. A basement, perhaps.

After spending a good half hour studying the Horseman and the background, Knox replayed the footage again. This time, he concentrated on Alethea. At that moment, she didn't look at all like an encantada—a female sex demon. Oh, her preternatural allure was still there, but it was tainted by the sheer terror in her watery eyes. Not just terror ... betrayal. She *had* known the Horseman. Known them well enough that she felt betrayed by their actions.

Her hair wasn't disheveled and, aside from her smudged mascara, her make-up was perfectly in place. As such, Knox doubted she'd been held prisoner. He couldn't be sure what length of time she'd been with the Horseman, but Knox didn't believe she'd been there against her will—at least not initially.

Watching it a second time, Knox concentrated on the part where she'd first mouthed something. Despite that he had a close-up view of her face, lipreading wasn't easy.

"Watching the clip again?"

Knox looked up as Harper walked in. "Baby, you don't want to see this, trust me on that. You certainly don't want to look at it when you not long ago ate."

Harper rolled her eyes. "Remind me when I've ever been delicate." She rounded his sleek black, U-shaped executive desk and peered at one of the multiple computer screens. She was so used to seeing Alethea smug and bitchy that it was a distinct shock to see the encantada looking so afraid. Harper knew how it felt to be held captive; to know that your life was in the hands of another. And death by hellfire—that would have been agonizing.

"I'm looking for clues that might help identify who this person was and just where Alethea was killed," said Knox.

Harper turned to him. "Any ideas?"

"At this point, I'm quite sure that the Horseman is, in fact, a man. Caucasian. Confident. He knew Alethea well, and she'd trusted him to some extent. You can see the hint of betrayal in her eyes if you look beneath the terror."

Harper leaned closer to the screen. "You're right. What's she trying to say?"

"That's what I'm trying to figure out." He rewound the clip slightly. "Here, it seems like she's saying, 'Please.' Then she pauses, licks her lips, and mouths, 'Don't do this.' The Horseman chats about how the US Primes must fall, and then—just before he sets her alight—she tries to say something else, but I can't quite work out what."

"Play it for me." Harper leaned toward the screen again and concentrated on the movement of Alethea's mouth. "You're. Dead. She's saying, 'You're dead.'"

Knox nodded, able to see it clearly now. "She says the next part so fast I can't understand it, but it seems like she's trying to tell him, 'He'll get through.' Get through what? And who's 'he'?"

Harper watched that part of the clip and then shook her head. "No, not 'get'. She's not mouthing a 'g' sound, she's mouthing a 'k' sound. He'll ... kill ... you. She practically spits the words, that's why it's hard to make it out, but I'm leaning towards, 'He'll kill you.' By 'he' I think she meant you."

It would make sense, since the Horseman had just been chatting about getting rid of Knox. "I think you may be right."

"Why couldn't she have mouthed something *helpful* like his name or something?"

Knox was thinking the very same thing. "I was hoping she might have tried to communicate something that would give us a clue."

"Have you tried calling Jonas yet?"

"Yes. He's not answering, which doesn't surprise me. If he's grieving, it's unlikely that he'll be interested in speaking with anyone."

Harper narrowed her eyes. "You said '*if*' he's grieving. Why wouldn't he be? You think he could be the one who killed her?"

"You don't?"

She thought on it for a moment. "He seemed pretty close to Alethea, so it's hard to imagine him ever hurting her. I was actually thinking that the Horseman could have killed Alethea because he knew that Jonas would never stop looking for her.

That made her a problem, didn't it? Because if Jonas had found Alethea, he'd have also found the Horseman."

Inclining his head, Knox said, "Yes, she was a liability."

"You know, I didn't figure Alethea for the kind of person who'd beg anyone for anything—not even for her life. She must have been truly terrified."

Knox hadn't thought of that. He nodded. "Alethea would never let anyone see her cry, let alone the entire world via a YouTube video. As you say, she must have been terrified." But of who?

As Jonas didn't answer any of his calls, Knox went to the Prime's home the following day. But when Levi spoke their names into the built-in intercom of the keypad near the front gates, the butler claimed that Jonas wasn't fit to receive visitors. In other words, he was drowning his sorrows.

"His control over his gifts isn't at its best," the butler told Levi. It was no surprise, since grief had a way of shaking a demon's control. "Perhaps Mr. Thorne could return in a week or so."

Knox lowered his window and spoke into the intercom. "It's essential that I speak with your Prime. If I could afford to give him time, I'd do so. But this is much too important."

There was a short silence, and then the butler sighed. "If you insist, Mr. Thorne." There was a loud beep, and then the iron gates opened.

As Levi drove toward the large mansion and Knox took in the expansive lawn, statues, fountain, and thick white columns, he recalled how Harper had once branded the place so showy that it was soulless. Knox could agree with her. He'd like to think his own estate possessed some character and personality. Jonas seemed too intent on being flashy to give this place a homey feel.

Levi accompanied Knox up the slate steps to the front door, where the butler waited, looking anxious. Their shoes clicked on the stone flooring as the butler led them through the open entryway, down a long hall, and into a large parlor that smelled of polish, wood smoke, and brandy.

The thick velvet drapes were closed, and the lights were off, but Knox spotted Jonas in the plush armchair near the fireplace. The flicker of the flames illuminated his vacant expression and red-rimmed eyes. He looked both dazed and devastated.

"I was clear that I wanted to be left alone, Rodger," Jonas slurred. He looked to the doorway and froze at the sight of Knox and Levi, who slowly crossed to him. The door closed quietly behind them as Rodger quickly scampered away.

Jonas snickered at Knox. "Why are you here? Come to gloat? No doubt you're glad my sister's dead. She can't cause your mate any more upset now, can she?"

Knox wasn't going to even credit that snipe with a response. He'd expected Jonas to lash out in such a way, which was why he was tremendously glad that Harper hadn't insisted on coming.

He wouldn't lie to Jonas and claim to be grieving Alethea's death. They both knew that, since she'd made a point of insulting his mate every chance she got, he'd felt nothing but distaste for Alethea near the end. His demon, who had never liked her, didn't feel even so much as an ounce of pity for her.

With a shaky hand, Jonas grabbed a crystal tumbler from the table and slurped the brandy. "I'll bet Harper's throwing a celebratory party. She probably plans to play the clip of Alethea's death in HD in your fucking home theater. Oh yes, she'll be loving this."

With an inner sigh, Knox arched a brow. "Are you done?"

Jonas glared at him. "God, you're cold. You took Alethea to bed countless times, yet you feel no grief at all, do you?"

"You're going to spew shit at me for not caring for her as you did? I would have thought you'd be more interested in seeing your sister's killer pay."

Jonas stilled, eyes sharpening. "You know who he is? Give me his name."

"I don't have his name. Yet. But I intend to ID him. I need your help to do that."

Sagging into the chair, Jonas glanced at the fireplace. "If I knew who he was, he'd be in my dungeon right now."

He has a dungeon? asked Levi.

Apparently so, said Knox.

Huh. Didn't expect that.

"What about the humans she spent time with?" Knox asked. "Have you interviewed them?"

"I already spoke to them after she first disappeared. None knew where she was. Since I couldn't have them reporting her disappearance to the human authorities, I had to tell them all that she moved away. None of them have contacted me recently, so I'm assuming they didn't see the video clip before I had my contact at YouTube take it down."

"I'm assuming you asked your contact if he had any information on the person who uploaded the clip," Knox prompted.

"All they had on the person was an email address. I had a technology expert from my lair try to track it. They said they couldn't. A proxy was used." Jonas stared hard at Knox, face twisting in resentment. "But maybe you already know that."

"Excuse me?"

"Maybe it was *you* on that clip. Maybe you're the fourth Horseman. Maybe you talked of being the next victim to draw suspicion from yourself."

"Maybe *you're* the fourth Horseman," Knox countered. "I saw her face at the meeting when she heard you wanted to make a pact with Lucifer—she was shocked. Anxious. Maybe she discovered what you wanted from Lucifer. Maybe she didn't like it. Maybe you then killed her to preserve your secret."

Eyes wide, Jonas snarled. "I would never have harmed my sister."

"And I would never have hidden behind a camera."

Sneering, Jonas slugged back more brandy. "I suppose you wouldn't have. You're so sure none of us can defeat you that—"

"You want to know who her killer is. I want to know who he is. Playing this game doesn't help."

"Just go." Jonas flicked a dismissive hand his way, but the move lacked strength. "I can't tell you anything that would lead you to the fourth Horseman because I don't know anything."

"He was no stranger to her, Jonas. They knew each other. Who was she spending her time with?"

He closed his eyes, replying, "I don't know. She disappeared, remember."

"Before that, who was she with?"

"*I don't know.*"

Trying a different tack, Knox said, "She was well-aware of what you wanted from Lucifer, wasn't she?"

"No, but she suspected why I wanted his aid."

"Aid with what?"

Jonas didn't respond. Just stared into the fire.

Patience thin, Knox bared his teeth. "Jonas, do not fuck with me right now. It's not the time to test just how much tolerance I possess. Someone recently posed as Harper to get to my son. We suspect they wanted to take him, and we're betting they were sent by the Horseman."

Jonas's face went slack. "Posed as Harper?"

"Took on her physical form. They left no scent or blood behind, and I don't have to point out that such a thing isn't at all common." Jonas went so deathly pale that Knox's muscles bunched with tension. "What do you know?"

Closing his eyes, Jonas shook his head. "Oh, Alethea, what did you do?" he muttered.

Knox took an aggressive step toward him. "*Tell me what you know.*"

Jonas pinched the bridge of his nose and let out a hard sigh. "Alethea. She . . ."

"She, what?"

"She had an incorporeal demon in her possession."

Everything in Knox stilled. Even his demon stiffened. Fisting his hands, Knox echoed, "An incorporeal demon? She had an *incorporeal demon?*" A demon without a body. A demon that could possess others. A demon that, if extremely powerful, could also temporarily maintain the physical form of anyone it chose. A demon that was as near to indestructible as anything in their world could get. Mostly intangible, it had no bones for you to break, no blood for you to spill, no heart for you to stop, no brain for you to damage. Very little could kill it . . . making it the perfect weapon, and one of the worst opponents imaginable.

"I don't know how long she had it. She was behaving strangely. Acting secretive. She also kept putting off our dinner plans, which was out of character for her. Concerned and annoyed, I went to her house to see her. She was angry that I hadn't called first, and I could tell she wanted me gone. I noticed a glass display case on the mantelpiece in her living room. It caught my eye because it was empty. But when I moved closer, I saw that there *was* something inside it. A sort of hazy vapor. So faint you could easily miss it."

Jaw hard, Knox exchanged a knowing look with Levi.

"I didn't need to ask what it was. I'd never seen an incorporeal before, but I'd heard enough about them to know what I was looking at. Still, I'd hoped she'd tell me I was wrong." Jonas tossed back the last of his brandy. "But she didn't. Of course, I demanded to know where the hell she'd gotten it."

"And?" prodded Knox.

"She said she stole it from a private collector. And that she meant to free it."

Levi swore under his breath.

"I insisted that she return the display case to wherever it came from," Jonas went on, "but she said that it was for protection. Said that she suspected you or Harper could be the fourth Horseman and that she thought one of you would come for her."

"But you didn't believe her," Knox sensed.

"No." Jonas rubbed his temple, as if a headache was building. "I knew that, whatever the case, I needed to somehow get rid of it. I also knew she would protest, so I pretended that I understood her motives, and I promised that I wouldn't say a word about it. But at the meeting, when you revealed that I wanted to make a deal with Lucifer, she became suspicious that I'd sought his help to destroy the incorporeal. That was why she disappeared—she ran from me, because she didn't trust me."

"And, knowing the type of destruction an incorporeal can cause, you didn't think to say something to someone?" clipped Knox, wanting to shake the other demon. So much could have been avoided if Jonas had just spoken up about it.

Jonas's eyes flared. "She was my sister. I knew people would come for the incorporeal, and I knew she'd never give it up easily—even if it meant risking her life. I thought if I could just get rid of it before anyone got hurt, no one would ever know. Besides, I didn't think she would truly be able to free it. She just wasn't strong enough for something like that. I spoke with an incantor about it—the same incantor people mistakenly believed

I was dating—and she said it would take several things to free an incorporeal, including the sacrifice of a demonic child."

Levi looked at Knox. "Harper's younger cousin, Heidi, could have been Alethea's chosen target."

Jonas's gaze snapped to the sentinel. "No. Alethea would never have done something like that. She may have thought about it, yes, but she wouldn't have gone through with it. She was vindictive, but she wasn't evil. *Someone* was using her. She was seeing someone else, but she wouldn't tell me who. Wouldn't even tell me if I knew them. The two must have worked together to free the incorporeal."

And now it was targeting Knox's son. His demon growled. "You should have *told* someone that she had one in her possession."

"I'd planned to destroy it," Jonas defended. "The incantor I spoke to said that nothing of the Earth could kill an incorporeal. Everyone knows that nothing is impervious to the flames of hell. Archdemons *are* the flames of hell. I wanted Lucifer to either banish the incorporeal back to hell or give me the brief use of an archdemon, but he wouldn't even *speak* with me. I was determined to undo what she'd done before it got her killed." He squeezed his eyes shut. "But I failed. I should have looked harder for her. I tried to find her, I really did, but it was like she didn't want to be found."

"Or she didn't want the incorporeal to be found," said Knox. "If she freed it, she would have given it an order; made a bargain with it. There would have been no other point in freeing one, especially since it could have turned on her. What do you think she asked it to do?"

A weary exhale shuddered out of Jonas. "I don't know."

"If you had to guess . . . ?"

"I don't know. Truly. I suspect that whatever order the

incorporeal was given came from the Horseman, not from her. And I believe deep down to my bones that she didn't know they were the fourth Horseman—the bastard wants to see the fall of the US Primes. I *am* a Prime. Alethea wouldn't have been party to anything that would harm me."

Knox could agree with the latter. "But she would have been party to something that brought harm to me, my mate, or my son, wouldn't she?"

Jonas looked about to deny the accusation, but then he sighed. "The temptation would have been there, but I don't believe she would truly have gone through with it. No, I think the Horseman lied to her about what his intentions were for the incorporeal. They told her whatever would gain them her cooperation."

"Yes, because Alethea was so naïve and easily manipulated," Knox said, sarcasm heavy in his tone. "Be real, Jonas. Your sister was cunning and devious; she would have recognized if someone was trying to play her."

"Then they were damn convincing or someone she trusted, because there is no way I will believe she would have knowingly worked with the Horseman. She obviously discovered who they were and wanted out, so they killed her to protect their identity. And now they're coming for you. Or, as it would appear, they're coming for your son. And if they really have an incorporeal in their arsenal, I'm sorry to say that he's doomed." Jonas turned back to the fireplace. "Now, if you don't mind, I'd like to be alone. There's truly nothing more I can tell you anyway."

Believing the latter, Knox decided to back off. But it was hard when anger still ravaged his insides. If Jonas hadn't kept the incorporeal a secret, the entity wouldn't now be targeting his son. If Harper had been here, she probably would have flown at the other Prime and gripped him by the throat. Knox was highly tempted to do that very thing, but it was possible that Jonas would later think of something else that could help. And considering Jonas wanted the Horseman as badly as Knox did, killing the Prime would mean there was one less person searching for the bastard. Knox would deal with Jonas at a later date.

"I'm holding a meeting with the other Primes," said Knox.

"Well, I do hope you enjoy it. I have no interest in going."

Knox had thought as much. "That's up to you. But a discussion about the Horseman needs to be had."

Jonas's gaze went inward. "I wasn't entirely convinced they were real."

"Many weren't."

"I should have looked harder for her."

"She didn't want to be found; you said so yourself." Too angry to have any interest in comforting the other Prime, Knox turned and left the mansion.

As he and Levi slid back into the Bentley, Levi said, "Well, that answered a lot of our questions. For instance, we now know that it was highly likely that Alethea was the one who went after Heidi—she needed a demonic child to sacrifice, and it would have given her a kick to kill a relative of Harper. It must have pissed Alethea off big time when her plan failed."

And while that was a relief, it also sadly meant that . . . "Some other child must have died in Heidi's place, otherwise the incorporeal wouldn't be free."

Levi nodded, expression grim. "We also now know that Jonas did in fact want an archdemon, just as Malden said. But it wasn't because Jonas had a nefarious plan, it was because he was trying to foil his sister's nefarious plan. An incorporeal demon . . . Damn, Harper's going to freak."

Knox felt his brow furrow. "No, she'll stay calm."

CHAPTER FIVE

"Alethea had a *what?*"

"Shh, baby, calm down."

Harper did a slow blink, thinking he had to be kidding. "Calm down? *Calm down?* Knox, that bitch had an incorporeal demon, it's now on the loose, and *it went after Asher.* There's also a damn high chance that Alethea meant to sacrifice Heidi in order to free the fucker. It's good for the damn dolphin that she's not alive, because I'd have smacked the motherfucking shit out of her. Really. I'd have put her through an eternal loop of soul-deep agony until she'd begged for a mercy that would never have come."

His cock inappropriately twitched—it seemed to love her bloodthirsty streak. Ignoring the "I told you she'd flip her lid" look from Levi, who was leaning against the wall, Knox spoke to Harper in a soothing tone. "I don't doubt that, baby. I'd have been right there with you, delivering my own brand of punishment. But we'll have to be content with knowing she suffered an excruciating—if much too fast—death and concentrate on dealing with those who'd worked with her, including the incorporeal."

"Deal with it how? Correct me if I'm wrong, but those fuckers are practically impossible to kill." Harper shoved a shaking hand through her hair. Fury and anxiety clawed at her insides. How the hell could she neutralize the threat to her son if she couldn't damn well destroy it?

Knox rested his hands on her shoulders. "They can be killed but, yes, they make tough opponents for a number of reasons. But so do we, baby."

Sitting on the sofa, Larkin lifted a hand. "I have to admit, I don't know a lot about incorporeals. Just that they're nasty little bastards."

Beside the harpy, Keenan gave Knox a look that said he wasn't much wiser on the subject. "I know they sure like possessing humans, pretending they're the devil himself. Do the exorcisms really weaken them?"

"No, but they weaken the human, which then weakens the incorporeal and so they switch to another body while they regain their strength," Knox explained.

"All I need to know is how the hell to kill it," said Tanner, sprawled on the other sofa with his legs crossed at the ankles.

Knox had summoned Larkin, Keenan, and Tanner to the mansion so that he and Levi could inform them and Harper of Jonas's revelations. It was vital that the sentinels were fully apprised of the situation so that they were not only prepared to deal with whatever came next, but so they could then impart the necessary information onto the Force—the demons who worked under the sentinels to help police their lair.

"Like archdemons, incorporeals are born in hell," said Knox. "For the most part, they remain there. But that's mainly because they can't survive outside of it unless they have a host. The only way they can roam the Earth is if they possess bodies. But they can only control them for a short time as it's draining, so they often sort of ... *linger* inside a person, surfacing occasionally to take command of the body and do whatever it is they wish to do. If they're very powerful and at top strength, they can even maintain a physical form of their own for a very limited amount of time."

At Knox's meaningful look, Harper hissed. "*Fuck*. I should have considered that she might have been an incorporeal. They're just so rare ..." Harper frowned as something occurred to her. "Wait, could she have still been in the room with Asher after the attack? I thought she'd gone, but maybe I just couldn't see her."

"It wasn't a 'she'," said Knox. "Incorporeals are neither male, nor female; they just are. As for whether it lingered, I doubt it. You hurt and weakened it, so it would have needed to quickly find a host. Without a body to possess, they die fairly quickly, especially since maintaining a physical form of their choosing drains them."

Cursing, Harper started to pace. "This isn't good at all. I mean, an incorporeal can look like anyone at any time, can't it? It can possess virtually anyone."

"It can possess virtually any human or animal," began Knox, "but only a powerful incorporeal could possess a demon. Incorporeals are uncommon, and *powerful* incorporeals are even less so."

"But they do exist," said Harper.

"Yes," Knox allowed. "Still, even powerful incorporeals generally don't bother trying to possess our kind. They can't use our abilities, so a human would be just as useful a host. Humans are also much easier to possess, not to mention a hell of a lot easier to control." He shrugged. "Logically, we're just not worth the effort."

"Have you ever come across one before?" Tanner asked him.

"Yes," replied Knox. "A long time ago. I killed it by calling on the flames of hell."

Keenan took a swig from his flask. "And if you're someone who can't call on the flames, how do you kill them?"

"It's not easy to harm an incorporeal," said Knox. "You can't do so by harming their host. You have to kill it while it's either bodiless or using its energy to manifest into a solid form. By stabbing it in the heart and dealing it soul-deep pain, Harper will have dramatically weakened it, but it would take much more than that to kill one."

"They can't leave hell unless they're conjured by a practitioner or an incantor, right?" asked Levi.

Knox nodded. "It would take a shitload of dark magick on the conjurer's part. It usually takes months and involves a lot of blood sacrifices. Not just any incantor or dark practitioner can call a demon from hell. They'd have to specialize in conjuring, and that often takes years of practice under the tutelage of another. There's nothing simple about the process, which is why there aren't many of them roaming the Earth."

"Is the conjurer then in control of the incorporeal?" asked Larkin, her eyes—sometimes gray-green, sometimes gray-blue—glinting with unease.

"To an extent," replied Knox. "They make a bargain. The conjurer will give it freedom, but the incorporeal must first do their bidding."

Keenan returned his flask to the inner pocket of his jacket. "And after the incorporeal has fulfilled its end of the bargain?"

"It can do whatever it wants," said Knox, flicking a concerned look at his mate, who was still pacing. "Remain on Earth. Go back to hell. Whatever it likes."

"Which means that the one we're up against could be acting alone," Tanner pointed out.

Knox pursed his lips. "Yes, but I don't see what it would gain from trying to possess Asher."

Harper stumbled to a halt. "Say that again."

Knox took her arms and pulled her to him. "I don't believe it was trying to snatch him, Harper. I believe it was trying to get close enough to possess him."

The thought made her stomach roll and her knees buckle. "But why?"

"Exactly. Why? It's not like an incorporeal would get any use out of a baby's body. Asher can't walk, and he relies on others to care for him. A baby would serve it no purpose." Knox just didn't get it. "He's simply not worth the struggle it would take to possess him—assuming the incorporeal even could."

"Does a person know they're possessed?" Larkin absent-mindedly toyed with the end of her long braid. "I mean, if the incorporeal is just hanging back, hitching a ride in someone's body like it's a cab or a train, will that person know?"

"Think of them as microparasites," said Knox. "Like bacteria. A host wouldn't feel the actual bacteria there. They wouldn't even be aware of the infection until they experienced physical symptoms. Incorporeals can, as you said, 'hang back' and hitch a ride. The host won't feel them. The incorporeals are a drain on the body as any parasite can be, so the host may feel tired and weary and have headaches. But unless or until the incorporeal takes control of the body, their presence won't be sensed. Well, not unless they talk to the host, anyway."

Tanner's brows rose. "Talk? They can talk to them?"

Knox nodded. "For the host, it's just like another voice

inside their head, which is why some often think they're
going crazy."

"Is the host fully aware of what's happening while the incorporeal is in control?" asked Larkin.

Pulling his mate closer, Knox slipped an arm around her as he
responded to the harpy's question. "Sometimes they're partially
aware. Afterwards, the host usually has no memory of what
happened. They might assume they blacked out or went into a
fugue state unless someone witnessed what happened."

Harper rubbed her arm. "So I could be possessed right now
and I wouldn't even know?"

"If an incorporeal were to attempt to possess you, you would
feel it." He gently skimmed his fingers over her head. "Like
sharp splinters trying to force their way into your brain. It's
highly unlikely that it ever happened to you, Harper. You have
extremely strong psychic shields that can shred and mutilate a
person's psyche. In other words, you wouldn't be a risk worth
taking when the incorporeal can just as easily use a human."

She swallowed. "You really think it meant to possess Asher?"

"Yes," he said, hating the answer. "I just don't see why. It could
have been ordered to do so by the Horseman, of course. But
there seems little point in it."

Tanner stroked his jaw. "I'm guessing an incorporeal can use
its own power just fine while possessing a host."

"It can," confirmed Knox. "But if you're thinking that it
was ordered to then strike at us while within Asher, I sincerely
doubt it. He's a baby. Limited with a baby's psychic strength, the
incorporeal wouldn't be able to do a lot of damage, no matter
how powerful it was."

"But it could drain Asher, right?" asked Larkin.

Massaging Harper's nape, Knox replied, "It could, yes, but that
would take time. Months. The entire estate is encompassed by

a protective shield that would prevent anything harmful from entering. Even if the incorporeal had managed to possess Asher while he was at Jolene's house, it would never have gotten past the shield. Would have literally been spat out of his body the moment Asher returned home."

"The incorporeal won't have known about the shield, though," said Keenan, but then he frowned. "Actually, I take that back. It's pretty much common knowledge among demons that your home is shielded, so it's unlikely that the Horseman ordered the incorporeal to try to possess Asher in order to drain him. That's probably why the incorporeal had to make its move when he was off the estate."

"It'll try again, won't it?" Edgy, Harper had to resist the urge to dance from foot to foot. "I mean, if it was ordered to possess him for some reason, it won't stop trying until it does. Not if it wants to be free."

Knox cocked his head. "That depends. If it *was* ordered to possess him and then reports back to the Horseman that Asher has a shield it can't bypass, it might then be given a different order."

But, whatever the case, they wouldn't give up, thought Harper. "The Horseman seems determined to succeed where the others within his group failed. If that's true, he'll—and I'm feeling confident that it's a 'he' after studying the footage—come at us with everything he has. Including an incorporeal demon."

Levi folded his arms. "Jonas said that Alethea claimed to have stolen it from a private collector. Knox, are you thinking what I'm thinking?"

Knox looked at him. "If you're thinking that Dion Boughton could be the collector then yes, I am."

Keenan's eyes lit up. "He collects the unique. Keeps them in his own personal museum at his home. If anyone would have an incorporeal in their possession, it would be him. Hell, he could even be the fourth Horseman. It's worth considering that Dion may have partnered with Alethea."

Tanner's brows lowered. "I don't recall ever hearing that he and Alethea spent time together."

"Unless we speak to Dion, we won't know anything for sure," said Knox. "Unfortunately, that's not something we can do straight away, since we can't simply call him to arrange a visit to his island."

"Ah, yes, he's a technophobe," Harper remembered. "Doesn't use phones or computers."

Knox nodded. "I still have his address somewhere. I'll write a letter to him, saying I wish to speak with him. It shouldn't take long for him to respond. Still, I don't like that we'll have to wait." He wanted answers *yesterday*.

Larkin crossed one leg over the other. "I still think we should look more closely at Thatcher. He helped us get to Harper after she was kidnapped by Nora, sure, but what better way to shift suspicion from himself than that? And he and Alethea did look a little cozy in the Ice Bar."

"But surely Thatcher wouldn't have been seen in public with someone he knew he might have to later kill if she didn't agree to go along with his plans," said Levi. "Plus, Jonas said Alethea was being secretive about her new boyfriend. Parading around with Thatcher isn't discreet. Not that I'm ruling him out as a suspect, I'm just saying it doesn't add up."

Knox felt his face harden. "As far as I'm concerned, while my mate and child are at risk, everyone's a suspect." He looked at Larkin. "Jonas says he had extreme difficulty tracking Alethea's movements after she disappeared, but maybe you'll have better luck with that. She's the key to uncovering the identity of the Horseman—he made a grave error in killing her so publicly. He more or less shouted, 'Just follow her past footsteps and you'll find me.'"

"He must be very sure those footsteps were covered," mused Levi.

Knox glanced at the reaper. "Let's hope the fucker made a mistake."

Harper sort of zoned out then. Conversation continued around her, but she couldn't take it in. Her thoughts were centered on the simple fact that an incorporeal demon wanted to possess her son. Possess. Her. Son. What mother would ever take that on the chin and get the fuck on with her day?

Like Knox, she had always suspected that someone would one day come for Asher. She'd planned to capture said someone and make them pay in a way that discouraged anyone else from even *daring* to try such a thing. But how could you capture something that had no body? How could you hunt something that had no scent? How could you attack something you could only see if it *wanted* you to see it?

The simple answer to each question was ... you couldn't. Not without a fuck of a lot of power and a shitload of luck.

Harper wasn't weak. Not by any means. And with her ability to call on the flames of hell, she could certainly destroy the incorporeal ... *if* it revealed itself. *If* it wasn't possessing another at the time. *If* it didn't learn from the mistakes it made with her at Jolene's house. She'd never been up against anything like it before, and it was easy to fear that she'd fail when the consequence of that failure would be the end of her son's life.

Her self-doubt weighed on her chest and left a sour taste on her tongue. She was Asher's mother; she was supposed to protect him. Right then, she didn't feel fully equipped to do it, and that absolutely terrified her.

Leaving the others to continue the meeting, Harper excused

herself and headed upstairs. She needed to be alone. Needed privacy. Needed time to assimilate everything and calm the fuck down.

On her way to her bedroom, she paused at the ajar door of the nursery. All was quiet inside. Still, she poked her head through the door. Asher was sprawled on his back in his crib, flat out, dark silky hair all mussed. Her heart squeezed.

Resisting the urge to go dab a kiss on his cheek for fear that she'd wake him, Harper headed into the lavish master bedroom, shed her clothes, and hopped into the walk-in shower of the opulent private bathroom.

She stood under the square rain shower head, arms crossed over her chest, head down, eyes closed as the hot spray pounded on her skin. Her muscles felt sore and cramped from the tension that had arrested her on hearing Knox's news.

An incorporeal demon. A goddamn, motherfucking incorporeal demon.

Dammit, why hadn't she just called on the flames of hell that day in Jolene's house? If she had, the incorporeal would be mere ashes right now. Then again, so would a good portion of Jolene's dining room, and there would be no hiding *exactly* how it had burned, since the flames of hell left a red residue behind.

People already worried that Knox could call on them. If they realized that she could also do so, they'd no doubt panic that she and Knox were so strong as a couple that they were a threat that needed eradicating. The other Primes were already nervous that Knox was mated—they didn't need an additional reason to worry.

Worse, people might even think that Knox had the ability to pass on such a power. She doubted there was a demon alive who wouldn't be greedy for such an ability. Some could then target him in the hope that he could give it to them. So, yeah, calling on the flames at Jolene's house would have brought on another set of problems.

That wasn't why Harper hadn't immediately called on them, though. She kept the ability in her "worst-case scenario" box, still spooked by how her demon had once gotten immensely drunk on the power. The fact was it wasn't an ability Harper should possess. She wasn't built to handle it. She could control it well enough, but not while angry. She wasn't like Knox, wasn't good at containing her emotions or keeping her composure. If she'd called on the flames in Jolene's dining room, Harper's out-of-control rage would have fed the flames and made them just as out of control.

In that sense, it was a good thing that Harper hadn't instinctively called on them. But the protective mother in her didn't care for logic—it wanted the incorporeal *dead*. And the dark entity within Harper craved that very same thing.

Knowing that stewing on the whole matter wouldn't help clear her head or calm her nerves, she concentrated on lathering the shampoo in her hair. Let herself enjoy the dig of her fingertips into her scalp and the vanilla scent of her soap surrounding her. Every time her thoughts strayed back to the incorporeal, she slammed a mental door on the subject. The last thing she wanted if Asher woke was for him to touch her mind and feel nothing but fury.

When she was finally done in the shower, she patted herself dry and then wrapped the lush towel around herself. Leaving the steamy bathroom, she grabbed her brush from the dresser on her way into the walk-in closet. Harper then combed the tangles out of her wet hair as she flicked through the underwear drawer.

She *felt* Knox enter the closet more than she heard him. He didn't speak. Just came up behind her and brushed her hair over her shoulder, baring her nape. Feeling his hot breath on her skin made a little shiver race down her spine. And the bastard no doubt knew exactly what he was doing to her.

Her eyes drifted shut as he nibbled and licked at her nape. Even through his clothes, she could feel his body heat blanketing her back and beating at her.

"Drop the towel," he whispered against her skin.

"Knox, my head's not in a good place right now and—"

He sank his teeth into the crook of her neck. The move was as territorial as it was dominant. "Never keep what's mine from me." He licked over the bite. "Now drop the fucking towel."

The soft command made Harper swallow. Knox's forceful nature wasn't an act; he didn't play a role. No, that assertiveness was part of him. He dominated from within. And damn if her body didn't respond to it every time, heating and buzzing with arousal. Sexual energy snapped the air taut. And as she felt his intense focus center on her, the outside world disappeared. Her mind cleared of all her worries, leaving only the need to have him inside her. And he'd known that, she thought. Known this was a distraction they both needed.

Clearing her suddenly dry throat, Harper let the towel puddle at her feet.

"Better," he said, sifting his fingers through her wet hair. "Now stay still for me."

Her eyes again drifted shut as he licked his way down her spine, scooping up any droplets of water. Goosebumps rose on her skin as a minor tremor quaked through her. She flinched as his teeth dug into one globe of her ass and he suckled hard. "Ow."

"Just renewing one of my marks," said Knox, unapologetic. "You know I don't like it when they fade." He shoved her towel aside and stood. He quickly shed his clothes, all the while enjoying the sight of his mate. Naked. Wet. Waiting for direction.

He knew her head was spinning with all he'd told her. His

own head wasn't in a much better state. Right now, he needed to feel her come apart around him. Needed the solace and peace that only Harper had ever been able to give him.

Pressing his front to her back, Knox fisted her hair, yanked her head aside and spoke into her ear. "Shall I tell you what I'm going to do to you? I'm going to get you so fucking wet, you can't take it. Then I'm going to rut on you the way my demon wants me to. Yeah, you're going to get fucked right up against that wall in front of you, Harper. Hard. Rough. Exactly how we both need it." He nipped her earlobe. "Turn around."

Cheeks flushed, Harper slowly turned. Her stomach twisted at the raw hunger and fierce possessiveness carved into his face. She knew that look. It said she was going to get ruthlessly fucked in a way that left her sore. "Knox, we—" He grabbed her chin and plunged his tongue into her mouth. And the world disappeared. All her thoughts were focused on him. On his mouth, so warm and demanding. On his taste, dark and rich. On the feel of his hands, skilled and confident as they skimmed over her.

Digging her nails into his back, she sank into the kiss as his tongue danced with hers; licking, flicking, and gliding against her own. Feel-good chemicals raced through her system, making her head spin.

A little desperate, Harper clawed at his back and tried taking over the kiss. It didn't work. His hand snapped around her throat and squeezed—a punishment and a reminder of who had the control.

With a growl, Knox pushed her against the wall, liking the way the breath left her lungs in a rush. He pinned her wrists at her sides, pressing her palms against the wall. "No touching me yet." The sapphire shade of her irises swirled, turned murky, and then darkened to a charcoal gray that blazed with need. The sight made his balls tighten. "Beautiful," he murmured.

He leaned his weight against her, making her feel crowded and overpowered, knowing she loved it. Knowing she even needed that bit of dominance, despite her defiant nature. He shoved his knee between her legs and pushed them apart. "Keep your palms flat on the wall, Harper." He slowly drew his finger down the column of her throat, between her breasts, along her stomach, but then veered down her inner thigh. She made a sound of frustration in the back of her throat. "What is it, baby?"

"Can we skip the you-getting-me-so-wet-I-can't-take-it part and just get straight to the fucking?"

His eyes slammed on hers, glittering with a need that matched her own. "No."

Yeah, she'd figured he'd say that. Harper watched as he continued to trace her with his fingers and tongue. She'd never get used to how his eyes roamed over her that way; it was the kind of appraisal one would give a rare, treasured artifact. No matter how rough or curt he was, she never felt anything but adored.

Taking in the sight of the little bites on her skin, pure masculine satisfaction welled up inside Knox. Never in his life had he or the entity been possessive of a partner—hell, another person—until Harper strolled into his office and turned his life upside fucking down. Knox sank his teeth into the side of her breast, renewing a fading mark. Honestly, he was as bad as his demon when it came to leaving marks of possession on her. He fucking loved her body. He knew every line, every curve, every dip, every sensitive spot. Knew how to drive her to a fever pitch of need. And that was exactly what he proceeded to do.

He relished every sigh, moan, and gasp as he mercilessly toyed with her body; licking over the thorny brand on her neck, tugging on her nipple ring, tracing the brand circling her breast with his tongue, twisting and plucking her nipples, and drawing as much of her creamy breasts into his mouth as he could get.

All the while, he ground his cock against her clit, tormenting her with what she couldn't yet have.

"I can't possibly get any wetter at this point!" she burst out, nipples tight and tingly from the overwhelming attention he was lavishing them with. Her clit and pussy throbbed, wanting the same damn attention. *But he was being an asshole.*

"Is that so?"

Harper gasped as icy fingers softly scraped over the swollen lips of her pussy. His psychic fingers—despite being so cold—gave off pure heat and made every nerve ending feel so electric she felt like sobbing. "Don't believe me? See for yourself."

Mouth curving at the dare, Knox dipped his finger inside her, almost groaning as her pussy, slick and inferno hot, clasped his finger tight. "Oh, you're wet all right. But I've had wetter."

Her mouth dropped open, but he just smirked. "If you're referring to *any* pussy than mine—"

"*Mine*, Harper. Not yours. This belongs solely to me." He thrust his finger deep and scooped out some of her cream to spread it over her clit. "Doesn't it?"

"Well—" A breath hissed out of her as he spanked her pussy. "*Doesn't it?*"

"Yes, asshole, it does." She gasped as he trapped her clit between two of his fingers and gave it a gentle, delicious squeeze. "I take the asshole part back."

Knox chuckled. "Good of you." She made him think of a hissing, spitting kitten when she was annoyed, and he couldn't help but find it cute. Of course, he'd never tell her that. He liked his balls exactly where they were.

Harper closed her eyes as his fingers glided forwards and backwards, stroking both sides of her clit. But then two icy psychic fingers shoved deep into her pussy, and her eyes snapped open. "*Fuck.*"

The strange heat that came from those shockingly cold fingers made her pussy flame and throb. Every thrust of his psychic fingers only made her burn hotter and coil tighter until she was so damn needy she couldn't stand it. Her sizzling nerve endings were so alive they fairly buzzed.

Knox bit her lower lip. "No one else can do what I do to you," he said, voice thickly possessive. "*No one*."

He was right, thought Harper. Not only because he was literally the only person who could take the burning ache away once he'd put it there, but because no one else could ever compare to him. From the first night, he'd become her sexual benchmark that would be impossible to meet. Everyone else would fall short.

Feeling her orgasm creep up on her, she warned, "I'm gonna come."

"Not yet you're not."

A sob caught in her throat as the psychic fingers dissipated inside her, leaving her inner walls tingling. "Knox—" He smoothly hoisted her up and dropped her on his cock, shocking the breath out of her. Harper's hands flew to his arms, nails digging deep. Thick and hard and long, his cock filled and stretched her pussy until it burned. Her tingling walls were so hypersensitive from the psychic fingers, she could feel every ridge and vein, and it was almost uncomfortable to take him.

"Palms flat on the wall, Harper," Knox ordered, voice guttural. Instead, she dug her nails deeper into his arms. He delivered a sharp slap to her ass. "Palms flat on the fucking wall." Her pussy—tight, slick, and scorching hot—quaked around his cock and soaked him in a rush of cream. He clenched his teeth, silently cursing. "*Now*, Harper."

Hissing, she slapped her palms on the wall at her back, eyes shooting fire. "There, asshole. You happy now?"

"Elated." He cupped her ass and spread the globes enough for it to sting just a little. She liked a bit of pain with her pleasure, and Knox knew exactly what line she rode between the two. "Now you get fucked."

He punched his hips hard, slamming into her tight pussy over and over. It was like burying himself in silken fire, and he loved every goddamn second of it. Loved feeling her slick inner walls squeeze and flutter around him. "I'll never get enough of this pussy. My pussy. Who owns you, Harper?"

"You," she rasped, too desperate to come to challenge him on that.

"Yes. Me." His demon rushed to the surface, chilling the air. "And me," it said. Then it was furiously powering into her.

"Fuck," hissed Harper. The demon was so much rougher than Knox. Gave her no reprieve or mercy, just jackhammered into her like it was trying to punch a hole through her back or something.

Still slamming deep, it shoved its finger into her mouth. "Suck."

She hesitated, because she knew where that finger would then go.

"*Suck*. It can go in wet or it can go in dry—make your choice."

Motherfucker. Harper sucked on the digit. Sure enough, the wet finger sank into her ass. No probing. No preamble. The demon just pushed it knuckle-deep. And then it was kissing her—no, *ravishing* her mouth, taking complete possession of it.

She *felt* the change in Knox's body—the kiss was no longer quite so bruising, and his thrusts lost their aggressive edge—and she knew the demon had retreated. Knox didn't withdraw his finger from her ass, though. No, he began to add another. *Bastard*. "Don't, or I'll come." The sting would throw her over—she knew it, he knew it.

"You'll fight it."

She shook her head. "Can't."

"You will." Knox shoved the second finger inside her ass and upped the pace of his thrusts, driving deeper. The hot clasp of her pussy, the little moans she made, the scent of her need, the sway of her tits, the feel of her ass squeezing his fingers ... He growled. "Wrap me up tight, baby." The moment she locked her arms and legs securely around him, he leaned into her so that he hit her clit with each brutal thrust. "Fucking come. Let me feel ... that's it."

White-hot pleasure violently whipped through her, making her eyes go blind, her mouth open in a silent scream, and her pussy spasm and clamp around his cock. Biting out a harsh curse, he swelled even thicker inside her as he brutally shoved himself deep and exploded. Every hot splash of his come soaked her quaking walls. And Harper just lost every ounce of her strength.

CHAPTER SIX

As his mate slumped over him, quivering with aftershocks, Knox kissed her temple. "Fuck, baby, I needed that."

Eyes closed, Harper hummed against his neck. "So did I." Hot, silky flames rose around them and licked at her skin, but she didn't stir. Knew they'd never burn her. Moments later, the fire eased away, and she opened her eyes to see that they were standing near the bed.

Knox toppled her onto the deluxe mattress, positioning them both on their sides with their heads on the super soft pillows that his mate adored. Usually, a look of pure contentment crossed her face when her head first sank into them, but not tonight. Lines of strain had settled there, and it didn't look as if they'd disappear any time soon.

The same anger and agitation lingered in Knox, twisting his stomach and riding his demon. Asher was just a baby. He hadn't done a damn thing to anyone. Knox wanted him happy, safe, secure. Not the target of a fucking incorporeal.

The fact that the Horseman would send one after a baby said he clearly had no conscience at all. To him, anyone was expendable. Even people like Alethea, who had aided him. All the bastard cared about was achieving his goal.

Knox wondered if behind the Horseman's determination to succeed lay a hint of desperation. So far, his plans had failed. Those failures were surely hits to his ego. Now he had something to prove—both to himself and to others. But he decided not to say as much to Harper. He wanted her to relax.

Combing his fingers through her hair, he whispered, "Sleep, baby."

"Can't. It's hard to sleep when you know there's a threat to your son at large. You know, I hate it say it, but sending an incorporeal after Asher was a smart move. We're now on edge, distracted, and need to be so alert for signs of the incorporeal that we can't concentrate on finding the Horseman. He was probably counting on that."

Knox skimmed his fingers over the curve of her shoulder. "I'd say so. It is imperative that we destroy the incorporeal. It won't stop. Not for anything. Ever seen a dog sitting near a store with its leash tied to something, keeping it from running off? That's the incorporeal's situation. It's stuck until it's fulfilled its end of the bargain, whether the person it made the bargain with is dead or alive."

"Everything in me itches to hunt the fucking Horseman and his pet incorporeal."

It was the sphinx in her, thought Knox. Her kind, like lions, would single-mindedly track, hunt, and run down their prey. That inborn instinct would no doubt taunt her until the incorporeal was caught. "I'll get them."

"*We'll* get them. You're not pushing me out of this fight, Knox. This isn't just about revenge for me. I *need* to be part of this. I need to be proactive in ensuring you and our son are safe. I know you would love it if me and Asher were here at all times because you're ridiculously overprotective of us both—"

"That's not something I can change."

"And it's probably something else that the Horseman is counting on. If I'm here all the time, I'm not searching for him. And it will look to others like either I'm hiding from him out of fear *or* that you're making me stay on the estate out of fear for me. If demonkind think *we* fear him, they'll fear him even more than they already do. People are easier to manipulate and control if they're afraid."

Knox wished to fuck that he could argue with that, but he truly couldn't.

"You know me, Knox. You know I couldn't stay home until this is all over even if I wanted to—it would only be a matter of time before I snapped." She'd never been good at staying indoors, even as a kid. And as much as she *loved* being with Asher, she'd miss adult company. Meg and Dan were great, but they were also busy people. "I don't want to leave Asher's side, but the best way to ensure his safety is to get the bastards who are threats to him."

Resting his forehead against hers, Knox sighed. "I need you safe."

"I know. But don't ask me to hole up here. I can't do it, Knox. Not even for you. Please don't ask me to."

Knox silently swore. He'd seen this coming, because he knew her so well. He'd long ago learned that Harper would never ignore the urge to protect those who mattered to her. She was protective right down to her core, much like her grandmother.

"Imagine if I asked you to stay home with me and Asher. Could you?"

He sifted his fingers through her hair. "No," he reluctantly admitted. "I couldn't."

She curled her fingers around his wrist. "We work together on this. I might not be as powerful as you, but I'm not weak."

"You're definitely not weak—I've never once thought you were anything but strong." Her expression dared him to prove it, and Knox sighed inwardly. He wasn't going to be able to talk her out of this. If their situations were reversed, she'd have no more success talking *him* out of it. So, going against every protective instinct he had, Knox said, "All right, we work together." His demon snarled, though it also understood and respected her need to hunt the fuckers presenting a threat to their family.

Letting out a long breath, she said, "Good. So what's the plan?"

"I have the feeling that the best chance we have of identifying the Horseman is if we find out what Alethea was up to before she disappeared. Larkin's working on that. We also need to find out where Alethea got the incorporeal. I'll write to Dion tomorrow and request a meeting with him. If he's not the collector we're looking for, he may know who is. While we wait for Larkin to gather information and for Dion to contact me, I plan to do the very thing that the Horseman won't expect—continue as normal and go about my daily business as if he's not on my radar."

"You'd be delivering the ultimate insult to him." Which Harper liked a fuck of a lot. "I'll do the same." She chewed the inside of her cheek. "But we need to leave Asher at home whenever either of us leaves the house. People would understand that—they'd see it as us being protective parents, not as us being afraid of the Horseman."

"You're only suggesting that Asher remain at home because you don't feel confident that you can fully protect him," Knox accused. She didn't deny it. He framed her face with his hands. "You didn't fail him the other day, Harper. You protected him." Knox needed her to believe that. Needed her to let go of her senseless guilt and remember just how strong she truly was. If his faith in her didn't do that, he wasn't sure what would.

"He protected himself."

"He *shielded* himself," Knox corrected. "He didn't get rid of the incorporeal. *You* did that. And I am absolutely certain that you could do it again if need be. You're strong. Powerful. You can call on the flames of hell, which means you can destroy the incorporeal. It doesn't know that, which gives you a major advantage."

Harper swallowed. "That incorporeal is damn powerful."

"But not invincible," Knox reminded her.

"If I'm forced to call on the flames in front of other demons, it could cause us a whole other set of problems, couldn't it?"

"Potentially, yes. We'll deal with that bridge if and when we come to it. There's no sense dwelling on something that may never happen—that's just borrowing trouble."

Harper inhaled deeply, taking in the comforting scents of clean linen, fragrant oils, and Knox's dark sensual cologne. "Can we talk about something else now? My head feels close to exploding."

"How about we go spend some time on the balcony and get some air?" His mate didn't do well with being cooped up indoors when stressed.

"That is not a balcony. It has a pool. An *infinity* pool, to be more precise."

His mouth curved. "We could take a dip in it now if you want."

Harper recognized the roguish glint in his eyes and stilled. "Don't you dare." But he held her tight as flames engulfed them both again. When the fire died down, she and Knox were suddenly submerged in water. She swatted him. *Bastard.*

The next morning, as she watched Asher chuck his spoon on the floor for the tenth time, Harper sighed. "I can't even be mad at him. I mean, look at that face. You can't be mad at something that cute."

Slicing into his omelet, Knox glanced at their son. Sitting in the highchair with his legs propped up on the tray, Asher grabbed his foot and started trying to shove it in his mouth. Everything went in the mouth. "At least he ate most of the porridge before he slung the bowl virtually across the room."

Harper humphed. Asher did the same thing pretty much every meal time. Of course, the bowl and spoon would initially be in *her* hands. But Asher would at some point pyroport them to himself and then proceed to paint his face and tray with what food he had left before then tossing the plastic dishware away. He'd often then pyroport the spoon back to his hand, only to throw it again.

Bracing her elbows on the dining table, Harper spooned some of her cereal as she asked Knox, "Has Dion responded to your letter yet?"

"No, but I expect he'll do so soon. Last time I wrote to him, he responded within a week." Knox studied his mate over the rim of his mug. She seemed better this morning. The lines of stress had smoothed away from her face, and he suspected it was because they'd agreed on how they would proceed. Now that she knew they'd be working together and had a plan of sorts, she probably felt more in control.

"Don't forget that the meeting with the other Primes will take place tomorrow," Knox continued. "Keenan and Larkin will stay at the mansion with Asher, so don't tense up and start panicking. He'll also have Dan and Meg with him—neither are weak in power. They'll all be under strict instructions not to allow anyone to step foot on the estate."

"Do you think Jonas will go to the meeting?"

"No, which is probably for the best." A grieving demon was an unstable one. "Especially since I know you'd like to—"

"Snap off his dick and shove it down his throat? Yes, I would. If he hadn't been so intent on dealing with Alethea himself, the incorporeal might not be free right now."

"You're not alone in wanting to see him hurt for that, but that will have to wait. We need to take care of the Horseman and the incorporeal first." Knox forked some of his omelet. "What are your plans for today?"

Harper snorted at his attempt to calm her by changing the subject to something mundane. Still, she went with it. "I thought about going to the studio to check how things are going." It was something she did once every two weeks.

"Good idea. Seeing you up and around, doing normal things, will stop people from panicking about the Horseman." Still, anxiety squeezed his heart at the idea of her off the estate while there was a threat at large. Of course, the very last thing he could do was let her see that anxiety when she'd lost a little faith in her ability to protect Asher. She needed to see only the confidence Knox had in her.

She reached for her coffee mug and took a sip. "I doubt it will stop them from panicking, but it might put some people at ease."

Knox went to speak, but then he paused as her gaze went inward and he felt the echo of a telepathic conversation. When her eyes once more focused on him, there was a hint of exasperation there.

"A skyscraper," said Harper. "Jolene flattened a skyscraper last night, according to Martina."

"You're honestly surprised?"

She sighed. "No, not really." Hearing that Heidi was meant to be sacrificed during a dark magick ritual was obviously going to infuriate Jolene. It only enraged the woman more that Alethea was dead and, as such, couldn't pay for her part in that plan. Jolene had a habit of demolishing buildings when she was pissed.

"She sounded deceptively calm and rational last time when I told her about the incorporeal situation, but that's something she's good at, so I hadn't bought it. Still ... a skyscraper? Good thing it was old and empty."

Knox gave her a pointed look. "Although you have the power to take down the incorporeal, I trust that you'll call for me if you come across it." The statement held a question, because he needed that assurance. It also held a warning. The past few times she was in danger, she'd called for him, but that had been when she was pregnant with Asher. Knox suspected that she never would have pulled him into a dangerous situation if it weren't for her determination to keep their son safe.

When she didn't respond, Knox narrowed his eyes. "You long ago made me a promise that you would call for me if you ever needed help. I know you hate the thought of drawing me into dangerous situations—I also understand it, since that works both ways." Not that he liked or approved of her habit of dealing with things alone. He respected her need to fight her own battles and to do her part in protecting their son, but he wouldn't agree to her going solo whenever it suited her. "We agreed to work together, remember. That means relying on each other."

Harper exhaled a heavy sigh. "I'll keep my promise and call out to you if I need you. But the same goes for you—if something happens, you don't tell me later just so that I can have an enjoyable day." It was something he'd done in the past. "You tell me *instantly*."

He inclined his head, though he didn't like it. Resting the cutlery on his empty plate, Knox pushed it aside. "What time are you leaving for the studio?"

"I'll probably head out in a few hours. Maybe I can have lunch with the girls while I update them. They need to be warned about the incorporeal."

"You don't think Jolene will have already told them?"

"If she had, they'd have called me by now. She's probably having a lair meeting later to reveal all. I'd rather the girls heard it from me."

"Fair enough." Knox sipped his coffee. "Keep Tanner with you at all times. The incorporeal can look like anyone. If somebody comes close who has no scent, he'll know and he'll pounce."

She cocked her head. "You think it will come for me?"

"No. What it did the other day, turning up at Jolene's house and making its move among all those demons, was arrogant. It will have known in advance that you were strong and could cause soul-deep pain. But now that it's been on the receiving end of such pain and knows exactly what it feels like, the incorporeal won't be so cocky. Especially since you overpowered it. Besides, it's bound to the conditions of the bargain. You're not the target. Still, I won't take chances."

Hearing a distinct fart, Harper looked at Asher. He glanced around, as if unsure where the sound came from. She snorted, turning back to Knox. "The idea of leaving him makes my stomach churn." She stilled as Knox's eyes bled to black and the room temperature lowered.

"You worry too much, little sphinx," the demon told her. "The boy will be fine."

The sheer confidence in that statement made her frown. "What are you keeping from us?" Because it certainly seemed to believe that it knew something about Asher that she and Knox didn't. "I can't properly protect him if I don't know the entire truth."

"That is my point . . . he doesn't need you to protect him," said the demon, voice flat and low. "Do not worry for the boy. Instead, pity the person who tries to harm him." With that, the entity retreated.

Rubbing her chest, Harper asked, "What did that mean?"

"I don't know," said Knox. "The demon may think it knows what Asher's other abilities will be."

"Maybe." It would be another couple of months before all Asher's abilities truly surfaced, and Harper wasn't at all sure *why* Knox's demon would believe it knew what those abilities would be, but she supposed it was as good a theory as any. "Your demon can be damn cryptic."

Knox nodded. "But it's never been arrogant. If it believes that Asher doesn't need our protection as much as we think he does, I'm inclined to trust its judgment." That didn't mean Knox wouldn't still worry or be as overprotective as ever.

As Knox's phone vibrated on the table, Asher blinked. "Ooh." And then the phone disappeared in a spurt of fire and reappeared in Asher's flaming hand. The *ooh* sound usually meant he'd seen something he liked, and that same something often appeared in his little hand.

"Asher," Knox gently complained as he pried the phone out of his son's grip. Asher frowned but then just shoved his foot back in his mouth.

"At least he didn't dump your phone in his porridge this time," said Harper.

"He probably would have done if he hadn't already flung the bowl away."

"Yeah, probably."

But she was right—it was hard to be mad at anything that cute. Knox ruffled his hair. "It's the Wallis in you."

Harper frowned. "You can't blame my family's blood every time he misbehaves."

"Sure I can."

At that moment, Meg walked in, shook her head at the sight of the spoon on the floor, and picked it up. "Did you enjoy your porridge?" she asked Asher, who was too busy gnawing on his foot to pay her any attention.

"Thanks for the omelet and toast, Meg." Standing, Knox shrugged on the jacket of his black suit. "Unfortunately, I have to leave now." Crossing to Harper, he kissed her. "I shouldn't be home late, but I'll let you know if I will be."

Harper plucked Asher out of the highchair. "Come on, let's go wave bye to Daddy." With Asher balanced on her hip, she followed Knox to the foyer. As he curled an arm around her, she melted against him and smoothed a hand down his shirt. "I'll miss you."

"Good. It's only fair, since I'll miss you." He kissed her again, indulging in a long, thorough taste of her. "Stay safe." He planted a kiss on his son's cheek. "Be good for your mom."

Predictably, Asher blew bubbles at him.

Harper walked out onto the stone step and tipped her chin at Levi, who opened the Bentley's rear door for Knox. Noticing that Asher was waving, she smiled. But then she saw that he wasn't waving at Levi or Knox. He was waving at something much higher up. "What is it, little man?" She tracked his gaze and grimaced. "Oh. More crows." There were at least five perched on the branches of a nearby tree. "Delightful."

Harper spent the next few hours with Asher—bathing him, dressing him, and then feeding him a slightly early lunch ... after which she needed to change him again, since he'd gotten puree all over himself.

Shortly after that, Tanner and Keenan arrived, just as she'd arranged.

In the living room, Keenan took Asher in his arms. "Wipe that anxiety off your face, Harper, he'll be fine here with me."

She forced a smile. "I won't be gone long." She pressed a long, noisy kiss to Asher's cheek and then waved. "Bye. Be good for

Uncle Keenan." He didn't wave back. His little face scrunched up in a way that made Tanner chuckle.

With one last wave at Asher, Harper turned and followed Tanner out of the room, down the hallway, through the foyer, and—

Something yanked her wrist, making her stumble backwards so fast she lost her footing. Landing awkwardly on her ass on the foyer hardwood floor, she hissed.

Tanner blinked down at her. "Damn, you okay?"

"No, I'm not," she clipped, scrambling to stand up. She spun, scanning the foyer, her heart pounding. Surely the incorporeal hadn't managed to get inside. Not with the amount of preternatural security measures in place. "Something just fucking *grabbed* me."

"Grabbed you?" echoed Tanner, muscles bunching.

At that moment, Keenan came striding toward them with Asher still in his arms. "What's the hold up?" He frowned at Harper. "Why are you rubbing your butt?"

"Get Asher in the living room, someone just—"

"What's that?" asked Tanner.

Her head whipped to face him. "What? What do you see?" He was looking at her wrist.

Gently, Tanner lifted her hand to study it. "What *is* that?"

"What's what?" Because she didn't see anything. But then he angled her hand a certain way so that the sunlight shone right on it ... and she frowned. "What *is* that?" It looked like partly translucent string was wrapped around her wrist. She touched it, half-expecting not to feel anything. But it was like she'd skimmed her fingertip over cold metal. "No, seriously, what *is* that?"

Tanner released her and stepped back. "Try leaving."

Moving more slowly this time, she stepped outside. No

problem. She kept walking, descending the stone steps nice and slow. One. Two. Three. Four—

And then she was pulled backwards again. No, not *pulled*, she realized. It was more like she was straining against a leash. Stomping back into the foyer, she shut the front door. "Is this supposed to be a cuff or something?" If Knox had done this to keep her home, she was *so* going to kill him.

Rubbing his jaw, Tanner replied, "I think so."

Keenan stepped forward to get a good look at her wrist. "The question is . . . what are you cuffed to?"

"Or *who* are you cuffed to?" Tanner made a speculative noise and then turned to Asher, who was chewing on his thumb while studying the pretty, freshly cut flowers on the circular table. "Let's take a look at those wrists, little man."

Harper snickered. "You can't think *he* did it, Tanner, he's just a—*oh, my God*." She felt the blood drain from her face. On his little wrist was a thin cuff identical to hers. Holding his chubby hand, she touched the cuff. Cold metal. "Asher," she drawled, pointing at her own cuff. "Take it off." He didn't; he tried reaching for her hair instead. She gave him her stern, "*I mean business*" look, and he mimicked her perfectly.

Tanner pointed at the other side of the foyer. "Harper, stand over there. I want to walk between you and Asher and see if anything tangible is actually *linking* the cuffs."

She did as he asked and then watched as the sentinel easily strode between them.

He shook his head. "Nothing."

Crossing to him, she pursed her lips. "So the cuffs don't have any links?"

"No," he replied. "I'd say the only thing linking them is power."

"Meaning they're psychic constructs. It's more that he's linked our psyches than that he's linked our bodies." Harper shook her head at Asher, but he was too busy twisting Keenan's nose to even notice her look of reprimand.

"I don't think he *meant* to shackle you to him," said Keenan, eyes dancing with humor. "I think he just doesn't want you to leave him. Couple that with all the power that lives in him and, well, this was the result."

Thrusting her hand into her hair, Harper blew out a breath. *Knox, our son has cuffed me to him. And no, I'm not kidding.*

Knox's psychic taste poured into her as his mind touched hers. *Cuffed how?*

I don't know. But we're both wearing thin, barely visible cuffs that feel like metal. There's nothing physical linking the cuffs, but I can't move far from Asher without being yanked back toward him.

She had the impression of pure male amusement and even a hint of pride. *Apparently, he doesn't want to be left behind.*

Her lips thinned. *How can you find this amusing?*

If our positions were reversed, you'd be laughing your pretty little ass off.

Yeah, okay, she would. *How do I get them off?*

He's just a baby, so he doesn't have the psychic strength to make the binding last long. They'll probably disappear in a few hours, maybe sooner.

With a sigh, Harper gave the sentinels a too-quick smile. "Well, it looks like you had a wasted journey. I can't go out now."

Keenan frowned. "Why not?"

"I can't leave Asher as long as I'm psychically cuffed to him, and he can't leave the estate."

"You'll only be gone a few hours." Keenan raised a hand when she went to argue. "Look, I understand why you want him to stay home. But there's no way someone can snatch him from you, thanks to these cuffs. And it will be good for him to get out, if you're intending to keep him confined to the estate for a while after this."

Tanner stuffed his hands in his pockets. "Keenan's right. It's just a few hours. The three of us are pretty powerful, especially as a unit. No one will get near Asher if he doesn't want them near him anyway."

Yeah, but ... "Taking him with me would be rewarding bad behavior." Very, very bad.

Tanner's mouth twitched. "True, but I agree with Keenan—I don't think Asher *meant* to bind the two of you together. He just didn't want you to leave without him."

Scrubbing a hand down her face, Harper reached out to Knox again. *I don't know what to do. Tanner and Keenan think we should all go to the studio, including Asher.*

Knox didn't respond for a long moment. *My demon isn't anxious at the idea.*

No, it wouldn't be, she grumbled. What was it the entity had said? Pity the person who tried to harm Asher. It was confident that he could take care of himself just fine. And as Harper looked down at the cuff on her wrist, she thought that just maybe Knox's demon had good reason not to be anxious.

Nonetheless, she wasn't keen on taking Asher off the estate. And she hadn't failed to notice that Knox had said his *demon* wasn't anxious at the idea, not that Knox himself was okay with it.

"It's your decision, Harper," said Tanner. "But I think it won't be such a bad thing to take him out for a few hours."

Have the faith in yourself that I have in you, Knox said to her.

Biting her lip, she exhaled heavily. "I'd better carry him, since I've no idea how long my 'leash' is."

A little while later, Tanner pulled up outside the nightclub that led to the Underground. As it was daylight, there was no thumping music filtering outside or a long queue of people behind the red ropes. For humans, it was a normal and highly popular club. Only demons knew what was beneath it.

Tanner walked in front while Keenan took up the rear as they all went inside the club and then ventured down the flight of stairs to the basement. Two burly, gruff demons guarded a door at the back of the large space. Both flashed huge grins at Asher, who shyly smiled back. With respectful nods for Harper and the sentinels, the doormen parted to allow them to pass. One then punched in a key code for the elevator, and the shiny metal doors opened with a *ping*. A short elevator ride later, Harper stepped into what was, literally, a demonic paradise.

Casinos, bars, nightclubs, hotels, restaurants, strip clubs, a rodeo, combat circle, hellhound racing stadium, a shopping mall—you name it, it was probably there. It was hectic of an evening, but it was also quite busy during the day.

Tanner and Keenan protected her from being jostled by pedestrians as they walked down the "strip", passing lots of stores and venues. The bars, clubs, casinos, and restaurants didn't have front walls, so it was easy to see people eating, drinking, chatting, laughing, and brawling.

Many stared as they caught sight of Harper, Asher, and the sentinels. Some whispered, some smiled, and others nervously averted their gazes. All looked surprised to see her and Asher, and many shoulders relaxed slightly. Knox had been right; people needed to see them carrying on with their day-to-day activities.

As she neared her studio, Harper smiled. Urban Ink was ideally situated in a hotspot that had top-notch security. It was near not only the best restaurants and the mall but Knox's main office too. It was also opposite a hotel wherein she and Knox had a penthouse suite.

Routinely, the girls all met at the coffeehouse next door to the studio each morning before work, and Harper missed their morning meetings almost as much as she missed her job. Still, as she'd told Raini, she wasn't ready to return yet.

"I guess you'll need to talk 'details' for Khloë's birthday party while you're here," said Keenan. "Does she know what she wants yet? Wait, let me guess . . . she wants the exclusive use of one of Knox's Underground clubs. Or maybe even a hotel."

"She wants a garden party," said Harper.

He blinked. "She wants a what?"

"A garden party—complete with champagne, flowers, sculptures, and other pretty things."

His brow furrowed. "That doesn't sound like Khloë."

"She also wants us all to dress like hobos so that we look ridiculous among all the finery."

"Yeah, that sounds like Khloë."

The bell chimed as Keenan pushed open the studio's glass door. Two clients were waiting on the sofa; one was watching the wall-mounted TV while the other was skimming through a tattoo portfolio. Both looked up as Harper and the sentinels filed inside the spacious reception area that smelled of ink, paint, coffee, and disinfectant.

There was a rock/art/Harley Davidson feel to the studio, which Harper loved. Metal art—which also happened to be enlarged copies of tattoos—hung on the bright white walls, including tribal swirls, Chinese dragons, bright flames, a flock of ravens, and a howling wolf.

Looking up from the obsessively neat reception desk that also doubled as a display cabinet for jewelry and other products, Khloë squealed in excitement. The noise made Raini peek around the checkered glass partition that separated the tattoo stations, and her eyes widened in delight. At the same time,

Devon turned away from the lighted tracing table with a 'What, what's happening?' look.

Heels clicked on the hardwood floor as the three girls *swarmed* Harper. But it wasn't her they made a fuss of—no, they didn't even say hello to her. It was Asher they fussed over, peppering his face, hair, head, and hands with kisses.

"Where's my little dude?" cooed Khloë who, despite being the smallest, managed to be the one who took Asher from Harper's arms.

"Careful," said Harper. She held up her wrist so they could see the cuff. "The little bugger bound me to him for a while, so you won't be able to move far before I get yanked along with you."

Raini's brows rose. "He did that?" She chuckled. "This kid cracks me up."

Tanner tugged on Devon's hair. "Hey, kitty cat."

Devon sniffed at him. "Go cock your leg and pee on some trees, pooch."

With an amused smile, Tanner took position at the door. Harper knew he intended to sniff anyone who entered. If they were without a scent, he'd pounce.

Khloë took Asher to the vending machine, bumped her fist on the side of it, and there was a whirring sound as it dropped a Hershey's bar.

Keenan shook his head. "I've tried to do that, I really have."

"We all have," said Harper. But it was a thing that only Khloë and her father seemed able to do.

Raini squeezed Harper's shoulder. "How are you?"

"Fine," replied Harper. "I have news you're not going to like, though," she added quietly. "It's not something we can talk about here in great detail."

Raini's brow furrowed. "We're closing for lunch in, like, twenty minutes. I'm almost finished with my client, and these guys are only here for a quick consultation. Can you hang around until then?"

"Sure. Me, Keenan, and Asher will stay in the breakroom out of your way."

Raini's gaze slid to the hellhound. "And Tanner's gonna stay right there?"

"I'll explain everything soon," Harper assured her. "Then you'll understand why we're being so cautious."

It wasn't much longer before the girls closed the studio for lunch. Khloë had apparently nipped to the deli first, because she entered the breakroom with a bag full of sandwiches. The smells of roast beef, peppers, and mayo made Harper's stomach rumble.

Once they were all gathered around the table, sandwiches in hand, Raini looked at Harper. "Spill."

Harper stroked a hand over Asher's hair, who was sitting on her lap and toying with her necklace. "Before Alethea died, she did something pretty stupid. She stole a jarred incorporeal demon from a private collector. She also set it free."

There was a shocked silence. Then the girls all muttered curses beneath their breath.

"If she was alive, I'd kill the bitch," spat Khloë.

"The she-demon who went after Asher, posing as you . . . that was the incorporeal?" asked Devon.

Harper nodded. "Which makes it an 'it', not a 'she'. I don't know if it will come here, but you need to be on alert just in case." As they ate, she told them everything that Jonas had told Knox. She also educated them on incorporeal demons before adding, "If you see me, don't automatically assume that it is in fact me. Ask me something that only I would know. Devon, you're a hellcat. Your sense of smell is strong. If someone approaches you who has no scent, it could very well be the incorporeal taking on a physical form."

Khloë absentmindedly tugged on her earlobe. "How do we know if we're around people who're hosting an incorporeal?"

"We don't," said Harper. "Not unless it wants us to know. That's why we all need to be alert and careful."

"Does Grams know about this yet?" asked Khloë.

Harper lifted a brow. "You didn't hear about the old skyscraper that freakily crumbled to tiny pieces last night?"

"I heard," replied Khloë. "I'd just hoped it wasn't Grams."

Asher's mind touched Harper's, and there was a question there. He'd clearly picked up on the tension in the air and wanted to know what was wrong. She smiled at him and gave his mind a reassuring touch as she said, "Nothing, baby boy."

"On a lighter note, let's talk party details," suggested Raini. "Khloë, are you sure about this garden party/hobo fancy dress thing?"

"Yep," replied Khloë. "And I want a fountain there. A *big* one. Maybe a mermaid fountain."

"Are you planning to drink from it?" asked Keenan.

Khloë's nose wrinkled. "Unless it's the fountain of youth, I don't see why I would."

"Well, that's good," he said. "It's one less thing we don't have to worry you'll do while smashed."

"I didn't say I *wouldn't* do it. I just said I don't *see* why I would."

"Knox said he has a fake flower garden here in the Underground for swanky events," said Harper. "You could use that."

Khloë grinned. "Cool."

"Okay, let's cover what else you want and then we can hand the matter over to one of Knox's event planners. They'll take care of the rest." It was while they were discussing the food menu—which was simple enough, since Khloë just wanted a burger van and a hot dog stand—that someone's cell phone began to chime.

Devon sat up straight. "That's mine." She dug out her phone, smiled at whatever name she saw on the screen, and answered, "Hey, Drew." She frowned. "Really? Oh. Okay. Just give me a sec." Ending the call, Devon said, "Drew's outside and, apparently, the pooch won't let him in."

"Tanner's just being cautious," said Harper.

"Well, unless he's not positive that it's Drew, there's no reason my brother can't come in." Devon stalked out of the room. Voices mumbled, someone growled, and another hissed. Then the doorbell chimed, and Devon welcomed Drew inside with a cheery voice.

Moments later, he entered the room. Gaze sweeping the space, he greeted everyone. His mouth kicked up into a smile when he spotted Harper. "Hey, didn't expect to see you here."

Awkwardness flooded her, but Harper managed to force a smile. "Hi, Drew."

CHAPTER SEVEN

Slipping his cell phone back into his pocket, Knox relaxed into the buttery leather seat of the Bentley as he said to Levi, "Did you find out anything about Clarke?"

On realizing that Devon's brother coveted Harper, Knox had asked the sentinel to do some digging on the male hellcat. Levi had been so thorough that he'd had a member of their Force, Armand, teleport him to Clarke's home earlier while Knox was in a meeting.

Levi briefly met Knox's gaze via the rear-view mirror. "As you already know, he's been living in Cuba for the past six years. He hasn't been a permanent fixture there, though. It's more like Cuba is his main base. He goes away for months at a time. Even went on a two-year trip to no-man's land on one of those 'unplugged vacations' where there was no phone service. He got back from there a month ago. When he *is* in Cuba, he rents a little shack on the beach. Works as a scuba diving instructor. Spends a lot of his time engaging in extreme sports. He also likes to party and socialize, and he sleeps around more than he dates. He has a type. Tall, blonde, stick-thin."

"The opposite of Harper," mused Knox. The surprise of that made his brows lower. "Find anything of interest in Clarke's shack?"

"The guy's as frugal as they come. The furniture couldn't be more basic. There are framed photos all over the house—they're all of Clarke doing extreme sports. None were of Harper or even Devon. I found a shoebox on the top shelf of his closet. There were little mementos in there and some pictures of his lair. Harper was on a few of them, but not alone or with him. There was nothing in his home that would suggest he's carrying a torch for her. But . . ."

Knox stilled. "But, what?"

"I noticed on his photos that he has an interesting tattoo between his shoulder blades. Not her work. At least, I *doubt* it was her work. I can't imagine Harper doing a tattoo like that without feeling damn awkward about it."

"Levi, tell me."

The sentinel sighed. "It's a picture of a sphinx—body of a lion, woman's head, but no wings. And there was a hellcat snuggled up to it protectively."

Knox swore. His rage bubbled out of him and filled the car, making the air so thick and oppressive it weighed heavy on his chest. "He *marked* himself for her." His demon roared, livid. By having what was essentially a symbol of Harper tattooed on his skin, Clarke had left a brand on her demon's behalf—as if it had claimed him. As if *he* had some claim to *Harper*.

Fists clenching, Knox forced his back teeth to unlock. "I have to say, Levi, I don't like that some guy's practically wearing my mate on his skin."

"Neither do I." A muscle in Levi's jaw ticked. "I was so pissed when I saw it, I ground the photo to dust—frame and all."

Knox would like to smash the bastard's fucking jaw. He drew in a breath through his nose. "I very much doubt that Harper knows about the tattoo."

"She'd never keep something like this from you, not even to stop you from hurting him." Levi slowed the car as they approached a red light. "There's something I really don't get. If he wanted her bad enough to brand himself for her, why stay away from her?"

"I don't know." Reining in his anger, Knox cricked his neck. "But I know someone who's likely to have the answer."

A little while later, they were stood on Jolene Wallis's porch. Opening the front door, she smiled. "Knox, always a pleasure." She stepped aside, allowing him and Levi to enter. Her brow creased. "No Harper or Asher?"

"They're at the studio."

"Ah. I was just about to make coffee for me and Ciaran. He's in the living area, watching TV." She gestured for them to follow her down the hallway, adding, "Come tell me what brings you here."

Following her into the kitchen, Knox positioned himself next to the island. He politely turned down her offer of a drink. Likewise, leaning against the doorjamb, Levi gave a quick shake of the head to her offer.

As Jolene pottered around the kitchen, Knox simply said, "Drew Clarke."

Jolene spared him a brief look. "What about him?"

"He wants Harper, but he stayed away from her. Why is that?"

With a sigh, Jolene turned to face Knox. "Because I told him to."

He'd suspected as much. "Why?"

Pouring coffee into her mug, Jolene explained, "Harper needed—and deserved—someone who would put her first.

Someone who would stay in one place and build a life with her. Drew is not that person. Like Lucian, he's very self-focused, enjoys partying and—though his base is in Cuba—he also travels a lot. Harper did enjoy her years of traveling with Lucian, but what she needed was roots, not someone who she'd come second to. So I told Drew to keep his distance until he was ready to give her what she did need."

"You were testing him to see if he'd step up," Knox guessed.

"Yes." Jolene's lips thinned. "He failed the test, just as I'd figured he would. He stayed in Cuba, living the regular bachelor lifestyle. I think he believed he had all the time in the world to take before offering Harper anything serious—back then, she only dated humans. Drew didn't feel threatened by that. He hadn't counted on her ever dating another demon, let alone mating with him."

"And yet, he didn't appear when I began dating Harper." Which made no sense, unless … "You told Devon not to tell him."

"Of course I did." Jolene blew over the rim of the steaming cup. "I didn't know how serious you were about Harper, but I knew that if Drew heard another demon was pursuing her, he'd have returned to stake his claim. He would have staked that claim for the wrong reason—not because he was ready for more, but because he didn't want to see her with another.

"I also knew that you, being possessive and a lover of challenges, would have fought for her. But I couldn't be sure whether it would have been because she meant something to you or because you simply weren't prepared to lose a challenge. You and Harper needed time without outside interference to see just whether you had anything worth keeping. So I told the lair not to mention your relationship with Harper to Drew."

Stuffing his hands in his pockets, Knox tilted his head.

"Why keep it from him for so long? She's been fully mine for a while now."

"I didn't plan to keep it from him for so long. He went on a trip to some God-forsaken place where he wouldn't be 'tethered by technology'. No one heard from him for two years, and he didn't hear from us. Which suited me fine, because I know he doesn't have a chance of luring her away from you. What I need is for *him* to know that. Once upon a time, he might have stupidly fought you and inevitably died. I'm fond of the boy, I don't want him dead. I also wouldn't want to deal with the clusterfuck it would cause."

Knox understood what she meant. If he killed the brother of Harper's close friend, it would drive a wedge between the two females. Harper would feel torn between her loyalty to Devon and her loyalty to him. Some of her lair would understand Knox's actions; the others would hate him for it. And Jolene, a master manipulator who was madly protective of her lair, would naturally do what it took to ensure such a future didn't come to pass—including keeping Drew blind.

"Like I said, he might have once fought you for her. Not now. The black diamond wouldn't have stopped him. But seeing her holding a baby boy, being part of a family? That screams to Drew that he lost his chance. He'll know that he has no one to blame but himself." Jolene sipped her coffee. "He'll brood and stew and whine, but he'll move on."

Knox wasn't so sure about that. "He has a tattoo of a sphinx snuggled up to a hellcat. A sphinx without wings."

Shock stiffened Jolene's shoulders. She sighed. "The dumb bastard."

Levi snickered. "He'll be a dead dumb bastard if he doesn't get rid of it soon."

Jolene went rigid. "Don't, Knox. Don't kill him. You're

understandably angry. But think what it would do to Harper and Devon's relationship if you were responsible for Drew's death."

Knox stared at her, incredulous. "You're asking me to drop this?"

"Of course not. I'm asking that you give me a chance to deal with this. I'll talk to him. I'll make him see sense and have the tattoo removed."

"You truly think you can?"

"I won't know until I try. Grant me this. For Harper's sake."

Exhaling a heavy breath, Knox nodded. "You have one chance to deal with this, Jolene. One. If he doesn't make the right decision and move the fuck on, I'll make him—even if that means doing something that causes problems between Harper and Devon." He would *not* allow another male to wear a symbol of his mate as if she'd branded him.

"I understand." Jolene rubbed her forehead. "You know, this only goes to prove what I've been saying. Despite caring deeply for her, Drew isn't able to put her needs before his own."

"Like Lucian," said Knox.

"Like Lucian," Jolene agreed. "She would never be as important to Drew as she is to you."

That went without saying, as far as Knox was concerned. She would never be as vital to another as she was to him. "I don't think he'll return to Cuba without trying to stir the sort of shit that will get him killed. Talk to him, Jolene. Make sure he gets rid of the tattoo, backs off, and moves on."

"I highly doubt he'll bother trying to cause trouble when he knows nothing could come of it."

Keenan's mind touched his. *Knox, I thought you might want to know that Devon's brother is at the studio, talking with Harper. I could be wrong, but it looks like he's trying to stir the pot.*

Knox's jaw hardened. He sighed at Jolene. "It seems you were wrong."

Watching Asher roll on the breakroom table like a dog performing a trick, Harper shook her head. The kid did the weirdest stuff.

"You were pretty shaken last week," said Drew, beside her. "How are you feeling?"

No less shaken, but ... "Fine." She'd feel a whole lot better if Drew would sit elsewhere, since Keenan kept glaring at them like they were having sex or something.

Drew folded his arms. "Do you miss working here?"

"A little. But I'd miss Asher more."

"I suppose you don't have to work, now that you're shacked up with a billionaire."

Harper blinked, shocked. She was used to cutting remarks like that, but she'd never expected to hear one from someone who knew her better than that; someone she considered a friend. Still, she only said, "True."

Drew swore under his breath and then held up his hands. "That was uncalled for, Harper, I'm sorry." When she only inclined her head slightly, he put his hand on her arm. "Harper, really, I'm sorry."

"It's fine, forget it." She shifted position so that his hand fell away from her arm.

"Smile for Khloë!" the imp sang at Asher, holding up her cell phone to snap a photo of him. Asher just kept on rolling from side to side. So Khloë snapped a photo of Keenan instead who, for some unknown reason, *hated* having his photo taken. The sentinel practically leaped on her, trying to snatch the phone so he could no doubt delete the photo. Khloë just laughed.

"Do you worry Asher won't have wings?" Drew asked Harper.

She did worry a little, since it had once been a limitation of hers. Although she had the tattoo-like markings of wings on her back, they hadn't surfaced at her call. Very few people knew that her wings finally came to her after Knox's power poured into her mind and body. Asher didn't yet have the markings on his back, but that wasn't uncommon since he was so young.

She also worried he'd share her inability to conjure orbs of hellfire. It was something the majority of demons could do, but although Harper could infuse it into objects, she wasn't able to shape it into orbs. "I don't want there to be anything that people could use against him. Weaknesses matter in the world of demons. Many people look down on me for not being able to call on my wings. Except for Knox. It never mattered to him."

"It doesn't matter to me or anyone else here either," Drew insisted.

Yeah, but they'd known Harper all their lives. She'd expected it to *totally* matter to someone as powerful and high-status as Knox, but he'd genuinely never batted an eyelid about it. She loved that.

"Devon tells me he's also your anchor," said Drew.

"Yep." Eager to move off the subject of Knox, she asked, "You met your anchor yet?"

"No, not yet." He drummed his fingers on the table. "Considering that your parents were anchors and that everything went to shit for them, I wouldn't have thought you'd ever get involved with your own anchor."

"I'm not Carla, and he's not Lucian."

"He's like Lucian in some ways."

That got her back up. "And you think you know Knox so well because, what?"

His mouth tightened. "It doesn't bother you that Thorne has a whole line of exes?"

"They're not exes per se."

"Excuse me, ex-bed buddies," he said, voice dry as a bone. "What-the-fuck-ever. It has to bother you."

Yes, it did, but she wasn't about to talk of her relationship with Knox to another guy—especially one who so clearly disapproved of it. "Everyone has a past."

"I heard that the encantada who was killed on the YouTube video was part of his past."

Harper narrowed her eyes. "Did you now?"

"Well, see, no one—not even Devon—told me about you getting together with Thorne or any of the things that followed. I've been catching up fast since I got back to the US. I also heard that the encantada was always flirting with Thorne and insulting you like it was her job."

Harper's fingers flexed. "You think Knox killed her? Is that what you're saying?"

Drew tossed her an incredulous look. "No. If he had, he wouldn't have broadcasted it on YouTube. But it made me wonder . . . what if the Horseman killed her *because* she was once with Thorne? What if the Horseman will target women from Thorne's past as he works up to the main event? And what if he then targets the woman in Thorne's *present*?" Keeping his eyes on hers, Drew gestured at Asher. "You need to take that little boy over there and go stay someplace safe, lay low for a while."

Her inner demon bristled, and Harper lifted her chin. "I don't hide."

He sighed. "Harper, you need to push your pride aside—"

"This isn't about pride. This is about my need to be proactive in keeping my son safe. Hiding isn't the answer. Finding the Horseman is what will keep Asher safe."

"Thorne doesn't need you for that. He's not a guy who'd ever need anyone." Drew's eyes hardened. "Definitely not a guy I would ever have envisioned you with."

She *so* didn't want to have this conversation.

"Ma!" shouted Asher, crawling toward her, saving Drew from a "Back the fuck off" glower.

"Hey, baby boy." She sat him on her lap and kissed his hair. "Done rolling around like a pup?"

As he squinted, nose wrinkling, his head abruptly snapped forward and he sneezed. Then he jumped, startled by the sound.

Harper chuckled. "Bless you."

He giggled, dimples deepening in that way that melted her heart. Drew laughed along with him, and Asher abruptly went quiet, studying him with a sober expression. It was almost like a . . . "Did I *say* you could laugh with me?" look.

Harper glanced at Keenan, who was smirking, shoulders shaking with silent laughter.

The air chilled slightly as Asher's eyes bled to black and his demon surfaced to study Drew with an unblinking stare. "Bye," it said, voice young but flat. It wasn't a farewell; it was a *fuck off and get out of here.*

Drew leaned back in his seat. "Whoa. Does it get like that around all strangers?"

"Only the people it doesn't like," said Keenan, offering Drew a toothy grin.

At that moment, the breakroom door swung open. Knox, Levi, and Ciaran entered the room. Demon retreating, Asher beamed. "Da!"

"What's this I hear about you cuffing your mom, little man?" Knox picked him up, kissed his cheek, and then bent down to brush a kiss over Harper's mouth. "Hey, baby. You okay?"

"Yeah." She shot Levi and Ciaran a brief smile. "This is quite the surprise."

"Ain't it, though?" Ciaran ruffled Khloë's hair. "Hey, bitch-face."

"Touch me again and I'll throw you out the fucking window," Khloë threatened, matter-of-fact. Her twin just laughed.

Harper stared up at Knox. "What brings you here, I wonder." *Keenan called you, didn't he?*

Knox's mouth twitched. *He doesn't like how friendly Drew is with you.*

Oh, my God, you actually called Ciaran to you just so that you could show up here and figuratively mark your territory? She tried to sound outraged but failed. Honestly, it was just far too dumb for her to be annoyed by it.

Not quite, replied Knox. *He was at Jolene's house when I paid her a visit.*

Her brow furrowed. *Why were you at her place?*

Long story. I'll tell you later. If Knox wasn't so pissed with Clarke, he'd be amused that the hellcat was doing his best to keep his mind clear right then—even to the point that he was internally humming a tune. Knox's demon found no amusement in it either. All it wanted to do was launch itself at Clarke and rip him to shreds.

It was incredibly tempting to do exactly that. But as Knox took in the way Devon smiled adoringly at his son and he recalled all the times she'd been there for Harper, he knew he couldn't. His mate and Devon had a solid friendship that had lasted a long time. For Harper, he'd give Jolene the chance to deal with it.

Levi crossed to Harper. "I'm curious about your brand-new cuff."

Drew's brows snapped together. "Cuff? What cuff?"

"It's a temporary gift from Asher," said Harper as she lifted her arm so that Knox and Levi could study the cuff. "Asher has an identical one on his own wrist."

Touching her psychic cuff and feeling the hum of power, Knox pursed his lips. "Hmm. It's strong." His demon was quite proud of Asher's show of power. It was also completely unsurprised. "Very strong, actually."

She frowned. "You can't take it off?"

"I could," said Knox. "But I'd much rather see how long the link lasts without interference. If the cuffs aren't gone by tonight, I'll take them off. Unless you're absolutely desperate to have them gone … ?"

Harper chewed on the inside of her cheek. "I'll wait till later. It would be handy to know how long they last, just in case he does it again."

"Wait a minute, your kid bound you to him?" asked Drew, casting Asher a wary look.

Before Harper could answer, Knox interlinked their fingers and squeezed her hand. "You done here, baby?"

"Yep."

"Good." Knox tugged her to her feet. "I'll walk you outside to the Audi before I head to my next meeting." Because there was *no fucking way* he was leaving her with Drew. Not after what Knox had discovered.

Slinging Asher's bag over her shoulder, Harper said her good-byes to everyone, adding, "Take care, and be alert."

"Be alert about what?" asked Drew, brow creased.

"I'll explain in a minute," Devon told him.

Drew waved at Asher, who frowned at him, expression once again sober.

Asher doesn't like him much, apparently, Harper told Knox, unable to hide her amusement.

Knox shrugged. *Kids can sense evil.*

Snorting, Harper let Knox lead her out of the studio. Tanner, Keenan, Levi, and Ciaran surrounded them protectively as they walked down the strip. Still in Knox's arms, Asher babbled to himself.

"I take it you fully warned the girls," Knox said to Harper.

She nodded. "I don't think the incorporeal will turn its attention their way, but it's best that they're warned just in case." The rest of demonkind would be warned after the Primes met and discussed the issue. Her demon's upper lip curled at the thought of the meeting. It had no time or patience for politics. Imps didn't take politics whatsoever seriously, but Jolene never missed a meeting.

On the subject of her grandmother . . . "I should probably give Grams a call and check she's okay," said Harper. "She was pretty mad when I first told her about the incorporeal. I'm worried she'll do something dumb."

"She seemed fine when I visited her just now."

Harper glanced at him. "Are you going to tell me just why you went to see her?"

"We'll talk about it later. We don't have enough time to cover it right now."

"Ma!" Asher pointed toward the rodeo, where a guy was struggling to hold tight to a wild bucking bull.

Harper smiled. "I see it."

Recalling the time Harper had engaged in such a sport and nearly took a hundred years off his life, Knox warned, "You'd better not try putting Asher on the back of a bull." Having been raised by imps, his mate had engaged in lots of dangerous and often highly illegal activities since a very young age—including breaking into bank vaults and indulging in high-speed car racing. He didn't want Asher doing the same.

Her mouth kicked up into a smile. "Not even once?"

"No."

"But it's fun."

Knox looked at her, incredulous. "It's the most dangerous eight seconds of sport." A sport that imps especially loved to do when *drunk*.

"What's your point?"

Knox shook his head. "Never mind."

His mate just chuckled.

"Ooh." Fire erupted out of Asher's hand, and then he was holding a little truck. Smiling, he showed it to Harper. "Ma!"

"I see it, but that's not yours." Gently prying the truck from him, Harper shook her head in reprimand. "We don't take people's things." She glanced around in search of the owner. A little boy in a stroller was hanging over the side, his teary gaze sweeping the floor like he was looking for something. Harper walked over and gave the little boy the truck, and he instantly calmed.

The kid's mother, who'd been gossiping with another woman, completely oblivious, turned.

"I was just handing him back his toy," said Harper, knowing the woman would assume he'd simply dropped it.

"Th-thank you," she stuttered, recognizing Harper and seeming a little intimidated.

"No problem." Harper returned to her son, whose eyes bled to black as his demon surfaced. It touched her mind, communicating its displeasure. "Don't be a brat," she told it. She cut her gaze to Knox. "It's not funny."

"I'm not laughing."

"You are in your head."

Yes, he was. Outside, Knox buckled Asher into the car seat of the Audi and then gave her a lingering kiss. "Unfortunately, I can't go home with you. I won't be long."

"Don't work too hard." She smoothed a hand down his tie. "See you soon."

He gave her nape a little squeeze. "Stay safe."

"Right back at you, Thorne." With that, she slid into the car.

Tanner and Keenan both gave him reassuring looks that said

they'd keep her and Asher safe, and then the sentinels hopped into the Audi.

Only when the car was no more than a dot in his vision did Knox then head back inside the club, where Ciaran then teleported them all back to Jolene's kitchen. She was waiting there, body tight, fists clenched.

"Is he still alive?" she asked.

"I told you I'd give you an opportunity to deal with it yourself, and I will," Knox told her. "Make the most of that opportunity, Jolene, because I won't give you another. No one gets to covet what belongs to me." He and Levi then exited the house and headed to the Bentley.

Inside the car, Levi clicked on his seat belt and said, "Didn't you mention the tattoo to Drew?" He tapped his temple to indicate he meant telepathically.

"No," said Knox. "I'll leave Jolene to deal with that problem. Clarke was careful to keep his mind blank, but it didn't take telepathy to sense his jealousy or bitterness."

Pulling onto the road to merge into the traffic, Levi smirked. "No, it didn't. I couldn't help but enjoy it. Did you notice that Asher doesn't like him?"

Knox smiled. "As I told Harper, kids sense evil."

"Are you going to tell her about Drew's tattoo?"

"Yes." Knox didn't particularly want her to know. Not that he worried she would be so moved by the news that she would try leaving Knox to be with the hellcat or something equally unrealistic. But he got the feeling that the situation was awkward enough for her as it was. Knowing about the tattoo would only make it worse for her. Still . . . "If she found out about it some other way and then realized I already knew, she'd be pissed that I didn't tell her."

"And you want to see her reaction."

Knox felt his brow crease. "I don't worry that she cares for him."

"No, but you still want to see her reaction. I think she'll be shocked."

Probably. Despite knowing her inside out, Knox could never predict her responses. Never. She continued to surprise and astound him. His demon loved that about her.

"What Clarke did was no little thing," Levi went on. "She knows him better than we do, but I don't think she even sees just how much jealousy is eating him up inside right now."

In agreement with that, Knox nodded. "Harper is very astute, but the insecurities that she carries make it easy for her to miss when someone is attracted to her." Being discarded by both parents had left her with what she called "textbook abandonment issues". Though Lucian, at Jolene's insistence, had later taken Harper to live with him, he'd never given her stability or been a true father to her. *She* had been the parent.

Harper persistently reassured Knox that, in spite of all that, she'd had a good childhood. It was clear to Knox that Lucian did care for her. He also seemed to adore Asher, but he could go for up to six months at a time before even making contact to ask about their welfare. Moreover, Lucian didn't find anything whatsoever wrong with that. Knox would *never* like or trust him.

"Personally," began Levi, "I don't think she'll be flattered to know that Clarke sort of had her on reserve."

"No, that won't flatter her," Knox agreed. "If anything, she'll be furious to hear that he thought she'd be waiting in the wings." For humans, it might seem odd that someone would spend years away from someone they cared for. But to creatures with extensive lifetimes, years were more like months. "And her demon will be outraged to hear that he marked himself on its behalf."

"Still, I don't think Harper will want him dead, considering he's her friend's brother, which is understandable."

"If he wants to live, he'll get rid of the tattoo. I'd be happy to do it for him. A little hellfire would burn it right off." The idea made his demon bare his teeth in a feral grin.

Levi's lips twitched. "Envisioning that shouldn't make me smile, but I'm a bloodthirsty son of a bitch." He paused as he turned a sharp corner. "Do you think Clarke will put up a fight? It would be a singularly stupid thing to do, but he'll probably feel that he chose her first; that he has rights to her."

Frowning thoughtfully, Knox licked his front teeth. "Maybe. Time will tell, I suppose." Hearing his cell beep, Knox fished it out of his pocket and answered the long-winded email from his business associate. Which led to yet another email. And another. And a—

"We have a tail," announced Levi as they stopped at a red light. "The pick-up truck two cars behind us. I turned off the freeway and drove into a rough neighborhood to see if they followed. They did."

Pocketing his cell, Knox peered out of the tinted rear window. It wasn't the first time they'd been followed. Sometimes it was paparazzi, sometimes it was someone hoping to pitch a business idea to him, sometimes it was a PI hired by a business rival or even a nosy Prime. Other times—though they weren't so common—it was a threat.

Squinting, Knox studied what he could see of the driver, which wasn't much. Scruffy dark hair. Scraggly overgrown beard. Red T-shirt. "I don't recognize the driver. It could be the incorporeal." The thought made his demon unfurl and rise close to the surface, ready to lunge and attack if needs be. It *wanted* a fight, craved revenge on the entity that could potentially be just behind them.

As Levi stopped the car at a red light, Knox glanced around, taking note of where they were and how many humans were walking along the drab street. Not many. There was an elderly woman struggling with an umbrella, a vagrant pushing a cart, a woman with a stroller, and a trio of teens that had just strode out of an alley. Still, he'd prefer to battle somewhere more secluded. If there were humans around, it would limit how Knox could retaliate against an attack.

"We need to lead the incorporeal into a more derelict area," said Knox.

"I got a place in mind." Tapping his fingers impatiently on the wheel, Levi sighed and tipped his chin toward the pedestrian crossing the street. "There's always a slow old lady when you're in a rush. Seriously, she's moving, like, an inch at a time."

If he wasn't so focused on the matter of the incorporeal, Knox might have smiled. Instead, he was running through battle plans in his head. His heart was pounding, and adrenalin was pumping through him. Preparing him. Invigorating him.

Like his demon, he relished the thought of fighting the demon that had *dared* to not only attempt to possess his son, but who had made his mate bleed. The delicious anticipation of it had his demon practically licking its lips.

Glancing at the traffic light, Knox rolled back his shoulders. It would go green any moment now, surely. Every second that ticked by seemed like minutes, winding him that much tighter with tension.

Amber.

Green.

"Fucking finally," Levi burst out, shifting the gear and exerting pressure on the pedal.

"Don't drive fast or try to lose it," said Knox. "We don't want it to know we've made it."

Further up the street, the woman with the stroller halted at the curb. As they neared, she looked their way. Smirked cruelly. And then shoved the stroller right into the road.

Levi slammed his foot on the pedal and sharply swerved the steering wheel, making the car skid until it was sideways. Tires screeched and the reaper swore a blue streak. His quick reflexes might not have been enough if Knox hadn't reached out with his psychic hands to yank the stroller to a standstill.

That was when a powerful gust of gale-force wind swept up the Bentley and tossed it in the air like it was no more than a leaf.

Even as the car flipped over and glacial air thrust into the open windows to freeze him, Knox grabbed Levi and pyroported them directly behind the woman, witnesses be fucking damned.

Just as the crackling flames eased away from him and Knox snapped a psychic hand around her throat, she went limp. He saw *it* leave her—saw the vaporous swirl that dissipated so fast, he could almost think it had never been there at all.

Shaking with rage and frustration, Knox sent hellfire blasting out of his hand like it was a flamethrower; aiming for what he could no longer see, even as he knew it would do no real damage anyway.

His heartbeat was pounding so loud in his ears that it took a moment to realize the woman in his psychic grip was screaming and struggling to get free, wanting to get to her baby. Knox released her so fast she stumbled, but he was too consumed by fury to feel bad for her. Just the same, he couldn't find it in him to feel any sympathy for the truck driver, who'd hopped out of the vehicle, looking equally baffled.

Spinning to face Knox, Levi hissed out a breath. "That motherfucking motherfucker."

Silently cursing himself, Knox flexed his fingers so hard his joints cracked. "I was so busy concentrating on what was happening behind me that I didn't think to focus on what was going on right in front of us."

"The incorporeal must have realized we'd made it, abandoned

the driver, and then possessed the woman in the hope of catching us off-guard with a frontal attack."

"It was a good plan," Knox ground out. "And now it could be anywhere." In a person, a bird, a rat—anyone. He scanned his surroundings slowly, but nothing set off his alarms.

"We have to get out of here before more people appear," said Levi, casting a meaningful look at the trio of teens that had gathered around the woman and her baby—one of the teens was snapping pictures. "You're going to have to plant a false memory in the minds of those witnesses over there. I'll take care of deleting the photos."

Muscles quivering, Knox forced himself to think past the anger clouding his thoughts. Levi was right; they needed to do damage control. Knox drew in a breath. "Let's get that done so we can send the humans on their way."

Although it was easy enough for Knox to thrust his mind into that of another, manipulating memories was a little more challenging. But he'd done it often enough over the years to cover their asses that it didn't take long to have the humans all believing that the woman had accidentally lost control of the stroller and that Knox and Levi had got out of the car to help.

As the truck driver's last memory was of driving along the freeway—at which point the incorporeal had either instantly possessed him or had taken control of his body after lingering inside him for a while—Knox planted false memories of the driver taking a series of wrong turns.

Once they were alone, Knox and Levi then headed to the Bentley. It lay on its side on the opposite side of the street, where it had knocked down a lamppost. All things considered, it should have been a wreck. But there were no dents, no smashed windows, and no smoke hissing out of the hood, thanks to its preternatural protection.

After Levi telekinetically righted the Bentley, they both hopped inside and quickly returned their personal objects to their rightful places.

Switching on the ignition, Levi said, "It came after you. It could have done a similar attack on Tanner's car to get to Harper and Asher. It didn't. It went directly after you. I didn't expect that."

As the impact of Levi's words hit him, they stole Knox's breath. If the same had happened to the Audi, Harper wouldn't have been able to pyroport her and Asher out of the flipping car as he'd done for Levi. No, his mate and son would have been tossed from side to side, thumped by loose objects flying around the car, and potentially been badly injured.

The Bentley rattled with the anger seeping out of him.

"I guess that wasn't the smartest thing for me to say." Levi gave him a sheepish smile. "I'm making the point that the incorporeal may well have abandoned the idea of trying to possess Asher. Either that or it's happy to keep us guessing about what it intends to do next. If it's the latter, it's working."

Knox nodded. "I didn't expect such a direct, public attack on me."

"But even though you're pissed, you're also relieved it targeted you," Levi sensed.

Of course he was. Knox shrugged. "Better it's me than my mate and son."

CHAPTER EIGHT

It was no surprise to Knox that Harper didn't share his relief that the incorporeal had targeted him. Naturally, she'd be glad that she and Asher weren't victims of yet another attack, but he could sense that she was nonetheless silently seething—not just with the incorporeal for making a move on Knox, but with Knox himself because she saw his relief.

At that moment, she was sitting on the sofa, arms folded, one leg crossed over the other. She was also crazily twirling one ankle and tapping her nails like they were claws. Every now and then she would shoot him a scowl that only deepened the lines of stress that seemed carved into her beautiful face. Knox couldn't—wouldn't—apologize for not putting as much value on his own life as he did on hers and Asher's.

Thankfully, Asher was currently taking a nap upstairs. Knox suspected that the amount of psychic strength he'd used to create the cuffs—both of which had now faded—had left him feeling drained and sleepy.

"We thought the incorporeal had been ordered to possess Asher," said Keenan, eyes narrowed in thought. "But maybe not, Knox. Maybe it had simply been ordered to destroy you, which gives it a lot of leeway about just how it will go about living up to its end of the bargain."

Knox's brow furrowed. "It couldn't have killed me using Asher."

"But if it had possessed him and tried attacking you through Asher, you wouldn't have fought back, and you certainly wouldn't have seen it coming," Keenan pointed out, to which Larkin nodded. "In that sense, Asher would make as much of a good shield as he would a weapon."

It was a valid point, but . . . "As I said before, the incorporeal would have been limited with a baby's psychic strength—it still makes no sense to use him in an attack." Knox rolled back his shoulders. His muscles were so tight with tension they ached, just as his jaw hurt from how hard he'd ground his teeth.

Beside Harper, Tanner leaned forward to brace his elbows on his thighs as he spoke. "Can an incorporeal kill from the inside out? Can it kill its host?"

"It could force the host to kill itself," said Knox. "You think it meant to make Asher harm himself?" His demon rumbled a menacing sound. The entity's anger was still fresh. It wanted blood, which it would never get from an incorporeal, since they didn't bleed. His demon would settle for the blood of whoever sicced the incorporeal on them.

"Possibly," said Tanner. "His death would have gutted you. The incorporeal might think that grief and shock will weaken you and leave you vulnerable to an attack. Of course, if it knew what you were, it would know better than to make such a move, since Asher's death would also send you on a killing spree that would leave the Earth a wasteland."

Yes, a killing spree would certainly follow. And since his grief would have weakened his control over his demon, the entity would then take control and set out to do the very thing it was born to do—destroy. Knox looked at Harper. "I'm not sure if even you could calm me and my demon if something were to happen to Asher." And that was a frightening thought.

Her face darkened. "I wouldn't try to calm you or your demon. I'd fucking egg the pair of you on. I'd be too deep in grief to care that the Earth would be purged. And don't think I'm just saying that because I'm mad. I wouldn't be rational enough to care about anything or anyone else."

Perched on the arm of the sofa, Larkin put a supportive hand on Harper's shoulder. "It won't come to that, because we'll catch this thing and then Knox will annihilate it."

"As for whoever has it on a leash," began Levi, lounging on the opposite sofa with Keenan, "not one goddamn thing will keep him safe from us. Not one. He's a walking dead man."

Harper gave a slow nod and drew in a steadying breath. "Thank God you were able to avoid colliding into the stroller. That baby would be dead by now if you both hadn't acted so fast."

"The incorporeal certainly doesn't care about collateral damage." Levi turned to Knox. "I think Tanner's theory is right—I think the incorporeal wasn't ordered to go after Asher, Harper, or you. I think it was simply ordered to end you, one way or another. If that's the case, there's no knowing what it will do next—only that it *will* act if it wants to be free. After having spent God knows how long in a fucking display case, it'll be determined to be free."

"It left the woman's body just as you reached her," Harper said to Knox. "It must suspect you can kill it. Probably heard the rumors that you can conjure the flames of hell. Still, it went after you. That's ballsy, just as striking while we were at Jolene's house was ballsy."

Knox nodded. "It didn't learn from its last cocky mistake. Arrogance is very clearly a weakness it possesses." He turned to Larkin. "Have you had any joy in tracking Alethea's movements after she disappeared?"

Larkin puffed out a breath. "That girl sure knew how to vanish. I broke into her old house, went through her computer, checked her bank account activity, internet history, cell phone records, and social media networks—that sort of stuff. It wasn't even hard, since her passwords weren't very inventive."

Knox folded his arms. "What did you find out?"

"Not much. Alethea hadn't used any of the accounts, her phone, or the computer itself for a long time. None of her status updates running up to her disappearance detailed anything about where she'd been or what she'd been doing. She'd just posted funny GIFs and selfies of herself all dolled up.

"You know she preferred to hang around humans, since they were easy for her to manipulate. I spoke to the people she was regularly photographed with on social media. None of them had seen or heard from her in over seven months. Of course, they're not concerned by that, since Jonas told them she moved to Australia and they don't appear to have seen the footage of Alethea's death."

"It was taken down *fast*," Levi pointed out.

"There's only one person I can't find from the photos," Larkin added. "A woman. She's not tagged in any of the pictures. In fact, she doesn't even seem to have a social media account. Give me a little time—I'll find her."

Trusting that she would, Knox nodded. The sentinels left, each heading to their respective cars. That was when Knox crouched in front of Harper and rubbed her thigh. She shot him yet another glower. As much as it was no fun to have her anger directed at him, he still couldn't help thinking of her as a cranky kitten. "I wish I could apologize for what's pissing you off, but it would be a lie."

Shoulders sagging, she sighed, and her scowl eased just a little. "I know, I get it. If our situations were reversed, I'd be glad the incorporeal went after me rather than you and Asher."

Knox's brows snapped together. "Never fucking ever be glad of something like that." She raised one imperious brow at him, and Knox honestly just wanted to bend her over something and fuck the haughtiness right out of her. Instead, he rose to his feet, plucked her off the sofa, and then sat with her straddling him. "Better."

Thrusting both hands into her hair, he soothingly massaged her head. Her eyes fell closed on a soft moan. He didn't want to talk anymore about the incorporeal or the Horseman. The bastards had stolen enough time from his day; he wouldn't give them even a second more of it.

"You're trying to distract me," Harper accused.

"I simply don't want either of us to spare another thought for those who would do us harm, let alone talk about them."

Neither did Harper. She was emotionally worn out by the whole thing, and she knew she'd have a difficult time sleeping tonight—if she even managed it at all. When Knox had strolled through the door earlier, she wouldn't have guessed anything bad had occurred if Levi hadn't been behind him with his eyes glittering and wearing an expression so grim that her stomach had knotted.

She hadn't just been angry because Knox had been relieved that *he* was the focus of an attack this time. She was angry with herself, because she'd assumed Knox wouldn't be directly targeted. She should *never* have made any such assumption. But as she figured such a revelation would annoy him, she instead said, "We could talk about what took you to Jolene's house." His fingers paused their massage as a new tension stiffened his muscles. Harper's heart leaped. "What? Is it bad? It's bad, isn't it?"

Knox combed his fingers all the way through her hair and settled his hands on her upper arms. "I had some questions that I suspected she could answer."

"About what?"

"Devon's brother."

Harper frowned. "Why the interest in him?"

"I don't like that he wants what's mine. He does, Harper; don't deny it."

Honestly, she still found it difficult to accept that Drew felt that way. But after the way he'd acted earlier, she'd reached one conclusion. "Okay, it's possible that he doesn't want me to be with you out of some misplaced concern. But Drew is totally focused on his own life—"

"Which was why Jolene told him to stay away from you until he was prepared to step up to the plate and give you what you needed."

Harper tilted her head. "She told you that?"

"Yes."

While it was the kind of thing Jolene would do, it was still hard for Harper to imagine Drew giving that much of a shit about her. "Well, he *didn't* step up, which tells you all you need to know. If he'd really wanted me as much as you think he does, he wouldn't have stayed in Cuba." There. That proved her point perfectly.

Sliding his hand around her neck, Knox gently breezed his thumb up the column of her throat. "Baby, he has a tattoo of a sphinx between his shoulder blades. A sphinx with no wings. Lying with a hellcat."

It took a moment for those words to truly sink in. Harper's

demon hissed, beyond enraged that another male would brand himself for it that way. "Seriously?"

"Do I look like I'm fucking kidding?"

"Wait, how do you know?"

"He likes to hang up pictures of himself doing extreme sports. Levi saw the tattoo on one of the photos when he visited Clarke's shack."

She decided not to ask what Levi had been doing in Drew's home. "You said the tattoo is on his back, right? Maybe that sort of represents him turning his back on what he once wanted and putting it behind him or something. I've had clients who want tattoos that remind them of what they're keeping in their past."

Knox slowly shook his head. "The hellcat was snuggled up to the sphinx protectively."

She swallowed. "There are other sphinxes out there."

"With no wings? Come on, Harper, accept the fucking facts. Why are you searching for reasons that I might be wrong?"

"It just doesn't make sense to me. Plus, I don't want you to kill my friend's brother." Even if the little bastard had marked himself for her, like he was under the impression she'd be his to claim whenever he was ready for it.

"I will if he tries to take you from me." Knox curled his hand around her chin and pulled her close. "Speak to Devon. Tell her to talk to her brother and keep him away from you. I've told Jolene to do the same and to make sure he gets rid of that fucking tattoo. Because nothing—not even you, baby—will keep him safe from me if he tries stealing you from me."

"That's dumb and immature. I had to deal with Alethea and countless other women trying to lure you away, but I didn't kill any of them." She'd toyed with them, sure, but that was all.

He did a slow blink. "Dumb and immature?"

"Yeah."

Stroking his thumb over her jaw, Knox cocked his head. "You still underestimate your importance to me, don't you? I'm beginning to think you always will."

"No, I don't. But I also don't see why you can't show the same restraint others do when people have a thing for their partners."

"I could show that restraint, Harper. I have more patience and self-control than most—I'd never otherwise maintain dominance over my demon. But if Clarke pushes this or refuses to have the tattoo removed, I won't want to show such restraint. I'll want to kill him. My demon will want his blood. And I don't have your goodness or mercy. So if you want Drew to live, talk to Devon and ensure that she makes him see reason." Knox's eyes narrowed. "What did he say to you earlier?"

Not willing to feed his anger, Harper kept her answer vague. "He was asking if I missed working at the studio and if I worried that Asher would have my weaknesses. I asked if he'd found his anchor—just general shit."

"What else?"

She sighed. "He expressed his surprise that I'd gotten involved with my own anchor. Asked if it bothered me that there were so many women in your past."

"A rhetorical question that would remind you of something that causes you pain," mused Knox. "Now that I'm dealing with Drew, I understand just how much hurt it actually caused you to be around women from my past. Before this, I could only guess." Splaying his hands on her back, Knox pulled her closer. "But, see, none of them meant anything to me. I suspect Drew did mean something to you, though. That's hard for me to stomach."

"I never loved him or anything. I had a crush on him as a teenager, and I always thought he was a decent guy. That's it."

"But if he'd stepped up to the plate as Jolene wanted him to, you probably would have given him a chance." Not that it would have stopped Knox from having her. He hadn't lied to her—he would have done whatever it took to have her, even if it meant somehow luring her away from another male. She did something to him. Fed something in him. Breathed life into his world. He couldn't be without her.

Harper shook her head. "You're forgetting just how opposed I was to dating demons. I fought you even harder because you were also my anchor. Not that it got me anywhere," she grumbled. "Bottom line: I don't want Drew. Nothing he says or does could make me leave you. Why is that funny?" He was giving her one of those highly amused, "you're so ridiculously cute" smiles that held a hint of condescension.

Brushing his mouth over hers, Knox lifted a brow. "You think I'd let you leave?"

"I could *totally* leave if I wanted to. You insist on ignoring my warnings about just how terrifying I can be when in berserker mode. It takes a lot for me to really lose my shit. But when I do, I do it in a spectacular fashion. Seriously, people have fled in fear when faced with—*stop laughing at me.*"

Shoulders shaking, Knox captured her face between her hands. "Only you could melt my mood when it's so foul." He kissed her, poured himself into her. Sipped and nipped and bit, alternating between gentle and rough. Then, grabbing a handful of her hair, he snatched her head back and traced the shape of her mouth with his tongue. "Mine."

Fisting his shirt, she swallowed. "Yours. Just as you're mine."

He dipped his head as he kissed his way down her neck. "Bed."

"Bed," she agreed.

Harper wrinkled her nose. The smell of the citrus air freshener was so strong, it almost burned her nostrils. The last time the Primes had gathered in this very conference room was to discuss the issue of her being hexed—something that it later transpired had been thanks to Nutty Nora. As she'd been pregnant at the time, Harper had stayed at home and missed the meeting. This time, however, she sat at Knox's side, her elbows propped on the long, smooth glass table.

She was also watching each of the Primes carefully. All looked grim aside from Thatcher. He kept sliding uneasy looks at the others, cheeks flushed with self-consciousness. He had to know that many of the whispers circulating the table were about him and his recent relationship with Alethea. He had to feel the suspicious glances aimed his way. To his credit, though, he jutted out his chin in a "fuck you all" gesture.

Dario, too, was on the receiving end of many suspicious looks. Considering that he was the most obvious suspect due to his grandmother being one of the Horsemen, it wasn't in the least bit surprising. Unlike Thatcher, he didn't appear dour. Nor was he displaying any "fuck you" language. No, he seemed intent on ignoring the attention and was in fact chatting amiably with Malden.

If Jonas had been there, he probably would have defended Thatcher against the whispers. Harper had been present when Knox called the encantado early that morning to remind him of the meeting. Jonas had reiterated that he had no interest in attending.

"Shame Asher couldn't be here," said Jolene, beside her. "He'd have melted all this tension easily."

Sitting on Jolene's left, Martina nodded. "He'd have had them laughing."

Just thinking of Asher made her tense. Intellectually, she knew he'd be fine with Keenan and Larkin, but that didn't stop her from worrying. Although Harper hadn't wanted to leave Asher, there was no way she'd take him to a meeting where

Thatcher and Dario were present. In her mind, one of them was most likely to be the Horseman.

She'd wanted Tanner to stay with Asher too, but the hellhound had just stared at her patiently. As her bodyguard, he went where she went . . . which was why he was currently stood behind her chair just as Levi was stood behind Knox's. Both were on guard, much like Jolene's anchor, Beck, who stood on Tanner's other side.

"I had to sneak out in case Asher accidentally cuffed me to him again," Harper told her grandmother and Martina.

Jolene cackled. "That will tickle me for a long time." *That's a very distinct mark on your neck.*

Harper resisted the urge to touch the bite. Knox had been rough with her in the shower that morning. It was part of that whole "you're mine and don't forget it" message he felt the need to drum into her brain on a daily basis. Basically, his possessive nature was live and electric due to Drew's behavior, and she was seeing the ass-end of it.

I'm assuming Knox told you about Drew's tattoo, Jolene added.

Harper shifted awkwardly in her seat. Her demon's upper lip curled at the reminder of the tattoo. *Yep, Knox told me. I keep thinking that maybe Levi didn't see the tattoo clearly on the picture.*

Oh, he saw it clearly. I had Drew show it to me. She sighed. *The boy always was reckless.*

Mouth quirking, Harper said, *That boy is in his late thirties.*

He won't live to see his forties if he doesn't do as I ordered.

Grabbing the pitcher, Harper poured some iced water into a glass. *What did you order?*

For him to allow Raini to remove the stupid tattoo and for him to return to Cuba earlier than he'd planned.

I spoke to Devon and told her about it all. She's sad to think that he could be hurting, but she also thinks he and I weren't "meant to be". She said she'll talk to him.

Jolene gave a curt nod of approval. *He listens to Devon.*

Beneath the table, Knox gently squeezed Harper's thigh. *Who are you talking to?* As her anchor, he could feel the echoes of her telepathic conversations but couldn't understand the words. The same applied to her when the situation was reversed.

Grams, Harper replied simply before sipping at her water. *Are you kicking this meeting off or what?*

Yes, I'd say it's time. Knox's demon wanted it over and done with. Despite that the others in the room held plenty of power, it had little respect for them. Mostly because of how they'd treated Harper. In their eyes, she was somewhat beneath them in that she wasn't from a powerful lair, didn't have a high-ranking or well-paid job, was an imp for all intents and purposes, and was part of a family that was notoriously criminal.

Knox agreed with Levi that people didn't truly look down on imps. Instead, they were wary of them. Daring, sly, wild, and uncontrollable, imps were wild cards, especially Wallis imps. They always retaliated, and they were never subtle about it. In any case, other breeds of demon tended to look upon imps as inferior. Not that it bothered them—imps took delight in irritating people.

For a while, the other Primes hadn't taken Knox and Harper's mating seriously, finding it much too difficult to comprehend that Knox would bind himself to a Wallis. Also, it was rare for Primes to mate, particularly since demons didn't like to share power, so they'd been shocked by the mating.

Knox had come to believe that the Primes also hadn't wanted to take the mating seriously, since a ruling pair—particularly a pair as strong as Harper and Knox—was far more powerful than a single Prime. He was enough of a threat as it was.

Keep a careful watch on Thatcher and Dario, Knox told his sentinels. Breaking the connection with them, he loudly cleared his throat. All eyes moved to Knox, and the low voices fell silent. The only noise in the room was the steady hum of the air conditioning. The tension was palpable, and he knew it wouldn't take much for an argument to ensue. He'd picked up enough thoughts filtering through weak shields to know that many suspected either Thatcher or Dario was the remaining Horseman.

"Unless you've been living under a rock," began Knox, "I'm sure you've guessed what prompted me to call for this meeting. Jonas is too mired in grief to attend, which is probably for the best since his gifts won't be very stable while he's grieving. Would I be right in presuming that you all saw the YouTube clip?"

"The whole world saw it," said Mila. "Including humans."

"Luckily, most of the human population sneers at the possibility of anything preternatural," said Jolene. "Plenty of comments were left about the clip, most of which went along the lines of 'terrible special effects' and 'bad acting'."

"But some names *were* mentioned—particularly those of the other Horsemen," Mila pointed out. "Alethea's killer also mentioned you, Knox."

"Only by surname," he said. "As such, I doubt it will be linked to me. Even if it was, the human authorities will hardly believe there's a death to investigate—people don't set others on fire and melt their corpse, do they? Not in the human world."

Pausing, Knox ran his gaze over each of the Primes. "If anyone here wishes to do as the Horseman asked and step down from their position, say so now." When no one spoke, Knox gave a satisfied nod.

Malden sighed. "Although I'd investigated the matter of the Horsemen, I'd held out hope that they didn't exist. Just the idea that demons might band together with plans to overthrow the Primes is bad enough. That such demons would also think to take *you* on means they're either powerful, delusional, or utterly stupid."

"Alethea's killer was powerful," said Mila.

Thatcher sighed. "I suppose I'm a suspect, just as I was a suspect during our last meeting."

Knox's eyes slammed on him. "At this point, Thatcher, everyone's a suspect."

"I watched that YouTube video several times before it was taken down," said Dario. "It seems obvious to me that Alethea knew her killer."

Knox nodded, watching the other Prime carefully. "He broadcasted her murder to create fear and panic and anger. But it was a mistake on his part, because he also gave us clues about his identity. For instance, we now know he's able to steal or replicate a person's voice. We know he's male. Caucasian. Well-built. We know he somehow knew Alethea—he said she was in his way."

Eyes narrowed in thought, Raul rubbed at his chin. "She may well have figured out that he was the last of the Horsemen. That seems the likeliest scenario."

"Alethea disappeared months before her death," said another Prime. "Do you think he held her captive all that time? If so, why? And why not kill her right away?"

"I don't believe she was his prisoner," said Jolene. "She looked rumpled, but not dirty or malnourished or beaten. Her make-up was close to perfect. Wherever she was all that time, it wasn't a prison of any sort." There were murmurs of agreement.

"I spoke at length with Jonas," said Knox. "Alethea was acting quite secretive before she went missing. Wouldn't even tell him who she was associating with at the time."

"I thought she was with Thatcher," a voice piped up from the opposite end of the table.

"Only for a short time," Thatcher told him. "It was nothing serious. Just a bit of fun."

"Maybe you didn't want that fun to end and so you punished her," that same Prime accused.

Thatcher sniffed at him. "If you're going to insist on playing Devil's advocate, at least offer more interesting theories. If you must know, it was *I* who ended the relationship. It was obvious that she was seeing someone else. I don't demand commitment from my sexual partners, but I do demand exclusivity." His eyes scanned the room. "Perhaps you've all forgotten that I aided Knox in reaching his mate before Nora could kill her. If I were one of the Horsemen, surely I wouldn't have helped him. I notice none of you are pointing fingers at Dario, even though he's a likely suspect."

Dario's brow slowly rose. "You do enjoy throwing accusations at others to divert attention from yourself, don't you?"

He's right on that one, Harper said to Knox.

Knox gave her an almost imperceptible nod. *It's a technique Thatcher often uses.*

"Nora was your grandmother," Thatcher said to Dario. "You were close, from what I heard. I find it difficult to believe that you hadn't sensed that she had such grand plans. And you were of absolutely no help when Knox asked where she might have taken Harper."

"Because I had no idea," Dario ground out, cheeks flushing.

Ignoring that, Thatcher added, "And let's not forget that you were also one of the Primes who campaigned to be the US Monarch, just as Isla did."

Dario's face hardened. "Malden also wanted the position, if you remember."

Malden tossed him a sour look. "Thank you, Dario, for shifting the suspicion so nicely onto me."

"I don't believe you are the Horseman, Malden," Dario told him. "I'm merely pointing out that my campaign to be a Monarch shouldn't be an indication of guilt. I also didn't associate with Alethea."

"Ah, but Jonas said she was being secretive before her disappearance," said another Prime. "I don't suppose either you or Thatcher have the power to steal or replicate people's voices, do you?"

Dario's lips thinned. "No, I do not."

"Nor do I," said Thatcher.

Before the conversation could become more heated, Knox cut in, "Jonas did manage to uncover one of the secrets that his sister was keeping." Again, all eyes went to Knox. "She stole something from a private collector of rare objects."

Raul's eyes sharpened. "What exactly did she take?"

Knox didn't answer for a long moment, studying each of the faces looking at him. "She stole a contained incorporeal demon."

People gasped and muttered.

"Stole it?" asked Raul. "From who?"

"*That* I don't yet know, but I intend to find out." Knox drummed his fingers on the table. "I believe she freed it."

The Prime opposite Jolene scoffed. "Alethea was strong, but not *that* strong."

"I believe she had help," said Knox. "The person who helped her may be the same person who killed her."

Frowning, Raul said, "You think he used her, just as the other Horsemen used Lawrence and Linda?" He pursed his lips. "It would make sense."

"Perhaps she got in his way by trying to prevent him from freeing the incorporeal," Malden suggested. "But can we be absolutely certain that it was freed?"

"Recently, a demon physically imitated Harper in order to get near our son," said Knox. "Asher wasn't fooled. He threw up his shield. Harper fought and overpowered it. She'd just stabbed it in the heart when it faded before her eyes and disappeared, leaving no scent or blood behind. Yesterday, I also had an encounter with it. I even watched as it left the body of a female human."

Thatcher sighed, looking genuinely weary. "Then it's true. The incorporeal was freed. My guess would be that the Horseman is using it to get to you, Knox. He said on the footage that you were next."

Knox draped his arm over the back of Harper's chair. "And that tells us another thing about the Horseman—he's not quite as powerful as he'd like us to believe or he wouldn't need a minion. Just the same, he wasn't powerful enough to free an incorporeal on his own; he needed Alethea's help."

"He must have promised her something good to get her to agree to be part of his plan," said Jolene. "Not just because it was risky, but because she wasn't a person who was interested in aiding others. Maybe she wanted you to be destroyed, Knox, just as the Horseman does. On the other hand, maybe she didn't want you dead and that was what he meant by her being in his way."

"He says the Primes must fall, but what does he expect to happen if such an event occurred?" asked Malden. "He can't truly believe it would somehow lead to something good. There would be anarchy. Demons mind their behavior because they will answer to their Primes if they don't. If they could act as they wished without consequences, the US would be in absolute chaos."

"Maybe that's what he wants," suggested Harper with a shrug.

"But why?" Malden pressed. "What could he possibly gain from that?"

"At this point, I'm not sure he expects to gain anything."

Harper leaned back in her chair. "The Horsemen wanted domination of the US, but none of their games to make it happen worked. Each attempt failed. With each failure, one of the group lost their life. On the clip, he just said the Primes needed to fall—not that he intended to take over. Maybe all he has on his mind is revenge. After all, demons always get even."

There was a short silence. People then nodded, murmuring that it was possible.

Harper continued, "On the other hand—because it's important to consider both sides of the coin—maybe he wants chaos so that he can then step in and take over. I mean, if he succeeded in killing the demon who's rumored to be the most powerful in existence, who wouldn't fear him enough to heed whatever he said?"

Raul pointed at her. "I'm leaning toward your latter theory."

"So am I," Knox said to her. "Ending my life would be a massive show of strength on the Horseman's part. However, we've already established that he doesn't believe he can kill me himself or that he's even powerful enough to free an incorporeal demon alone. As such, he doesn't deserve to be as feared as he hopes to be."

"You're quite friendly with Lucifer," Raul told Knox. "Maybe you can ask him to banish the incorporeal back to hell for you. I've heard that only the flames of hell can kill their kind. Unless you truly can call on the flames, you have yourself a major problem."

Knox said nothing to that and kept his expression blank, not willing to even hint at whether the rumor was true or false.

"We'll deal with it somehow, just as we'll find out who the Horseman is," said Harper, eyes hard. "*Nobody* gets to go after my son without paying in blood. And he'll pay for a very, very long time."

CHAPTER NINE

With Harper at his side, Knox made a public announcement the next evening while sat in his main Underground office. It went live on every screen throughout the subterranean 'strip'—including in the bars, restaurants, casinos, and hotel rooms. He revealed his suspicions about Alethea's killer, the matter of the incorporeal, and even the recent attempts by the incorporeal to get near Asher and to kill Knox. Just as he'd told the Primes, he also expressed his opinion that the last of the Horsemen obviously wasn't as powerful as he'd like people to believe if he needed a minion to do his dirty work for him.

Yes, the latter would enrage the Horseman and might even prompt him into making another attack on Knox, but that would happen at some point anyway.

Afterwards, he settled Harper on his lap in his office chair and massaged her nape as he made some calls. It was just as he was ending one of said calls that there was a knock at the door. Recognizing the rhythmic rap of knuckles, Knox invited, "Come in."

As he'd expected, Levi stalked inside. "I talked to Armand and others within the Force," the sentinel said. "They made rounds of the strip, as ordered. Hearing you point out that the Horseman needed a minion seems to have lessened people's fear. They're naturally nervous that there's a powerful incorporeal on the loose, but *your* lack of nerves appears to be keeping them from stressing over it—especially since you and Harper went strolling along the strip earlier and then had a meal like all was well."

Knox gave a satisfied nod. "That was my intent, so good."

Levi flung himself in the seat opposite his. "Our lair is *pissed* that the incorporeal went after Asher. I'm telling you, your kid has them all head over heels in love with him."

Harper smiled. "Who wouldn't love Asher? He's too adorable for words."

"True," said Levi, mouth quirking. "He didn't cuff you again when you tried to leave?"

"No. But he might have done if I hadn't snuck out just to be on the safe side." She'd touched Asher's mind several times since she left the house and felt nothing but contentment and amusement. Larkin and Keenan were with him, and what better babysitters to have for your child than two badass, tough-as-fuck sentinels?

"How long do you think it will be before the Horseman strikes again?" asked Levi.

Knox twisted his mouth. "He'll be livid that I practically dismissed him and branded him weak. Whether he retaliates quickly or slowly will depend on just how impulsive he is."

Levi's gaze slid to Harper. "I know you both said you wanted to resume your day-to-day activities. Does this mean you're returning to work soon?"

Just the thought made Harper's stomach go rock hard. "Not yet. Especially while all this shit is up in the air."

Levi nodded. "Figured as much, but I wanted to check. Heard anything from Dion yet?"

"As a matter of fact, yes," replied Knox. "His letter came earlier today. He's invited us to visit him tomorrow."

Hiding her annoyance that he hadn't told her of the letter sooner, Harper asked, "What time will we be leaving?"

"Not you, baby. Levi and I will go."

Harper hiked up a brow. "Is that a fact?" So much for working together, she thought. Glaring at her mate, Harper said, "Levi, could you give Knox and me a minute alone, please?"

"I'm done here anyway." The smile was clear in his voice.

Good luck, Levi said to Knox, pushing out of his seat.

Fuck off, Knox retorted. The second the door shut behind the sentinel, Knox put a finger to Harper's mouth. "Before you light into me, hear me out. I'm not pushing you out of this fight—I said we'll work together on dealing with the Horseman and the incorporeal, and we will. But I don't want you coming with me to visit Dion. If I have my way, you'll *never* be in the vicinity of him."

"Why?"

"He collects the unique, and you are very much that. Your eyes alone would fascinate him. I want his focus on me and the matter of Alethea when I speak to him, not on you."

She snorted. "I seriously doubt I'd fascinate him *that* much. Also, if he *is* the Horseman, his attention will *definitely* be on the matter of Alethea because he'll worry he's a suspect."

"I know, but I don't want him to worry he's a suspect. I'll make out like I'm there purely because I mean to speak with each of the people who Alethea spent time with before she disappeared. Of course, I'll be taking a stab in the dark by implying that Dion was one of those people, but he doesn't need to know that. He won't buy that he's not a suspect if you and I—*two* Primes—go there together. It will seem something much more formal. Threatening, even. And then he'll likely shut down, and we won't get the answers we need."

Harper swore under her breath and then snapped her mouth shut. She wanted to poke holes in his case, but he made sense. Uncovering the identity of the Horseman was far more important than whether she got to accompany him to his meeting with Dion. Still, her demon was gonna sulk for sure. "I hate that I can't argue with that."

Knox kissed her forehead. "I know you do. And I'm sorry if it makes you feel left out, but we have to be smart." Wanting to move off the topic before his very astute mate thought of a reason why it *would* be a good idea for her to accompany him, Knox curved his hand around her chin and said, "I saw your face when Levi asked if you intend to return to work soon. You don't like the idea of going back to work, even though you miss it. Why?"

"I'm just not ready yet." Harper had told herself that she'd begin working part-time once Asher reached nine months old. Maybe she'd be ready by then. Maybe not.

"It doesn't make you a bad parent that you eventually want to return to work."

"I know that. I really do."

"But you stupidly feel guilty about it."

She sighed, admitting, "But I stupidly feel guilty about it. You think I should go back?"

Releasing her chin, Knox glided his fingers down the column of her throat. "I don't care whether you choose to return to work or be a stay-at-home-mom as long as you're happy." Knox doubted she'd find contentment in the latter, though. He knew how much she loved her job. He enjoyed watching her work. She had raw talent, a steady hand, immense focus, and a flair for design. "In any case, there's no rush to decide." He dipped his head, letting his mouth follow the path of his fingers as he brushed kisses down her throat. Latching onto her pulse, he sucked hard the way she liked it.

Harper tensed at the sound of her phone chiming. It had been like a hotline all day, and the main caller had been Drew. She'd canceled each call, believing it best not to speak to him. It would only piss Knox off and, well, there was nothing to say anyway. Plus, it was making things hard for Devon. Recalling the female hellcat's phone call the previous night, Harper remembered how strained her voice had sounded . . .

"Hey, how are you?" Harper asked on answering the call.

"Fine," said Devon, her tone friendly but awkward. She cleared her throat. "I wanted you to know that I spoke to Drew. He's . . . upset that you found out about the tattoo. He wants to talk to you. I told him that it wouldn't be possible and he should just get rid of the tat and go home."

Harper swallowed. "Thanks, Devon. I hate that you must feel in the middle here."

"I'm just grateful for the restraint Knox has shown so far. He's so incredibly possessive of you that I'm honestly surprised he hasn't kicked Drew's ass."

"If Drew wasn't your brother and killing him wouldn't cause a massive clusterfuck, I think he'd be nothing but ashes by now," Harper admitted.

There was an awkward silence. "I have to go. Take care. And give Asher a kiss for me."

Heart squeezing at the almost tortured note in her voice, Harper said, "Will do."

The feel of Knox's fingers doodling on her nape snapped her

out of the memory. She noticed then that her phone had stopped ringing, thank God.

"Was that Drew again?" Knox asked, voice deceptively casual.

Harper gave a nonchalant shrug. "I don't know."

"Check."

She flexed her fingers. "I'd rather not talk about him or—"

"Check."

Knowing by the determined set to his jaw that he wouldn't let this go, Harper pulled out her cell and saw that she had nine missed calls from Drew. The guy was nothing if not persistent. She almost jumped as it began to ring again, screen flashing. And, unsurprisingly, the caller was Drew.

Knox held out his hand. "Give it to me."

She shot him a pained look. "Knox, just leave it. Answering the phone would only give him attention—"

"Baby, give me the phone," Knox said, voice soft but insistent.

With a resigned sigh, she reluctantly handed it over to him for one reason only—if the situation had been reversed and another female was constantly calling him, Harper would have insisted on speaking with the bitch.

Knox swiped his thumb across the screen and answered, "Hello, Drew."

Harper was close enough to hear Drew's response: "*I want to talk to Harper.*"

"I guessed that much, since you've been calling her all day. I don't know how you got my mate's number, but this stops now. No calling her. No texting her. Don't even think about her."

"*I'm leaving, just like you want. But I want to talk to her first.*"

"I couldn't give two fucks what you want, Clarke."

"*I wonder what she'd say if she knew you were taking her calls for her.*"

Knox's eyes met hers. "She's sitting right here. On my

lap. Wearing my brands. About to get fucked by me on my office desk."

There was a loud hiss.

Eyes narrowing, Harper mouthed, "That was mean."

"*She can do better than you, Thorne.*"

"And you think you would be better for her? Someone who put his need for a high before the needs of her?" Knox sounded mildly curious, toying with Drew.

"*So maybe she can do better than both of us,*" Drew allowed.

"She can. She's singular. Extraordinary. No one in the world could compare to her. And she's mine. I can't stress enough just how important it is that you accept that. I've killed people for lesser reasons, and I would rather enjoy killing you. Don't tempt me any more than you already have done." Knox ended the call and slipped the phone back into her jacket pocket.

Face hard, Harper clipped, "Was that whole 'she's about to get fucked on my office desk' really necessary?" She was annoyed with Drew, but she didn't want to aggravate the situation.

"Yes, it was. For three reasons. One, I want him to have that image in his head just I have his memories of you in my head. Two, he needs to get the message that you're mine and only mine." Knox smoothed his hand up her thigh and dropped his voice an octave. "Three, you *are* about to get fucked on my desk." He'd been imagining it since she first walked into his office, and he wasn't going to let Clarke's call mess with his plans.

"Oh, is that a fact?" Harper thought she did a good job of sounding disinterested, even as her body reacted to his dominant tone—heating, flushing, and practically humming with anticipation. It knew what that tone meant and was trained to respond to it.

"Yes, it's very much a fact."

"Well, maybe I don't want to. Maybe I—" She gasped as

he cupped her pussy hard above her jeans and pushed up with his palm.

"What have I told you, baby? Never keep what's mine from me."

Harper swallowed. His words were soft and gentle, but they carried a wealth of steel. He stroked her pussy, rubbing her clit with the heel of his hand and, God, that felt good. He'd been rough and demanding with her lately because Drew's behavior was grating on his possessive streak. It was understandable. It also got her fucked *a lot*.

Knox's mouth grazed her ear. "Countless times I've imagined spreading you out on my desk. Just as I've imagined you kneeling between my legs, sucking me off, right here in my office." Sinking his hands into her hair, he plundered her mouth. Greedily feasted and savored until he was sure his head would spin. "Love this mouth. My mouth." He angled her head and kissed her deeper. Hungrier. Claimed and possessed her lips just as he intended to possess her body. "Stand up, Harper."

She should say no, Harper thought. She should tell him he didn't need to constantly remind her that she was his. She should—

"*Baby*." Again, his voice was soft, but there was steel there.

Standing, she sighed. "Look, Knox. You don't have to keep . . ." She sort of lost her train of thought as he unzipped his fly and pulled out his cock. It was thick and long, and looked almost aggressively hard. She felt herself go damp.

"Don't have to keep what?" Fisting his cock, Knox pumped it once. Twice.

"Nothing."

Knox spread his legs wider. "Come here, baby. I want that pretty mouth of yours wrapped around my cock." He watched her reflexively stiffen. Watched her fight down the urge to defy him. "That's my good girl." To reward her, he thrust a psychic finger into her pussy and swirled it around, wrenching a soft moan out of her. Then he let it dissipate, giving her a look that said if she wanted more, she'd have to work for it. "Now do what I told you to do." Placing her hands on his thighs, she slowly got to her knees. He swept her hair away from her face and said, "Very good."

The moment Knox released his cock, she reached for it. She got a tight grip on the base, but she didn't suck as he'd expected. She proceeded to torture him instead. Licked, nibbled, scratched, and stroked his dick, balls, and perineum until the muscles in his thighs bunched tight enough to ache. He hissed as she circled the head of his cock with her tongue and then flicked his frenulum just right.

He grabbed a fistful of her hair. "Quit playing, baby, I don't have the fucking patience for it right now." She didn't make him wait any longer. She took him into her mouth and sucked so hard her cheeks hollowed. He groaned. "That's it."

Using his hold on her hair, Knox guided her movements, forcing her to suck at his pace; knowing just how deep she could take him before she choked. At the same time, he drove a psychic finger in her pussy and began to finger-fuck her. Her soft moans vibrated around his cock, making him ache to be in her. "Fuck, baby, that's good." So good he felt a telling tingle in his balls and knew he couldn't take any more.

Snatching her head back, he traced her lips with his finger. "I like how swollen your mouth is right now." He also liked how flushed her cheeks were. Liked that he could smell her arousal even from there. "Stand up and strip for me." Rising fluidly, she kicked off her shoes and then shed her shirt and jeans. Knox grabbed the gusset of her panties and began pulling them down her legs. "Look how wet you made your panties, baby." He held them up to show her, and her eyes flared. "Want me to eat you, Harper?"

A fine tremor worked through her body as he let the psychic finger dissipate inside her. "You know what I want," she said, voice shaky.

"To come."

Harper blinked, taken off guard, as psychic hands clasped her hips and lifted her. They propped her on the edge of the desk and then spread her legs wide, exposing her pussy. The cool air purring out of the air conditioner blew over her pussy. The way he stared at it—hungry, intense, like a predator that had honed-in on its prey—made her inner walls quiver.

With a wave of his hand, Knox shoved aside the objects on the desk. "Lay back. Good girl." He grabbed her thighs and pulled her closer. "Don't come."

Harper's back arched as he pushed his face into her pussy and swiped his tongue between her folds. Jesus, that felt good. He sank his tongue inside her, tasting and swirling and scooping up every bit of cream. She moaned, bucking her hips, needing more.

Thanks to his psychic finger, her pussy felt on *fire* and was unbelievably sensitive. Each lick of his tongue both soothed and fed the blazing ache. Her orgasm was creeping toward her, and she knew it wouldn't be long before she tipped over the edge. "Knox, no more."

His fingers tightened on her thighs, and the bite of pain brought her release that little bit closer. She squeezed her eyes shut, fighting the need to come. But it became harder and harder to fight as his mouth just kept on devastating her pussy.

"I love how you taste." Like warm, sweet honey. Knox's tongue did a little foray over the brand in the V of her thighs and then lapped at her once more. "Addictive." He latched on her clit and suckled gently.

Hissing, Harper reached down to grab a tuft of his hair. She missed, because he rose to his feet. His predatory gaze raked over her, heating her even more, and his mouth then quirked in pure masculine satisfaction. That smugness should have rankled, but she was too damn turned on to care. "Why am I naked when you're fully dressed?"

"Because I want you to be, baby." Knox yanked her to him as he thrust forward, ruthlessly slamming his cock home. He closed his eyes as her pussy clamped around him like a hot fist, squeezing and rippling. Nothing in his life had ever felt better than his mate's pussy—inferno hot and deliciously slick—wrapped so tight around him.

Knox closed his hands around her breasts and squeezed the creamy mounds. He could feel her heart beating through her pussy. "Hook your legs over my shoulders, baby. Good girl." He fucked her hard. Brutally rammed into her like there was a fever in his blood. Because there was. *Her.* She was the fever.

She wasn't just deep under his skin. She was in his blood, bones, cells—everywhere. Filled and soothed every fracture and void inside him.

He plucked at her nipple ring, loving the way it made her inner walls quake around his cock. He would have leaned over and sucked that ring into his mouth if he wasn't so busy watching his cock—shiny with her cream—slamming into her over and over. The sight made his balls tighten. He kept driving hard and fast, unable to get enough. It had always been that way with Harper. She was a thirst he couldn't quite quench. A hunger he'd never fully sate. A drug he'd forever crave.

Harper blinked as he suddenly yanked her to feet, roughly spun her, and then bent her over the desk. "What the—" Her mouth fell open as he forcefully shoved every long thick inch of his cock deep in her pussy, hitting a spot that made her groan. Keeping her pinned with a hand on her nape, he hammered into her again. Merciless. Frantic. Winding her tighter and tighter.

She would never admit aloud that she liked it when he held her down, giving her no choice but to take what he gave her. Never admit she liked the dominant way he often—

He landed a sharp slap on her ass, and Harper's head snapped up. "Ow! That was hard!" Ignoring her, he did it again. And again. Each slap was harder than the one before. She scowled at him over her shoulder. "Stop slapping my ass!"

His eyes bled to black as his demon rose. "You don't want to be spanked, little sphinx?" it asked.

Not at all liking the dark note in its tone, she hedged, "Um, well . . ." A prickly heat suddenly blazed from the palm pressed on her ass—a burn that quickly became pleasure. Her eyes widened as realization hit her. "Oh God, no." The fucker was *branding her ass*.

The demon upped its pace, pounding into her like it wanted her sore. The sadistic shit probably did. "One day, I'm going to leave a brand *inside* you," it told her. "Yes, little sphinx, I'm going to shove my fingers deep and brand you right there."

Harper's hands curled, nails scraping the desk. Pleasure, pain—both had blended until she didn't know the difference. Her release was so damn close she could almost taste it, and she was sure that it would strike hard and hit her like a freight train.

Just as the prickly burn on her ass began to fade, the pounding thrusts eased a little, and she knew Knox had resurfaced. "Knox, I—" He landed a harsh slap on her throbbing, newly branded flesh. Like that, a powerful shockwave of pleasure/pain jolted through her, and that was it—she was gone.

Her mouth opened in a silent scream as a powerful orgasm forcefully *ripped* through her, imploding her, making her pussy contract and milk the cock still slamming into her. Teeth sank into the back of her shoulder as Knox stiffened above her, and then she felt every hot splash of his come.

Slumping on the desk, Harper panted. Thoughts hazy, she started to drift up until a hot tongue lapped at the bite on her shoulder. She almost shivered when he then straightened, baring her back to the cool air. As fingers lightly probed the new brand on her ass, she squeezed her eyes shut. "I can't decide if I want to know what it looks like."

He hesitated. "It's a very pretty intricate swirl of thorns."

Was that amusement she heard in his voice? Harper stiffened. "What aren't you telling me?"

"I'm not sure you'll want to know."

Yep, that was *definitely* amusement. She lifted her head. "Seriously, what's funny? What did your damn demon do this time?"

"There. I've snapped a photo of it."

"What?" She tried to stand, but his body covered hers once more. "Don't take photos of my ass, you—*oh, my God.*" She could only gape at the screen of his cell phone as he slid it in front of her face. The brand was, as he'd said, an intricate swirl of thorns . . . in the shape of a "K". "Your demon's territorialism knows no boundaries."

"Hmm." Still fluttering his fingers over the brand, he pressed a kiss to her neck, his mouth curved.

She twisted her head to meet his eyes, and found that they were glittering with male satisfaction. "You like it," she accused.

He shrugged one shoulder. "You have the initial of my first name on your ass. What's not to like?"

Harper shook her head, gaping. "You're unbelievable. Really." And so was her inner demon, since the weirdo also liked it.

He pressed another kiss to her neck. "I should have guessed my demon would brand you again. Drew's presence is playing on its possessiveness."

"And on yours."

"And on mine."

Feeling his cock thickening inside her once more, Harper's brows rose. "You really, *really* like the brand, don't you?"

He scraped his teeth over the crook of her neck. "I want you again. But this time, you'll ride me while I sit in my chair."

The entire time she did, his hand cupped the brand on her ass. Hell, yeah, he liked the brand.

CHAPTER TEN

The following day, Knox had Armand teleport him, Levi, and Larkin to Dion Boughton's private tropical island. As they waited for the bridge to descend over the moat that bordered Dion's large stately home, Knox studied the building. It looked out of place amongst exotic plants and coconut trees. Instead, it looked like it belonged in a period drama.

"What's the point in living on a tropical island if you're not near the beach?" asked Armand. "Why build it smack bam in the middle of the island?"

"Isolation," said Knox, watching as a blond, tanned, broad-shouldered male crossed the bridge. *Nightmare*, Knox immediately sensed. Such breeds were rarely powerful, but this one was strong. He was also brave, because he met Knox's stare without flinching.

"Mr. Thorne," he greeted simply before giving the others a brief nod. "Please follow me."

Levi walked in front while Larkin covered the rear as the

four of them followed the Nightmare across the bridge, through a pretty courtyard, and into the building. It was extravagant and ostentatious with its marble floors, rich dark woods, and chandeliers. It also burst with antiques, expensive vases, unusual ornaments, and vintage items. Many of the servants were rare breeds of demon—more collector's items, really.

Knox's demon liked shiny things, but it wasn't impressed by the place. Found it far too pompous and flashy. Perhaps it was Dion's way of compensating for how very average he was.

The Nightmare led them into the parlor, where Dion waited on his throne-like chair. Only Levi followed Knox inside the room. Larkin and Armand stayed in the wide hallway outside the door, on guard.

Clasping his hands, Dion stood and smiled brightly at Knox. The smile seemed genuine. "It truly is a pleasure to see you again, Knox. I don't particularly enjoy having visitors, but I do like your company."

No, he liked having the opportunity to observe Knox in the hope of figuring out what he was. Dion was also fascinated by anything unique, and Knox was certainly that.

He gestured for Knox and Levi to sit. "Would you care for any refreshments?"

"No, thank you," said Knox, taking a seat on the plush upholstered sofa opposite Dion's chair. Levi stood near the wall, feet wide apart, arms crossed. The sentinel managed to look cool and casual even as he projected a "Make no wrong moves" message.

Dion sank into his chair. "May I ask how your mate and son are doing?"

"They're both well, thank you." Despite the fact that Harper couldn't argue with Knox's reservations about it, she'd still wanted to come along. Knox had managed to talk her into staying at home, pointing out that they'd left Asher with the sentinels a lot lately and that their son would benefit from some one-on-one time with her. Yes, Knox had thoroughly played and manipulated her. She'd also been well-aware of it. Still, she'd agreed that Asher would enjoy having her to himself for a while.

"I heard through the grapevine that your little boy is quite the character," Dion went on.

"I can agree with that," said Knox, ignoring the prompts for him to speak more about Asher. He would do nothing to pique Dion's interest in his son.

As if resigned to that, Dion let out a long breath. "You told me during your last visit that you don't do social calls, so I'm guessing this is business."

"Of a sort."

Clasping his hands again, Dion offered him a cordial smile. "Tell me, how can I help you?"

"I'm sure you heard about what happened to Alethea."

Distaste crossed Dion's face. "Awful. Just awful. And to have such an undignified death be shared with the world ..." He shook his head. "It would be truly maddening to know your final moments would be uploaded onto the internet for all to see, especially for someone like Alethea."

Knox tilted his head. "Did you know her well?"

"Not really, no." Dion stilled, eyes widening just a little. "Am I a suspect? Again?"

"No," Knox lied. Personally, in Dion's position, Knox wouldn't have been reassured, but his response immediately put Dion at ease. "I discovered from Jonas that Alethea was acting strangely before she disappeared."

Dion's brow creased. "Disappeared?"

"She wasn't seen by Jonas for at least five and a half months before her death."

"Really?" Dion blinked. "I had no idea."

"I've been speaking with everyone who spent time with Alethea running up to her disappearance," Knox again lied. "You were one of them."

"Well, yes, but it was at least ten months since I last saw her. I was quite surprised when I received her letter, requesting permission to visit. We had history, but that history was rather ancient. I was curious about what she wanted."

"And?" Knox prodded.

"She said she'd broken up with Thatcher but that he was harassing her, constantly reaching out to touch her mind. She remembered that I have a psychic barrier here stopping telepathic contact from reaching the island—people can talk mind-to-mind while here, but not with someone who isn't on the island with them. She was hoping I'd give her sanctuary for a short while." Dion spread his hands. "She said she simply wanted to be left alone. I, of all people, understand the need for solitude."

"Would you say she acted strangely at all while here?"

"She was tense. Edgy." Dion paused. "She spoke of you."

"Did she?"

"She said she'd always considered you a friend, and she felt that she'd lost that friendship since you met your mate. It saddened her. Especially since, right then, she felt you were the only person who could help her."

Knox couldn't imagine Alethea ever admitting to needing aid with anything. He had to wonder if she'd been playing Dion. But for what purpose? "Help her with what?"

"She wouldn't say. I tried to get her to open up about her problems, but she would always give me this sad look and then shake her head."

Knox twisted his mouth. "Did you give her a tour of your museum?"

"Several, actually."

"What about the incorporeal demon you keep in there? Did you show her that?"

Dion went rigid. "How do you know about the incorporeal?" he asked flatly.

"I know many things."

When Knox didn't elaborate, Dion cleared his throat and spoke. "Yes, well, I did show her. I keep it in a display case—you can see the demon moving around, if you look close enough." His eyes lit up, as if just talking about one of his collectibles got him excited. "Sometimes it even glows, you know. I'm not sure if that means it's attempting to use power, but that would be my best guess."

"Did Alethea show any interest in it?"

"Yes, she was quite fascinated by it, in fact. She wanted to know all about how I came to own it. Wanted to know if I'd ever free it or consider making a bargain with it. Of course, I have no intention of doing either." Dion gave him a wry smile. "According to Alethea, that makes me a bore. If that is the case, so be it—an incorporeal on the loose can never be a good thing."

"I agree. Do you still have the incorporeal?"

Dion's brow puckered. "Yes, of course."

"Can I see it?"

Eyes brightening, Dion stood. "If you have the time, I can give you a full tour of the museum. But if you're in a rush, I can simply bring the display case to you."

Remaining seated, Knox said, "I'm afraid I don't have very long."

"Ah. Another time, then. I'll just be a moment." Dion's shoes clicked along the marble floor as he left the room.

I'm not sure if I believe him, said Levi without moving from his spot across the room. *He seems genuine, but I don't trust him one*

172   Suzanne Wright

little bit. If he is telling the truth, I've got the feeling that Alethea toyed with him for sympathy or something.

The comment echoed Knox's thoughts. *Alethea would never admit to needing help. And I seriously doubt that she ever considered me or anyone else to be a friend. I also can't envision Thatcher harassing her.*

Do you think she needed a place to hide? Or do you think it's possible that she already knew Dion had an incorporeal demon and she came here with the intention of taking it?

Either is possible.

A minute or so later, Dion reentered the room, carrying a display case. His steps were slow, his expression one of utter confusion.

"This is it?" Knox asked, standing.

Dion shook his head. "No. It's a copy of my case. A very good copy. It's also empty." He stared at it, expression thoughtful. Then his eyes cut to Knox. "Odd that you would ask if I'd showed it to Alethea and then also ask me if I still have it. You think she took it?"

"Yes, I do."

Dion's gaze turned inward. "If she had a duplicate of the case in her possession, she must have come here specifically to steal mine," he said, though he appeared to be talking to himself. "But how could she have known about the incorporeal or what the case looked like? I've never taken her through the museum before."

"She could have had someone teleport a replica of the case to her after giving them a description of it," Levi suggested, but Dion didn't seem to have heard him. He seemed lost in his own thoughts.

"It hadn't even occurred to me to check if she'd taken anything when she left. I'll have to search the entire museum from top to bottom to see what else she stole." Finally, Dion looked at Knox. "Do you think she meant to free the incorporeal?"

"I think she *did* free it," Knox told him.

"No," said Dion with a sharp shake of his head. "No, it's not as easy as it may sound to free an incorporeal from a container. It would not have been as simple as merely smashing the display case."

"Why not?" asked Knox.

"For one thing, it would take an extremely strong spell to break the glass—the ritual is quite complicated. Secondly, the incorporeal would have been in no fit state to follow her instructions. It was in captivity for a very long time. The spell that kept the case locked also kept the incorporeal from dying without a host."

Planting his feet, Knox folded his arms. "Humor me. Let's say she managed to free it. What would have happened next?"

"Well, when first released, the incorporeal would have been extremely weak—so much so that it wouldn't have been able to survive outside of a human host for more than a few seconds. It also would have been unable to control the host and, as such, would have been forced to simply lie in the background while it 'fed' on its host's energy."

Rubbing at his chin, Knox asked, "How long would it have taken the incorporeal to reach such a level of strength that it could maintain a physical form of its own choosing for a short time?"

Dion was silent for a moment as he considered it. "Providing it was given a strong host to drain on being freed, I'd say it would have taken somewhere between four and six months. But only if the incorporeal was extremely powerful."

"I have reason to believe that she did manage to free it." Knox told him about the demon's attempt to get near Asher and its attack on Knox. Dion actually paled, and Knox wondered if it was because he worried the incorporeal would kill him in revenge for holding it captive.

"Alethea couldn't have freed it without help," Dion insisted. "She simply wasn't strong enough."

"I don't believe she had help. I believe she *was* the help. Someone else—most likely the last of the Horsemen—wanted the incorporeal and recruited her to aid him in obtaining it. Together, they then freed it and nurtured it back to full strength. Then he made a bargain with it."

"But he said on the clip before killing her that she was in his way."

"Maybe she didn't like the bargain he made with the incorporeal. Maybe she hadn't known he was the Horseman until right then. We can't be sure why he killed her, but we can be certain that the incorporeal is free."

Urgency in his manner, Dion slung the duplicate of his display case on the sofa. "If the incorporeal is gunning for you and your family, you need to find a way to have it banished back to hell or destroyed. It won't stop until it's done whatever it is that will free it. Only the flames of hell can destroy an incorporeal. And, despite the rumors, I don't believe that's an ability you possess. There would be no reason for you to hide it." He swallowed. "I will do what I can to discover where Alethea spent her time running up to her death."

Levi looked at Dion through narrowed eyes. "You fear the incorporeal will come for you, don't you?" It wasn't really a question; it was a confident statement. "Well, if I were kept in a museum for centuries, confined to a small case and gawked at by passersby, I'd certainly want vengeance on my captor."

"You'll need to be careful who you let on your island, especially if they're human," Knox advised Dion. "You wouldn't know they were possessed by the incorporeal until it was much too late."

Dion swallowed nervously, but he set his jaw in determination. "It will never reach me here. I wish you luck in dealing with it."

Yeah, I'll bet he does, Levi said to Knox. *If it's destroyed, he's safe.*

You can't blame him for being so disturbed by the idea of the incorporeal coming for him, said Knox. *They're not forgiving creatures, and I would imagine they would be eager to make their captor pay for a very long time.*

After Armand teleported Knox and the sentinels to Knox's office within the Underground, the teleporter left the room. Knox sank into his leather chair behind his desk and brought Larkin up to speed on all that Dion had said. "Well, now we know for sure where Alethea got the incorporeal," Knox added. "By all appearances, it does seem that she stole it right from under Dion's nose."

"For a minute, I did wonder if maybe he *gave* the incorporeal to her and then fed us a load of shit to cover his ass," began Levi, "but he could have just denied ever owning an incorporeal—we would never have been able to prove that he had. He could have also denied that Alethea had spent a lot of time with him before her disappearance—again, we wouldn't have been able to prove it was a lie on our part."

Perched on the sofa near the window that overlooked the combat circle beneath them, Larkin spoke, "I agree that it's unlikely he was in cahoots with Alethea. It seems extreme that he'd have gone to the trouble of having a replica of the display case made purely on the off-chance that our investigation would have led us to him."

"We don't know that it *is* a replica," said Knox. "We never saw the original case. Only Jonas knows what it looks like. Dion could have shown us any damn case."

Larkin bit her lip. "Shit, I never thought of that. I guess we could ask Jonas to describe the case he saw at Alethea's home."

"He won't do us any favors," said Knox. "He won't even take my calls anymore. Despite that I can't be sure the case truly was a replica, I'm no longer inclined to consider Dion a suspect. If he were the Horseman and needed Alethea's help in freeing the incorporeal, it seems highly unlikely that he wouldn't have given it to her. They could have just worked together in secret on his island."

Levi nodded. "Letting her take the case off the island risked someone else, like Jonas, seeing it. Plus, I doubt Dion would have wanted it so far out of his sight and reach."

"I don't think Dion's the fourth Horseman either, but that's not to say that he isn't one of the bastard's minions," said Larkin. "Honestly, though, my suspicions lean more toward Jonas. Maybe it's just because I've never liked him and something about him rubs me up the wrong way. And it still bugs me that he wanted an archdemon."

"He said he wanted one so that he could use it to kill the incorporeal," Levi pointed out.

"But I can't help wondering if maybe what he *really* wanted was an archdemon for a minion, so that he had extra power against Knox," said Larkin. "Jonas did seem to put a lot of effort into looking for Alethea, but that could have been for show. You said he was adamant that she wouldn't have known she was working with the Horseman, but that's exactly what you'd expect him to say. You'd be suspicious if her own brother did anything but defend her."

Levi tilted his head, allowing that. "True. But if you ask me, Dario is the most obvious suspect, since he had a connection to both Nora and Isla. He campaigned to be Monarch of the US like Isla, but it's possible that they weren't really competing for the position. Maybe they both did it in the hope that at least one of them would be elected."

Knox twisted his mouth. "Dario does seem to be the most logical suspect. He also had a connection to Alethea. In Malden's words, Dario's 'ancient history' with Alethea hadn't ended well, but that's not to say that she and Dario hadn't recently rekindled what they once had." Alethea had never been difficult to seduce, which was partly why his demon hadn't found her in the least bit interesting.

"And, if the rumors are right, Dario's no stranger to rituals," Levi added. "It's alleged that he regularly engages in voodoo sex rituals with his harem."

Larkin's brow puckered. "Was his concubine part of the harem? The one who died?"

"Most likely," replied Knox. Many Primes had harems consisting of several concubines. Personally, he'd never seen the appeal in having a harem.

"Maybe he replaced her with Alethea. I heard she was pretty adventurous in bed." Larkin's gaze turned inward. "I wonder how the concubine died."

Levi shrugged. "No idea."

Touching Harper's mind, loving the way it rang with her fire, iron will, innate sensuality, and the soft streak she did her best to hide, Knox said, *Hey, baby, how are you and our boy doing?*

We're fine, she replied. *He seems very pleased with himself after peeing in the air while I was changing his diaper. Honestly, it was like a fountain.*

Knox's mouth twitched, able to imagine the impish grin on his son's face. *I'd say it was the Wallis part of his nature at work.* They were mischievous to their core.

Yeah, probably. How did it go with Dion?

Alethea got the incorporeal from him. It seems that she stole it

*and replaced his display case with a replica, which suggests she was
either prepared and went there specifically to take the incorporeal or
she had someone teleport a replica to her.*

Harper was quiet for a moment. *I'm more inclined to think that
she already knew he had an incorporeal. The Horseman probably
knew and sent her to get it, allowing her to take the risks. She'd have
gotten a kick out of the danger. But we can't be sure, can we?* She
sighed. *At least we know where the incorporeal came from. Are you
going to tell the other Primes about it?*

*Yes, I'll hold a teleconference later today to bring them up to
speed. I don't want them wasting resources on trying to find out
where she got it from.*

"So," began Larkin, "you no longer think that Thatcher's a
possible suspect?"

Knox gave Harper's mind a soft stroke with his own before
breaking the connection and responding to Larkin. "I didn't say
that. They could have chosen to continue their relationship in
secret for one reason or another. Whatever way you look at it,
Dario is the most likely suspect. But it bothers me that it seems
so obvious."

"Just because something is obvious doesn't mean it isn't the
right answer," said Larkin. "If you're leaning so much toward
Dario, why haven't you paid him a visit?"

"I feel as if I'm missing something. Something important." But
damn if Knox could figure out what.

CHAPTER ELEVEN

"Ew, Asher, don't eat the sand—" Too late. Harper sighed, shaking her head. Sitting in his sandbox where he'd been digging out half-buried toys, Asher grimaced as he worked to spit out the gritty sand.

Mouth curved, Keenan declared, "I got it." Taking a tissue from Harper, he crouched and wiped Asher's mouth.

It was no more than twenty minutes ago that she'd stopped Asher from licking stagnant pond water from his fingers. The landscapers had added the shallow pond especially for Asher, keeping it close to the playground—complete with a little bridge, a rock formation, and beautiful plants. Asher *loved* it. He always had a grand time tossing rocks in the water, ripping apart the high grass, watching frogs plop into the water, and playing with the silky petals of the wildflowers. What he most loved was feeding the geese and ducks.

The playground was his favorite place on the estate, though. In terms of equipment, there was everything a child could want, some of which he was too young to use yet. Sandbox, swings, seesaw, slide, jungle gym, rock climbing wall, tube maze, monkey bars—you name it, it was there. All were brightly colored, just like the rubber matting on which they were situated.

It was a little distance from the house, so the playground was pretty quiet. At that moment, all she could hear was the gentle rustling of grass and the slight creak of the swing-chains, thanks to the breeze. A breeze which was a very welcome reprieve from the glare of the sun.

"What's with the crows?" asked Tanner, who was lazing on a wooden bench in the shade.

Tracking his gaze, Harper squinted at the gathering of crows in the high trees. "I don't know. Dan keeps chasing them off, but they keep coming back. And they bring friends. At first, I worried the incorporeal might be hitching a ride in one of them."

"It wouldn't get on the estate—not even while possessing a bird," said Keenan. "The psychic shield encompasses every bit of land, every tree, every blade of grass. A demonic presence would rebound right off it."

Harper nodded, since Knox had already assured her of the same thing many times. "Dan said there's no maliciousness in the crows' minds. He said it's almost like they're drawn here."

Tanner's gaze cut to Asher. "If he's drawing them, he's not doing it on purpose."

"No, he's not." She smiled at the way Asher kept trying to grab the sand, frustrated that it kept pouring out of his little fist. "It might not be him. I mean, he doesn't draw other animals to him. And if he had some kind of affinity for birds, the ducks and geese near the pond would be drawn to him, right?"

"True. Never thought of that. In that case, you're right, it might not be him. I don't know what else it could be, though."

No, neither did she. But no matter what way she looked at

it, it made no sense that it was Asher. Taking in a deep breath, Harper felt her nose wrinkle. The spongy material beneath their feet might be a good safety measure, but sun-warmed rubber wasn't a pleasant smell. At the least there were the scents of tree blossoms, pine sap, and flowering plants to make up for it.

"No!" yelled Asher, glaring at the sand as it once again sifted through his fingers. "*Ma!*"

She stifled a smile. "I can't make it stay in your hand, baby."

He patted the sand hard in a huff, grimaced when a cloud of it hit him in the face. Worse, he went to lick some from his little fingers.

"No, Asher, don't eat—" Too late. Again. Plucking another tissue out of her pocket, she wiped his mouth. He gripped her hand as he pulled himself to his feet. She smiled. "Big boy, aren't you?" Holding her hand, he toddled out of the sandbox.

Keenan crouched and held out his arms. "Come on, little man. Try walking over to me."

Keeping his little fingers curled around hers, Asher walked toward him. Harper moved with him, step for step, impressed by his balance and speed. As Keenan urged him to keep going, she ever so gently let go of Asher's hand, hoping he'd carry on walking. Instead, he stopped dead and then deliberately plopped right on his ass.

Keenan chuckled. "Let's go for a wander." Taking Asher's hand, he guided him around the play area.

"His balance is getting better," Tanner commented. "He'll be walking on his own in no time."

She nodded. "Then I'll really be in trouble, because he'll go searching for it."

"It's the Wallis in him," Tanner said with a grin.

Yeah, it certainly was. Just then, Jolene's mind touched hers, bold and strong. *Sweetheart, is there anyone around who can watch Asher for you for a little while?*

Harper frowned. *What's wrong?*

Nothing. I just have something to show you. It won't take long.

Wondering if Jolene was being deliberately and annoyingly vague just for the fun of it, Harper turned to the incubus. "Keenan, would you be able to watch over Asher for me for a little while? Jolene wants to see me. She said it won't take long."

"Of course," Keenan replied.

Tanner fluidly rose from the bench. "I'll go with you."

Reaching out to her grandmother, Harper said, *Keenan will stay with Asher. I'm ready when you are.*

Good, Jolene instantly responded. *I'll send Ciaran for you.*

Mere moments later, the male imp appeared in front of them. He grinned at Harper. "Hey."

Asher's head lifted, and he smiled.

Ciaran saluted him. "Hey, kiddo! I'm just borrowing your mom for a few minutes."

"What's this about?" Harper asked him.

He shrugged. "No idea. I'm just following orders." He teleported her and Tanner to Jolene's kitchen.

Sitting at the island, flicking through a magazine, Jolene looked up and smiled. "Harper, thanks for coming so fast."

Harper returned her smile and accepted the one-armed hug. "Hey, Grams. What's going on?"

Jolene looked the personification of innocence. "As I said, I just have something to show you."

Uneasy, Harper narrowed her eyes. "You're being very mysterious."

"Tanner, Ciaran will keep you company while we're upstairs," Jolene told him. "We won't be long."

Shrugging at Tanner's questioning look, Harper followed her

grandmother out of the room, up the stairs, and toward Harper's old bedroom. "Seriously, Grams, what's this all about?"

Stopping outside the closed bedroom door, Jolene said, "Drew's inside. He wants to say his goodbyes."

Harper gaped. "*What?*" Her inner demon hissed, furious. He hadn't called her since Knox warned him to stop, but he also hadn't cut his visit to the US early, promising Jolene he'd keep his distance. This was not keeping his distance, and it would piss Knox the fuck off. "Grams, don't put me in this position."

"He's agreed to leave and have the tattoo removed tonight, but he wishes to speak with you first. He's very insistent about it. If you want him in Cuba, away from Knox, just give Drew five minutes of your time. He was your friend once. And it would mean a lot to Devon if all this awkwardness could be a thing of the past."

The latter comment made Harper's hackles lower. She'd spoken with Devon just last night, who was mad at Drew for "not using his brain" and just letting the whole thing go. But she also felt sorry for her brother, and she was upset that he was so angry with her for not giving him a heads-up when Knox first began pursuing Harper. She hated that Devon was hurting and there was such friction between the siblings—they'd never really argued before. Harper wanted to see an end to all this shit.

She blew out a breath. "Two minutes, Grams. I'll give him two minutes, but that's all."

With a pleased smile, Jolene patted her upper arm. "Good girl. I'll wait downstairs. And don't be too hard on him. He made a mistake, he knows that. Let him put it right."

Harper twisted the doorknob and pushed it open. Drew was standing at the window, watching the traffic go by. He turned to face her as she closed the door. She only took a single step into the room.

He gave her a weak, too-quick smile. "Hey."

"Hi." God, could this be any more awkward? Nope.

"Thanks for coming."

She didn't say anything. Didn't know what *to* say.

"So ... you know about the tattoo."

"I don't understand why you had it done," she said with a shrug. Marking himself for her demon was not only wrong but *huge*. Dramatic, even.

He tucked his hands into the pockets of his jeans. "My demon needed it. It chose you a long time ago. *I* chose you. My demon was ready, but I wasn't. Not then. Now ... *Fuck*." He thrust a hand through his hair. "If I hadn't stayed away, if I'd just come home—"

"It wouldn't have made any difference to Knox if I was with someone else."

"No, it wouldn't have." He took a step toward her. "But you're loyal to the bone. You wouldn't have given in to him if you'd already been claimed by another."

"You're taking for granted that I would have let you claim me." Her inner demon snorted at the idea.

"If you had—"

"I wouldn't have cheated on you, no," Harper allowed. "But, as my anchor, Knox would still have been a part of my life. And I'd be lying if I said I wouldn't have grown to care for him just as I do now. I wouldn't have betrayed you, but I also wouldn't have stayed in a relationship with you if I felt so strongly for another person—that wouldn't have been fair to you, me, or him. Things would have ended up exactly as they are right now. Me with Knox and Asher." She wholeheartedly believed that.

Lips thinning, Drew threw up his arms. "I don't get it, Harper."

"Don't get what?"

"You and Thorne. You don't make sense as a couple. You come from completely different backgrounds, you've lived totally different lifestyles, and you don't seem to have a single thing in common. Beneath that hard shell, you're giving and softhearted—don't even deny it—while he's . . . *him*."

Bristling, she clipped, "Well, I don't need you to '*get*' it. It's none of your damn business."

"Don't you want someone who cares for you?"

"Yes, I do. And that's exactly what I have."

Drew tossed her a disappointed look. "You can't honestly tell me he loves you with the intensity that demons are known for. He sees you as a possession. A thing. Something he won't share but can never love."

"Wrong. But you believe whatever makes you feel better—I really couldn't give a fuck." She raised her hands, palms up. "And I'd say we've now officially reached the end of this conversation." She turned to the door.

"I almost didn't leave."

Glancing at him over her shoulder, she frowned. "Excuse me?"

"The night after I came so close to having you, I almost didn't go back to Cuba. I thought about staying and seeing if there was any way to get behind those walls of yours. They were always sky high and ten inches thick. But I figured you weren't ready—even shitfaced, you'd pushed me away before it went too far. So I went back to Cuba. And, yeah, part of the reason it wasn't so hard was that I wasn't ready either. Not for anything serious."

"Drew, this is old—"

"I took it for granted that when I came home you'd still be kidding yourself that you could be happy with a human, even though you knew your demon would never accept one as a mate. That was my mistake." He let out a short, humorless laugh. "I couldn't fucking believe it when I heard you were mated. Devon didn't tell me about him. Said she kept it from me because Jolene didn't want you to be with someone whose priority was chasing the next rush. But it wouldn't have been like that, Harper. *You* would have been my priority."

"It really doesn't matter. I'm mated. I'm happy. I have a son. I'm totally committed to Knox."

"Which makes no sense unless you've deliberately chosen someone who won't demand everything from you. The kicker is ... you won't get all of him either." Drew took another step toward her. "Your little boy is bright and warm and playful—*all* you. Do you want him living every day of his life with someone as cold and dangerous as Thorne? Because if he does, he'll lose that warmth bit by bit. *You'll* lose that little boy."

So tired of this shit, Harper planted her hands on her hips. "Pray tell, Drew, what should I do instead?"

"Leave Thorne. Leave him."

"Why exactly would I do that? I love him, and he loves me. You don't have to believe that. I really don't care if you do or you don't. But it's the truth. *I* know he loves me, and that's all that matters."

"Did you also know that he was sleeping with one of the Horsemen? Isla? They were close, Harper. They'd known each other for centuries. But he killed her. You think *you're* any safer with him?"

At the reminder of Isla, Harper's demon curled her upper lip. "He killed her because she hurt me. And yes, I do believe I'm safe with him." She fumbled behind her for the doorknob. "Look, you need to go back to Cuba, Drew."

"Nothing I say could change your mind on Thorne?"

"Nothing." With that, she turned to the door again.

"I know that Asher's not a sphinx."

That comment had her hand freezing on the knob. Whirling

to face Drew, she scoffed, "Of course he's a sphinx. It's perfectly easy to sense."

"Did you forget I have the ability to identify a demon's breed on sight?"

Yes, actually, she had forgotten. But she remembered now that he didn't even need to be in the vicinity of the person in question. Drew could look at a photo of a demon and simply *see* what they were. Stomach rolling, she nonetheless stated, "Asher is a sphinx."

Eyes soft with sympathy, Drew shook his head. "No, Harper, he's not."

Fisting her hands, she advanced on the asshole and then jabbed a finger at him. "Don't you dare fuck with me just because you're bitter about my—"

"This is not me fucking with you. I would *never* lie about something like this. I'm telling you, Harper, your son is not a sphinx."

"Then do educate me, Drew . . . what is he?" she spat sardonically, humoring him.

"Each breed of demon has a sort of aura. Not a spiritual glow like what humans talk about. The auras I see are faint ribbons of light that twine around a person. Thorne's light is black, which sounds like a contradiction in terms, doesn't it? But the color black is really just the complete absorption of visible light; it's the absence of color. I have no idea what he is, but it's dark and old and I've never come across one like it before."

"And Asher's light?" she asked, voice cracking.

"He doesn't have one, Harper. He has a shadow instead. It's like a dark smudge. Do you know what that means? It means he doesn't belong to a breed. He's a demon, yes, but he's nothing . . . *natural*. Whatever he is doesn't have a marker because it shouldn't exist."

Her spine snapped straight. "My son has every right to exist!"

"I'm not saying he should be fucking killed, Harper, I'm saying he isn't a natural breed of demon. I haven't told anyone, before you ask. And I won't. But you need to be careful, Harper, because that dark smudge … it pulses. Like an irregular heartbeat. I don't know what the fuck that means, but it can't be anything good. You wouldn't have fully committed yourself to someone who kept secrets from you, so I'm sure you *think* you know what Thorne is. But I doubt he's told you the truth because whatever that guy is, he couldn't even conceive a normal demon. What does that say about him?"

Overwhelmed, she swallowed. "I have to go. *You* have to go."

"You really think I could go back to fucking Cuba when I know there's an incorporeal demon out there who came at you and is highly likely to do it again? I'd spend my days going insane with worry. No, I'm staying until the threat has gone and I know you're safe."

"Knox won't stand for that."

"He's already taken my future from me. What more can he do?"

"Your future?" she echoed, blood boiling at the sheer nerve of him. "If you'd really thought of me that way, you'd have done something about it a *long* time ago. And you're goddamn arrogant to assume that I was that much of a sure thing." Her demon surfaced with a hiss. "You had no right to mark yourself for me," it said.

Drew shrugged. "It's done."

"You have to get rid of it."

"You think I'll let Thorne or anyone else tell me what I can do to my own damn body?"

Retaking control, Harper glared at him. "And how would you like it if you knew there was someone out there wearing your female on his skin?"

"Someone out there *is*." He gave her a pointed look.

Harper snarled. "*I'm not yours.* Never have been. Never will be. You need to accept it or—"

Behind her, the bedroom door flew open.

"You've gotta be fucking kidding me," growled Tanner. He rounded Harper and stalked into Drew's personal space. "Do you want to die? Is that what this is?"

Sidling up to Harper, Jolene put a hand on her back. "I tried to keep him downstairs, but he got suspicious."

"Call Thorne here," Drew dared. "Even better, ask Ciaran to go get him. Harper has a right to know why her son—"

She jerked as fire roared to life in front of her. Hissed. Popped. Crackled. And there was Knox. No, there was Knox's demon. *Oh, shit.*

Everyone froze, eyeing it warily. Its attention was on Drew. Although it looked the image of utter composure, fury gleamed in those obsidian eyes. The air turned bitterly cold and so oppressive that it hurt to breathe it in.

Chest tingling, Harper coughed. "Knox?" *Knox, please get your demon to dial it down.* If anything, the air thickened even further. Then they were all coughing. Rubbing her chest, she tried again. "*Knox?*"

Black eyes slid to her, and the fury there receded just a little. Either the demon chose to subside or Knox wasn't taking any of its shit, because then he surfaced and the air cleared. *Want to tell me why you're in a bedroom with the fucker who wants to steal you from me?*

She winced. Yeah, it did look bad, didn't it? *I didn't know Drew was here. Grams just said she had something she needed to show me.*

He arched a brow. *And you didn't think to walk out when you realized why she really brought you here?*

Grams said he just wanted to say goodbye. I figured I could just let him get it over with and then leave.

Knox's gaze cut to her grandmother. "You fucked with my trust, Jolene."

Smoothing a hand down her blouse, Jolene said, "Drew just wanted to say his goodbyes." It wasn't a defense; it was a statement. Jolene didn't justify herself to anyone.

"No, he didn't want that," said Knox. "Not at all."

Harper frowned, wondering if he'd taken a dip in Drew's mind and seen a wholly different intention.

Knox turned to Drew. "Did you have it removed?"

Drew lifted his chin. "If you mean the tat, no." And his expression said that he had absolutely no intention of doing so. Jolene groaned in exasperation. Tanner shook his head, mouth tightening. Knox? He just looked at the hellcat blankly.

"That's fine. I can remove it for you." Knox gripped Drew, and then fire erupted around them.

"Knox, no!" Harper shouted, but it was too late. They were gone. Sighing, she shoved a hand through her hair. "Well, Grams, I can't say you didn't fuck this one up."

Jolene fingered her pearl necklace. "Will he kill him?"

"I don't know." Harper rubbed her temple. The day had started off so well . . .

"If Knox can pyroport," began Jolene, "why has he been using Ciaran like a cab all this time?"

"He likes to keep people guessing about what he can do."

Jolene gave a slow nod of understanding. "His secret is safe with me."

"I'd like to say your hellcat is safe with Knox, Jolene," Tanner told her, jaw hard. "But he's not. Not one little fucking bit."

*

As the flames eased off, Knox grabbed the hellcat with psychic hands and rammed him into the cracked stone wall. The breath slammed out of Clarke's lungs. He coughed, body shaking, eyes burning with rage. He would no doubt have stupidly lunged at Knox if the psychic hands weren't pinning him to the wall like a butterfly.

Knox's demon bared its teeth in a feral grin, pleased to see the hellcat helpless and—better still—in what was effectively its playroom. Unlike Knox, it didn't mind the scents of sweat, metal, mildew, and iron that were swirling around them.

Drew glanced around the dull, shadowy space, taking in the tiny cramped cells, the iron maiden, the Judas chair, the rack, the cages hanging from the ceiling, and the sets of manacles attached to the walls. If it wasn't for the dim recessed lighting, the large space would have been as dark as it was grim.

"Where are we?" Drew asked, voice warbled. Fear seemed to light his eyes from within.

"My sentinels call it the Chamber." Knox's footsteps echoed on the hard, stone floor. "Not very original, I suppose. It's located beneath my prison, and it's where members of my lair are brought for punishment. Some are then incarcerated. Others are released after paying their penance." Knox had had a lot of fun punishing Roan in this very room. "It really all depends on the severity of the crime. I also bring here those who have ... *wronged* me or mine. Can't you hear them?"

The sounds of weeping, screaming, begging, raving, and the sound of whip hitting flesh filled the air.

"Don't you see them?"

Suddenly they were surrounded by people straining against manacles, being stretched over a rack, forced into the Judas chair, and laid on a bed of spikes.

Squeezing his eyes shut, Drew shook his head fast. "It's not real!"

"It was real." Knox let the echoes of the events fade away.

Tanner's mind brushed against his. *Knox, I know you want Clarke dead—you're not alone in that. But if you haven't already killed him, think about whether it's what you really want. His death at your hand could cause a massive rift between Harper and Devon, and that would affect Harper's life in a substantial way. He'd affect her life. And it could slowly eat at what you and Harper have. Do you want to give him that power? Because I honestly think he'd be happy to die if it meant it gave him that.*

Knox didn't respond. His demon paid the sentinel no mind—it wasn't interested in reason or rationality right then. Its rage was like a fire in Knox's veins. The bastard had *dared* to corner Harper, get her alone, and try to turn her against Knox. There was no way he wouldn't pay for that. "You should have stayed away from Harper."

Drew's eyes snapped open. "She needed to know the truth."

Knox lazily raised a brow. "About what?"

"That whatever you are, you couldn't even conceive a normal demon. Jolene didn't tell you I see auras?" Drew snickered. "I've never seen one like yours before, but at least you have an aura. Your kid? No. He has a black smudge where an aura should be. A smudge that *pulsates*. Whatever you impregnated Harper with isn't natural."

"Whatever I impregnated her with?" Knox echoed, enunciating every word carefully. "Asher is a person, just like you and me. He's not a thing. He's not unnatural."

"Well, he's not a natural breed of demon. He's something else. Something that doesn't have a marker. Something I've never—" Whatever he saw on Knox's face made Clarke's eyes narrow. "You knew. You knew he wasn't a sphinx. You know what that black smudge is, too, don't you?"

"Forget all of that."

"You think I'll honestly forget—?"

"I'll *make* you forget." Knox thrust his mind into Drew's, allowed him to feel his presence there. "I can erase memories. All I have to do is find them and—" Finding a particular thread of memory, Knox smiled. "There." He snipped the thread. Like that, Drew could no longer remember Harper's taste.

His eyes widened. "What did you just do? You can't take my fucking memories!"

"If you had simply removed the tattoo and returned to Cuba, we wouldn't be in this position. You put yourself here." Seeing that Drew was trying to visualize a brick wall in his mind, as if it would bolster his shields, Knox's demon rolled its eyes. "You can't keep me out of your mind. You're simply not strong enough for that."

As he surfed through the hellcat's thoughts, it surprised Knox to find that ... "You see me as someone who sauntered in and stole Harper right from under your nose. But that's not really accurate, is it? Someone can't steal something from you if it never belonged to you. And Harper was never yours. She never would have been yours. She was meant to be mine."

Drew said nothing. Just kept on visualizing a brick wall, cheeks flushing red.

Ignoring the hellcat's futile attempts to keep him out, Knox went deeper into his mind. "My, my, my, you do like to lie to yourself, don't you, Clarke? You've managed to convince yourself that you're on a good and noble path; that your efforts to separate her from me is 'right' for Harper. But there's a little part of you that keeps shaking its head sadly—a part of you that finds it somewhat distasteful to try to tear apart a family."

Drew's eyes flickered.

"You don't even hope to gain anything from it at this point. You're not under the illusion that you have a chance with her.

You know she doesn't love you. You know she'll never belong to you. But you'd hoped that you could scare her into fleeing with Asher. You don't even care if she flees with you or not. All that matters to you is that she's away from me. You don't even care if it means that she'll be miserable without me. Tell me, Clarke, where's the nobility in that?"

"She's not safe with you," Drew gritted out. "I'd rather she was safe than happy. And if I'm going to lose her to someone, it should be to someone who deserves her. Someone who I know will care for her and give her what she needs. You're not that person. Never will be. I don't know how the fuck you managed to make her care for you—"

Knox laughed, and it was a dark sound that made the hellcat tense. "Don't lie, Clarke. You think I somehow manipulated her into believing she loves me. I'm guessing you haven't shared that belief with her. She'd have slapped you for thinking her so weak-minded."

"She's not weak-minded, but she's soft inside. She wants to be loved. You know that, and you've played on it."

"The only person who's been manipulating Harper is you." Knox stepped closer to him. "You know she finds it difficult to believe that people can truly love her and will stick around, and *you* played on *that*. Only it didn't work, did it? She's secure in what I feel for her. But if you'd tried that in the beginning when I very first met Harper, it might just have worked." A smug smile tugged at Knox's mouth. "I suppose that only makes it worse for you that Jolene insisted on you being kept in the dark about my presence in her life. How very sad."

Clarke sneered. "She would have chosen me if I'd come for her back then."

Knox laughed again, and there was a hint of genuine humor in it this time. "You really do enjoy deluding yourself, don't you?

Perhaps I should pity you. It must be difficult to have a mind that simply can't deal with reality and has invented its own version of it. You've not only blinded yourself to what Harper feels for me, you've blinded yourself to why you're so intent on separating her from me. Do stop with the pretense that you're doing what's best for her. Oh, you do want Harper safe, that's true. But you mostly want her away from me because you're jealous that she loves me and not you."

Clarke shook his head. "It's not—"

"Lie to yourself if you must, but I've been in your mind. When you get down to the bottom of all the bullshit in your head, Clarke, you can clearly see that this is just a very simple case of jealousy. But then, people have been doing extreme things out of jealousy since the beginning of time, haven't they? It's a very potent emotion." Something that Knox hadn't truly experienced until recently. "And it only makes it worse for you that I can offer her things you can't. It also annoys you that, power-wise, my dick is a hell of a lot bigger than yours. You know you're nothing close to my equal, and you hate that."

Hands curling into fists, Drew pointlessly struggled against Knox's psychic grip.

"I'd like to say that, in your shoes, I would walk away and let her enjoy the happiness she'd found with another, but I'm not sure if that's true," said Knox. "I know I'm a ruthless bastard. Whereas you . . . you truly believe yourself to be a good, honorable person. But wouldn't a good, honorable person tip their hat and walk away in such a situation?"

Drew ceased struggling and lifted his chin. "If you're going to kill me, get it over with."

"I'm not going to kill you." Because Tanner had been right. It would impact Harper's life. Clarke was nothing to her, and he needed to *stay* nothing to her. Knox didn't want any of her thoughts centered on the hellcat. But Knox couldn't guarantee that he'd have the same restraint if such a thing happened again.

Experimentally, Knox shot a laser of hellfire out of his finger. He saw understanding light Clarke's eyes. "I gave you the chance to get rid of it yourself." With his psychic hands, Knox twisted Drew, slammed him face-first into the wall, and held him there. "This shouldn't take long. But I won't lie to you, Clarke, my demon wants me to make it last. And, well, I've decided to give it what it wants." Knox tore open the back of the hellcat's shirt. "Do feel free to scream."

Drew hissed. "Do your worst."

"I will." Knox was quite sure the hellcat meant to suffer in silence. But the moment Knox honed that laser of hellfire onto the tattoo, Drew screamed.

CHAPTER TWELVE

Fire thundered to life in front of her. Harper looked up from the sofa, where she was embellishing her new jeans with rhinestones and diamantes. There was Knox; body stiff, shoulders square, dark stare fixed on her.

"So, you're back," she said, keeping her tone even and resisting the urge to ask if Drew was dead.

"It would seem so," Knox said silkily, pouring himself a gin and tonic.

Choosing to ignore that snippy response, she took another rhinestone from the box at her side. When Knox had disappeared with Drew, she'd wanted to reach out and try to calm him, but she'd worried that if she showed any concern for Drew's welfare it would only anger Knox further. While she couldn't find it in her to give much of a rat's ass about the hellcat after the shit he'd pulled, she couldn't feel good about anything that would upset Devon.

Having glued the rhinestone onto the back pocket of her

jeans, Harper reached for another. The box also contained crystals, gems, beads, sequins, sash, lace, and other appliques. She'd started personalizing her clothing when she lived with Lucian. They traveled light and weren't always able to afford new clothes. At those times, Harper would simply revamp her old ones.

She'd decided to work on her new jeans because she'd needed a distraction. She'd needed to think about something other than whether she'd have to explain to her friend that her older brother was dead. Mostly, though, she'd needed something to stop her from stressing over what Drew had said about Asher. None of it could be true. *None* of it.

"The hellcat's alive," Knox told her, sensing she wanted to know. He'd dumped Clarke on Jolene's doorstep; trembling, teeth chattering, sweat and blood gleaming on his back—and minus a series of memories, including the one of Knox's ability to pyroport. And Knox felt absolutely no remorse for it.

He'd given Clarke enough warnings. The male's sister had warned him. His own Prime had warned him. Still, Clarke had ignored them all. It wasn't like the hellcat was unaware of Knox's merciless nature. He'd known what he was risking. If he'd thought that Harper would save him from Knox, he'd thought wrong.

Hiding her relief in case he misinterpreted it as her caring for Drew, Harper said, "I'm guessing the tattoo is gone."

"You guessed correctly." Knox took a swig from his tumbler. He'd exorcised much of his anger when he "toyed" with the hellcat. But as he looked down at his calm and collected mate, who didn't appear in the slightest bit remorseful, he felt that anger building once again. "You should have called for me when you realized that Jolene and Drew had played you. At the very least, you should have walked out of that bedroom."

From the way he was glaring at her, looking all self-righteous, it was clear to Harper that he expected her to feel guilty. While he had reason to be upset, she refused to feel shamefaced when she'd only been trying to fix the complicated situation they were in. It wasn't like she'd arranged some kind of secret meeting with Drew, was it?

She was betting there had been numerous times when Knox had been alone with women who coveted him. She hadn't freaked out on him, and it pissed her off that he was looking at her like she'd cheated on him or something.

Feigning calm, Harper rummaged through her box in search of a tiny skull head. "I decided to hear him out because I wanted him gone. This whole thing isn't just hurting you, Knox, it's hurting Devon. I wanted to save you both that pain."

"It didn't work, did it?" Knox clipped. "Drew had no intention of leaving Vegas, Harper. He simply wanted an opportunity to convince you to leave me."

"Well, I know that *now*. But I didn't then."

"Would you even have told me about it if Tanner hadn't already done so?"

"Of course I would have told you—I had nothing to hide." Putting her jeans aside, Harper crossed her legs and folded her arms. "I also have nothing to prove or justify, so you can stop looking at me like I somehow betrayed you."

But that was exactly what Knox felt: betrayed. "I told you that I didn't want you near him. I made that very clear. And what did you do? You had a private conversation with him in your old bedroom. I swear, Harper, if I ever hear that you're alone with him again—"

"*Don't* threaten me," she hissed. Bristling, her inner demon unfurled and pushed against Harper's skin, ready to jump in and defend her.

"I'm not threatening you," he said, voice low. "I'm making

the situation abundantly clear, since it seems that you haven't listened to a single word I fucking said on this. I didn't kill Clarke just now for the simple reason that I don't want him on your mind or to impact your life. But I only have so much restraint in me. If he tries to get you alone again, I *will* kill him."

"You don't think you're overreacting just a little?"

"Overreacting?" Knox's hands curled. "He wants to take you from me."

"Just like Alethea and plenty of other women wanted to take you from me."

"If you'd wanted to kill them for it, you would have had every right. An 'overreaction' is the very last thing I would have called it. You chose to deal with it in a different way—I respected that decision, even though I hated what their actions did to you."

"But you didn't order them to stay away from you, did you?" Raising her chin in challenge, Harper rose from the sofa. "You expect me to stay clear of Drew, but I'm sure there were times when Isla or Alethea or other women that wanted to get in your pants went to see you at one of your offices. I'll bet you didn't tell them to fuck off and keep their distance. Am I right?" He didn't respond, but she knew she was right. "Thought so. You certainly never called out to me, so why the fuck would you expect me to call out to you? It's not like Drew's a physical threat to me."

"Those situations were different."

Her inner demon curled its upper lip in disgust. "Really? How? You knew the women wanted you; you knew they wanted me out of the picture, but you didn't call out to me or send them on their way immediately. No, you knew you could deal with those situations alone, so you did. How is that any different from what I did?"

"For one thing, I didn't have them in *my old fucking bedroom*."

"Like them being in your office makes much of a difference.

You fucked me in there not long ago so, yeah, you don't get to use that one."

He advanced on her, closing the distance between them, and pushed into her personal space. "How many times did you imagine those women touching me or vice versa, Harper? Hurt, didn't it? You didn't want those pictures in your head, but your imagination went wild on you. What if those pictures hadn't simply been your imagination at work? What if they had been actual memories that belonged to those women and you knew *exactly* what I did to them and what they did to me? How well would you have dealt with that?"

Not well at all. Harper would have *hated* having that shit in her head, but she'd like to think that she wouldn't have made Knox suffer for it. "Look, I'm sorry you have Drew's memories—"

"They're no longer his memories."

"What does that mean?"

"It means I erased them. He no longer remembers what you taste like, how your pussy feels around his fingers, how your breasts felt in his hands, or what you look and sound like when you come." Knox had thoroughly enjoyed snipping each thread of memory. Drew also had no memory of his reservations about Asher. As long as the hellcat didn't come into contact with Asher again, Drew never would. "That drunken encounter no longer has a place in his mind."

It kind of scared Harper that he could completely erase an event from a person's mind. It made her extremely grateful that she had tough psychic shields that he couldn't penetrate without shredding his own psyche.

"If Jolene has any sense, she'll put him on a plane tomorrow and he'll be gone. But maybe you're not relieved by that. Maybe you *like* the attention he gives you. Maybe you even want him."

Her head jerked back. For a moment, words failed Harper.

"Repeat that." It was a dare. Although he didn't repeat it, he gave her a look that said he meant every fucking word. An angry flush heated her cheeks. "You son of a bitch."

"Why else would you willingly be alone with him?"

"I already told you why, so stop with this crap. I won't pay for your pointless jealousy. I've given you no reason not to trust me."

"*Except that you were in a bedroom with another man.*"

"Fully dressed. Arguing, because he'd called our son 'unnatural' and claimed that he wasn't a sphinx. I'm assuming he said the same thing to you, since you don't look surprised by that."

"Yes, he did. But we're not talking about Asher, we're talking about you."

Harper froze. There had been a brief flash of something in his eyes just then that made a tingling sensation creep up her neck and face. "You were always careful about what you said whenever I mentioned how relieved the Primes were that Asher was a sphinx. You never once referred to him as a sphinx. And whenever Jolene made jokes about how much trouble baby sphinxes were, you never said a word. Just smiled absently or changed the subject."

Knox said nothing. Just casually tossed back the rest of his gin and tonic.

"You suspect that Asher might not be a sphinx, don't you? You motherfucker, you do. And you said *nothing.*" Her demon bared her teeth in the same fury that bubbled through Harper's veins. It lunged to the surface and glared at him. "You had no right to keep such a thing from us. It's time you got off your high horse and stopped trying to make her hurt as you hurt. I will put you through a world of pain if you do not."

If the entity glaring at him had lived within anyone other than his mate, Knox probably would have laughed. No one had ever taken him on and lived to tell the tale, but he would never retaliate against Harper or her demon; he'd never hurt them. In that sense, they had the upper hand. They wouldn't even need to engage him in a fight—one touch would have him writhing in soul-deep agony. And while he didn't believe Harper could stomach harming Knox any more than he could stomach harming her, he didn't doubt that her fierce and protective inner demon would do whatever it took to shield or avenge Harper—even cause him pain.

As if satisfied that its warning had been heard loud and clear, the entity subsided. Then Harper was once again sneering at him. "You don't even see anything wrong with the fact that you didn't share this with me, do you?"

"We're not done talking about Clarke."

"Oh, we're done with that," Harper said, knowing he was stalling for time. "We're *totally* done with it. Unless it's more important to you than our son?"

He didn't answer. He returned to the small bar and refilled his glass.

"How long, Knox? How long have you suspected Asher isn't a sphinx?"

"A while. As you know, each demonic breed has an 'air' to it. A sort of psychic scent which makes it possible for people to sense what breed of demon they're facing. That doesn't mean that all hellhounds smell the same, of course. Similar, yes, but not the same because each person's psychic scent is that *little* bit different. Yours is very subtle and elusive, so it's not simple to 'read'. It took me a good few minutes to detect that you were a sphinx." Glass full once again, Knox turned to face her. "Like you, Asher has the air of a sphinx. Like yours, that air isn't so easy to read."

"Yeah, he takes after me that way. Lucian's air is subtle too. I really don't see where you're going with this."

Knox took a swig of his gin and tonic. "Maybe it's because I've walked the Earth a very long time and so have a lot of

experience at it, or maybe it's just something that comes naturally to me, but I can read airs much better than most. I can pick
a psychic scent apart and find each individual note."

"Fascinating. But I still don't see where this is going."

"As your anchor, someone who's psychically bound to you, I
know your psychic scent better than anyone else ever could or
ever will, Harper. I know every single delicate note to it. And,
as Asher's father and someone who's touched his mind hundreds
of times, I also know every note to his." Knox took a step toward
her. "There are no variations between yours and his. Not a single
one. You don't just have *similar* psychic scents; you have the
exact same one."

Harper's breath caught in her throat. "That's not possible.
Maybe he's able to mimic psychic scents. My cousin can do it.
It's not an uncommon ability, and it certainly doesn't have to
mean that Asher's not a sphinx."

"But does your cousin mimic one particular scent twenty-four/
seven? Is it something he even *could* do?"

Probably not, but Harper shrugged. "If anyone could do it,
Asher could. And just because he's mimicking me doesn't mean
he's not a sphinx."

"Which is why I only *suspect* it. The fact is that demons don't
birth hybrids. A demon is either like their mother or like their
father. Asher's not an archdemon. *Can't* be an archdemon, since
we're not born from wombs. If he's not a sphinx, I don't see what
else he could be. The more abilities he shows, the more clues I
have. Individually, the powers tell me nothing. Collectively, they
form a picture. So far, I'm still unsure of just what the picture
could be."

Stomach hardening, she swallowed back bile. "What about
the black smudge?"

"I didn't know about that until Clarke mentioned it. He

thinks it indicates that Asher isn't a natural breed of demon. He's wrong." Knox swirled his glass and then sipped at his drink. "It's a veil. A psychic shadow. Its presence could suggest that Asher's inner demon is disguising itself. I've met demons who can cloak themselves. It's an extremely rare ability, but it's not limited to a particular breed."

Baffled, Harper frowned. "If the demon is cloaking itself, how come people don't sense that?"

"Because part of that ability is that they can mimic psychic scents."

Harper felt the blood drain from her face.

"Cloaking means he can assimilate himself into any group and be seen as whatever it wishes to be seen. Asher won't physically change, but his 'air' will—in fact, he can even hide it completely so that he appears human. Depending on just how strong he grows, Asher may even be able to ensure that he isn't seen at all. Not in the sense that he becomes invisible. No, but he will be able to socially cloak himself to the extent that he garners no attention or sticks out in no memories."

Well, fuck a duck. "Why would the demon cloak itself?"

"Because it can, maybe. I don't know. As I said, the point of cloaking is to assimilate. To fit. Blend. It wouldn't surprise me if my own demon influenced its decision—sending some kind of 'impression' that safety equaled mimicking its mother. After all, masquerading as a sphinx *will* keep him safe."

Knox stepped toward her. "Asher is very much like you, Harper. Good. Mischievous. Expressive. I fear that his demon is very much like mine. Exceedingly cold and dark. Something to rightfully fear." He tilted his head. "But you've already figured that much out for yourself, haven't you? For a while you've suspected—deep down in a place you weren't ready to face—that he wasn't a sphinx. Haven't you?"

She'd wondered about it, yes, but she hadn't given any real weight to her suspicions. She'd thought she was just letting her fears toy with her mind. "Why didn't you tell me you believed he might not be a sphinx?"

"Probably for the same reason that you didn't tell me of your own suspicion. I wanted to be wrong. Saying it aloud felt like taking the suspicion too seriously. Plus, I didn't want to worry you when it could have been needless. I intended to simply watch him and wait until I at least had a theory as to what else he could be. So far, I have nothing."

"You didn't want to worry me? I'm not made of fucking porcelain."

"Don't put words in my mouth, Harper."

"Why? You certainly enjoyed twisting my motives, accusing me of meeting with Drew because I like having his attention."

He set down his glass. "I'm glad we're back on the subject of Clarke, because I'm not finished."

"Well, I am. You did your best to hurt me by spouting all that shit earlier. Guess what? It worked. I have no interest in giving you the opportunity to spew more of that crap and hurt me all over again." Whirling, she stalked away.

"Harper, *we're not done.*"

"I am." She *needed* to go. Needed space. Needed air that wasn't tainted with tension and anger. It took everything she had not to storm up the stairs. She wanted out of there—not just the room but the mansion itself. Wanted distance from him. Mostly because "alone" was her default zone, especially when she was hurting or confused.

The first time they'd had a major fight, Harper had fled to Jolene's house. Naturally, Knox hadn't reacted well to that. And since she couldn't deny that she'd have felt like shit to have searched their home for him, hoping to mend things, only to find that he'd left her, she'd promised him that she'd never again leave after an argument. She'd made it clear, though, that she'd likely walk away to get some space and cool down. He'd better damn well give her that space, no matter how hard he'd find it not to push.

Upstairs, she returned her things to the closet, got ready for bed, and then slipped under the covers. Using the remote to lower the blackout blinds, she plunged the room into darkness. Honestly, she wasn't tired. Emotionally drained, yes, but not physically exhausted. But Jolene had always said that a rest could be as good as a sleep. Speaking of Jolene . . .

Harper telepathically reached out to her. *How is Drew?*

First, I want to know if you're all right, sweetheart, said Jolene.

Knox hasn't hurt me, if that's what you're asking.

I know he wouldn't physically hurt you, but that's not to say he wouldn't lose his mind and lash out at you. Men tend to do that when they're hurt—apparently, they prefer that to admitting they're upset.

Oh, Knox had definitely lashed out, but he rarely lost control. *He's pissed at me, but he didn't blow. How bad is Drew?* For a moment, there was only silence. *Grams?*

He's bad, Harper, Jolene admitted. *The pain was so terrible he's gone into shock. I had Beck put him to sleep. He'll be healed by the time he wakes. He was very confused about what happened—he doesn't remember your conversation. There seems to be large gaps in his memory.*

Harper closed her eyes tight, thinking that if she'd just refused to go into that damn bedroom, the guy would be okay. Not that she was assuming responsibility for what happened. No, he'd ignored every warning he'd been given, effectively poking at the hornet's nest. Still, refusing to talk to him alone would have been smarter. *Does Devon know yet?*

She's with him now, holding his hand.

Tell me the truth, is she pissed at me?

No. She appreciates that you agreed to let him say goodbye. Still, she's upset with Knox. She feels he overreacted to seeing you and Drew speaking alone. Intellectually, she knows it was more than that.

Figuring that calling Devon wouldn't be the best idea until she'd had time to cool down, Harper sighed. *I don't know how to fix this.*

There's nothing for you to fix. You were placed in the middle of an impossible situation. Drew made it worse, and Knox reacted exactly as we all anticipated that he would. I'd hoped that you speaking to him privately, allowing him to say his goodbyes, would have prevented that. Instead, it only exacerbated the situation. If I'm honest, it surprises me that Drew is still breathing.

Rubbing her forehead, Harper said, *Keep me updated on his progress.*

Will do, sweetheart.

Thanks, Grams. With that, Harper cut the connection. She knew Knox would have sensed that she'd been speaking telepathically with someone. Ordinarily, he'd ask who she'd been talking to. This time, there was only silence from him. That suited her just fine.

Harper woke to a young mind poking at hers. Opening her eyes, she saw that Knox's side of the bed was empty. Unruffled. Cold. He hadn't come to bed. Apparently, he was still sulking. Whatever.

Giving Asher's mind a reassuring stroke, she quickly did her business and pulled on her sweats. Walking into the nursery, she found him standing in the crib, hair all tousled from sleep. He gave her a huge grin.

"Hey, baby boy." Harper lifted him out of the crib and kissed his cheek. He was so adorable and loveable that her heart squeezed. "So, your demon hides from us, huh? Why?" She didn't get it. Not at all. Did the entity think she wouldn't accept it? Or maybe Knox's demon thought that she'd struggle to accept it and, as such, urged Asher's demon to hide. Still, why? "Whatever you are, I don't care. You're still my boy. I accept your dad's demon, and I'll accept yours just the same."

Of course, she knew Asher didn't understand a word she'd said. In fact, he wasn't even paying her any attention. He was staring at the tree mural on the wall while chewing his finger. Still, she'd just needed to say it out loud.

Harper kissed his cheek again. "Hungry?" He blew bubbles at her. "Thought so. First, let's get you sorted." After changing his diaper, she lay out some fresh clothes for him before heading downstairs. Given his little habit of making a mess of himself in the morning, she always dressed him after he'd eaten.

Tanner was at the kitchen table, munching on a Danish pastry. He was also alone. Reaching out with her mind, she searched the house for others. Meg. Dan. No Knox.

The hellhound flashed a smile at Asher. "Hey, big guy. Stop chewing on those little fingers." He looked at Harper, expression sobering. "You all right?" he asked softly.

"Fine." She settled Asher in the highchair just as Meg came in with his porridge. "Morning, Meg. Thanks."

She beamed. "Not a problem. Bagel and creamed cheese?"

Stomach churning, Harper grimaced. "I'm not hungry, but thanks."

Meg's brow furrowed. "Not hungry? That's unlike you. Not pregnant again, are you?"

Harper sighed. "No, I'm not." She was just pissed and off-balance. "I wouldn't mind some coffee, though." Sinking into a chair, she spooned some porridge for Asher and blew on it to cool it down.

"Mmm," drawled Asher, stretching toward her. He opened his mouth wide and practically gobbled the food.

"Knox headed out a few hours ago," said Tanner. "He didn't say where he was going. I take it you two had a spat."

"Why would you think we had a spat?"

"Because his face might have been blank, but his anger was tangible. Also, you look ready to commit murder when you aren't smiling at Asher."

Deciding to keep the matter of Asher's cloaking ability private for now, she said, "He accused me of wanting Drew around and relishing the attention."

Tanner winced. "Knox didn't mean it, Harper. He doesn't just fucking adore you, he trusts you. Guys say stupid shit when they're mad."

"That include you?" she asked, feeding Asher another spoonful.

"Yep."

"The whole thing rankles because I know for a fact that there were times he was alone with women who wanted me gone from his life so that they could get in his pants. I didn't like it, but I didn't take out my frustrations or jealousy on him."

"Yeah, but you're more emotionally mature than he is."

Harper gave a soft snort of amusement. "Damn fucking right I am." They talked about general things as they finished breakfast. After that, she cleaned and dressed Asher. While he played with Tanner, she tried calling Devon. It wasn't a total surprise that the female didn't answer. It still hurt.

A little later, Keenan turned up at the house. As he played on the rug with Asher, she and Tanner filled him in on what had happened the night before. Relaying the tale and reliving each moment of it rekindled the anger she'd somehow managed to let go of the night before. Now, it was back with a vengeance, leaving her restless. Twitchy. Her fingers tingled with the urge to do something—anything.

An hour later, when she could take it no more, she pushed up from the sofa and declared, "I'm going for a drive."

Looking up at her from where he was sprawled on the sofa with a napping Asher on his lap, Keenan frowned. "A drive?"

"Yes."

Tanner stood. "All right. Let's go."

"No, I mean *I* need to go for a drive," she said. "You can come, but I'm driving."

"Fine," said Tanner, because his expression was pained.

"Asher and I will be okay here," Keenan assured her.

She nodded. "I won't be long."

She'd driven Tanner's Audi a few times and, as usual, he handed over the keys with a whole lot of reluctance. If her mood hadn't been so grim, she might have smiled at the way he awkwardly settled in the passenger seat ... as if finding it weird to have a woman driving him around. Maybe it was an alpha male thing or something.

The Audi was a total dream to drive. Smooth and easy. She missed driving. She'd had her driver's license revoked due to her impatience with traffic lights, unpaid parking tickets, and speed restrictions. But she was a damn good driver, so it didn't seem fair. Having a chauffeur was great and all, but there was something relaxing about sitting behind the wheel of a car and just going for a drive.

Tanner didn't speak as they journeyed around Vegas, as if sensing that she needed the time to just lose herself in what she was doing—not think or dwell or brood. Just *be*.

She didn't even realize she'd been heading toward her old studio in North Las Vegas until she found herself turning onto the street where it was situated. She pulled to a stop outside the building, which was now a hair salon. It made her remember a time when things were different. Simpler in some ways. A time when things were easy between her and the girls.

A time before Knox.

She didn't regret meeting him. Didn't regret accepting him as her anchor or taking him as her mate. Definitely didn't regret having Asher. She just hadn't envisioned herself ever being in a situation where she may have to choose between him and one of the girls.

"You think Devon's going to partially blame you for what happened to Drew?" asked Tanner, correctly guessing where her jumbled thoughts had taken her.

Harper sighed. "I don't know. But she's not taking my calls."

"Maybe she doesn't trust herself not to say something that will fuck things up in a way that they can never be fixed."

"According to Jolene, she thinks Knox overreacted."

Tanner snorted. "If anything, Knox *under*reacted."

"I know that."

"So does Devon. She's not stupid. But she is emotional. Drew's her brother; she's protective of him and will naturally be pissed at anyone who harms him. That's the way it should be. Give her time."

Knowing he was right, Harper nodded. As she took a deep, centering breath, the scent of coffee filtered through the open window and filled her lungs. The smell came from the café across the street—a café that she and the girls had frequented once upon a time. "I feel like a vanilla latte. You want anything?"

Tanner glanced at the café. "Is this a good idea? That place is run by the sister of your human ex-boyfriend, right?"

"What's your point?"

He just sighed. "I'll have a cappuccino."

With a nod, she hopped out of the car and headed into the

café. There was a line but she didn't mind waiting; she liked being surrounded by the scents of coffee beans, spices, fresh desserts, and even acrid burned coffee.

Around her, people were sat at bistro tables—drinking, eating, talking, reading, working on their laptops. She could hear dishware clattering, the whirr of machines, and music playing low in the background. The line moved at a steady pace, thankfully, so—

"Harper?"

Looking to her left, she saw none other than . . . "Royce." Her ex. She silently swore. It was just her luck that he'd be there. She thought about walking right out, but he'd see that as her fleeing from him. She wouldn't give the cheating bastard the satisfaction.

He cleared his throat. "Um, how are you?"

"Fine."

He gave her a quick head-to-toe scan and said, "You look well. Marriage to a billionaire suits you."

At those words, the woman in front of her turned and gave Harper a cursory look, as if to check she wasn't a celebrity or something. Harper and Knox *had* been featured in magazines, but it seemed that this woman hadn't read any of them because she turned right back around.

Ignoring the bitter edge to Royce voice's, Harper smiled. "It does suit me pretty well, doesn't it?"

"I bumped into one of your work colleagues the other day," he said. "They took great delight in telling me that you're happily married. With a kid. A boy, right?"

"Right," she said, tapping her nails on her thigh.

"Is he with you?" Royce glanced at the Audi, which was parked among a row of other cars.

Harper narrowed her eyes. "How did you know the Audi was mine?"

His eyes shot back to her and widened slightly for a brief moment. "Okay, I'll admit, I saw you hop out of it a few minutes ago. I was debating whether to come talk to you. I almost didn't."

"I see."

"What's your little boy's name?" asked Royce.

"You really want to talk about my son?"

Royce shrugged, nonchalant. "I'm just interested in what's happened in your life since we parted."

"As you know, I got married and had a kid. Why don't you tell me what's been happening in your life?"

"Nothing interesting. My life's been pretty dull since you left it." He swallowed. "Do you have time to talk?"

"No." And, really, what was there to say anyway?

"Come on, Harper. It would be good to catch up."

She frowned, finding it odd that he would even want to speak with her, considering she made a habit of giving him shit. "No, it really wouldn't."

His face hardened. "You know, they're right in what they say. Money changes people."

"No, but it does change how the people around you treat you. Take you, for example. I haven't been civil with you since the moment you cheated on me. Instead of shouldering that blame, you're blaming it on the fatness of my purse. Mature, Royce. Real mature."

He sighed. "I just want to talk. Please."

Quite frankly shocked that he would ever plead with her for anything, she felt her frown deepen. As she looked at him again, seeing the out-of-character kicked-puppy look on his face, her pulse quickened. And then it hit her. He'd said, "your work colleagues". But Royce believed they'd closed the studio down, not *relocated* it. As such, he would have said her "old" work colleagues . . . if it were Royce.

Motherfucker, she was talking with the bastard incorporeal. Her realization must have shown on her face, because his eyes narrowed in suspicion.

He clasped her hand and, *Jesus*, it was like someone poured ice-cold water into her veins. It went rushing up her arm, into her shoulder, spreading and spreading through her body. The shock of it took her breath away. Still, she instinctively slapped his chest, sending soul-deep agony out of her prickling fingertips and blazing through him. She was fast.

But she hadn't been fast enough.

The incorporeal burst out of his body just as Royce sagged to the floor. The whirling vapor plunged right into a little girl of about eight or nine, and the impact almost knocked the kid off her feet.

Harper stumbled toward her, shaking from the cold that had invaded her body and seemed to weigh her down like lead. But, in control of the child, the incorporeal righted itself, shot a creepy smile at Harper, and thrust out its palm. A bitterly cold wind soared out of its hand, slammed into Harper, and tossed her aside.

There was a crack as her head hit the wall hard. *Motherfucker*. Harper slid to the tiled floor with a shaky moan just as the incorporeal swept out its arm, sending a blast of glacial air that froze the humans around them.

Harper's mind told her to get up. Attack. Fight. But her body helplessly curled into a ball, trembling from the cold. It reminded her of the time she'd fallen into a frozen lake, only this was ten times worse. God, she was so cold her skin *burned*; it felt like she was being stabbed with needles.

Her demon raged, urging Harper to rise and charge at the little fucker. She wanted to get up. Tried. But she could barely breathe, let alone *move*. Hell, it was hard to think about anything other than the pain.

Hearing pounding, she realized that Tanner was kicking and punching the door. A door which was covered in the same ice that had crept along the walls. He couldn't get inside, and there was no way for her to help him. She just couldn't get up. Every muscle contracted painfully. Each breath she took chilled her throat and lungs, as if she was breathing in ice-cold air. It made her chest hurt like holy hell.

Even as the cold began to fog her brain and cloud her thoughts, she retained enough presence of mind to call out, *Knox, need you here.* Her telepathic voice was soft and weak, but she knew he'd hear it.

The incorporeal skipped over to her with a giggle. "You don't look too good. Don't worry, the pain will be gone soon . . . because you'll be gone." She giggled again.

Harper snarled, but what could she do? Even if she was prepared to hurt a kid on the off-chance that it would also hurt the incorporeal, she couldn't have moved to do so. Numbness had crept into her fingers and toes, like her hands and feet were submerged in snow. Her demon surfaced with a hiss and said, "You will die for this."

"That would have sounded scary if you weren't chattering your teeth."

The air thundered as fire erupted out of the floor. The incorporeal wasted no time in attacking. The moment Knox stepped out of the dying flames, it sent a blast of glacial energy at him. The blast had no effect. Just skimmed over him, barely even ruffling his hair.

Harper? It was a demand to know if she was all right.

I'm fine, Harper told him. *Kill it.* Her demon didn't settle now that he was there. It wanted to fight alongside him. Harper wanted it too, she really did, but she couldn't stop shaking. Hell, she couldn't even *speak.* Every breath hurt. It felt like shards of ice had splintered her throat and lodged in her lungs. The air in the room sliced at her skin like it was a bitterly cold wind; making her nose numb, her ears throb, and her cheeks feel windburned.

Smiling up at Knox, the incorporeal let out a nervous girly giggle. "You wouldn't hurt a little girl, would you?"

Glaring hard at the incorporeal, Knox flexed his fingers. Fury lived and breathed inside him right then, making his heart pound and his blood sing with the need for vengeance. His demon ached to take charge and annihilate their enemy, but Knox didn't trust that it wouldn't annihilate everyone else in the process, considering them collateral damage. The demon only cared for the safety of its mate and son.

"I see you have something in common with your owner," said Knox. "You hide behind others—or, in your case, *within* others."

The incorporeal narrowed its eyes. "I am not owned."

"Sure you are," he said, tone derisive. Taunting. Cutting. "He holds your leash and tells you to go fetch. You obey his orders like a good . . . little . . . dog."

She hissed and bared her teeth. "I am no one's *dog*."

"And yet, here you are, doing your master's bidding at the promise of a treat. You may have escaped your glass case, but you are still very much a captive."

"Once I am free of this bargain, I will find Dion and make him pay for keeping me in that case," she snarled.

Well that confirmed that it wasn't Dion who had helped Alethea free it.

"If you persist in coming at me and mine, the only freedom you will find is in death." Knox slipped an arm behind him and shot a wave of raw power at the front door. The moment it burst open and Tanner rushed inside, Knox clipped, "Get Harper out of here."

The hellhound probably would have done exactly that if the incorporeal hadn't hit him with a wave of glacial energy, encasing him in ice—it happened in a mere millisecond.

The incorporeal giggled and put a hand to its mouth. "Oops. Wasn't that one of your big, bad sentinels? Frozen is a good look for him."

Harper shot a hard glare at the incorporeal as she spoke to Knox. *Kill it for fuck's sake.*

With a sudden sharp cry, the incorporeal slapped its little hands to its head.

"You feel me inside the child's mind, don't you?" taunted Knox. "I see you have a good grip on it. But to make you loosen your hold on her ... all I have to do is *this.*"

Harper winced because whatever 'this' was made the incorporeal scream like a banshee. It thrust out both chubby little hands, and a harsh wind whooshed out of its palms and whirled around Knox like a tornado. He stood inside it, looking unimpressed. Even a little bored. Which only pissed the incorporeal off beyond measure.

He was *playing* with the incorporeal, Harper knew. Letting it see and feel just how outmatched it was. And she suspected his demon was thoroughly enjoying that.

Finally, he stepped out of the mini tornado, nary a hair out of place. "Enough. I think we've established that the glacial energy has no effect on me."

The incorporeal's mouth sagged open. "Impossible," it spat. Another gust of wind rushed out of its hands. But Knox slammed up his own palm and sent a blaze of fire streaming at the incorporeal. Wind and fire crashed together like swords, and a backlash of the colliding energies swept across the room in a bright sheen of light that almost blinded Harper.

Again, her demon urged her to rise and fight, but she simply couldn't. Instead, she could only watch as the archdemon and incorporeal battled hard.

"I will have my freedom, Thorne, you cannot—" Once again, the incorporeal's hands snapped to its head as it let out yet another high-pitched scream. The sound went on and on and on, until Harper thought the windows would smash. A blizzard suddenly whipped up around them, ruffling her clothes and tossing her hair everywhere. It would no doubt have also sent objects sailing around if they weren't frozen in place.

Knox merely flapped a hand as if swatting at a fly. Just like that, the blizzard seemed to shudder and then abruptly die off. "When will you learn that you stand no chance against me?"

The incorporeal once again screeched, knees buckling under the strain of whatever mental pain Knox was causing it. The girl's body bucked as the incorporeal lunged out of her . . . which was what he'd been waiting for.

A raw dark power buzzed and pulsed in the air just before flames instantly erupted out of the ground—vivid flames that were red, gold, black, and deadly. The incorporeal dove straight back into the kid's body to escape them. Eyes wide and afraid, it stared at the flames of hell as they inched around it, barricading it in. "You can truly call on them."

"There's no way out of this," Knox told the incorporeal. "I can do this all day."

Panting, it hissed. "But your mate cannot. Do you not see what is happening to her? She is freezing from the inside out. Soon, her heart will fail and rupture into tiny pieces."

Harper knew the incorporeal wasn't exaggerating. She could feel her heartbeat beginning to falter. Could feel the cold invade and surround the organ. Her vision was starting to darken around the edges, and a deep sleep beckoned her.

"You could save her, but only if you move now and make her

warm. At a guess, I would say you have mere seconds before it is too late for her."

No, kill it, Harper insisted, but Knox instantly pyroported to her. At the same time, the incorporeal surged out of the child's body. The hazy vapor flew over the flames and rocketed out of the front door, fading as it did so.

Knox crouched in front of her, eyes glinting with panic. "Baby."

You should have killed it. Then darkness swept over her.

CHAPTER THIRTEEN

For a second, Knox didn't move out of sheer terror. His mate was curled up on the floor, shivering violently, teeth chattering, arms wrapped tight around her body. His demon let loose a deafening roar. "Shit, baby."

Knox lifted her and held her close, shocked that her skin was so cold it was uncomfortable to touch. Her system seemed to literally soak up his body heat—he could practically feel the warmth leaving him.

With a single thought, he reined in the flames of hell before they could do further damage or harm the little girl within them, but he never moved his eyes from Harper. She was gulping in breaths like she'd just surfaced from the ocean after being submerged for too long. Each shaky breath fogged the air.

He stroked her face. "I need you to breathe for me, baby. Relax. Slow it down."

She clumsily tried fisting his shirt but seemed barely able to move her fingers, as if they were too numb.

"I'll get you warm, you'll be fine." But she didn't look fine. Not at all.

There was a loud, birdlike screech just before a black harpy eagle soared inside the café and landed on the floor. A billow of smoke swirled around it, blanketing it for a mere moment, and then Larkin was stood in its place.

She glanced around, taking in the frozen people, the little girl unconscious on the floor, and the block of ice encasing Tanner. "Oh, God. Tanner called me and—what the fuck happened to Harper?"

"The incorporeal happened." With a quick wave of power, Knox freed Tanner from the block of ice. The hellhound blinked, as if surprised to see that time had passed. "I need to get Harper home, Tanner," said Knox, urgency in every syllable. "You and Larkin need to take care of the situation here."

Concern lighting his eyes, Tanner said, "Consider it done."

Knox unfroze the rest of the café and then pyroported his mate to the walk-in closet of their bedroom. Although he wanted to put her straight into a hot bath, he knew he needed to slowly increase her core body temperature first.

Snatching a fleecy blanket from a top shelf in the closet, he stalked over to the bed and lay her down. He then quickly shed their clothes, which wasn't easy when her jeans were stiff with cold. Her eyes fluttered open. She tried to talk through blue lips that were dry and bleeding.

"No, baby, don't talk. Just get warm." Lifting her, he held her tight, sharing more of his body heat even though her icy skin made him flinch. As he pulled the fleecy blanket around her, she huddled inside it, chin dropped down to her chest.

Flipping back the coverlet, Knox settled in bed with her tucked close to his body and then dragged the coverlet over them both. She burrowed into him, placing her hands on his chest as if to greedily absorb more of his warmth. Her hands and feet were like blocks of ice.

Under the blanket, he rubbed at her skin, hoping the friction would warm her. Inside him, his demon roared and raged. Knox's own fury was tangible. The fucking incorporeal had tried to *kill* her. Tried to freeze her from the inside out. Tried to take from him the very thing that had brought *life* to his existence.

He'd known she'd taken a hit from the incorporeal, but he hadn't known it was fatal, assuming Harper would have told him if it were. But she hadn't. And she'd almost died right in fucking front of him and his demon but, so focused on toying with the incorporeal, they'd been completely oblivious to just how seriously hurt she'd been.

He didn't need to ponder why Harper hadn't drawn attention to her condition. But he already knew the answer to that: she'd sooner die along with the incorporeal than have it be free to harm Asher. His demon wanted to spank her pretty ass for being so ready to sacrifice herself. Knox wasn't at all averse to the idea.

He telepathically reached out to Keenan. *Harper and I are home, but I need you to keep Asher downstairs.* He gave the sentinel a brief summary of what had happened at the café.

Son of a bitch, spat Keenan. *Will she be okay?*

Yes, she will. Knox wouldn't have it any other way. *Reach out to Levi and explain what happened.* Knox's focus needed to be on Harper. Breaking the connection with his sentinel, he touched his housekeeper's mind and said, *Meg, I need hot water bottles for Harper. She was attacked, and she's ice-cold. Bring them to the master bedroom.*

I'll be as quick as I can, replied Meg, sounding frantic.

Just as frantic, Knox stared down at Harper. His mate never looked weak. But right then, huddled into a tight ball, she looked so delicate it made Knox's chest tighten. Every rough breath sounded like it was sawing at her throat. Being upset with her, letting her sleep alone and then leaving before she woke—it all seemed so stupid now. Stupid and petty and beneath him. She'd deserved none of it.

He kissed her hair. "I'm sorry I was a shit, baby," he said, unsure if she was even properly aware of where she was or who she was with.

One by one, the other sentinels telepathed him questions, wanting to be sure that Harper was fine. He answered their queries but was far too furious to sound reassuring.

Meg bustled into the room with a hot water bottle that was wearing a chunky knitted cover. "I could only find one," she said, anxiously. "Here, put it near one of her major arteries."

Satisfied that it wasn't so hot it would burn her skin, Knox tucked the water bottle under Harper's armpit and then pulled her blanket tighter around her, hoping to trap the heat and hot air inside it.

Twisting her fingers, Meg asked, "Should I make her a hot chocolate?"

"I don't think she could drink it, Meg. She's shaking too badly."

"Watch out for chilblains and frostbite. Can she get those things if she hasn't really been out in the cold?"

"I don't know." He gently touched her dry mouth. "Get her some lip balm or something," he ordered, and Meg swiftly disappeared. He should have felt like a bastard for being so gruff, but he didn't have tact in him right then. Not when he was so worried for Harper. He didn't like how slow and shallow her breaths were. Didn't like how weak her pulse was or how her muscles kept spasming.

"Baby, I need you to be okay," he whispered, breezing his fingers over her cheekbone. Like her lips, the skin on her cheeks and forehead had cracked. "You hear me? You have to be okay."

Her chapped lips trembled, but she didn't respond.

With Dan trailing behind her, Meg came back into the bedroom holding a tub of Vaseline. "This will help."

When she unscrewed the lid, Knox dipped his finger inside and then gently spread the Vaseline over Harper's lips.

"Is there anything I can do?" asked Dan.

"Help Meg and Keenan watch over Asher for me," said Knox. "I'm not leaving Harper's side until I know that she's fine."

As both Dan and Meg melted out of the room, closing the door behind them, Harper's eyes fluttered open again. She stuttered words that he couldn't quite make out.

If you really need to talk, do it mind-to-mind, Knox told her.

My skin is prickling and tingling, she said.

That's good. It means it's beginning to thaw. But that didn't bring him any relief. Even when her pulse began to steady and her trembling eased a little, he didn't settle. Couldn't. Not until she was one hundred percent okay. Maybe not even then.

Still, taking a deep breath, he did his best to rein in his anger. She'd be fine, he assured himself. She was safe. Alive. Right there in his arms. But it was hard to find calm when his demon's own anger still bubbled within Knox's veins. Stroking her skin, he inhaled deeply, letting the feel and scent of her calm the chaos in his mind.

Knox glanced down at the ring on his finger that was studded with black diamonds. He hadn't imagined he'd ever completely commit himself to another person, let alone ever wear a symbol of commitment. But he wore it with pride—even smugness. That same satisfaction always filled him when he looked at the rings on her own finger.

He was not an easy anchor, and he was an even more difficult mate. It would probably always astonish him that Harper had accepted his claim on her. She'd changed everything. Brought out emotions in him that he'd never before felt. Emotions he'd never thought he could feel. He needed her. Fucking adored her. And now he needed to fix his fuck-up.

He lay there with her for what could have been hours, holding her close, rubbing her skin, talking to her in a low, soothing voice. Her skin eventually warmed, and she slipped into a restless sleep. He just continued to hold her, stroking her hair and skin.

At one point, Tanner's mind touched his. *How's Harper? Any better?*

A little, replied Knox. *How is the clean-up going?*

Once you unfroze the people in the café, I pushed the smell of smoke into the air and yelled that there was a fire. Everyone other than Royce—who was shaking on the floor from what I'm pretty sure was soul-deep pain—rushed outside. With regret, I carried the asshole out of there instead of leaving him to burn in the fire that Larkin then started. Once the building was destroyed, she let the hellfire ease away. It was the only way to cover up the scorch marks left behind by the flames of hell.

What was Harper doing in the café? asked Knox, rubbing a silky strand of her hair between his fingers.

She was restless and wanted to go for a drive. I don't know if she meant to drive to her old studio, but she pulled up outside and just looked at it. She's hurting that Devon won't take her calls.

He knew that. Hated that he hadn't been more sensitive about it. If he had, if they'd talked last night instead of arguing, just maybe she wouldn't have felt the need to go for that drive. Then the incorporeal wouldn't have almost killed her.

She went into the café to grab us both some coffee, said Tanner. *I saw her talking to Royce, but I figured she could handle him. It happened so fast—one second she was talking to him, the next thing he collapsed to the floor and a weird vapor shot out of him and into the little girl. I bolted out of the car, but the café door iced over before I could get inside.*

So Royce had been possessed by the incorporeal. Harper had clearly figured it out if she'd delivered him soul-deep pain, but that pain obviously hadn't reached the incorporeal. *If the incorporeal was in control of Royce, he won't remember any of what happened.* That was a good thing.

Larkin and I slipped away before the human authorities could question us. I'm glad Harper had the presence of mind to call out to you while she was being attacked, because I was too frantic to get inside that fucking café to even think about it.

Just as Knox had been too frantic about her condition to even care much about damage control—he'd left it to his sentinels. *You would have called me. She just beat you to it.*

Breaking the telepathic connection, Knox glanced down at Harper. She was looking up at him, eyes a little glazed over. His relief at seeing her awake almost felled him. "Hey, baby," he whispered, mouth curving. A hint of wariness entered her eyes, as if she suddenly remembered their argument and expected him to continue it. As if, worse, she thought he'd verbally strike out at her again. Fuck if that wariness didn't gut him.

Drawing her closer, he pressed a kiss to her forehead and stroked her back, letting her know without words that the last thing he intended to do was snap at her. All he wanted was to hold, comfort, and soothe her.

"You shouldn't have let the incorporeal go," she said, voice a little croaky.

Knox skimmed his thumb over her jaw. "Your life is a billion times more important than its death."

"It will keep coming."

"And it will keep failing."

Harper hoped to God that was true, because she was *so* done with assholes hurting her and the people she loved. She shifted a little, flexing her toes and fingers. She felt drained and drowsy, but her lungs and throat no longer burned. Still, her muscles were tired and stiff. That didn't stop her body from reacting to his nakedness—it was a total traitor.

Tossing the hot water bottle aside, she said, "I feel like I've been in a car wreck."

Knox played his fingers through her hair. "You scared me. I could feel you weakening ... feel your pulse slowing." Resting his hand on her chest, he let the steady beat of her heart soothe him. "Too close. I came too close to losing you. Again."

She swallowed at the torment in his voice. She wanted to be mad at him for what he'd said last night and for keeping things from her. She *was* mad at him, but it was hard to keep a firm grip on that anger when he looked so tortured. Her demon, on the other hand, had no problem holding onto its rage—it sniffed haughtily at him, unmoved.

"If the incorporeal hadn't warned me what was happening to you, you would have died right there in front of me." As the dark reality of that once again hit him square in the chest, Knox tightened his hold on her. "You should have reached out to me and told me how bad it had hurt you—if I'd known, I wouldn't have spent so much time antagonizing it in the hope that it would make a mistake. I'm not asking why you didn't. I know why you didn't. But it's not a good fucking reason. There'll never be a good reason for you to die." But she just stared at him, unapologetic. He dropped his forehead on hers. "You're going to drive me into an early grave."

"I'm going to *put* you into an early grave if you ever purposely hurt me again," she warned.

Knox stifled a smile. Ah, there was his hissing, spitting kitten. "I'm an asshole."

"Yes, you are."

"I didn't consciously set out to purposely hurt you, but it doesn't change the fact that I did—I know that. And I'm sorry. I fucked up. Majorly. But I need you to forgive me, baby, because the way you're looking at me right now—all wary and sad—is killing me."

Harper wanted to groan. Why did he have to be so good at apologies? Was it so wrong that she wanted to be mad at him for a while? She didn't think so, but he knew just how to take the wind out of her sails.

"I didn't mean what I said last night," he continued. "I don't think you want Drew. Nor do I think you like having his attention. I said that shit because I was pissed."

"And hurt."

"And hurt," Knox admitted, though he'd never have confessed that weakness to anyone other than her. "It's been an extremely long time since I had someone in my life who had the power to hurt me. I'm not yet used to it. I can't say I like that you have that power, but I wouldn't give you up for anything. No matter how much of a bastard I am, never think that you're not everything to me."

"You weren't here when I woke up," said Harper. When she'd promised she wouldn't walk out after arguments as long as he gave her what space she needed to calm, he'd agreed on the condition that she'd never sleep anywhere except beside him. He'd given her space last night, but she suspected that was also because he'd been brooding. "You didn't sleep beside me."

"Because, like I said, I'm an asshole."

"And you were brooding."

He couldn't deny it. His demon—whose temper ran quick and hot—had lost its anger with her within the hour. It had pushed at him to seek her out, but Knox had been too busy ruminating on everything. As such, his demon had sulked all damn night and morning.

Harper hiked up a brow. "You're not honestly going to deny it, are you?"

Knox's mouth quirked. She was the only person who expected him to explain himself. She was also the only person he ever would explain himself to. "No, I'm not." He tucked her hair behind her ear. "I always thought I was too emotionally disconnected to ever have a mate. Of course, I knew what love was—I'd felt it for my parents. But after so many years without them, the memory of the emotion had faded. Still, I'd sensed the emotion in others and I'd known full-well that it wasn't something I'd felt for a woman. Then there was you.

"I've never had someone as deeply enmeshed in my life as you are, Harper. Never wanted anyone to be. I don't have any real experience with emotional intimacy, which means I'm often flying blind here. Not being good at something pisses me off. But you . . . you're something I need. I absolutely refuse to live a life that doesn't have you in it. I hate that I hurt you, but I can't change that I did it. I can't even promise I won't do it again, which doesn't help my cause here. But, as I said, I need you to forgive me. Can you?"

"You kept something huge from me, Knox."

"I truly do think I might be wrong about Asher being something other than a sphinx—it just seems so impossible. But the black smudge . . . that could suggest otherwise. The demon is cloaking itself."

"Hiding."

"In a sense, yes, it's hiding. I don't see why it would."

She narrowed her eyes. "Your demon knows if Asher's a sphinx or not."

"Probably. I've asked it dozens of times for answers, but it's being very tight-lipped. I truly don't know what we're dealing with here." And Knox hated that, because he detested blind spots. He liked to have the facts. "The only thing we can do is the very thing we've both been doing, though you didn't consciously acknowledge that you were doing it. We watch and wait."

"Do you have any theories at all?"

"Not at present. Asher hasn't shown any abilities that are limited to a particular breed of demon. Every demon has at least *one* power that's exclusive to their kind. We just have to wait for Asher's to show itself, which could happen any day now. Probably within the next month. But I'm still hoping I'm wrong."

Her hand twitched into a fist. "You should have told me."

"And you should have shared your suspicions with me."

True, Harper thought. She could understand why he'd kept it from her, since it was the same reason she'd kept her own concerns from him. In that sense, the blame for this shit lay with them both. "From now on, we communicate fully. No holding back—not even to protect the other's feelings."

Knox nodded. "No holding back."

She let out a long breath. "I guess you're forgiven. Sort of. Maybe."

He sighed, relieved, even though he knew there was a very good chance that he'd go to grab a suit from the closet in a few days' time only to find that she'd sewed pink sequins onto it. His mate might forgive, but she never forgot. "What about your demon?"

"It's no longer imagining jerking you off with a pencil sharpener." At his wince, she smiled. "But it's by no means a happy bunny."

"What if I promise it a nice sparkly necklace?"

The sad thing was that her demon genuinely perked up just a

little at that. It had a huge weakness for shiny things, especially the jewelry he often bought—Knox had good taste. "I don't think that's necessary," said Harper. Her demon frowned, finding it *totally* necessary. As if Knox sensed that, his mouth twitched into a smile. Harper scowled. "You shouldn't exploit my demon's weaknesses. It's not fair."

"I don't fight fair, as you well know. If I have to buy my way back into your demon's good books, that's what I'll do. As it happens, I did see a diamond necklace that I thought would be perfect for you." Knox gently tapped her earlobe. "I think some matching earrings wouldn't go amiss."

"Okay, stop. Just stop." Because her demon was beginning to salivate.

Smiling, Knox pulled her even closer and took a deep breath, inhaling her scent. "I hate it when we argue."

"Me, too." But they'd undoubtedly do it again, she thought—particularly since they both had such strong personalities. He didn't bend to please others any more than she did. "I didn't mean to hurt you. I was trying to fix the situation."

"I know." He feathered his fingers down her throat. "It isn't your fault that it isn't something you have the power to fix." Knox landed a soft kiss on the corner of her mouth. "But I don't want to talk about that."

"Don't you?"

"No. I don't want Clarke in our bed."

No, neither did she.

"And I don't want to think any more about all the shit going on around us. Right here, right now, it's just you and me."

Harper closed her eyes as he began to skim his hands over her skin, petting her, tracing her, soothing her. But those touches soon lost their comforting edge; became sexual and teasing. His cock, hard and thick, dug into her lower stomach.

As he swirled his tongue in the hollow of her throat, she raised a brow. "You really think that sex will soften me up?" He should, since it worked every time. And, really, how could she resist him after such a heartfelt apology? Especially when the need to reconnect beat at her. Even her demon had backed down, though it was more placated by the promise of sparkly jewelry than by his apology—typical.

His mouth kicked up into a smile. "I hope so."

"What if I'm not in the mood?"

Knox almost laughed. She was already wet—he could smell it. "Then I'll have to get you in the mood." He slid his hand up the back of her neck and thrust it into her hair, liking her sharp intake of breath. "You're easily the best thing that ever happened to me." Knox swiped his tongue along her lower lip. He loved the shape and softness of her cherry mouth. Hungered to delve and taste and dominate. And that was exactly what he'd do.

Harper's lips parted on a surprised gasp as he pinched her nipple hard. His tongue sank into her mouth. He didn't kiss her. He consumed her. Greedily ate at her mouth like he'd been starving for her.

Fisting his hair, Harper shamelessly rubbed against him like a cat. Her breaths turned short and rapid as a ravenous need built inside her, making her restless. He was grinding his cock against her clit, but it wasn't enough. She needed more. But whereas she was a hot mess, he was in complete control, the bastard.

Hoping to eat at said control, she dug her fingers into his scalp and let him feel the edge of her nails, knowing how much he liked it. Sure enough, he groaned—the guttural sound made her pussy clench. But his composure didn't falter.

Refusing to give up, she sucked on his tongue. A growl that vibrated with power rumbled out of his chest and poured down her throat, making her nipples pebble and a shiver quake through her. Still, he remained in control. Both her and her demon snarled. "You're such a dick."

"I can't deny that." Knox closed his hand possessively around her breast, loving the feel of her skin. She was a taunt to his senses with her petal-soft flesh, sweet honeyed taste, cock-hardening raspy moans, and the beautiful sight she always made.

Demons were prone to developing addictions, and this little sphinx had long ago become Knox's. She was a drug he would never get enough of—one he had no intention of ever giving up. A drug that pumped through his veins, invigorated every nerve ending, and stimulated every part of him.

Lifting her breast, Knox swooped down and sucked her pierced nipple into his mouth, relishing the taste and texture of her. With a low moan, she arched into him, thighs clenching. Using his teeth, he tugged on her nipple ring just enough for it to hurt a little. Fuck, he needed to be inside her, assuring himself that she was fine, but he wanted to savor her just a little first. His demon had no such patience; it wanted to take her there and then.

"Fuck me. I want you in me," she rasped.

"I know." He bit the skin between her breasts and sucked hard, leaving a mark there. "But I'm busy. So you just lie there like a good little girl." She spat a curse, and he couldn't help but smile. But then the little witch slid her hand down his chest and fisted his cock. He thrust into her grip with a snarl as she pumped him. "You think you can make my control crack, baby?" His demon sure fucking hoped so.

"Shh, I'm busy. You just lie there like a good little archdemon." Tightening her grip on his cock, Harper pumped faster, feeling quite pleased with herself. Of course, she expected him to match her move for move, so she wasn't the least bit surprised when his hand cupped her pussy and he slid his finger between her folds.

Harper moaned as this thumb circled her clit, making her pussy spasm. He didn't touch her clit, though. No, he zoomed in on the hood. Stroked it in circular motions that made her see stars. Lightly pinched it just shy of pain, which only made her want more. And then he was rolling it between the pads of his fingers, and she thought she'd cry if he didn't *finally* touch her clit.

Using the tips of his fingers, Knox spread her plump folds. "Put your finger inside you. Tell me how wet you are."

She licked her dry lips. "I'd rather you did that."

"I know." He thumbed her clit hard enough to make her hiss. "Do what I told you to do."

The dominant rumble almost made her shiver. Releasing his cock, Harper slipped a finger inside herself; automatically, her pussy clenched it tight. "I think I'm wet enough for you. But you might want to check for yourself." Before she could move her hand, his own was there, keeping hers in place. She gasped as a long finger thrust inside her pussy, joining her own finger.

"Nice and slick," Knox agreed. "But I want you soaking wet."

Harper made a sound of annoyance in the back of her throat. "No, you're just playing 'let's torment Harper' because you're a sadistic asshole."

"Who wouldn't want to play with a pretty little fuck-toy like you?"

Harper gaped. "Bastard."

He chuckled and took her mouth again. Licked and bit and dominated. Swallowed every moan and relished the tightening of her fist around his cock. "Now we're both going to finger-fuck your pussy. Don't come until I tell you."

Keeping a firm grip on her hand, Knox withdrew both their fingers and then thrust deep. He did it again and again, watching pleasure and desperation play across her face. When her pussy started to heat, he drove a psychic finger inside and upped the pace of his thrusts. He could sense how close she was to the edge; could sense how hard she fought off her orgasm. "Good girl. Come when you're ready."

Harper almost sobbed as he forced all three fingers to fuck her with hard, rough digs. She didn't last long. Pleasure swept over her like a tidal wave, sucking her under and sending her thoughts scattering. She might have sagged against the mattress, but the psychic finger dissolved, causing her pussy to blaze and quake unbearably. "Hurts."

Knox scraped his teeth over the hollow beneath her ear, where he'd left a small mark that indicated she was anchored, and then spoke into her ear. "Want me to take the pain away, baby?" She only nodded.

Rolling her onto her back, he tugged her down the bed so that her head slid off the pillow. He then eased himself on top of her, giving her his weight, and she wrapped her limbs tight around him. Knox shook his head. "No, baby." He shackled her wrists. "I want these above your head." One-handed, he pinned them down on the pillow.

As his free hand cupped the branded globe of her ass and tilted her hips, Harper said, "You like touching that brand while you fuck me, don't you?"

Mouth curving, he lodged the thick head of his cock in her pussy. "You know I don't like rhetorical questions." He slammed home, forcing his way past swollen muscles and shocking the breath from her lungs. Her scorching hot pussy clamped down on him so hard, he ground his teeth against the urge to come right there and then. "Look at me."

Opening her eyes, Harper curled her legs tighter around him. "I need it hard."

"Do you now?" Tightening his grip on her wrists, Knox

mercilessly fucked in and out of her. He was done teasing her. Didn't have the control for it. Not while something wild and primal was clawing at him, driving him to plunge deeper, faster, harder. Not while his demon was riding him just as hard, feeding Knox's hunger with his own carnal greed.

Harper gasped as ice-cold psychic fingers dug into her thighs, hiked them up and then spread them wide, letting Knox slide even deeper and hit some magical spot inside her. "Fuck, Knox, I'm going to come with or without you."

He bit her lower lip. "Then come." He pounded harder, his pace furious, and then he watched as her orgasm crashed into her, making her eyes go blind. She screamed as her spine arched like a bow. Knox jammed his cock deep just as her pussy contracted and rippled around him, greedily milking every bit of come from his dick. And then they both collapsed.

CHAPTER FOURTEEN

Pausing in pulling on a fresh sweater after Asher had spilled milk all over her other one, Harper looked at Knox. "What do you mean, you're not going to work?"

Leaning his hip against the doorjamb of the closet, Knox said, "I mean, I'm taking the day off. We're going out. You, me, and Asher."

"We are? Where?"

"I was thinking we could pyroport to the spot on the Grand Canyon where I taught you to fly. He loved it last time—especially since we both took turns flying him around."

Harper pursed her lips. They didn't get enough days out, in her opinion. And it would be good for Asher to leave the estate for a little while. "Sounds good."

"It does." Crossing to her, Knox drew her to him and slid his arms around her waist. "How do you feel about getting away from Vegas for a week or so? The three of us need some uninterrupted time together. I was thinking we could take a trip out on the yacht."

She sighed. "You apologized last night. I accepted your apology."

"I know you did."

"Then you also know you don't need to make it up to me by doing nice stuff or—"

"I *want* to do things for you. I want to spoil you. I like spoiling you. I don't get to do it as often as I'd like, because I'm conscious of how awkward it makes you feel." He was introducing her to the concept, little by little, but Knox suspected that awkwardness would always be there. Since he found it sort of cute, that didn't bother him in the least. "But this isn't just about that. The three of us could really use some time and space away from all the shit that's going on around us."

Unable to deny that, Harper relented, "Okay. A little break would be nice. But I think Asher would prefer another trip to the island over some time on the yacht."

Knox traced the brand on her throat was his fingertip. "You're right, he'll enjoy the beach. And he likes the nursery we had built for him in the hut." At Harper's specifications.

She sighed. "It's not a hut. It's a giant beach villa with a thatched roof."

Knox's mouth quirked. "Call it whatever you like. Can you be packed and ready to leave tomorrow morning?"

"So soon?"

"Like I said, we need the time and space away."

"Tomorrow morning's good with me. But since you'll be taking some time off work for a vacation, you really don't need to stay home today."

"I know. I *want* to stay home." Not only because they needed quality time together, but because *he* needed her to be in easy reach for a little while so that he could touch her whenever he liked. After what happened, Knox didn't want her out of his sight. He wasn't leaving her side until the fear that had struck him last night had completely faded. If that made him irrational, so be it.

They'd spent much of the night talking and fucking, enjoying some alone time. When Asher woke at six in the morning, they brought him into their room and let him play on their bed while they watched TV. It had been peaceful. *Normal*. They didn't get much "normal" these days. Which was why Knox then said ...

"Later, you and I are going out for dinner."

She lifted a brow. "Is that a fact?"

Mouth twitching at her haughty tone, Knox kissed her. "I'll rephrase. I'd like to take you out to dinner later. Does that work for you?"

"And if it doesn't?"

"I'll hound you until you agree."

Harper snorted. She didn't doubt that he would. "Where do you want to go?"

"You choose."

Harper leaned back a little to study him, narrowing her eyes. "You, a total control freak, want *me* to choose? I think the last time you did that was when I was pregnant. You'd messed up then too. Knox, I told you, you don't need to do nice things for me—your apology has been accepted."

"And I told you that I *want* to do things for you, so suck it up." Before she could chew a chunk out of his ass for that remark, he kissed her. Took her mouth, pouring that consuming and overpowering emotion he felt for her right down her throat. Moaning, she melted against him, and something in him settled. Just as he pulled back, Larkin's mind touched his.

Knox, we need to talk, the harpy told him. *I'm in the living room when you're ready.*

We'll be right down. Cupping Harper's hips, Knox said,

"Larkin's here. She no doubt wants to check on you. I assured her that you were fine earlier this morning by telepathy, but she'll naturally want to see that for herself."

Knox hadn't been surprised when Tanner and Levi turned up a few hours ago, wanting to check on Harper first thing. Keenan had actually stayed the night, worried for her. Knox was quite sure his little sphinx would be surprised by just how protective his sentinels were of her. It wasn't about her being their Prime; it wasn't about duty. They cared for and respected her. She had a way of winning people's loyalty without even trying.

"I'm ready," said Harper, straightening her sweater. "We can—" Hearing her cell chime, she walked out of the closet and over to the nightstand, where she grabbed the phone. The name flashing on the screen made her blink in surprise and caused her stomach to knot.

"Who is it?" asked Knox, who'd followed her into the bedroom. "Clarke?" He'd kill the fucker if it was.

"Not the one you're thinking of. It's Devon." The other girls had called last night to check on Harper after Jolene—who'd lost her everloving mind when she heard about the café incident—passed on the news of what happened. It had hurt Harper that Devon hadn't bothered to even send her a text. Noticing that Knox was lingering, arms folded, Harper said, "Can I have a little privacy while I take the call?"

"I'm staying until I'm sure she's not calling to give you grief." He held her gaze with his own, telling her without words that he wouldn't budge.

Sighing, Harper swiped her thumb across the screen. "Hello?"

"Hey," Devon greeted shyly. "I meant to call you last night but ... well, I wasn't sure if you'd want to hear from me, considering I've been such a bitch lately. Now I've decided I don't care if you don't want to talk to me, I need to know you're okay. Khloë promised you were fine, but . . . "

Shoulders losing their stiffness, Harper said, "I'm okay. And I'm glad you called." She gave Knox an "it's fine" look, but he still didn't move. She rolled her eyes.

"Khloë said that you would have died if Knox hadn't been there at the café." Devon's voice shook a little. "He's handy to have around."

Harper gave a soft snort of amusement. "Very true."

"It wasn't fair of me to be mad at him. Drew was warned, and he ignored every one of those warnings. I just felt torn. And guilty, because I was pissed at him even while he was so hurt. He's my brother. I felt like I should have sided with him, but I couldn't. It ate me up."

"I get it. I'm not upset."

"Not sure if Jolene's already told you, but Drew left for Cuba. We escorted him to the airport and watched the plane take off. He's gone so . . . Look, I know Knox probably won't care, but tell him I'm sorry for not being fair to him. I'm guessing he's right there, since there's no way he wouldn't monitor a call you received from someone he suspected might upset you."

Harper met his eyes. "He's here."

"And that's why I like that you have him. I want someone who'll always look out for you, even if that means my brother suffered his wrath." There was a short pause. "So, are we okay? You and me, I mean?"

"Of course we're okay. We'll always be 'okay', Devon."

There was a distinct sigh of relief. "Maybe we could have dinner later or something. I've missed you."

Harper bit her lower lip. "I have plans for tonight. I can't do lunch either—me, Knox, and Asher are going out for the day."

"That's no problem—a family day out is *much* more important. We can get together another time."

Harper smiled. "We'll definitely meet up soon."

"I'll hold you to that. Have a great time. And give Asher a kiss for me."

"Will do. Take care." With that, Harper ended the call and tossed her phone on the bed.

Knox crossed to her and rubbed her back. "Feel better now?"

"Yes." Being at odds with Devon had made things feel … off-balance. Out of whack. Now that the knot in the pit of Harper's stomach unraveled, she took a deep, cleansing breath. "She wants you to know that she's sorry for being mad at you. She knows it was unfair."

"She felt torn, I understand that. I'm not at all grieved by it." Other people's opinions of him mattered little to Knox. "But she upset *you*, and that's not whatsoever acceptable to me." He didn't believe the female hellcat deserved to get off with it so lightly.

"You upset me, too," Harper reminded him gently. "You asked me to forgive you, and I have. She's asked me to accept her apology, and I have. It would be hypocritical of you to begrudge her the forgiveness I gave her when you wanted it from me, too." Before he could grumble about that, she kissed him. "How about we go see Larkin now?"

Allowing her to distract him from a conversation that he had no real desire to continue, Knox took his mate's hand and led her down the stairs and into the living area. All four of his sentinels were scattered around the room.

Raking her gaze over Harper, Larkin smiled, "Hey. You look good for a girl who almost died."

Knox let out a low growl. "Don't remind me of what a close call it was."

Larkin lifted her hands in a placatory gesture, but she seemed
to be stifling a smile.

"Thanks for cleaning up the mess at the café, Larkin," said
Harper. "Knox told me what you and Tanner did." Harper had
already thanked the hellhound earlier.

Larkin just shrugged. "That's what we do."

Glancing around, Harper frowned. "Where's Asher?"

"In the playarea with Meg," replied Keenan, juggling toy
bricks. "When Larkin said she had some news, I thought it would
be better if the little guy wasn't in the room."

"Thanks, Keenan." Taking a seat on the sofa beside Tanner,
Harper lifted a brow at Larkin. "So, coming to check on me isn't
the only reason you're here."

"No." The harpy looked at Knox. "You wanted me to track
Alethea's movements before she disappeared. I told you that
I'd spoken with the humans she was regularly photographed
with, right?"

Knox gave a short nod and settled on the sofa next to Harper,
pulling her close. "You said there was only one you couldn't
find. A woman."

"Yes." Larkin scooted forward on her seat. "I figured that
speaking to her wouldn't really help, since it was likely that Jonas
had given her the Australia story, just as he had the others."

"But he hadn't?" prodded Levi.

"*That* I don't know. I haven't spoken to her." Larkin's eyes flit-
ted between Harper and Knox. "I think she's much more likely
to give you answers than she is me."

Knox arched a brow. "Why is that?"

"Because she's not human," said Larkin. "She's a demon, so
she'll know exactly what a mistake it would be to play dumb
with you."

Tanner blinked. "A demon? One of ours?"

Larkin shook her head. "She's one of Thatcher's demons. I ran her picture through facial recognition software. Her name is Sherryl Malloy."

Brow furrowing, Harper tilted her head. "Why does that name sound familiar?"

Larkin hesitated. "Because she's dating your cousin, Ciaran."

Knox had performed several interrogations in the boathouse on the grounds of their estate, but he was wary of having any strangers near his home and son right now—even if those strangers wouldn't live long. As such, he would have asked Levi to grab Sherryl Malloy and take her straight to the Chamber ... if Harper weren't insisting on being part of the interrogation. Nothing he'd said had made her change her mind, and that meant he'd have to conduct it at the boathouse, because there was no way he was taking her to the Chamber.

He didn't want her to ever step foot inside there. Didn't want her to see the torturous implements and devices, or to be stained by the grim and hopeless air of the place. Of course, she knew Knox had a specific place where he punished those who deserved it. She was also well-aware that none of those punishments were even remotely merciful. But she never asked for details. Never even asked *where* the punishments took place. And that suited Knox just fine.

It would suit him just as much if she'd leave the interrogation up to him, but she'd point-blank refused. So, at that moment, his mate was walking between him and Larkin as they made their way to the boathouse. Tanner and Keenan had agreed to remain with Asher, but Knox suspected they would join them at some point out of sheer nosiness, if nothing else. They didn't like to miss anything.

Knox briefly glanced at his mate. Harper looked composed,

but her fiery anger brushed the edges of his mind. His demon wanted to nuzzle and calm her, even as it also fairly vibrated with its own fury.

Technically, since Malloy was one of Thatcher's demons, Knox should contact the Prime about the situation before performing any interrogation. It was Thatcher's right to deal with it himself and to take care of any punishments that needed to be dealt out. But since Knox hadn't been able to cross Thatcher off his suspect list, he had no intention whatsoever of involving him in this.

Harper gave Knox a sideways look and said, "Let me lead this time. This bitch may well have been using Ciaran to get an in with my family and spy on them somehow for Alethea. She might have even recommended that Heidi be the perfect kid to use for the ritual to free the incorporeal. You can have your turn when I'm done."

"You're all heart," Knox said dryly. She just snorted.

"I don't think Malloy had anything to do with what happened to Heidi," said Larkin, frowning. "From what I could gather, she's only been dating Ciaran for a few months, off and on."

"Yes, but I called Khloë a few minutes ago," Harper told her. "She said that Ciaran and Sherryl have been working together at a retail store for a few years now. They were friends well before they started sharing a bed. I wouldn't be surprised if Sherryl pushed for more so that she could get closer to him and get more info."

"How much did you tell Khloë when you asked about Malloy?" Larkin asked.

"Not much. I assured her that I'd answer her questions later, once I had the answers I needed." And Harper would do whatever it took to get them from this bitch who'd endangered her family. Anticipation filled her inner demon, who was anxious to vent some of the rage it had been forced to contain for far too long.

"Does Ciaran care about Malloy?" asked Larkin.

Harper considered it for a moment. "I doubt it, or he'd have brought her to family gatherings. He's never once mentioned her to me. It was Khloë who talked about her, saying she didn't like Ciaran's new girlfriend."

Harper also knew from Khloë that Sherryl was a familiar—a breed of demon that could change into small animals such as cats, dogs, birds, and ferrets. As such, Harper had been able to warn Levi that the bitch might try to escape him by shifting into an animal. She had indeed tried it, but Levi had bound her quickly with the preternatural rope he'd been given by his incantor friend—a demonic witch. It not only trapped a person, it blocked them from being able to use their gifts. Only a very powerful demon could escape it.

Generally, familiars were rarely powerful. However, they were often annoyingly immune to the compelling tone that all sphinxes were gifted with, which meant that Harper probably wouldn't be able to force the she-demon to confess all. But that was okay. There were other much more fun ways of extracting information from people.

As they neared the boathouse, Harper shot Knox a look. *Remember, let me lead.* He only inclined his head, which would have to be good enough. Blanking her expression, she pushed open the door. Three gleaming chrome and fiberglass boats were separated by narrow walkways. At the end of the central walkway was a curvy redhead, tied to a chair, her eyes wide, her freckled face pale.

Keeping her gaze locked with Sherryl's, Harper slowly stalked toward her, wooden floorboards groaning beneath her feet. The rough nylon ropes creaked as the boats swayed gently. Beneath the scent of the briny salt water that lapped at the hulls were the smells of wax and motor oil ... and the little bitch's fear. Excellent. That fear was like catnip to Harper's demon.

Coming to a halt, Harper bared her teeth in a feral smile. She was conscious of Knox sidling up to her while Larkin joined Levi in standing near the wall, but her focus was on the familiar in front of her. The familiar who had quite possibly passed on info that led to the *attempted attack on her son*. As far as Harper was concerned, an effort to possess Asher counted as an attack. An attack that, if successful, could have led to any number of bad things for her little boy.

Harper tilted her head. "Sherryl, isn't it? I have some questions for you. I'd advise you not to choose silence over honesty, but I truly can't say I'm *hoping* you'll choose honesty. I'm in a real bitchy mood, so torturing answers out of you would bring me nothing but supreme joy."

Sherryl studied her. "You're not a killer," she said, voice shaky but sure. "I see into a person. You'll kill in self-defense or during combat. But you won't kill someone who isn't fighting back."

Not usually, thought Harper. "But my demon will. And since I'm quite sure you've been working with the remaining Horseman—"

Sherryl's eyes bulged. "What? No! I'm not working with him!"

"Alethea was. And you were doing her bidding." Harper pursed her lips. "How did you meet her?"

The familiar snapped her mouth shut and raised her cleft chin slightly. Ooh, she apparently felt some loyalty toward the encantada. How silly and pointless.

"You really don't want to test my mate's patience," Knox told Sherryl, tone silky smooth yet coated in menace. "She doesn't have a lot of it at the best of times. Right now, she's dangerously low on it." But Sherryl, obviously dumb as a crumb, still said nothing.

Face hardening, Harper carefully removed the jeweled metal sticks from her hair. Then, holding Sherryl's eyes, Harper infused hellfire into the sticks.

Sherryl jerked back a little in her seat, breaths coming hard and fast now.

"I'm going to count to four," Harper said, calm and pleasant. "If I get to two and you haven't yet spoken, I'm going to stab your thighs with these. Believe me, it'll hurt like a motherfucker. If I get to three and you still aren't talking, I will set your fucking nipples on fire and watch the hellfire eat at them—with utter joy and a mental happy dance. And if I reach four and you're *still* not singing like a canary, I will proceed to torture you with a slow, sadistic meticulousness that will *blow your mind*. And Sherryl, you *really* don't want that."

Eyes wide, Sherryl licked her trembling lips.

"One." No response. "Two." Still no response. Quick as lightning, Harper rammed the flaming metal sticks into Sherryl's thighs. The familiar screamed, face reddening, spine snapping straight. Harper didn't pull out the sticks; she held them tight, glaring right into the bitch's pain-filled eyes. "Told you it would hurt like a motherfucker. Now, where was I? Oh, yeah. Thr—"

"Alethea came to me when she was dating Thatcher!" Sherryl burst out, eyes tearing.

Harper's demon sighed, disappointed. It had been looking forward to setting her nipples alight. Disturbingly, it was slightly comforted by the sound of their prey's blistering flesh sizzling. "Go on."

"They didn't seem serious, but she said she hoped they could have something good," Sherryl went on, pain dripping from every syllable. "She was ... she was nice to me."

"Nice to you?" Alethea wasn't *nice*.

"She said I reminded her of her when she was younger," said Sherryl, words coming sharp and fast. "She took me shopping, clubbing, and introduced me to her friends. She was surprised when she realized I was friends with Ciaran."

Harper gave her a look of mock pity. "She wasn't surprised. That was *why* she befriended you. She wanted to use you. But I don't feel in the least bit bad for you, since *you* used *Ciaran*. You started dating him so that you could try milking him for info on our family."

Roughly, Harper yanked out the metal sticks and took a step back, mostly because being so close to the scent of burning flesh was not fun. Sherryl sagged slightly in her chair, fists clenched, tears dripping down her face, flesh still sizzling. "Why would you help Alethea?" Harper asked, but Sherryl was busy gaping at the blood seeping out of her charred jeans. "Why did you help her?"

Sherryl swallowed. "All she wanted was some info on what the Wallis imps did with their time. Said she was worried they intended to attack her at some point so she wanted to monitor their movements and habits. It seemed harmless to tell her stuff."

Harmless? Harper's demon hissed, tempted to lunge to the surface. For now, it was content to let Harper lead. "And just what did you get out of it? Don't tell me you were just being *nice* like Alethea."

Sherryl hesitated, gaze darting to the side. Would she never learn?

Harper thrust one of the sticks into the familiar's shoulder, and the air was filled with the sound of yet more skin sizzling. She waited for Sherryl's horrific scream to die down before she spoke. "I believe my mate warned you that I was very short on patience. Now, answer my damn question."

Taking a shuddering breath, Sherryl squeezed her eyes shut.

"She paid me for the info, and she said she'd arrange for me to transfer to her lair."

Knox arched a brow. "You don't like having Thatcher for a Prime?"

"It's not that," replied Sherryl, opening her eyes. "My ex is part of Thatcher's Force. He's making things difficult for me. I just want out."

"Hmm." Knox twisted his mouth. "Where did she go when she left her home?"

"I don't know. She wouldn't tell me. She just said it was someplace safe."

"But you stayed in communication with her?" asked Knox.

"Only through telepathy."

Tipping his head to the side, Knox said, "You must have known that Alethea was working with someone."

"She never mentioned anyone else." Sherryl's brow puckered as something seemed to occur to her. "Though she did once say that she had it 'on good authority' that the Wallis imps would target her."

Harper narrowed her eyes. "What else did she ask you to do?" When the familiar hesitated, Harper twisted the stick that was still stuck in her shoulder. Sherryl cried out through her teeth. "*What else did she ask you to do?*" Harper demanded.

Sherryl's pained gaze cut to Knox. "She wanted to know what you are. She thought the imps might know; that you might have told them."

"So you asked Ciaran," prompted Harper.

Sherryl nodded. "He said that my guess was as good as his. I knew he was telling the truth. I can smell lies. They have a distinct scent. Like smoke." She swallowed. "I got the feeling he wouldn't have told me, even if he did know."

She was right to have that "feeling". Harper knew her cousin wouldn't have told an outsider jack shit. "What else did Alethea ask of you?"

"She wanted to know about your kid. Said if I heard anything at all about him, I should tell her. But no one ever spoke of him in front of me. I asked Ciaran about him, said I'd love to meet him, but Ciaran blew me off without even being rude. He's good at that."

Evasiveness was a trait that every imp possessed, so Harper didn't see why the familiar would be so surprised. "Just what info *did* you pass to Alethea?"

"I didn't know anything *to* pass on."

"But she kept in touch with you. She wouldn't have done that unless you were being useful. So, what did you tell her?"

"I kept her updated on the imps' movements. And, okay, I lied to her a few times."

"And just what lies did you tell her?" asked Knox, voice a lethal purr.

Sweat beading on her forehead, Sherryl flexed her bony fingers. "I told her I'd met your kid and that he didn't seem powerful. I said he didn't use any abilities in front of me."

"And?" Knox pushed.

"And I told her I overheard imps say you were a hybrid, but that I didn't know what breeds your parents were."

Knox arched a disbelieving brow. "She bought that I was a hybrid?"

"No, she thought you'd lied to the imps about what you were. That pissed her off. When I asked why she cared so much about what breed you were, she said that she suspected you were the fourth Horseman and that you would come for her; she wanted to be prepared. I said I didn't think you were the Horseman; that if you wanted to overtake the Primes, you could do it easily and you wouldn't need any help. She seemed to think about that for a minute, but then she said she'd heard from a 'reliable source' that you could be him."

Knox exchanged a brief look with Harper. Either Alethea had been feeding Sherryl excuses or the Horseman had worked to convince Alethea that she'd soon be a target. It could even have been a bit of both. "I'm guessing you asked who that source was." *He* would have done, in her position. "What did she tell you?"

"Only that it was someone whose word she trusted."

Trusted? Knox's brows knitted. Alethea had never been the trusting type. "When was the last time you heard from her?"

"I contacted her telepathically a few days before the imps' tea party to tell her about it," said Sherryl. "She thanked me for the info, asked how I was doing, and how things were going with Ciaran. You know, girl stuff."

Keeping up the best friend act while also checking that Sherryl and Ciaran were still an item, Knox thought. "Did she ever talk to you about her own boyfriend?"

"She said she didn't have one. But one time, when I went to her home, she acted weird and wouldn't let me inside—told me she was tired. I saw a man's long, navy blue cashmere coat hanging on her hallway coatrack. Cirque du Soleil tickets were sticking out of the pocket—they only caught my attention because my friend is going to the show and she'd showed me her own tickets. And I smelled tobacco coming from inside."

Knox licked over his front teeth, trying to remember if he'd ever seen Jonas, Thatcher, or Dario either smoking or wearing a cashmere coat. "When exactly was this?"

"I don't know. A month before she moved out, maybe."

"Does Thatcher know you were passing on info to Alethea?"

"If he does, *I* didn't tell him." Sherryl's eyes filled with yet more tears. "When I saw the clip on YouTube, I was hoping to God that it wasn't real. But when I tried to contact her telepathically, there was nothing. And I knew she was really dead."

"I wouldn't grieve too hard," said Harper, yanking the stick out of the familiar's shoulder. "She used you. But, if it's any consolation, you'll be joining her soon enough."

"What?" Sherryl sounded genuinely baffled.

Harper leaned forward. "Your self-centered actions made my family vulnerable. They led to an attack on my son and the attempting kidnapping of my cousin. Don't play dumb. Heidi is Ciaran's little sister. You would have heard that someone attempted to snatch her and—since it's highly likely that you passed on info about how Heidi often went to the playground after school—it must have clicked in your head that Alethea had something to do with it."

Sherryl shook her head madly. "I went to her home and asked her! She promised it was just a coincidence!"

"And you can smell lies, so you would have known if she was telling the truth. She wasn't, was she?"

Sherryl looked away.

"Yeah, you knew she was involved. But you hadn't cared. It didn't matter to you that a little girl was almost kidnapped. Didn't matter that what lay in store for her wouldn't have been good. Hell, you even risked it happening again when you did *nothing*. You could have told Ciaran. Jolene. Me. Any number of people. Instead, you kept on feeding her info, didn't you?"

"I fed her *lies*, sure. That's all."

Harper shook her head. "I don't believe that. You told her about the tea party."

"It didn't seem like a big deal. No one would attempt an attack in a house full of people—especially when those people are Wallis imps."

"Someone did. And that someone was sent by Alethea's

reliable source. But they wouldn't have known to go there if it hadn't been for *you*," Harper spat, pointing the blazing stick at her. "In fact, if you'd just come to us *months* ago with what you knew, this all could have been avoided. But you didn't. I doubt you ever even considered it. My son was attacked, Sherryl, and you *profited* from it." Her demon shot to the surface and hissed. "Anyone who was even the slightest bit involved in what happened to the child will pay in blood, including you," it told her.

Hate gathered behind Sherryl's eyes until they practically shone with it. "And I should be afraid of a sphinx that doesn't even have fucking wings? I should care about the fate of a kid that's probably just as much of a freak as its mother? *You* should have been the one who died in that video. Or better still, your brat should have been the one crying and screaming while his flesh blistered and melted. At least I have the comfort of knowing all three of you will be dead soon. The Horseman, whoever the fuck he is, will come for you."

The demon's smile was rather serene. "I know," it said. "And he'll die too." With that, the demon jammed the flaming stick into the bitch's eye.

CHAPTER FIFTEEN

Knox stared down at the charred, bloodied, battered body in front of him. Sherryl Malloy had taken a long time to die. Both Harper and her demon had put the familiar through a shitload of well-deserved pain—a pain that might have ended sooner if Malloy hadn't screamed her hope that Asher died a dreadful, agonizing death at the hands of the Horseman. Maybe she'd thought that such words would drive Harper into delivering a killing blow. They hadn't. His mate had remained completely controlled.

Harper had warned him that she could be scary. Warned him time and time again that a sphinx in 'berserker mode' was a dangerous creature. But he hadn't been able to imagine his mate ever truly losing her shit in a spectacular fashion. Now he understood that a sphinx's version of 'berserker mode' didn't involve an explosion of rage. No, their rage remained relatively contained, but they showed no mercy whatsofuckingever.

Harper had been almost robotic in the way she'd systematically subjected Malloy to several rounds of excruciating torture. A lesser man might have been freaked out by it. Her demon had surfaced occasionally to join in on the fun, but Harper had taken the lead. Sensing that she'd needed it, Knox had stood back and left her to it.

He knew her actions were driven by not only anger but her fear of what *could* have happened to Asher and Heidi. The fact that they were safe and unharmed just wasn't the point. Not when their fates were intended to be utterly horrific.

In order to ensure Asher's safety and survival, Knox and Harper needed to send a clear message that anyone who had even the tiniest role in a plan to target Asher would suffer inconceivable agony.

No one who looked at what was left of Sherryl Malloy could miss that message.

His demon was proud of its mate. Approved that she'd showed no mercy. While Knox also approved, he was concerned that Harper's conscience would feel the strain of it later. She wouldn't regret what she'd done, but she'd be upset that she didn't regret it. Might even be a little disturbed to learn just how far she'd go to protect and avenge their son.

Keenan and Tanner had entered the boathouse moments ago, curious about what was taking so long. They'd been taken aback by the gruesome sight they found, but not horrified—they'd seen Knox dole out much worse torture. Hearing that it was *Harper* who was responsible, however, had been a huge shock to them. Not a bad shock, though. No, like Knox, they approved of their Prime's actions even as they knew Harper's soft heart would pay a price for it later.

"Conference call's scheduled to start in thirty seconds. You both ready?" Larkin asked from behind him.

Turning to face the sentinel, expression blank, Harper lifted her chin slightly. "Ready." She hadn't said much since Sherryl took—well, croaked—her last breath.

Knox moved closer to his mate's side so that their bodies brushed, giving her space yet also letting her know he was there. "Let's get this done," he said.

The harpy pressed a few buttons on the laptop. "And we're live." She turned it to face them. The wide screen was a grid of faces as the other Primes stared back at them. Only Jonas, who hadn't accepted his invite to the video conference, was missing. As Harper had telepathed Jolene with a heads-up about the situation, the female imp was the only one who wasn't completely clueless as to why Knox had arranged the video conference.

If he and Harper weren't blocking their view of Sherryl, they would have no doubt all jerked back in horror. Yeah, the view was *that* bad.

"I know many of you are exceptionally busy," said Knox, not bothering with any preliminaries, "so I appreciate you all cutting your activities short to take this call."

"Is this about the Horseman?" Raul instantly asked. "Have you discovered his identity?"

"No," said Knox, "but we're getting closer and closer to finding him. It's only a matter of time before we do." He truly believed that.

"Then what is the big emergency?" asked Malden.

Knox looked at Thatcher, face hardening. "I believe we have something that belongs to you. Or someone. Sherryl Malloy is one of your demons, correct?"

"Yes," Thatcher confirmed, thick brows drawing together. "Why is she with you?"

Knox kept his eyes on Thatcher to monitor his reaction closely as he and Harper parted, revealing Malloy. The Prime recoiled in horror, eyes wide. There were gasps, curses, and horrified mutters from the other Primes. Only Jolene, expression grim, stayed silent.

Face reddening and contorting with fury, Thatcher demanded, "What happened? What did you do to her, Thorne?"

"He didn't do it," said Harper, voice hard. "*I* did. She was passing on information to Alethea—information that led to the attempted kidnapping of my niece and to the incorporeal's attack on my son."

The Primes fell silent, all looking varying degrees of shocked. Harper suspected they were more shocked to hear that *she'd* killed Malloy than they were to hear *why* Harper had killed her. After all, the Primes had always insisted on viewing Harper as someone who was playing out of her league; a fluffy bunny trying to hang with feral wolves. That was their mistake.

Thatcher's lips parted in surprise. "You're certain?"

A flash of anger sailed through Harper. "Do you think I'd do that for shits and fucking giggles?" She had no regrets about what she'd done, but she hadn't enjoyed it. Her demon, on the other hand, had been on cloud goddamn nine.

Incredulous, Thatcher shook his head. "It makes no sense that Sherryl would have placed your family in danger. She was dating your cousin." Watching as Harper slowly lifted a brow, realization seemed to dawn on Thatcher. He sighed. "She was using him to get information." His eyes flicked to Knox. "I suppose the reason you didn't call me until now is that you suspect me of being the Horseman. I would have taken care of her punishment."

A low hiss came out of Harper. "That kill was *ours*," she told Thatcher, jabbing her finger in the corpse's direction. "That creature—or what's left of her—endangered our son. The Horseman wanted us to know what happened to people who got in the way of his plans. Well, *that* is what happens to anyone who even plays a *part* in any harm that befalls my family. And when I get my hands on the Horseman—and I will—he won't get off so lightly."

"You call that *lightly?*" asked Mila, tone mild.

"Her pain is over, isn't it?" Harper retorted. "His will *never* be over."

The Primes studied Harper as if they'd never seen her before. There was a newfound respect in their gazes and, in many cases, a healthy dose of apprehension. Knox suspected the Primes would also be both unnerved and irritated to learn they had totally underestimated her. Though she was strong, they'd never really considered her a threat in her own right—only in the sense that she was mated to Knox and, thus, they made *each other* stronger.

"I am assuming you interrogated the she-demon," said Dario, flicking a look at the corpse. "Did she know anything useful that will lead us to the Horseman?"

"Nothing that would lead us directly to him," said Knox. "But she gave us information that would help—information I'm quite sure the Horseman didn't know she possessed."

Jolene gave a slow nod. "He would have killed her if he'd thought she had anything on him, but he apparently didn't consider her a loose end."

"Will you not share with us the information she gave you?" Raul asked Knox.

"No, just as I'm quite sure none of you will share anything that you uncover." Knox was unsurprised when none of them denied it. "Sad as it is, we do not know who we can trust. If the Horseman should learn what I now know, it would give him the opportunity to wipe away any evidence. I won't risk that."

Dario sighed. "Very well."

Exhaling heavily, Thatcher rubbed at his brow. "I'll send

some of my sentinels to collect Sherryl's body. It is custom in my lair to give each demon a proper burial, no matter their crime."

"Is it?" drawled Harper, eyes narrowing. "Levi."

At the one-word summons, Levi stepped out of the shadows and into the camera's line of sight. He then clicked his fingers, and the corpse burst into cinders that quickly faded away. It was an ability that came with being a reaper. And it made Harper's inner demon smirk. Now that the entity had vented some of its rage, it was much mellower.

Glaring at Thatcher, Harper said, "There's no such custom about burials in my lair. Even if there were, that bitch would get no courtesies from me."

"Nor from me, in your position," Mila said to Harper. Others murmured their agreement.

Knox ran his gaze over each of the Primes, who—except for Jolene, who looked at her granddaughter with pride—were once again eyeing Harper warily. He didn't blame them. "I think my mate and I have made our standpoint blindingly clear. I hope you convey this message to the demons within your lairs. We wouldn't want anyone else getting ideas about targeting Asher, would we?" He nodded at Larkin, who cut the link for the video conference and then closed the laptop.

Harper's shoulders lowered slightly, and she let out a long breath. "I need a drink." Or a bottle. Maybe then her nerves would finally fully settle.

Keenan pulled his flask out of his pocket and offered it to her. "Here."

She didn't even take a cautious sniff. Just chugged it down. And nearly choked as her throat and the roof of her mouth started to burn like holy hell. She coughed. "Jesus, what is that? Battery acid?"

The incubus smirked. "Everclear vodka with a little something mixed in."

Deciding she didn't want to know what that little something was, Harper handed him the flask, still coughing. Knox rested his hand on her nape and gave it a comforting squeeze.

Staring down at her, Tanner said, "You weren't kidding."

She blinked at him. "What?"

"You can in fact be terrifying. And no, I'm not teasing you."

"I don't think you'll have to ever again deal with shit from the Primes, Harper." Levi moved the chair back to its spot near the wall and hooked the rope over it. "It's fucked up that this gained their respect, but if that respect and fear keeps them from messing with you, that can only be a good thing."

Keenan knocked down a huge gulp of that vodka, the weirdo. "You still plan on playing a clip of Malloy's slow-death throughout the Underground?"

"It's the only way to be sure that the Horseman and any minions he might have will get our message," said Harper. "Besides, everyone needs to be sure *exactly* what happens to those who go after my family."

Larkin nodded. "Fair enough. I'll get on it."

With his hand still on her nape, Knox led her out of the boathouse and into the fresh, open air. Harper inhaled it greedily, needing to drown out the scents of blood, pain, and hate that seemed to be clogging her nostrils and lungs.

"Are we all thinking that the Horseman was Alethea's 'reliable source'?" asked Tanner as they walked back to the house. Mansion. Whatever the beautiful monstrosity should be called. "That he told her she was a target to scare and manipulate her?"

"It seems likely," said Knox. The others nodded. "We can cross Dion off our list of suspects. The incorporeal said it intended to find and hurt him once it had earned its freedom."

Levi twisted his mouth. "That leaves us with Thatcher, Dario, and Jonas."

Holding the laptop against her chest, Larkin sighed. "It's a crying shame that the only clues Malloy gave us about Alethea's partner in crime are that he wears a cashmere coat, smokes tobacco, likes Cirque du Soleil, and that the encantada trusted his word."

"The only person I can imagine her investing any trust in is Jonas," said Tanner. "But I saw her face when she realized that Jonas wanted an alliance with Lou. If the siblings were working together, would it really have bothered her that he wanted such an alliance? It makes more sense that she suspected Jonas would betray her and try to have the incorporeal destroyed or banished back to hell, just like he claimed. Also, I've never known him to smoke. Nor Dario, for that matter. Never smelled tobacco on them."

"I've seen Jonas smoking a time or two," said Knox. "I've also seen Thatcher with the occasional cigar at gatherings, but I got the feeling he only smoked them to look distinguished."

Larkin drummed her fingers on the closed laptop. "Malloy was one of Thatcher's demons. He could have turned Alethea's attention her way—pulled her strings, so to speak. But I don't think he's the Horseman. I mean, if he is, he would have just asked Sherryl for the info himself; he wouldn't have done it through Alethea."

A thoughtful silence fell. After a long moment, Harper broke it. "The Horseman's not very hands-on, is he? He likes to use people. And it makes me wonder if he was pulling the strings of the other Horsemen. Sitting back and letting them take all the risks and do all the work."

Knox's eyes narrowed slightly. "You think he was their ring-leader? That he might have even been the one who brought them all together?"

Harper shrugged. "It's just a theory."

"It's a good one," said Knox.

Levi rubbed at his nape. "If we go with that theory, it would suggest that Dario isn't our guy. He campaigned to be Monarch, like Isla. That's not 'sitting back', is it?"

"No, it's not." Knox frowned, still feeling like there was something he was missing.

"Where do we go from here?" asked Larkin. "Malloy didn't exactly give us any useful clues, did she?"

"Maybe she did," mused Harper, coming to a standstill as something occurred to her. "She said that she and Alethea only communicated through telepathy. It's an ability that pretty much all demons possess, but it's not always strong. Some don't have a very wide telepathic range." She turned to Knox. "You'd known Alethea a long time, you must have some idea of how wide her range was."

Knox thought about it for a moment. "It couldn't have been very wide. There were many occasions when she called my cell phone. Especially when she was out of the country, which was often."

"What about when she was *inside* the country?" asked Harper. "I'm sure you were often invited to her home here, but maybe there were times when she called to say she was near one of your offices and wanted to know if you were interested in hooking up?"

"Yes," he remembered. "There were also occasions when she called to say she was near the estate."

"Hoping you'd grant her entry and she could wangle her way into your bedroom, even though you never 'shit where you slept', as you once so aptly put it." Harper snorted. "Okay, and where were *you* at the time of these calls?"

"Various places. I was rarely ever home. I worked a lot." Knox searched his memories, eyes narrowed. "I remember I once agreed to meet her in the bar of a hotel on the strip. I was running late, so I tried telepathing her to let her know. I couldn't reach her, so I had to call her."

Harper took a small step toward him. "And where were you at the time?"

"In a hotel further along the strip. Four kilometers away, at most."

"Then her telepathic muscle didn't stretch very far," Harper mused. "But she was in regular contact with Sherryl Malloy, who lived smack bam in the middle of North Las Vegas." Which meant that . . . "Motherfucker, Alethea must have been hiding in North Las Vegas all that time—the last place anyone would think to look for her."

Levi bit out a harsh curse. "So close yet so fucking far. If she was relying on Malloy for info, she wasn't getting out of her hideout much. She holed herself up somewhere."

Keenan nodded. "Still, she would have caught *someone's* attention. She was a sex demon. Encantadas easily entrance humans."

"I should get my family on this," said Harper. "They can show her picture to people and ask around. We may just be able to find out where she was staying."

"The Force can do that," said Knox.

"Yes, but my family knows the area better than they do." Pretty much all of the Wallis imps lived there. "People are more willing to talk to them than they are to any of our lair."

Knox inclined his head. "We'll still have our Force make enquiries. The more people working on this, the better."

Harper gave a satisfied nod. "The odds are good that he cleaned wherever she was staying of anything that could implicate him, but someone will have seen something. People mind their business in shady areas, but they stay alert, too. If they saw a stranger walking around, they'd have gotten a good look at them."

Feeling a tingle of optimism, she wasted no time in telepathing Jolene and bringing her up to speed as she walked back to the house. Her grandmother offered to assist in questioning people in the area before Harper even got the chance to ask. With the combined efforts of their lairs, they would surely learn *something* important.

Entering the foyer, she asked her grandmother, *How's Ciaran?*

Jolene sighed. *Outraged would be the best word. He wasn't serious about Sherryl, but he'd considered her a friend, if nothing else. He's mad at himself for not seeing what she was doing—which is dumb, of course, and I've expressed this to him several times. He'll be all right. I wish you'd told me about Malloy before you killed her. It's not fair that you got to have all the fun.*

Sorry.

Jolene gave a soft, almost delicate snort. *No, you're not.*

No, I'm not.

It's a good thing that the other Primes got to see what you're capable of. It's also good that they saw you're not someone who will hide behind Knox or leave the dirty work to him. You could have left the punishment to him, who would certainly have made Malloy suffer. But you didn't. Nor did you invite him to get in on the fun—which does make me feel a little better about being left out. Instead, you took care of it yourself, and you did it in a way that conveyed a very powerful message. They'll highly respect that.

Hopefully the message would be heard loud and clear, Harper thought, as she followed Knox into the living room. Asher was nowhere to be seen, so she figured Meg had him with her somewhere. *Gotta go, Grams. Speak soon.*

Take care, sweetheart.

Breaking the connection with her grandmother, Harper

turned to Knox, who was watching her closely. She also realized they were alone. "Where'd the sentinels go?"

"To their respective cars." Crossing to her, Knox cupped her hips, fighting the urge to eat up every bit of her personal space and hold her tight. "You okay?"

She placed her hands on his chest. "I'm fine."

"You're not feeling bad for what you did, are you?" he asked, searching her eyes and getting caught up in the way the chocolate-brown color swirled, faded, and then settled into a warm honey shade.

"No." Harper jutted out her chin. "She deserved every second of pain she got. I don't need to go journal about it or cuddle a teddy bear."

"But it unsettles you that you can deliver such pain and feel no remorse for it."

She shrugged. "Maybe." When he just looked at her expectantly, she sighed. "Okay, yes, it unsettles me that I have that kind of cruelty in me."

Knox couldn't relate to that, because he never experienced any such guilt—that wasn't something he was proud of, though. "You are not cruel, Harper. You didn't hurt Malloy because you're heartless or sadistic. You did it because she was partly responsible for what happened to our son. That primal, mama bear protectiveness in you was *never* going to let that go. Nor was it going to be satisfied with anything other than her death. The very fact that you're unsettled by your lack of remorse shows that you're not a bad person."

Harper swallowed, comforted by his words, and walked into his arms. He held her close, stroking her back and pressing gentle kisses to the side of her face. She sighed, content. "I was kind of looking forward to our day out." Malloy had fucked that up.

"Some quality time on the island will make up for it."

"You still want to leave tomorrow?"

"Yes, I do."

"Then I'd better get packing."

CHAPTER SIXTEEN

Sitting in the inflatable paddling pool, Asher again tried pouring water over his head with his plastic sieve. Once again, the water dripped through the holes of the sieve before he could get it near his head. "Ma!" he practically barked, frustrated.

Sprawled on her stomach on a sun lounger, Harper leaned over and handed him a fish-shaped tub. "Use that instead."

Asher took it, studied it carefully, and then tossed it aside in favor of the sieve.

Harper sighed, shaking her head. She wished there was some room in that inflatable pool for her, because she was *seriously* freaking hot. The heat was prickly and smothering, which was why they were sticking to the cabana on the deck that overlooked the rippling turquoise sea. The sand was simply too hot for him to play on this early in the day, but Asher was having an absolute ball in the paddling pool, stomping and splashing like he'd never seen water before.

"Ma!" he barked again, utterly exasperated, when he once more failed to drench his head in water.

"So use this." She held out the fish-shaped tub again. Asher began furiously shaking his head back and forth. Honestly, she didn't know how it didn't leave him dizzy. "You're just like your father—determined to do everything your way." Which just made her smile.

They had been at the island for a week now, relaxing, sunbathing, swimming, and even venturing out on Knox's new mini yacht. Asher loved it there. He'd also loved their time on the private jet. For the first ten minutes. Then he'd gotten bored of looking at clouds and simply played with the toys she'd brought in his bag.

He'd seriously enjoyed the mini trek through the jungle, though, as they'd walked from the jet to the villa. His beautiful dark eyes, sparkling with fascination, had drunk in the thick lush canopy, colorful birds, rough ropy vines, and meandering stream. Every sound had tugged at his attention—the calls of the birds, the trickle of the stream, the chirping of the crickets, and the distant hoots of the monkeys.

Harper had heard the occasional chuffing that made her think of a large cat. She also hadn't failed to miss the shadow in her peripheral vision, following and watching them. "I'm pretty sure we're being hunted by something," she'd said.

Knox had glanced at her over his shoulder and said, "It's just curious. A predator always senses other predators. It'll have more sense than to try to attack."

He'd been right, luckily. Nothing had followed them to the villa. Two-stories tall, the spacious building was all bright walls, high windows, and gleaming marble floors. It also had a private pool and was surrounded by palm trees and white sand. With the housekeeper and maintenance guy—both of whom were members of their lair and natives of the neighboring island—the place was always pristine and there was no need to cook. Knox would make a *mint* if he rented out the island, but he was much too territorial to share what was his.

Resting her crossed arms on the lounger, Harper propped her chin on her hands. Even with the jet skis thundering by—Tanner and Levi were currently racing, and neither appeared to be winning—she could hear the peaceful sounds of waves crashing into rocks and tumbling onto the shoreline. It was the first time in a while that she'd felt truly relaxed. Maybe that was because she also felt safe. Knox had been right—they needed this. And how could she not love having quality time with her guys?

Speaking of her guys … Knox was padding up the narrow wooden walkway that led from the villa's deck to the shoreline, bucket in hand. *Well, damn.* Little drops of water were sliding down all that hard muscle and sleek tanned skin, making her want to lick it all up. He was as mouth-watering and magnetic as he was intimidating.

It made her glad they were on a private beach, or there would be females ogling and batting their eyelashes at him. Then Harper would have to kick some skanky ass.

"Hey, baby." He bent and pressed a soft kiss to her mouth, tasting of salty water. Her body hummed, and her toes curled. The feel of his wet hand sweeping across her back felt *so* good on her heated skin.

A loud splash was followed by, "Da!"

Knox ended the kiss with a nip to her lower lip and then straightened to smile at Asher. "I got something for you." Squatting, he emptied the bucket of sea water into Asher's pool to top it up, and the little guy flashed his dimples. "I half expected him to climb out of the pool and crawl everywhere, looking for trouble," Knox said to her. "But he really does love the water. When the temperature cools, we'll take him to the shoreline, so he can paddle in the sea. You sure you don't want to take another dip? Tanner and Levi will watch him when they're done racing."

It was tempting to have a reprieve from the heat, but . . . "I'm not taking any chances with the jellyfish." No way.

Knox sighed. "There are no jellyfish."

"I saw it with my own eyes. It came right at me."

Fighting a smile, he slid onto the double-lounger and traced the length of her spine with his finger. "You need more sunscreen."

She snorted. "No, I don't." She was in the shade, for God's sake. "You just want to put some on me."

He gave her a very boyish smile. "Busted."

She chuckled and handed him the tub of lotion. "There. Have at it." He sprayed the lotion on her back and then rubbed it in, digging his fingertips into her skin just right. Closing her eyes, she moaned.

"You can't make that sound in public, baby," he admonished, voice dropping an octave. "You know what your little moans do to me."

She shot him a glare over her shoulder. "And you know just what *you're* doing to me right now." His smile said that, yes, he did. Maybe that bit of smugness should have annoyed her, but his self-assurance *totally* flipped her switch.

"When Asher has a little nap later, I'll show you what else I like doing to you."

"Promises, promises." Hearing jet skis whizz by, she looked up in time to see that . . . "Oh, Tanner's now winning." Though he and Levi had come along to the island, they were giving her, Knox, and Asher enough space to enjoy family quality time. Meanwhile, Larkin and Keenan were working with the Force to find where Alethea had been staying in North Las Vegas.

Before they left, Knox had made a short announcement throughout the Underground that Sherryl Malloy had been working with Alethea and, as such, was partly responsible for what almost happened to Asher and Heidi. His announcement had been accompanied by a short excerpt of Malloy's torture. According to Keenan, most had been as shocked as the Primes to realize what mercilessness lived inside Harper.

Jonas had called Knox after seeing the clip, insisting that Alethea would only have worked alongside the Horseman if she'd had no idea who he was. Jonas had also wanted to know what Malloy had had to say, but Knox hadn't told him any more than he'd told the other Primes over the video conference call.

Harper had worried that Ciaran might be hurt by Malloy's death, but he'd assured her that the only thing he felt about it was utter satisfaction. As far as he was concerned, if the female was truly the type to risk the safety of a child—*his own sister*—Malloy wasn't the person he thought he knew, and he couldn't grieve a person he'd never known.

Feeling Knox's hand slide into her bikini bottoms and massage the lotion into her skin, she said, "I really don't think my ass is at risk of getting sunburned."

"You know something, baby? This lotion would act as a really good lube."

Harper tensed. "Don't you dare try shoving your finger up—"

"I'd never do that in Asher's presence," said Knox, chuckling. "But later, when we're alone ..."

Rolling onto her side, she propped herself up on her elbow. "Want to know what I think?"

"Always."

"I think you've been far too preoccupied with my ass ever since your demon put the damn brand on it."

Knox smiled at her haughty tone. "Know what I think, baby?"

"What?"

"I think you like that brand far more than you're willing to admit."

"Why would I like having a 'K' on my ass?"

"I'm sure that, given your line of business, you've seen crazier tattoos than a simple initial on someone's ass." Which he didn't really want to think about, since he didn't like the idea of his mate looking at another guy's bare ass.

A slow smile spread across Harper's face. "A woman once came into our studio blitzed out of her mind, wanting a tattoo on her ass that said: 'Exit Only'. You should really think about that."

A cell began to chime. "That's yours," said Knox as he dug the phone out of the bag next to the lounger. The name he saw on the screen made his lips thin. "It's Lucian."

Taking it, she answered, "Hello?"

"Baby girl, why have you not called me?" Lucian whined.

She sighed. "I take it you got wind of all the trouble that's been going on."

"If you mean the incorporeal on your tail, yes, I did. Why didn't you call?"

Honestly, it hadn't occurred to her. It wasn't like he could help, and Lucian had never cared to receive "courtesy calls" in the past. Plus ... "Because then you might have come home, and I don't want to spend yet more time trying to stop you from tempting Knox to kill you."

"That psychopathic bastard—"

"Enough with the 'psychopathic'," she snapped.

"Fine." He sounded like a rebellious teenager. "Tell me how my grandson is."

Glancing at her son, a smile automatically curled Harper's lips. "He's currently having a grand time playing in an inflatable pool."

"Good, good. I'm coming for a visit in the next few weeks."

"Great," she said, though she wasn't convinced. He always *meant* to come, but he often got distracted by one thing or another.

"I'm going to take my baby girl and my grandson out for dinner." He gave a long-suffering sigh. "You can bring the psychopath if you must."

"*Lucian*."

"Just because he hasn't yet tried to kill you doesn't make me wrong."

"I'm hanging up." Because there was no reasoning with him—he was determined to hate Knox, probably due to the simple fact that her mate had once called Lucian on his poor idea of parenting.

"When you find yourself locked in a basement where you're routinely tortured for his own sick pleasure, you'll wish you'd listened to me."

"And I'm done." Ending the call, she groaned. Lucian was a trial at times.

Knox took the phone from her and returned it to the bag. "I've said it before, Harper, and I'll say it again: that demon is a waste of skin." His mate believed that by raising her to not need anyone, Lucian had been trying to ensure that she wouldn't be anything like him. Maybe that was true. Maybe it wasn't. But it didn't change that Lucian had let her down in a whole host of ways.

If Jolene was right, Lucian hadn't been *purely* selfish in dragging his daughter around the world—he'd actually thought it would be good for her to be exposed to different cultures and lifestyle and, in doing so, he'd shared with her the only thing other than Harper that brought him joy. Even if that were true, Knox didn't find it a justifiable excuse for Lucian's emotional neglect.

Before she could start jumping to her father's defense—something that would piss Knox off, since the bastard didn't deserve it—Knox said, "Thought you might want to know I had a call from Elena. McCauley's doing well." The annoyance on her face faded, just as he'd hoped.

"Really? Good." Little McCauley was a cambion who had been switched at birth with a human child by his late mother, a demon drug addict who'd been raped by a human. Oblivious to the switch, a human couple had taken him home and raised him, but they hadn't done a great job of it. As such, McCauley's inner demon had sort of stepped in and become the parent, which explained why the kid was robotic.

"It is indeed good," agreed Knox. "Especially since he helped us by telling you that Nora had taken me into a portal. I'll always be grateful for that even though he did it for a selfish reason." McCauley had wanted Harper's protection from Linda, a woman who had killed most of his maternal relatives and had also helped Nora in the hope that she'd get her hands on Asher. McCauley was now staying at a house with other demonic children who had no family to care for them.

"I think that—" Seeing a spark in her peripheral vision, Harper looked to see hellfire flaring in Asher's hand. It winked away fast. "Did you see that?" she asked Knox.

"I did."

Asher's little face scrunched up, and then hellfire once more flickered in his hand. It wasn't quite an orb. More like a spurt of fire. Again, it vanished quite quickly. He glanced at his hand curiously, and then his mind touched hers—there was a question there.

"I saw it, baby," Harper told him. "Here, play with this instead." She handed him his sieve and, *bam*, he was distracted. Which was good, because she'd rather he didn't set his pool on fire. "It wasn't an orb, but that's not to say he won't be able to shape the hellfire into a ball once he's had a little practice, right?"

Knox stroked her arm. "I know you think it a weakness that you can't conjure an orb of hellfire. Maybe it would be if you couldn't produce hellfire at all, but you can. I don't see your ability to only infuse it into objects as in any way a limitation. In fact, I'd say it's more destructive."

"Yeah, unless I need to throw a ball of hellfire. Then it's a problem." Glancing at Asher again, she asked Knox, "How old were you when your abilities first started to surface?"

"I'm not sure," said Knox. "I don't remember ever *not* having abilities. It wasn't a question I'd ever asked my parents. I remember being excited whenever a new ability surfaced. My parents would always panic, though, and urge me to hide them. They didn't want the other demons to know what we were." As an archdemon, Knox would never stop growing in power. That was one of the things that made his breed so dangerous.

People believed that what was born in hell should remain in hell. His breed tended to live in hordes deep within hell itself. Despite that the children were born from the flames, the adults all shared in the care of them. Some adults "adopted" children, treating them as their own, just as his parents had done.

"You said your horde separated when it came to Earth. What happened to the others?"

"Lou told me they'd returned to hell of their own accord well before the law had passed that archdemons were forbidden from leaving it." After a rogue archdemon once almost destroyed Earth, Lou agreed to keep the breed in hell. But since he hadn't agreed to round up any archdemons still roaming the Earth, he left Knox well alone. "People here don't exactly welcome our kind. No lairs would accept them. No one trusted them. They felt they had no place here."

"Why didn't you go back to hell after your parents died?" Harper asked.

"It would have felt too much like running. Hiding. Accepting defeat. That's not who I am."

"So . . . you're, like, the *only* archdemon on Earth?"

"Yes."

Her eyes clouded. "Must be lonely to be one of a kind. Cool too, in some ways. But mostly lonely."

"It never really affected me one way or the other. And how can I be lonely when I have you?" Cupping her nape, he took her mouth, keeping the kiss slow. Deep. Lazy. Indulging in a thorough taste of her that never failed to enliven him . . . so it was pretty annoying that they were disturbed by the laughter of the sentinels.

Knox looked to see them traipsing through the shallow part of the sea, heading for the shoreline. "Who won the race?" he called out.

Tanner snorted, as if offended by the question. "Me, of course. I wanted to—shit, jellyfish!"

Harper raised a brow at Knox. "What did I say?"

He just shook his head.

Digging her fingers into his shoulders, Harper did her best to keep her moans low as he ate at her pussy but, dammit, it was hard. God, he was ravenous as he licked, nipped, and savored. Every flick of his tongue to her clit made her wind that much tighter. Every light scrape of his teeth made her stomach clench. And when he began pumping his tongue inside her, stabbing and swirling, she felt herself start to fracture. He growled, the vibrations rumbled up her pussy, and then her release barreled into her, making her back bow and her fingers claw at the bedsheet.

Cock as hard as a steel spike, Knox kissed his way up her shuddering body. "Fucking love making you come, baby." He latched onto her nipple and suckled, plumping her other creamy breast with his hand. Her skin was soft as silk. He loved fucking her breasts, but not tonight. Tonight, he needed to be inside her.

As her lips parted and she went to argue, he took her mouth. Sank his tongue inside and glided it against her own.

Her fingers dug into his shoulders, and she arched into him with a throaty moan he felt all the way in his balls.

The moment his mouth had touched hers, her entire body just lit right up. No one had ever kissed her the way Knox did. He didn't just stroke her tongue with his. He licked at her teeth, nipped at the corners of her mouth, sucked on her bottom lip, rubbed the inside of her top lip. Devoured her until her brain was mush and her emotions were spinning.

The sexual aggression pouring off him made her pulse quicken, her nipples pebble, and her pussy clench. His cock, hard and long and thick ...

He pulled back, and she would have chased his mouth for more if it wasn't for the hand fisting her hair and holding her in place.

As she wrapped her limbs around him and arched her back to grind against his cock, Knox delivered a sharp tweak to her taut nipple. "Roll over."

She frowned. "Huh?"

"Roll over."

Knowing he just wanted to look at his brand while he fucked her, Harper almost rolled her eyes. "Will you just fuck me already?"

"I won't tell you a third time, baby."

"But I want—"

He slapped her clit. "Right now, this isn't about what *you* want. You're here to make me come. To satisfy me. Once you've done that, you'll get what you want."

Her mouth dropped open. "You mother—"

He gave her clit another slap. "Last chance to do as you're told, baby."

Grinding her teeth to hold in the stream of curses going through her head, Harper slowly rolled over.

He stroked over the brand on her ass. "There, that wasn't so hard, was it? Now arch your back. Push your ass in the air. Good girl." Knox lodged the head of his cock in her pussy, and they both sucked in a breath. She was so hot and tight and deliciously slick that he could have come right then. "All mine." He slammed home.

Harper's breath got caught in her throat as she found herself stuffed full of his long, hard cock. He felt almost impossibly thick as he stretched and filled her until it almost hurt. She could feel him throbbing inside her. What she needed was to feel him *coming* inside her.

His body folded over hers. "Feel good?"

She nodded, nipples tightening at the weight of his hard body and the graze of his teeth on her throat. She felt crowded. Unable to move. But she liked it.

Bunching her hair in his hand, Knox snatched her head back. She moaned, pussy contracting around him. A low growl rumbled in his chest. "Don't come."

Harper fisted the bedsheets as he pounded into her pussy, riding her so hard he took her breath away. All the while he grunted and whispered in her ear, telling her how good her pussy tasted, how he loved going down on her, how he loved that no one else would ever have her.

"You're close, aren't you?" he gritted out as her pussy tightened and fluttered around him. He slid his hand around her body and thumbed her clit.

Harper groaned. "Oh, God."

"Don't come yet."

Her eyes snapped open. "*What?*" He couldn't play with her clit and expect her not to come! But he did. He thumbed, circled, plucked, and rubbed at it until she wanted to cry. "You bastard!" She couldn't hold back. She just couldn't. She—

He pulled out.

Harper blinked. "What the—"

Knox flipped her onto her back, slid a hand under her ass, and tilted her hips just right. "Wrap me up tight, baby."

She locked her limbs around him, and then he was fucking in and out of her like he'd never get enough. She clawed at his back, relishing every hard slam of his cock, wanting more—always more. His teeth scraped over the hollow beneath her ear just as an icy-cold psychic finger stroked her clit just right.

"Come," Knox rumbled.

White-hot pleasure lashed through Harper like a whip of lightning as she came with a silent scream. He bit out a harsh curse against her neck as he hammered into her even harder, his pace *furious*, his cock filling her to bursting, making the headboard slam against the wall. She felt pure power gather in his muscles just before he jammed his cock deep and exploded inside her, his hot come splashing her quaking inner walls.

It could have been minutes or hours that they lay there, panting, shuddering. She didn't mind having him slumped over her. Liked that she could make him so sated he was reduced to a dead weight. "You bring real game to this sexual relationship," she slurred.

Shoulders shaking, he slid a hand under her back and then

rolled, taking her with him. "You've got enough 'game' of your own." Skimming his fingertips down her spine, he asked, "You okay?"

"Will be when I can feel my legs again. Playing with my clit and ordering me not to come was just plain mean."

"It made you come like a fucking freight train, though."

"I really wish I could argue that." He chuckled, but the sound cut off fast, making Harper frown. She felt the echo of his telepathic conversation. Felt as he began to tense beneath her. But she didn't speak until she was sure the conversation was over. "Who was it?"

"Keenan," replied Knox, expression grim. "They found where Alethea was staying."

Well, damn.

CHAPTER SEVENTEEN

Glancing around the living room, Harper raised her brows. "Even in this neighborhood, she couldn't resist having her comforts, could she?"

The little house was in the exact sad state that you'd expect to find any house in such a rough, poverty-stricken area. Yellowed wallpaper was peeling from the walls. Black splotches tarnished the ceilings. Cheap, grubby carpets boasted dubious looking stains.

The furniture, however, was another matter. Honest to God, they were something out of a freaking palace, especially the classic, imperial gold sofa, matching chairs, and piano. As she and Knox strode through the house, they saw that the rest of the furniture was just as luxurious—particularly in the bedroom, with its royal bed and old-fashioned vanity set.

The contrast was just plain weird.

Around them, the sentinels and a number of the Force were examining the two-story house, searching for anything that might have belonged to Alethea's ally and maybe help identify him. So far, they'd found nothing.

Taking a slow turn around the bedroom, Knox flicked her a brief look. "It surprises me that Alethea agreed to stay here, given how much of an elitist she was. The Horseman really did have her dancing to his tune." Halting, he turned as Tanner and Larkin entered the room. "Any scents?" Knox asked the hellhound.

Jaw hard, Tanner shook his head. "I can't even smell Alethea. This place has been 'wiped' clean somehow. It smells fresh as a fucking daisy. Like it was magickly cleansed."

"If someone had the house cleansed, it had to have been the Horseman," said Harper. "I mean, if Alethea had done it to cover her tracks before moving elsewhere, she'd have taken her stuff. Yet, all this furniture is here."

"And the fancy wardrobe and drawers are full of clothes and shoes," Larkin added. "Plus, the trinket box on the vanity is almost bulging with expensive jewelry. I can't imagine why she'd have left all this behind." The harpy sighed. "I've searched every drawer, shelf, cupboard, nook, and cranny. There isn't a single clue that could lead us to the Horseman."

"No, he's done a good job of ensuring there's no trace of him here," said Knox.

Tanner tipped his head to the side. "I wonder why he didn't remove *all* her stuff after her death."

"Maybe he figured the people here would steal it and, in doing so, do the job for him," suggested Larkin with a shrug.

Tanner pursed his lips. "Maybe."

"She must have had someone teleport it all here," said Harper. "If the locals saw this stuff being moved in here, she'd have been robbed within a week."

Knox nodded. "I was just thinking the very same thing."

"Knox!" Levi called out from downstairs. "You might want to come and take a look at this!"

Exchanging a look with Harper, Knox walked out of the room and then headed downstairs with his mate and the two sentinels behind him. He found Levi in the hallway, hanging out of a closet door. Crossing to the reaper, Knox realized that the closet led to a basement. "What is it?" Knox asked him.

"You need to see it for yourself," said Levi.

Following the reaper, Knox descended into the dark space. The wooden steps creaked beneath his feet, and the banister shook as Knox slid his hand down its surface. He glanced at Harper over his shoulder. "Watch the banister, baby. It isn't stable."

"Neither is this staircase," said Harper. The steps gave slightly, unable to fully support her weight. Stepping onto the cement floor, she frowned. No scents of must or mildew met her nose. It smelled just as fresh as the other floors, which meant that . . . "It's been cleansed."

"It has," Tanner confirmed as he and Larkin joined them. Keenan was already there, drinking from his flask as he searched the shadowy corners.

Harper moved to the center of the space and did a slow spin, canvasing her surroundings. It wasn't easy, since the single, bare bulb buzzed and flickered. But she could see that, like the rest of the house, there were damp spots and cracks in the floor and walls. There was nothing down there except for the furnace, water tank, breaker box, utility shelves, and stacks of dusty boxes, yet the space strangely didn't feel unused.

She flexed her fingers as unease weirdly slithered through her, making her stomach quiver and her scalp prickle. "I don't like it here. At all."

"Me neither," said Larkin.

"Do you feel it?" Levi asked Knox.

Gazing at a particular wall, Knox nodded. "There's a ... wrongness. Like something is out of place. Or as if we simply can't see the space as it should be." He stepped forward and laid his hand on the cold wall, "feeling" magickal energy, "reading" it. "Someone cast some sort of concealment spell."

Harper's brows shot up. "Concealment spell?"

"Yes," said Knox, backing up. "We'll need an incantor to unravel it."

Harper looked at Levi. "Your friend's an incantor, right?"

"I'll call her," said Levi, digging out his cell phone before heading upstairs to make the call.

Knox turned to Harper. "While we wait for her to arrive, we can interview the human outside."

It was Khloë who had found someone that recognized Alethea's picture. Harper had asked her to stay with the human to make sure he didn't disappear. She'd also asked Khloë not to fully question him as Harper and Knox wanted to do that themselves.

Following Knox out of the house, she saw Khloë across the street, standing beside a dark-skinned kid who was straddling a bike. Spotting Knox, his brown eyes flickered nervously. The kid might not know that Knox was a demon, but he could still sense the danger in him.

Harper exchanged a quick, grateful smile with Khloë and then slid her gaze to the boy. "It's Isaiah, right?" Khloë had told her a little about him.

He nodded curtly, trying to look tough. "Yeah."

"I'm Harper. This is my husband, Knox."

The kid tipped his chin in a "Sup?" gesture. He was cute with his small afro and the shaved lines at the sides of his head, Harper thought. There was also a badass swagger in his manner that most of the kids in that area had.

"Khloë tells us that you recognize the woman in the picture she's been showing around," said Knox.

Isaiah shrugged. "I saw her in the doorway of that house a few times. Never saw her leave, though."

"Did she ever have visitors?" Knox asked.

"Dude, she had a *lot* of visitors. Only saw one person go there more than once, though. A guy. Most of the time, he'd take someone with him. Weird thing was he always left them behind. I figured he was her pimp or dealer or something."

Knox narrowed his eyes. "Can you describe him?"

Isaiah's brow wrinkled. "He only came at night. He was tall. Walked like he could handle himself, but he wasn't built. Wore a long coat."

"What color?"

"Dark. Not black, but dark."

Perhaps navy blue like the cashmere coat that Sherryl had described, Knox thought. "Did you ever hear him speak?"

"The walls of these houses are thin as fuck, but I didn't hear a damn thing come from inside that place."

"Hmm." Knox had to wonder if a spell had also been cast to contain sounds. "Anything about him ever catch your attention?"

"Him? No. I paid more attention to his ride than him." Isaiah's mouth curved. "The dude had a sweet ride. Aston Martin."

Khloë snorted. "I'm surprised no one tried *borrowing* it."

Isaiah's gaze cut to her. "Probably would have done if he hadn't always had his dog with him. Big fucking brute of a dog. He'd leave it in the yard, and it would lie next to the car. Didn't move an inch until the dude came back out."

Knox tilted his head. "Can you describe the dog?"

"Like I said, it was big," said Isaiah. "It had black shaggy hair. Always looked wet."

Probably a black shuck, Harper told Knox, referring to shape-shifting demons that were considered death omens by humans.

Sounds like it, agreed Knox. "Did you recognize any of the people that entered the house, Isaiah?"

"Some. A couple of them were meth addicts. That's why I figured that dude was a dealer or pimp." He flexed his grip on the bike's handlebars. "Our local dealer confronted him; didn't want anyone else selling shit on his turf. The dude said he was no dealer."

Knox tensed briefly. "Where can we find this dealer?"

"Graveyard. He was shot dead sometime after that." Isaiah's gaze sharpened. "You think that guy had something to do with it?"

"It's unlikely," lied Knox. The Horseman wouldn't have wanted there to be someone who could describe him to anyone who came asking questions. "When was the last time you saw him?"

"Months ago. Haven't seen anything of the woman in a while either. But I don't *watch* the place, so I can't be sure when anyone was last there. Can I go now?"

"Yes. Thank you for talking with us, Isaiah." He handed the kid some cash, who nodded in thanks and then disappeared on his bike.

Cupping Harper's elbow, Knox led her across the road to where the four sentinels waited. He quickly brought them up to speed, adding, "We now know our suspect drives an Aston Martin and has a black shuck working for him."

Tanner's brow furrowed. "I'm pretty sure one of Dario's sentinels can shape-shift. He could be a shuck."

"Look into it. We also need to find out if any of our suspects own an Aston Martin." Knox looked at Harper's cousin. "Your help was appreciated, Khloë."

Doing a long, languid stretch, Khloë yawned loudly. "No problem."

Harper's mouth quirked. "Tired?"

Khloë's shoulders slumped. "Haven't slept in, like, a week. I was too determined to find someone that could lead me to Alethea. And I did. Am I *the shit*, or what?"

Deciding not to tell her cousin that she *looked* like shit, Harper gently squeezed her arm. "Yes, you are indeed *the shit*. I'm totally in your debt. Now go home. You need sleep." Although demons could go days without it, it wasn't good for them.

"You don't need to tell me twice."

"Want a ride back? Tanner won't mind."

Nose wrinkling, Khloë began to back up. "Nah, I'm good."

Keenan sighed at the imp. "Should you be out alone?" he snarked.

Khloë blinked up at him, as if she'd only just noticed he was there, but Harper knew that wasn't the case. Khloë was aware of everything. "Why wouldn't I be?" she asked.

His mouth tightened. "Because you attract trouble like it's your job."

"And you drink Everclear like it's your job," Khloë shot back. "Do you hear me commenting on it?"

"You just did."

"Only to make a point."

"My point carries more weight."

"Probably not as much weight as your monster cock."

"*Khloë!*" Harper exclaimed.

She turned to Harper, eyes widening in innocence. "It's not like he doesn't know. He sees it every day. I'm sure there have been many times when he's jerked himself—"

"*Khloë!*" Seriously, Harper was going to kill her one day.

"Fine, fine. I'll call you tomorrow." She spun on her heel and walked off, whistling a merry tune.

Keenan turned to Harper. "Are you really going to let her walk home alone?"

"Let?" Harper frowned at him. "Do you not know Khloë at all?" There was no forcing her cousin to do anything she didn't want to do.

Keenan sighed again. "I'll be back in ten minutes." With that, he jogged to his car.

Sidling up to Harper, Larkin leaned into her. "Do you think she'll agree to let him give her a ride?"

"It'll give her the chance to torment him some more, so, yeah." Harper twisted her mouth. "Think he'll ever ask her out?"

Larkin bit her lip. "That will depend."

"Yeah? On what?"

"On whether he can get over his little issue."

Before Harper could ask what that meant, her attention was snagged by the white Toyota Prius that pulled up. Moments later, a willowy, leggy female hopped out. Her rich ruby red hair was tied back in a chic, hobo knot that was dotted with flowers—Harper seriously liked it. Inky blue eyes swept over them, stopping as they found Levi. She made a beeline for him.

Harper gave Knox a sideways glance. "I take it this is the incantor." He only nodded.

As she came to a stop in front of them, Levi inclined his head. "Thanks for coming, Ella. I'm sure I don't have to introduce my Primes, though I don't think you've ever officially met them."

"No, I haven't," confirmed Ella. She nodded respectfully at Harper and Knox. "It's nice to meet you both."

Harper smiled. "Likewise. This is Larkin, one of our sentinels." After the two females exchanged nods, Harper added, "I know Levi's consulted you many times in the past when we've had magickal trouble, so I just want to say thank you for all your help."

"No thanks needed." Ella looked at the house. "Levi tells me someone cast cleansing spells and possibly even a concealment spell here."

"We don't know whether it was an incantor or a dark practitioner," said Knox. "Will you be able to unravel the spells either way?"

"I won't be able to unravel a cleansing spell—they sort of bleach the air," replied Ella. "There's no way of undoing that. As for the containment spell? It's possible that I'll be able to untangle the threads. It won't matter if it was an incantor or a dark practitioner; it will only depend on the complexity of the spell."

"Then let's go see how complex it is." Knox took Harper's hand as they all walked back into the house and then down to the basement. He watched as Ella strode straight to the wall where he'd earlier sensed the spell, as if she was drawn there. Her fingers moved along the wall, looking as if they were plucking at strings.

Finally, she turned to them. "You're right; there's a containment spell here. It was cast by a dark practitioner. A very talented one." She skimmed her fingers over the wall, brow furrowing. "It's not a typical enchantment."

"In what sense?" asked Knox.

Her gaze cut to him. "It was boosted by another spell, so the two are tied together."

Knox frowned. "What other spell?"

"Glamor. What you see there isn't real. The wall is fake. I can still untangle the threads of the incantations, but it may take some time."

"We can wait," said Knox.

"All right. I'll get started."

Harper wasn't really sure what she'd expected Ella to do, but there was no lighting of candles, no drawing of symbols, no calling on the natural elements. She simply stood there, plucking, snapping, untying, twisting, and unknotting "threads" that they weren't able to see. This was the difference between incantors and practitioners. The latter were able to *practice* magick, but incantors were born to use it. The magick was part of them.

While they waited for Ella to finish, Larkin updated Harper and Knox on everything they'd missed during their vacation— sometimes telepathically, since speaking of lair business around outsiders simply wasn't done, even if said outsider was untangling spells for them.

Keenan reappeared, exasperation lined into his face, and announced to Harper that her cousin badly needed a keeper. When Harper had asked if he was volunteering for the job, he'd flushed and adamantly stated, "*Hell, no.*" And he'd been a little *too* adamant. Harper had to wonder why the guy preferred to live in the land of denial. She was just about to telepathically ask Larkin what Keenan's "little issue" was when Ella spoke.

"I have one last thread to snap. Everyone needs to back up."

With the exception of Ella, they all moved to the center of the basement. Satisfied, she then turned back to the wall and tugged sharply on an invisible thread. Just like that, the fake wall disappeared, revealing a space that was roughly thirty-five square feet . . . that featured a small bare, iron prison cell. Taking up so little room, it was no more than a cage, really. Manacles hung from its walls. Blood and other bodily fluids stained its floor. Misery, despair, and pain seemed to hover in the air.

"Jesus," breathed Levi. "A lot of people died here. And they're severely pissed about it."

Harper's eyes shot to him. "Their souls are still here? They're talking to you?"

"Not in the way that you think," said Levi. "I don't hear full sentences. Just snatches of what they want to say. Someone brought them here—someone who promised them drugs and sex. But they were chained. Starved. Brutalized."

"They were brought here to feed the incorporeal," Knox realized. "Maybe Alethea and the Horseman thought that putting the hosts through pain would somehow make the incorporeal strengthen quicker—maybe it did." Or maybe the fuckers had done it for the sheer pleasure of it, he thought. Alethea had always had a mean streak.

Harper rubbed at her nape. "When Isaiah said that people were brought here but he never saw them leave, I had a feeling they were for the incorporeal. It makes sense that Alethea and the Horseman would choose rough areas as their hunting grounds. There are so many drug addicts, prostitutes, and other people who wouldn't be missed."

"So, basically, Alethea holed up here while she pretty much nursed the incorporeal back to full strength." Larkin bit the inside of her cheek. "Maybe *she* was also killed here. We speculated that she might have died in a basement."

"If she did, her soul isn't here," said Levi.

Keenan frowned. "Why didn't the practitioner cleanse the area? Why conceal it instead?"

"No amount of cleansing could completely wipe away so much violence and pain," said Ella. "The containment spell kept everything in that little area from reaching your senses. The glamor helped reinforce the illusion. They were strong spells. The practitioner was talented."

"But you're better," said Harper with a smile that Ella returned.

"I'm better," agreed Ella.

Tanner stalked over to the prison door, nostrils flaring. "None of the blood in there belonged to anyone we know." Moving away from the prison, he patrolled the area around it that had also been concealed by the spell. And then he tensed, cursing a blue streak.

"What is it?" asked Knox, voice sharp. "What do you scent?"

Tanner turned to face them. "I can smell Alethea here plain as fucking day."

"It's hardly surprising, since she was the one nursing the incorporeal," said Knox.

Tanner gave a curt nod. "Yeah, but it's not just *her* I smell. Someone else we know was here—their blood isn't here, just their scent. And the scent isn't heavy with pain or death. They weren't a victim. They were *with* her."

Knox took a step toward him. "Who?"

CHAPTER EIGHTEEN

Back at the villa, Harper slapped her clothes into the suitcase. "I won't believe it's him, Knox," she clipped. "I will not believe he's the Horseman. How could he be? He's been in Cuba for fucking *years*."

"Or so we thought," said Knox, voice soft. He stood a few feet away, giving her space, letting her reason it through. If he was honest, he was just as surprised as Harper to hear that Drew's scent was in the basement, so he couldn't blame her for finding it so difficult to absorb. Knox didn't like the hellcat whatsoever, but he wouldn't have suspected him of being the Horseman or party to anything that would harm Harper.

"What possible motivation could Drew have for wanting to see the US Primes fall?" she challenged.

"He wants me dead, Harper. In his mind, I stole you from him."

"Yes, and you know that because you've literally been in his mind. If he was the Horseman, you'd already know."

"That's not how it works, Harper. The mind is a vast space.

Trillions of webs of memories, thoughts, views, wants, likes, dislikes, regrets, goals, et cetera. I didn't root through his mind as a whole, I only explored the web of thoughts and memories he had that were related to you. Still, I'd like to think that I'd have seen *some* indication of him being the Horseman if he truly was."

"But you didn't, did you?"

"No, but why else would he have been with Alethea? What other reason could he have had for being in that house? He wasn't killed there, Harper. He wasn't used to feed the incorporeal. Either he was working with her, or he had some other reason for going to that house. Whatever the case, *he was with her.* I picked up how badly he wants me dead—"

"It's one thing to want to see *you* dead. But why take all the other Primes down too?"

"I don't know. Maybe he's bitter that Jolene wouldn't make him Prime—I called her a few minutes ago; she said he told her long ago that he wanted to take her place one day, and he'd seemed upset when she made it clear that she wanted *you* to replace her."

It had made Knox wonder if just maybe that was part of why Drew had wanted Harper for himself so badly—as her mate, he would have then also been her co-Prime if she'd taken Jolene's place. It could even be that the reason he'd waited to claim Harper was that he'd been waiting for her to be declared Prime first. But Knox decided not to say that, since she was hurting enough.

Shooting him a look of impatience, she snorted. "Knox, practically all demons want to be a Prime. We're typically power-hungry creatures."

"I'm simply saying that maybe we failed to see that Drew is as power-hungry as Isla, Nora, and Roan were."

Harper jutted out her chin. "I won't believe it."

"You don't *want* to believe it," he corrected.

"No, I don't." Because it would *kill* Devon, and Harper didn't want to see her friend hurt. Regardless, it just seemed *wrong* to her. It didn't add up. "You have to admit there are some holes in this theory. Did Drew ever seem power-hungry to you?" Harper had never sensed that quality in him.

"No, but Tanner scented him in that basement, baby. Why else would he have been there?"

"I don't fucking know." Slamming the suitcase shut, she sharply yanked on the zip as she secured it shut. "But I just can't accept that Drew is the freaking Horseman. I can't."

Knox crossed to her and rested his hands on her shoulders. "There are a lot of people trying to track Drew right now. He can't hide for long. We'll find him, and we'll get our answers. For now, we have to operate on the assumption that he was—at the very least—involved with Alethea somehow."

Sighing, Harper raked a hand through her hair. "I only just got Devon back, Knox," she said, voice small. "If you're right, the whole thing will shred her, especially if we have to kill him."

"I know. I wish that wasn't the case." Killing Drew wouldn't bother Knox, but causing a divide between Harper and her friend would. Still, there was no way he would—or even could— let the male live if he was the Horseman. Deciding to change the subject, he asked, "You packed?" At her nod, he gave her shoulders a little squeeze and pressed a soft kiss to her mouth. "Good. The jet's ready. Let's go get Asher."

Minutes later, they were walking to the clearing where the private jet waited. Levi led the way, using a machete to clear a path through the thick vegetation. The pilot, Davis, and his mate, Noelle—who was also the flight attendant—were already there. The sentinels got settled in the front cabin while Knox, Harper, and Asher seated themselves in the rear cabin for some privacy.

She sat Asher on her lap, who was busy poking Hound's eyes. God, she hated that she was taking him back to a place where danger awaited him. She'd considered leaving him on the island with Tanner, but she couldn't. Maybe it was selfish, but she wouldn't cope with having so much distance between them. She also couldn't bring herself to leave Knox to deal with the Horseman situation alone, even though he was fully capable of doing so. They were a team, and that need to be proactive in eliminating the threat to her son wouldn't be satisfied with leaving it to Knox. No way.

Before the jet took off, Noelle came to offer drinks and snacks. Knox ordered a gin and tonic, but Harper declined—her churning stomach wouldn't handle food or drink very well. Soon enough, they were in the sky.

Sitting opposite her, his thighs bracketing hers, Knox squeezed her knee. "It'll be okay, baby."

She kissed Asher's head, inhaling his scent. "No, I don't think it will." Because there was a very good chance that Drew was going to die. "If we kill him, it will always sit smack bam between me and Devon, no matter how justified the kill is."

"Which is why I'll be the one to kill him, if it needs to be done. I'm fine with Devon hating me, but not with her hating you. Have you spoken with her about his scent being present at the house?"

"Not yet." But she suspected that Jolene, as Devon's Prime, might have already done so—her grandmother wouldn't want the female hellcat to find out from someone else.

"You don't want to speak with her about it because you're still searching for a reason that might excuse why he was there—something innocent," Knox gently accused.

"Is that so wrong?"

"No, but perhaps you should consider that the Drew you

thought you knew doesn't truly exist. Or maybe he did once exist but has long since changed. You're right that some things don't make sense, but that's only because you have a certain impression of him in your head. Plenty of people wear masks, baby."

Harper felt her brow furrow. "Yes, but Devon would have seen right through it."

"Are you sure? She rarely sees him these days. He's been gone six years now, and she wasn't frequently in contact with him. People change—sometimes for the better, sometimes for the worse. Drew likes a rush. What better rush than to be a Prime? And how much bigger would that rush be if you got the position by dominating the other Primes, making yourself the only ruler?"

Closing her eyes for a moment, she rubbed her forehead. "Okay, it would be a huge rush, but it doesn't automatically follow that you're right."

Knox took a sip of his drink. "Would the Drew you thought you knew have been so disobedient? Several times he's ignored warnings from Jolene. He's even lied to her. She was under the impression that he was in Cuba right now. She escorted him to the airport herself a few weeks ago—even walked him to the departure gate and watched the plane take off. He either got off the aircraft somehow before it left, or he took a flight back to Las Vegas."

Harper thought on that for a moment. "He's never been rebellious, no. He always seemed to respect her authority."

"His recent actions would suggest otherwise, baby."

She scrubbed a hand down her face. "It doesn't even make sense that he'd work with Alethea. You've been in his head; you say he wants me. Why would he have ever worked with someone who would have *loved* to see me dead?"

"I don't believe he was working *with* her, I believe he was *using* her. We agreed that the Horseman probably lied to Alethea about his plans. Maybe Drew told her that he wanted you dead. That would have gained him her cooperation. In using her, he also kept her away from you."

"What about Heidi, Knox? The Horseman arranged to have her kidnapped so that she could be used in a damn ritual. No matter how much Drew wants to be a Prime, he would *never* hurt Heidi. I firmly believe that."

"So maybe, unknown to him, it was Alethea who chose Heidi. Maybe the reason that there wasn't another attempt to snatch her was that he disapproved of Alethea's choice. But don't be so sure he wouldn't harm Heidi. You said Drew was a decent person who would never try to break up a family, but he did. He tried to turn you against me. Tried to convince you to leave me. And he spoke of our son as if Asher were a thing, not a person. Does that really sound like the Drew you thought you knew?"

She swallowed. "No. No, it doesn't. I just wish that—" The jet jerked to the side, struck by something hard. "What the—?" She cuddled Asher tight, eyes wide, mentally fumbling as the jet shook. Swayed. Tipped to the side. And then they were falling.

Jaw hard, Knox let out a wave of raw power that punched a hole through the jet. "I'll get the others. *Go!*"

Harper called to her wings, tightened her arms around an alarmed Asher and—hating that she had to leave Knox behind but trusting him to get himself to safety—shot out of the aircraft like a bullet out of a gun. The air whipped at her hair and face, almost taking her breath away. They were above an island that neighbored theirs, she realized, and—

Something slammed into her wing, sending her dipping into the trees. Her wing got caught on a branch, yanking her backwards so sharply that it felt like someone was trying to *pluck* the wing stem right out of her back. Grinding her teeth through the blinding pain, she wrenched free, wincing as the branch tore a long, wide strip through her wing.

Panicked, Harper flexed her back muscles hard. Yet more pain assaulted the stem, and her injured wing failed her. *Knox, we're going down!* All she could do was helplessly and shakily glide her way down, navigating her way through the tight clusters of trees.

As they neared the ground, she curled herself even tighter around Asher and snapped her wings around them to cushion their fall. It helped, but her head still connected hard with the spongy moss ground. Stars burst behind her eyelids and fiery pain knifed through the stem of her injured wing, making the breath explode out of her lungs.

She heard a sob build in Asher's chest, but the sound seemed so very far away. "Shh, baby," she whispered, voice lacking in strength, head spinning. "We're fine. Let me get a good look at you." But even as she said it, she could do no more than loosen her hold on him before the darkness pulled at her. She fought it, she really did, she fought it so fucking hard ... but it was mere moments before it swallowed her whole.

Knox felt it the moment that Harper lost consciousness—his own vision darkened around the edges, making him almost lose his footing on the moss-covered earth. His heart leaped, and his ribs suddenly felt too tight as panic tore through him.

Baby, don't fucking do this to me. Wake the fuck up. He had no chance of sounding gentle when a soul-wrenching terror was strangling him with a vice-like grip.

Pulse racing, Knox touched Asher's mind and felt vibes of fear, confusion, and shock. But no pain, to his utter relief. That didn't calm Knox's demon—the entity was going fucking insane.

Knox soothingly brushed his mind over Asher's, trying to ease his anxiety. *It's okay, I'll find you*, he said, hoping the reassurance in his tone would somehow comfort his son.

Asher's mind slid against his own, cold and composed, and he knew it wasn't Asher responding to him. It was his son's inner demon, giving him the "impression" that it would keep Asher safe. That would have to be enough for now.

Knox scanned the area, as if he'd miraculously see some sign of Harper and Asher. He didn't. Hell, they could have been twelve feet away and he probably wouldn't have noticed, since the undergrowth was so dense. Ropy vines curled around thick tree trunks and draped over branches that boasted long-ass leaves. If he'd thought it would help, he'd fly over the island in search of them, but the canopies were too thick—he could easily skim right over Harper and Asher without knowing it.

He'd managed to pyroport the sentinels, Davis, and Noelle to the ground before the jet crashed somewhere in the distance, but they had no fucking idea where they were. None. Worse, he had no fucking idea where his mate and son were. *Baby, wake up and tell me where you are.* Nothing. Not a fucking thing.

"Harper's unconscious," Knox told the others, voice thick, stomach rock hard. He wouldn't be surprised to hear that his eyes looked as feverish with rage as he suspected.

"Shit," cursed Levi, sidestepping a spiky pineapple bush as he sidled up to Knox, fists clenched. "Asher?"

"He seems to be okay." But while Harper was unconscious, Asher was extremely vulnerable. As if the heat, insects, and wild animals weren't enough of a problem, there was the added danger of the Horseman. Who else would have taken out the jet? "We have to find them." Even he heard the fear in his voice—the emotion left a metallic taste on his tongue.

Tanner's nostrils flared as he drew in the scents around them.

"They're not close, but that doesn't mean they're at the other end of the island or anything. We will find them, Knox."

Oh, they'd find them. What worried Knox was that the Horseman might find them first. The very idea of it made his chest tighten unbearably, taking his breath away. "But we don't know which direction to head in, do we? Until we have even a hint of an idea where they landed, we don't know where to start." *Harper, fucking answer me!*

"Am I the only one thinking that the Horseman was responsible for the jet crashing?" asked Davis, taking his mate's hand in his.

"It had to have been him," said Knox. "He wasn't able to get on my island—it's too well-protected—but he knew what direction we'd take to get home, so he waited." If Knox hadn't erased the memory of himself using his ability to pyroport from Drew's mind, leaving the hellcat clueless to it, Drew probably would have taken another course of action.

Noelle flicked a frown at the giant termite nest a few feet away. "Do you think he thought the crash would be enough to kill us?"

"I doubt it." Levi used the bottom of his tee to wipe at the sweat on his forehead. The air was hot, thick, and heavy. "But I think he thought it would badly injure and weaken Knox."

"Can't Harper fly above the canopies when she wakes?" Noelle asked Knox. "You'd easily spot her if you then did the same."

Knox shook his head. "He hurt her. Damaged either one or both of her wings bad enough to make her fall." And the fact that she couldn't fly her way out of danger made it even more important that Knox find her and Asher *fast*.

Tanner rubbed at his nape. "I have to say, I can't imagine Drew harming her. Unless he's given up on winning her to his side. Some people have that whole 'If I can't have you, no one will' mentality."

Harper, baby, I need you to wake up. When she didn't answer, Knox growled and kicked aside one of the pieces of overripe fruit that littered the ground. "Whoever the Horseman is, he's somewhere on this island. Where, I don't know. But my guess is that he'll be intent on tracking Harper and Asher, just like we are."

Levi nodded, jaw hard. "They're your only vulnerabilities. Moreover, they're your demon's only vulnerabilities."

The reaper had that right. It was taking every inch of control Knox possessed to keep his demon in check. The entity wanted to hunt and annihilate the person who it knew was daring to hunt its mate and child.

It was filling Knox's mind with images of them hurt and in pain, trying to goad Knox into surrendering control. But he didn't. Even though he felt close to drowning in a soul-eating rage, he maintained control. Because the demon wouldn't think. Wouldn't wait for Harper to wake and give them some clue as to where she was. It would only do what it had been born to do—destroy.

"I don't think he'll hurt them, Knox," said Tanner. "At least not until you're there to watch."

That didn't make Knox feel much better. He again touched Asher's mind. The vibes of fear had eased, which told Knox that it was highly unlikely they'd been found.

It galled him that he couldn't get moving—he needed to act, but they needed some idea of what direction they should move in first. That left him feeling both helpless and fucking useless.

Harper, wake up, baby. Harper? Harper, WAKE THE FUCK UP!

Harper's eyes snapped open as the telepathic shout seemed to rattle her brain, making her wince. She blinked rapidly, struggling to bring her surroundings into focus, groaning at the throbbing pain in her head. The smudge in her vision cleared, and she saw Asher sitting on the ground a few feet away, babbling to himself while shaking Hound, like he was playing on the rug at home. But they weren't at home. They were ... in a rainforest? What the hell—

The jet went down.

Her heart leaped in horror, slamming against her ribs, as memories flickered through her mind. The distance between her and Asher suddenly felt like miles. Fuck, fuck, fuck.

She tried bolting upright. And she instantly regretted it as pain exploded in her skull, streaked down her back, and lanced through her left wing-stem. The shock of the white-hot pain made her muscles lock tight. *Motherfucker*. She clenched her teeth, but a long hiss escaped. The sound caught Asher's attention.

He looked at her and—unbelievably—a smile creased his face. There were dried tears on his cheeks, but he didn't appear to be in any pain. In fact, there didn't seem to be even a scratch on him, thank God. Her body and wings had protected him.

A growl rumbled out of Knox. *Harper, you need to—*

I'm awake, I'm awake, she assured him. A vibe of relief reverberated against her mind.

How long had she been out? Looking up, she saw snatches of sunlight through the thick, lush canopy. The sky hadn't darkened. The fact that her wings hadn't melted into her back suggested that she hadn't been unconscious long.

Where are you, baby? Knox asked, urgency in every syllable. *I need to know where you are.*

Give me a sec, I can't see shit from the floor. Moving slowly, she plastered her hands onto the damp, slick moss beneath her and pushed herself onto her hands and knees. Wooziness hit hard, and her head swam. "I will *not* pass out again," she said through her teeth. "I will *not*." Because then her baby would be vulnerable.

Breathing through the wave of dizziness that had rushed over her, Harper took stock of herself. Nothing was broken. But she had a few aches here and there, and she could feel little licks of fire on her skin. She suspected she was covered in cuts and scratches.

Standing, Harper glanced back at her wings. She winced. One had a long tear running through it, like it had been raked by the claw of a big jungle cat. It was also numb, so the stem must have taken a hard hit. Her demon bared her teeth, *beyond* pissed and raring to hunt the fucker responsible.

Where are you? Knox demanded. *Tanner will track you, but we could do with a little help here.*

If she'd been able to throw fireballs, she would have launched one in the air like a flare. Taking a tentative step toward Asher, she glanced around them. There were no landmarks. Only thick trees, ropy vines, thorny plants, hanging moss, and gleaming leaves of all shapes and sizes. Green, green, and more fucking green.

Beneath the birds calls and the crickets chirping was … *Waterfall. I can hear a waterfall close by. And monkeys shrieking.* Damn, she hated monkeys.

Tanner says he can hear a waterfall in the distance, along with some monkeys fighting. Stay where you are. We'll track you. There's no sense in me doing a flyover to search for you. The foliage is too thick and heavy.

We won't move, she promised him, swiping her hands together, trying to dust the grit from her fingers.

Tell me you and Asher are okay, Knox urged.

We're okay. Sort of. The biggest issue was that her wing was fucked, preventing her from flying her and Asher to safety. Thankfully, though, he seemed to be fine.

Who the fuck had shot them down? *That* she'd really like to know. She had the feeling she'd find out soon enough. It was highly likely that they'd search for her. Her hope was that Knox found her first.

Head still pounding, she made her way to Asher—well, staggered her way to him. The spongy moss didn't help her balance at all. With a single thought, she made her wings melt into her back until they were once again tattoos. It hurt like a bitch, since the stem was damaged.

Crouching down, she kissed Asher's head, wishing she could pick him up and hold him tight but not trusting herself not to fall just yet. "Sorry I passed out, sweetie. Thank God you're okay."

Smiling, Asher reached out and made a grab for her nose. Taking his hand, she pressed a kiss to his little palm. "Daddy's coming soon. Daddy and Tanner and Levi. We're going to be fine." She skimmed her knuckles down his hot cheek, wishing they had water. Mouth dry and sticky, she licked her lips, tasting salty sweat. Swallowing was almost painful as the air was just so thick on her tongue—

A twig snapped.

She froze, attention sharpening. Her eyes narrowed as a large black cat prowled out from behind a huge tree on Asher's far right-hand side. Heart pounding in her chest like a drumbeat, she shot to her feet and—ignoring the explosion of pain in her head—rushed to block the animal's path, having *no* intention whatsoever of letting it get to Asher.

As it neared them, she realized it was no jungle cat. No, it was a hellcat. One she *knew*. Betrayal curdled her stomach, and Harper snarled at Drew's demon as a red haze fell over her vision. "You son of a bitch."

It curled back its upper lip—the act almost seemed like a taunt.

Before she even thought about it, she was stalking toward the bastard, fingers tingling with the protective power that had rushed from her belly to her fingertips. While her blood roared in her ears, it was a wonder that she heard leaves rustling behind her . . . but she did.

Twisting, she saw a big black fucking shuck standing in front of Asher. Dread and realization crashed into her, making the blood drain from her face. Oh, God, Drew had *baited* her. Lured her away from Asher. And she'd *fallen* for it. Mouth dry, pulse racing, she could only stare as the shuck snarled and snapped its teeth at her little boy.

Her demon hissed, wanting to lunge at the shuck but anxious that it would react by attacking Asher . . . which the shuck was no doubt counting on.

"You tracked them," said a male voice. "Well done."

Her head whipped to the side as two men slowly came into view, halting a good ten feet away from Asher. Every muscle in her body tensed. One of the males was short, gray-haired, and completely unfamiliar. As for the other one . . . that was another matter. A matter that made her blood boil and her mouth drop open in utter shock.

It couldn't be him. Really. It just couldn't be him. Because if it was, it would mean he'd fooled them all. *Played* them all. Because even though she'd learned from Knox that the guy had in fact smoked on occasion, and even though she recalled once hearing how much the asshole enjoyed attending Vegas shows—which would have made him a likely purchaser of Cirque du Soleil tickets—she just wouldn't have imagined that he'd *truly* kill his own sister, especially in such a gruesome way.

Suddenly, it was too quiet. No bird calls, no crickets chirping, no droning of mosquitos. Only the distant roar of the waterfall.

Jonas flashed her a grin. "Evening, Harper. You're looking a little worse for wear." He gave Asher that same smile, but her son was too busy staring at the shuck. Not in fear, though. No, Asher looked utterly fascinated by it.

The sight of him sitting there, vulnerable and alone, made her want to cry. Shame curdled in her stomach. She was such a fucking idiot. How could she let herself be baited that way? How could she be *that* fucking stupid?

She had to get to Asher. *Had* to. Although she couldn't cover six feet in one lunge, she could certainly get to Asher a lot fucking quicker than Jonas could. Sadly, the shuck would get there first. Plus, the hellcat—who was now standing a few feet behind Asher—would probably rush to block her path anyway.

Godfuckingdammit. Knox, Drew's here. But he's not the Horseman. It's fucking Jonas.

And she needed to get the bastard away from her son. Needed to think. Plan. Act.

She needed the flames of fucking hell, *that* was what she needed.

Jonas? Knox echoed, his voice a guttural growl.

Yes. Which still boggled her mind. *But I can't fry the fucker. Asher doesn't have his shield up, even though he has a black shuck in front of him and a hellcat behind him. Also, Jonas has some guy with him. If I call on the flames to burn one of them . . .*

The others could attack Asher before you get the chance to direct the flames their way. Knox bit out a harsh expletive. *Keep them distracted as best you can, baby. I'll be there soon.*

"Asher, put your shield up, sweetie." Harper knew he wouldn't understand the words, but she hoped he might respond to the urgency in her voice. He didn't. Instead, he beamed at the shuck and waved, apparently unfazed by its snarls. Yes, he *waved*.

She just hoped to God that his inner demon would encourage Asher to protect himself. It had done a decent job of that so far.

She spoke to his demon as she said, *I'm trusting you to protect him*. She didn't receive a response.

God, she wanted to cry. Scream. Rave. Beat her fists into something or someone. Preferably Jonas, the motherfucker. She had the power to kill him and it was oh, so close. All she had to do was tap into her link with her wings and use it as a bridge to the power that waited on the other end of it. It would be so very easy, but she couldn't call on the power right then.

As the shuck released a loud growl at Asher, she tensed, coiled to spring even as she knew it could be a very bad idea. She couldn't just fucking stand there while it hurt her son!

"I wouldn't move if I were you," Jonas warned her. "If you do, I'll have Drew rip out your son's throat. I believe you're well-acquainted with him, aren't you? He's been rather helpful these past couple of weeks. Who can blame him for standing with me after what Knox did to him?"

Harper narrowed her eyes, hands fluttering slightly with a desperation she tried to hide. She suspected the only reason Jonas hadn't directed the shuck to attack Asher was that he didn't want to risk him raising his shield. The Prime was also enjoying her fear for her son. It would be damn good if Asher felt that same fear, but he was still smiling at the shuck.

"You don't really think you can keep me from my son, do you?" Harper asked, keeping her tone controlled and flat, hoping to hide the sheer terror choking her.

"Maybe not. But he can." Jonas clicked his fingers at the man at his side, who sputtered a brief chant. And then, just like that, she was enclosed in an iron cage much like the one in the basement where Alethea kept her captives to feed the incorporeal, only its bars covered in what looked like lava. *What the everloving fuck?*

As her demon predictably lost its shit, ranting and raving and determined that these fuckers would die today, Harper grabbed the iron bars, intending to shake the cage, but the liquid fire coating it burned like a goddamn son of a fucking bitch. She snatched her hands back, grinding her teeth as her skin sizzled. *Knox, don't come into view. Jonas has a dark practitioner who can cage people with magick.*

You're caged? Fuck. I'm going to rip out their fucking spinal cords.

She could *so* get behind that plan. *Stay downwind of the hellcat and the shuck.* It was a wonder she'd managed to sound composed when her mind was in chaos at being separated from Asher this way. She wanted to pound her fists against the cage. But Jonas would love that display of emotion. The flames of hell would sever the iron bars, but she couldn't call on them without risking the others harming Asher.

Please, baby boy, put up your shield, she begged him. But still, Asher didn't.

Jonas studied her. "You lied about not having wings, I see." He exhaled. "I suppose that was Jolene's idea. She no doubt suspected you'd be hunted due to how unique they are, so she advised you to claim that you had none. Sensible. They're quite beautiful—the colors of the flames of hell." His eyes darted to the shuck as it weirdly whined and shook its head. "I did intend to cage the boy ... but I think the sight of him surrounded by hellish beasts will terrify Knox much more than seeing him confined."

Harper knew he'd be right on that, since it had instilled the same terror in her.

"Since you don't appear to be deep in grief, I'm guessing that Knox is still alive." Jonas sighed sadly. "I had doubted that the crash would be enough to kill him, but the hope was certainly there. I suppose you've already telepathed him with news of my presence. Good. I want him afraid for you. And what better way to frighten him than to slather your mind with a spell that will prevent anyone from sensing you—he'll think you're dead."

Harper stiffened, stomach rolling. "That's not possible."

Jonas shot the practitioner a sideways glance. "Charles."

She felt an oily tendril of magick poke her mind like a fingertip . . . and then she watched with a smile as Charles winced and rubbed at his temple. "Her mind is protected with sharp psychic barbs," he complained.

Jonas's mouth tightened. "What about the boy?"

A hiss slid out of her before she could stop it, which only made Jonas give her a gloating smile.

Charles plucked at his collar. "He may well have inherited her psychic barbs. Even if he hasn't, touching his mind would be a bad idea if you really don't want him to slam up his shield. A foreign psychic touch could make him and his demon feel threatened."

"True," Jonas ground out. "Look at him, Harper, just sitting there staring at the shuck—completely unafraid. Your son is either very brave or very stupid."

"Funny. I was thinking the same thing about you. This won't end well for you, Jonas, and you know it. I can't even imagine why you started it." She frowned as a hazy swirl appeared in front of the cage. Then, suddenly, an imitation of Heidi stood in its place, smiling slyly. Harper gave it a scathing look and then spoke to Jonas, "Ah, it's your little pet dog again." The incorporeal bared its teeth.

"That's such a mean thing to say."

The words didn't come from the incorporeal. Or Jonas. Or the practitioner. They came from the person who strolled out of the trees and sidled up to Jonas.

Harper's mouth dropped open. What. The. Fuck?

"It was the incorporeal you saw burn on the YouTube video,"

said Alethea, smirking. "It took on my form so I could fake my death. *Ta-da*," she sang, like she'd performed a magic trick. "Oh, come on, that was clever—admit it."

"You didn't even consider it, did you?" The incorporeal sighed, as if it pitied Harper. "I can maintain a physical form. And just as I can choose what form to take, I can change that form. Make it appear as though it is wet, burning, decaying—whatever I want."

Harper slid her gaze back to Jonas. "You faked her death so that you wouldn't be a suspect?"

"I did believe it was unlikely that you would suspect me of ever harming my sister. But, mostly, I did it because Thatcher was suspicious of her—he was having her watched because he suspected she was the remaining Horseman. Killing him would have been stupid of me, since some believed *him* to be the Horseman. It was far better to have him as a scapegoat. But I needed him to stop keeping tabs on her. Charles here was good enough to slather her mind in a spell that protected her from being sensed."

Hearing the shuck snort and shake its head, like something was jammed up its nose or something, Jonas paused a moment to shoot it an exasperated look. Turning back to Harper, he went on, "I was rather hoping Alethea's 'death' would make you and Knox suspects, considering how much you both detest her, but—alas—that did not pan out." His eyes flicked to the hell-cat. "I should really give Alethea the credit for bringing Drew to our side. I have to say, you don't look very surprised to see him, Harper."

"You made a mistake taking him to the house and showing him the prison in your basement," said Harper.

"Ah, so you found a way to untangle the spells." Jonas gave a delicate shrug. "No matter."

Well, it seemed to matter to dear old Charles—he looked pissed that someone had undone his work.

Harper's eyes helplessly slid to Asher as she reached out to Knox. *Alethea is alive. The incorporeal posed as her on the YouTube clip.*

Anger crashed into her consciousness. *That bitch,* he growled. *We're close.*

Clenching her fists, Harper felt her nails digging into her blistered palms; the pain distracted her from the debilitating fear. "I thought it was the *Four* Horsemen. Alethea would make that *five*." He gave her a look that questioned her intelligence, and her brow knitted as she suddenly recalled something. "Isla recruited Roan *after* she started the campaign to be Monarch. He was never really a Horseman, was he?"

"Oh, he *was* a Horseman," said Jonas. "He was the one who came up with the pathetic name. He would have branded us the Five Horsemen if he'd known I was involved."

"Why didn't you tell him?"

"I didn't trust him not to keep his mouth shut. He wasn't as easy for Isla to recruit as you might have thought. It wasn't that he felt any loyalty toward you. But he did fear Knox. I'm sure you noticed that Roan was somewhat egotistical. Isla appealed to that; told him that she, Alethea, and Nora needed a man to help them; that they'd been looking for someone who they thought was strong, smart, and brave enough to help them take Knox on. He practically rolled over in delight." Jonas sighed. "So easily manipulated. But then, so were Isla and Nora."

It was Jonas who had started and led the group, Harper realized. "I don't think Roan was the only person scared of Knox. I think you're pretty terrified of him. You sat back and let the other Horsemen take all the risks. Hell, you basically set them up as sacrifices. And now you're here with your sister and a practitioner to hold your hand—not to mention you have an incorporeal, a shuck, and a hellcat to protect you." She gave a snort of derision. "Oh yeah, very brave, Jonas."

Face tightening, he cut his gaze to the incorporeal and tipped his chin. The entity abandoned Heidi's form, fading and then bursting into vapor. Harper winced as she felt a sudden pressure against her mind; like knives trying to slice through her skull. Then the pressure abruptly disappeared, and the vapor jerked back, obviously hurt by her psychic shields. It whooshed through the air and plunged into Charles, who blinked rapidly, but it didn't seem to take control of him; simply needed to hitchhike on him.

Looking put-out, Jonas pressed his lips together. "I had a feeling you'd be too strong for it to possess you. Shame."

With a snarl, her inner demon lunged for the surface, making Harper's eyes bleed to black. "What do you want?" it asked.

Jonas's eyes flickered. "Mostly, we want to see Knox die. Killing his mate and child is just a bonus."

The demon laughed—a dark, unnerving sound that seemed thick with power. "How very foolish you are. You started a war you stand no chance of winning, and you are too dimwitted to see it. I look forward to watching you and your sibling plead for death." Satisfied by the apprehension that flashed across his face, the entity retreated.

"Your demon is clearly very confident that Knox will save you," Alethea said to Harper. "You yourself appear to be quite calm for someone who is caged and unable to protect your son. Relying on Knox to save you, sphinx?"

Calm? Harper was so far from calm it wasn't even funny. She was also fighting the urge to plead with them to leave Asher be. Begging them wouldn't work. They would get nothing but sick satisfaction from it. Her only hope was to seem confident in his ability to protect himself. "Asher isn't as helpless as you seem to think he is."

"Because he can raise a shield?" Alethea scoffed. "That doesn't make him invulnerable. But don't worry, we're not quite ready for you both to die yet. Not until Knox is here to watch the show."

Harper shot her an incredulous look. "Are you out of your mind? Seriously? You can't kill Knox. And he's not going to let you hurt us. As plans go, this one is a total flop."

"Oh, I don't think so," said Alethea. "You escaped the jet, but the others didn't. They'll be badly hurt. I doubt that even Knox could walk away from a magick-induced plane crash without being severely wounded." And the idea of that appeared to delight her.

Harper's demon bared its teeth, wanting to wrap one of the ropy vines around the little bitch's neck. They wanted him weak, Harper thought. Well, they hadn't got what they wanted, but she didn't let her satisfaction show in her expression.

Asher clapped, chuckling to himself, eyes on the encantada.

Alethea looked from him to Harper, brows knitting. "Why is he clapping?"

"He seems to find you funny." Though fuck if Harper knew why.

Alethea's face hardened. "Does he now?" She took a step toward him. Although Jonas snapped out his arm to bar his sister's path, Harper found herself snarling.

"Bitch, you try to touch my son and—"

"You'll do what?" Alethea asked, hiking up an amused brow.

"I never said I'd do anything. I won't have to."

Alethea faltered—hell, even Jonas and the practitioner seemed a little spooked by the sheer confidence in Harper's voice. That was good, because it meant they hadn't sensed that deep inside she was screaming.

"Do not advance on him," Jonas told his sister. "If we make any quick or aggressive movements, he'll pop up the shield."

Alethea gave a dismissive flick of the hand. "I have it on good authority that he's not very strong. I could probably punch right through it."

"I'm not sure I'd ever describe Sherryl Malloy as 'good authority'," said Harper.

Alethea's eyes narrowed. "So, she told you about our 'friendship' during that interrogation you subjected her to."

"We didn't see the clip of the interrogation, since neither of us were in the Underground at the time it was aired," Jonas told Harper. "But I certainly heard about it from my sentinels. They were rather surprised and impressed by your voracity."

A snort popped out of Alethea. "Killing a person who is bound and tied is easy. That doesn't require power."

But the interrogation hadn't been a show of power. It was a warning not to fuck with Harper and Knox. And it seemed that the siblings were refusing to heed that warning. They weren't willing to deviate from the plan they'd put in place years ago— they may have felt they'd come too far to turn back. Of course, they probably wouldn't be feeling quite so confident if they didn't have their minions with them.

Alethea sighed at Jonas. "You can move your arm—I won't approach the child. You're right; it would be best not to risk him raising his shield. We want Knox to be afraid for himself, his mate, and their spawn. But he won't be so afraid for his son's life if the child is safe within his shield."

Barely stopping herself from grabbing a fistful of her hair, Harper lifted her chin. She wouldn't show them her fear or desperation. No way. "Wise decision on your part."

"Back to the subject of Malloy's interrogation," began Jonas. "Your video clip had the desired effect, Harper. People received the message loud and clear. That's not good for us, since it is *us* they need to fear. We're going to make a video of our own.

A video of my sentinel and Drew's hellcat ripping apart your son while both you and Knox are helpless and can do no more than watch."

Just the idea of it made Harper almost retch. The protective power that lived within her was tingling her fingertips so intensely, they were close to numb—she craved to deliver some soul-deep pain upon these bastards.

"They will not only see our power," added Alethea, "they will see how we lured one of your old lair to partake in this."

Harper's mouth flattened. "He's just a baby."

"But he won't always be a baby," said Jonas. "He will grow, and I can't risk him coming after us for revenge."

Another whine whistled out of the shuck as it danced from foot to foot, seeming uneasy. The siblings gave it an odd glance, but it was staring at Asher.

Just then, Asher looked to Harper. His little face scrunched up at the sight of the cage. He reached toward her and flexed his hands, making a fussy 'Ma' sound.

She gave him a reassuring smile. "It's okay, baby boy. I'm fine." She expected him to cry or attempt to crawl toward her, but he didn't. He calmed, and she suspected she had his demon to thank for that.

"No, it's not okay. It's really, really not." Alethea licked her front teeth. "I'm going to enjoy watching you die, sphinx. And I'm going to enjoy that Knox will watch you die. What I'll enjoy even more is that you *both* get to watch your son die first."

So much bitterness, thought Harper. This whole thing was about far more than Knox being an obstacle to their goal. This was personal. "What's your beef with Knox? Tell me it's not because the black diamond isn't on *your* finger. Because if so, that's just sad."

Alethea sniffed. "Rejecting me was a massive mistake on his

part, but no. That's not what this is about." Her expression made it clear that she had no intention of explaining.

"You really think you can take him on?" Harper shook her head. "The incorporeal has to have told you that Knox can call on the flames of hell. You can't cage him with dark magick, if that's your big plan. It's been tried before. It's never worked."

"Ah, but that's because those other practitioners didn't know what he is." Jonas smirked. "We do, thanks to Drew, which means Charles knows exactly what kind of containment spell he needs to use. It also means we know how to kill Knox."

Harper inwardly frowned, wondering how Drew had discovered that Knox was an archdemon.

Jonas shot his sister a brief look of annoyance. "Of course, we'd have known that a lot sooner if *someone* hadn't failed at their job of getting close to Knox."

Hands balling into fists, Alethea glared at him. "I didn't fail at getting close to him. He simply wouldn't tell me what he is."

"We knew in advance that he wouldn't," said Jonas, "which is exactly why I told you that you'd need to seduce him into taking you as his mate. How hard can that really be for a sex demon?"

Alethea's cheeks flushed. "It is hardly my fault that he's so closed off. If *she* wasn't his anchor, she would never have gotten close enough to Knox for him to lower his guard and let her in."

Hearing not only scorn but jealousy in Alethea's tone, Harper knew that . . . "You might have reason to want him dead, but you also grew to care for him."

The encantada tittered. "Wrong, sphinx."

Ho, ho, ho, what a lie. "Unless dear Charles can create a cage that's impervious to the flames of hell, you won't succeed in containing Knox. How can you not see that?"

"It won't hold him permanently, that's true," said Jonas. "The flames will certainly eat at the cage. But it will contain him long enough for us to kill him, which is all we want."

Whimpering, the shuck walked in a tight circle, as if chasing its tail.

Brow furrowing, Alethea asked, "What is *wrong* with him?"

Jonas lifted one shoulder. "You know he gets restless when he's forced to wait before he plays with his food." That made Alethea chuckle.

It made Harper clench her fists. Asher wasn't going to be anyone's food. *Please tell me you're close,* she said to Knox.

His mind slid against hers. *I see you.* There was a wealth of rage in that rumbled response. *Just hold on for me.*

Relief breezed through her. *Pyroport to Asher and get him the fuck out of here.*

The shuck is standing very close to him, Harper. It's probably been ordered to attack Asher at the slightest sign of anyone trying to save him. Do you really want to risk it?

She squeezed her eyes shut. *No, I don't but, dammit, Knox, he needs to be safe.*

My demon is urging Asher's to raise the shield, but it seems to be paying it no attention. I have a plan. Keep those fuckers distracted.

Resisting the urge to glance around for some sign of Knox's presence, she spoke to Jonas. "So, all this is just about you wanting Knox dead? The big Horsemen-goal was never really to have a power structure put in place or even to elect a Monarch—you knew yourself that it would only result in war . . ." Harper trailed off as she caught an odd glint in Jonas's eyes, and she *knew* . . . "You *want* war. You want chaos. Why?"

His face darkened, and he touched his sister's arm in what seemed to be a gesture of support. "Our world became one of chaos when we were very young. The Primes are as much to blame for that as the person who caused that chaos."

"The Primes think of themselves as *superior*," Alethea scoffed. "They claim that the current power structure keeps us all safe. Well, it doesn't. Not even close. A Monarch could have put an end to the suffering we endured, but there was no Monarch. The other Primes knew what was happening, but the majority did *nothing*. Now, they will all fall. And they will fall hard."

"By 'world of chaos' are you talking of when your old Prime turned rogue?" Harper asked.

Jonas's face scrunched up in scorn and revulsion. "Cordell never should have been Prime. It was no surprise that he turned rogue—the sadistic bastard was insane."

"I can agree with that," said Knox, stepping out of the trees. Eyes wide, the siblings and practitioner spun to face him. And, considering she'd informed him of exactly what their plans were for him, Harper had to wonder if her mate was fucking high.

CHAPTER NINETEEN

Asher looked at him with a delighted smile and clapped. "Da!"

Knox brushed his mind over Asher's—it was a greeting and a reassurance. He didn't dare go to him, though. Black shucks could kill with a single bite. Not that Asher seemed at all worried by its close proximity. On the contrary, he seemed pretty content. As for Harper . . . she didn't appear so happy to see Knox. In fact, she was glaring at him *hard*.

This is your big plan? she clipped. *Walk right into the line of fucking fire? Seriously, are you out of your everloving mind?*

"Charles," clipped Jonas.

A mere moment later, a band of dark magick surrounded Knox. Then, suddenly, he was inside a glass cube. No, not a cube. It was a large display box, much like the one that the incorporeal had spent God-knew-how-long trapped inside. Knox didn't react other than to casually stuff his hands in his pockets.

His demon did nothing more than bare its teeth. Its anger was no longer hot and out of control. It was now vibrating with a cold fury that allowed the entity to *think*. It knew Knox's plan and had confidence in it. Moreover, it had confidence in Asher's demon; believed it would protect him.

Knox didn't say a word as the siblings exchanged smug smirks, practically bouncing in delight. He'd purposely approached them from behind so that they'd have to turn their backs on Harper and Asher to look at him. Knox wanted their attention divided. Wanted to make it hard for them to keep tabs on him, Harper, and Asher at the same time.

Eyes bright, Alethea laughed and pointed a finger at Harper. "And you thought he couldn't be caged." She laughed again, turning to face Knox. "See, no one is omnipotent."

Knox simply looked at her, bored. Her smugness faded. She seemed . . . disappointed. As if she'd expected panic and anger.

Alethea jutted out her chin, defensive. "It was easy enough to capture you once we discovered what you are."

They know what I am? Knox asked Harper.

They seem to think they do.

Jonas tilted his head. "I must admit, I was surprised when Drew told me that you're a phoenix. They are so few of them left. No more than a handful. But it makes sense. They're strong, powerful, and dangerous. They're also practically impossible to destroy, since they are reborn from their ashes over and over. But there are ways to kill them for good. And we know just how to make sure you're not reborn this time."

It didn't surprise Knox whatsoever that they were still clueless as to what breed of demon he was. Still, he said nothing.

How tough is that damn box? Harper asked Knox.

It can't keep me contained. It's designed to keep a phoenix contained. I'm not a phoenix. He could pyroport out of it, no problem. *Let them relax in the illusion that they're safe, baby. The shuck and the hellcat will relax too and hang back a little, giving Asher space.*

Then I can pyroport to him and take him to Davis and Noelle. Levi and Tanner will deal with the hellcat and the shuck, and you and I can then take out these other motherfuckers.

I absolutely adore my part in your plan, but don't wait too long to act. Alethea and Jonas plan to get a video of Asher being torn apart by the two beasts while we're caged and forced to watch.

Bastards. His demon roared its fury, but it kept a grip on its control. *Is there a reason the shuck keeps whining and acting odd?*

If there is, I haven't the faintest clue what it could be. Where's Levi and Tanner?

They're close. And they'd follow what orders Knox had given them.

A smirk spread across Alethea's face as she tapped her nail on the glass box. "I'll bet you're surprised to learn that Jonas and I are Horsemen. I'll bet you didn't think I was smart enough to carry out such a plan. Wrong. Jonas and I have worked together every step of the way." She slung a put-out look at Jonas, adding, "Except for the part where you tried getting an alliance with Lucifer and the use of an archdemon, of course. You'd failed to tell me about that."

"Which I apologized for," Jonas said through gritted teeth. "Let it go."

She sniffed. "Fine. Let's get on with this. I've been looking forward to the moment when Knox would be forced to watch his mate and child die."

Harper glared at them. "You could really stand there while two beasts tore an innocent child to pieces?"

Pursing his lips, Jonas was quiet for a moment. Then he smiled and glanced at Harper over his shoulder. "Yes, I believe I can."

"I guess it's not like you haven't killed a kid before," Harper clipped, referring to whatever demonic child was sacrificed to free the incorporeal.

"No, it's not," Jonas freely admitted. "I first killed a child when I was seven. Cordell ordered it done. As I said, he was insane. Being without an anchor was too much for him."

Harper's face fell. "He forced you to kill other children?" She sounded unable to wrap her head around it.

"I can't count the number of times I whipped or caned another child for 'rebuking' his advances or some imaginary slight." Fury blazed in Jonas's eyes. "That sick fuck liked children, you see. He would take in stray demons and their children; then he would kill the adults and keep the children for himself."

"He had a household full of them," added Alethea, voice flat, gaze focused inward. "He liked to hurt them. Abuse them. Most of all, he relished their fear."

"If they bored him—and by bore him, I mean if they didn't show the appropriate amount of fear when he hurt them—he would make one of the other children kill them." Jonas swallowed. "His sentinels were of the same ilk as him, and so he sometimes shared us with them. Some were particularly brutal."

Despite what they'd been through, Knox couldn't find it in him to feel any sympathy for two people who were planning to sic two beasts on his son and then kill his mate.

Harper frowned. "You were initially stray demons?"

"Little history lesson," said Jonas. "There was once a Prime by the name of Houston Steward—Knox will remember him. He was my father; Alethea's father. He wasn't extremely powerful, but he was strong. Good. Honorable. A true leader. But his lair was small, and larger lairs kept coming along, plucking the strongest members out of our lair. It got smaller and smaller, until it was too weak to stand on its own. The remaining demons were forced to become strays or join other lairs. Only those who were utterly loyal to my father stayed."

"The other lairs were well-aware that ours was so frequently targeted," added Alethea. "Some did try to help when he appealed to them for aid. Nora—she was Prime of Dario's lair at the time—tried. Isla's old Prime, Rhea, also tried; Isla was actually one of her sentinels at the time, so she did what she could at Rhea's command. But did the other Primes offer to help him? No." Her upper lip curled. "They were happy to take in those who fled the sinking ship."

Jonas placed a supportive hand on her shoulder. "It wasn't until the death toll got too high that the other Primes acted. Our father was dead by then. The other Primes didn't care about that. They didn't care about the lives that were lost. They only stepped in because those deaths came close to attracting human attention," he said bitterly.

"Our mother fled with us." Alethea's eyes dulled with pain. "Cordell took us in, killed her, and made our lives a living hell. We had another sibling. Isaac was only three."

Jonas let out a shaky breath. "He was so small and frail. His body couldn't take Cordell's brutal ways. He died of internal injuries. And all that could have been avoided if the other Primes had just united to stand with our father. Instead, they turned a blind eye." He glared at Knox. "*You* turned a blind eye. If you had stood with my father, the others would have left him alone out of blind terror."

"You're not being realistic," said Knox, bluntly. "Either that or you aren't fully aware of the truth."

Alethea's hands balled up into fists. "We know the truth."

"Then you know that your father aimed to build an army and declare war." He noticed the way both siblings stiffened, but Knox went on, "He approached demons from many lairs and tried persuading them to join his side and be an 'inside man' for him, much like you did with Roan."

Houston had even tried it with Knox's demons. Loyal to the

bone, they'd come to Knox about it. He'd warned Houston that if he attempted such a thing again, Knox would put him through a world of pain. Houston hadn't bothered him after that.

"The Primes that targeted your father didn't do so merely because his lair was small," said Knox. "They did it because he was trying to turn their own demons against them. He'd even succeeded with some and ordered them to kill certain members of the lairs—often the anchors of the Primes or sentinels. Such a thing would *never* go ignored. I'm not sure who led you to believe he was good and honorable, but that isn't the truth."

"Then why would Nora and Rhea have stood at his side?" Alethea challenged, red-faced, eyes blazing.

"He had strong alliances with them. The rest of the Primes, including me, suspected that Nora and Rhea had agreed to band with him to form an army, but we couldn't be sure, so no action was taken against them. Your father brought that devastation upon himself. His family, however, didn't deserve to suffer for it. It's regretful that you did—"

"Regretful?" Alethea sneered. "Don't pretend to feel compassion. It's not an emotion you're capable of. What you *are* very capable of doing is manipulating others, and that's exactly what you're trying to do to us right now. You're feeding us lies, hoping to shake our faith in our father. It won't work."

Yeah, Knox could see clearly enough that they wouldn't believe him. "No one knew Cordell was abusing children. Not until after he'd turned rogue."

"Probably not," said Jonas, face hard. "But I strongly doubt they would have intervened even if they had known. Nora and Rhea would have, but no one else would have given a damn."

They were wrong. Generally, Primes didn't interfere in the business of other lairs unless their actions attracted human attention, but Knox would never have overlooked children being abused. Still, he didn't say as much. The siblings would only think he was trying to placate them.

"And now I'm done talking." Jonas turned to Charles. "Get your iPhone out and be ready to start recording."

Knox, if you plan to do something, you need to—

The shuck dipped, coiled to spring, and growled long and low in its throat. The noise made everybody stiffen. Except for Asher. Knox's heart would have skipped a beat in panic, but it didn't for the exact same reason that Jonas, Alethea, and Charles exchanged confused looks. The shuck wasn't growling at Asher; it was growling at them.

"Grant, stop pissing around," Jonas snapped.

The shuck barked and snapped its teeth so hard Knox was surprised they didn't crack. The hellcat rounded Asher and sidled up to the shuck with a hiss of warning at Jonas, as if it also planned to protect Asher.

It was the perfect moment for Knox to pyroport to his son and get him to safety, but his demon ushered him to remain still. To watch. To have faith in Asher and his own demon. *Fuck* if Knox would stay right where he was while his son was in danger, but then he froze as his demon did the unexpected. It finally told him what breed of demon Asher was.

Not a sphinx. Not an archdemon. Not a hybrid. But a breed that had qualities of the two.

Knox, do something, Harper urged.

Knox met her eyes and echoed words he'd heard her earlier say to Alethea. *I won't have to.*

Just then, Asher's face blanked and his eyes bled to black as his demon surfaced. It opened the palm of its little hand. Narrowed its eyes. And then the shuck—lightning-fucking-fast—lunged at the practitioner with a roar. It knocked him flat and ravaged him with teeth and claws. Charles screamed in agony, but it wasn't just the shuck causing that pain. No, the practitioner was *blurring* around the edges. Like he was splitting. And then he did. His body sagged to the floor, eyes wide open, and his soul whooshed over to Asher and seemed to sink into his open palm.

Looking at his mate's face, Knox watched as shock, dread, and realization slammed into her. There was only one breed of demon that could call to souls that way. A rare breed. A feared breed. One that tended to remain in the abyss of hell.

Jonas shook his head. "No. No, he's a sphinx. Sphinxes cannot harvest and deliver souls to hell."

Anubis. The soft whisper came from Harper.

Yes, he's an Anubis, said Knox. It fit. Like sphinxes, they were of Egyptian descent. But instead of walking the Earth, they dwelled in the depths of hell and served it faithfully ... just as archdemons did. Asher had a mother who could touch souls and a father who could kill as easily as he could breathe. Anubis demons could call to souls and deliver them to hell just as effortlessly as they could call to objects around them. They could also kill a person without even touching them, much like Knox could.

What's more, Anubis demons also drew and communicated with living death omens such as black cats, crows, owls ... and black shucks.

Breaths coming short and fast, Alethea bit out, "No. I am *not* dying today."

Jonas shot two balls of hellfire at the shuck and telekinetically sent it careering into a tree just as Harper's cage abruptly went up in tri-colored flames that began to quickly eat through the iron bars.

The incorporeal surged out of Charles's body and flew at the hellcat just as the beast was leaping at Alethea, causing it to topple on the floor and whimper as it fought the incorporeal's attempt to possess it.

"Die, you little bastard!" Alethea shot a ball of hellfire at Asher, who let out a wave of gold energy that dissolved the orb and knocked her flat on her back.

Levi and Tanner skidded out of the trees and went straight to Asher protectively just as Knox pyroported out of the box and moved to stand behind Jonas. Trusting Harper and his sentinels to deal with the hellcat and shuck, Knox snapped his hand around Jonas's throat, baring his teeth. "Really, Jonas, how stupid can two people be?" Knox tossed him at a thick tree. Of course, Knox could have snapped his neck and killed him instantly, but he didn't want him dead. No, he had much more interesting plans for Jonas and his bitch of a sister.

Levi, Tanner—stay with Asher, Knox ordered. *The hellcat and the shuck tried to protect Asher, but I don't trust them. Don't let them near him or allow them to escape.*

Struggling to his feet, Jonas threw an orb of hellfire at Knox, who sharply side-stepped it. Grabbing Alethea's hand, Jonas dragged her toward the trees. Both tossed more balls of hellfire as they ran.

Neatly avoiding the orbs, Knox asked, "And where is it you think you're going?"

*

Harper stiffened as the ground tremored. Mere seconds later the air buzzed, pulsed, and thickened with a power that purred against her skin. It was a power that lived inside Knox, and he was apparently setting it free. The sheer, raw force of it stung her eyes, squeezed her chest, made her teeth rattle and caused her ears to ring.

Striking, ten-foot high flames erupted out of the ground in

front of Jonas and Alethea, forcing them to skid to a halt. Cursing loudly, they changed direction and fled. A jagged line of red, gold, and black flames devoured the undergrowth as they raced past the motherfuckers and cut off their escape. Harper's demon grinned.

Branches snapped, leaves crackled, and trees groaned as the flames consumed them while quickly forming a circle around the siblings and Knox. He wasn't just trapping them, thought Harper. He was toying with them. And now she couldn't see shit.

Asher looked up at her. His demon had now retreated. *Good.* She kissed Asher's head. "I'll be just a minute, baby."

There was a loud, feline whimper. Harper turned just in time to see a whirl of hazy vapor erupt out of the hellcat, which it had obviously failed to possess. And she knew it would flee. Knew it would thrust itself into some animal and hightail it out of there. *Not a fucking chance.*

She called to the radiant flames that were consuming the last of her cage. A pretty red one snatched the incorporeal out of the air and curled around it. The haze squirmed and twisted, attempting to escape, but the flame tossed it into the fire. There. Done. Which was anticlimactic, since she would have liked to torture it a little first, but she had no way of containing it. Besides, she was much more interested in hurting the fucking dolphin.

The hellcat staggered to its feet and looked at her, eyes unreadable. Taking a leaf out of Knox's book, she directed the crackling flames to form a circle around the beast, imprisoning it until she could figure out what the fuck to do with it.

"The shuck's dead," Levi told her. "Little bastard tried to rip my throat out." Which meant that Asher didn't have control over such creatures for long. God, he was an *Anubis*. Later ... she'd think about all that later.

Harper gave Levi a thankful nod. Looking from him to

Tanner, she said, "Stay with Asher." There was something else she needed to take care of—or some*one*.

She headed right for the large circle of flames. They roared, crackled, hissed, and spat. The air shimmered with the waves of heat. It was a horrendous heat that seared her skin but, as always, caused her no harm—not even when she walked right through the flames like they weren't even there, making Alethea's mouth drop open in shock.

Harper sidled up to Knox, eyes on the siblings. "I don't know why they look so shocked that their plan failed," she said to him. "I mean, I did warn them. Why do the bad guys never listen to me?"

Knox shrugged. "No idea, baby."

"You won't find me easy to kill," growled Jonas.

Knox blinked. "Why ever would you think that I intend to kill you?"

Jonas seemed thrown by that question, but then he scoffed. "Don't expect me to believe you will allow us to live."

"I'm not going to kill you," Knox told him. "Even a long, painful death would be merciful, considering all you've done. And I've never been merciful, have I?"

"Oh, Jolene will want her shot at you, too," Harper told the siblings. "And my uncle Richie, Heidi's dad. Oh yeah, he'll want some quality time with you both. Hey, Knox, we don't have to take these fuckers straight to the Chamber, do we? I don't want to kill the bitch, but I do intend to kick her skanky fucking ass. It's been a *long* time coming."

Torturing her would be fun, sure, but it wouldn't be enough. Harper needed the bitch to feel defeated. Needed her fear. Not fear of pain that Harper would inflict, but fear of Harper herself. She also needed to vent every bit of the helplessness she'd felt when they'd kept her separated from her son.

"No, we don't have to take them straight away," replied Knox. He liked the idea of toying with his prey for a while. "There's no harm in you and I having a little fun first, baby."

"Excellent. Why don't you—"

Alethea stomped her foot like a kid having a tantrum, which would have been funny if the ground beneath Harper's feet didn't suddenly give away. Harper threw out her arms, swaying. A crack spiderwebbed along the ground in front of her and Knox, who grabbed her arm and pulled her backwards as the cracks widened. Her body shook, and her teeth clattered as tremors bucked the earth. The earthquake seemed contained within the circle of flames, as only the trees inside the area swayed and cracked.

Knox raised a brow at Alethea. "You don't think a few cracks in the ground will truly be enough to keep us away from you, do you?"

The ground beneath their feet settled, and Alethea narrowed her eyes. A strange haze then rippled the air, blurring objects and muting colors. The trees began swaying again, but there was no earthquake this time. Instead, a harsh wind built around them, tossing Harper's ponytail, flapping her clothes, and sending leaves skittering along the ground.

She planted her feet wide, standing firm against the biting, buffeting wind. She had to squint and raise a hand to her face to guard her eyes. It howled and moaned as it rushed around them. Trees creaked, branches splintered, and loose leaves hit her face and arms—it was truly surprising the wind hadn't uprooted any of the trees.

"Lower the flames!" shouted Alethea, wind whipping her hair into her face. But, of course, Knox didn't.

The wind went from cold to glacial as snowflakes whirled around them. The blades of icy wind sliced at Harper's skin just as the flakes pelted her hard enough to sting. Within moments, a carpet of snow began to build on the ground and weigh down branches. Harper had to admit that the raw power of it was impressive.

"The cold won't put out the flames, Alethea!" Knox yelled over the sound of the whistling wind. A wind that began to ease, lowering the onslaught of snow until the blizzard finally stopped.

Their once-green surroundings were now almost completely white, and Harper honestly felt like she was in freaking Narnia or something. *I'll take care of this bitch. You concentrate on Jonas.*

Trusting that Knox could deal with the asshole alone, Harper put the two of them out of her mind. In that moment, no one else existed but her and the bitch in front of her. Harper smirked. Oh, she was going to enjoy this. It had been a *long* time coming. "There's nowhere to go, dolphin," she taunted in a little sing-song voice.

"No one plays with me like I'm prey," Alethea spat, glaring at Harper with utter hatred. Then the weirdest fucking thing happened. Black cables shot out of Alethea's sides. No, not cables, Harper realized, as she spotted the octopus-like suckers. Tentacles. Worse, they were barbed tentacles.

Harper whipped her stiletto knife out of her boot, infused it with hellfire, and braced herself. The tentacle lashed at her like a whip. She sliced at it, making it jerk back as Alethea hissed in pain.

Two tentacles came at her this time. Harper ducked, avoiding one. But the other wrapped around her waist and lifted her from the ground, contracting around her body like a snake. The suckers felt like rough sandpaper, and they scoured their way through cloth and skin, drawing blood. Worse, the barbs lodged themselves in her arms and sides.

With a war cry worthy of a highlander, Harper stabbed the tentacle hard over and over. Alethea let out a cry of her own, though it seemed to be a mix of pain and fury. The tentacle threw Harper at the ground, which earned her a mouthful of snow. Spitting it out, Harper pushed to her feet and faced the dolphin. And she noticed something ... odd. There were *stab* wounds on the dolphin's arms ... as if each wound that Harper had inflicted on the tentacles had somehow transferred to Alethea's limbs. Maybe the appendages were linked somehow due to the tentacles functioning much as an extra set of arms—Harper didn't particularly understand it. Didn't care to. But she *did* like knowing that the more injuries she delivered onto the tentacles, the more hurt Alethea would be.

So each time one of the tentacles tried belting, flaying, or grabbing her, Harper slashed and stabbed and sliced at them. The hellfire ate at the flesh of Alethea's arms, and each screech of pain made Harper's inner demon laugh.

At the same time, Harper tried digging the barbs out of her skin, but there were some she couldn't quite reach. It wasn't until she found herself feeling strangely weak and lethargic that she realized that—*fuck a duck*—the barbs had released some kind of drug in her system. If she wasn't powerful and anchored by Knox, they might have knocked her on her ass long ago.

Swaying, vision blurring, Harper couldn't brace herself for the next attack. A tentacle struck her hard, sending her flying through the air. The breath gusted out of her lungs as she hit a tree hard and then fell to the snow. Oh, this bitch needed a few of those barbs lodged in her rectum.

Snatching her knife from the depression in the snow, Harper charged at Alethea on unsteady feet. She stumbled to a halt as her foot got caught in something. It was a crack in the ground, she realized. Fuck. She struggled to pull herself free. Couldn't.

A tentacle lashed her face, scraping strips of skin away. "*You motherfucking bitch!*"

*

As his mate focused her attention on Alethea, Knox locked his on Jonas. The male kept glancing around, as if hoping a gap would appear in the flames surrounding them. "There will be no escaping this, Jonas. You'll have to face me. Or do you prefer letting your sister fight your battles for you?" he taunted. The male's eyes narrowed to slits and—

Knox blinked, suddenly finding himself stood in a boardroom with his sentinels and the other Primes. It wasn't real, he knew. It was an illusion. But he didn't know how the fuck to break out of it and—

Red-hot pain slammed into his chest, burning and sizzling his flesh, and Knox was once more in the rainforest. He didn't need to look to know he'd been hit with a ball of hellfire. *Fucking asshole*. With a snarl, he conjured a lethal orb and launched it at Jonas.

The bastard stretched and arched his back at an odd angle like he was boneless and fucking elastic, avoiding the orb—but barely. Jonas tossed an orb of his own. Knox returned the favor. And on and on it went.

Snowflakes and tree bark flew in the air each time a ball of hellfire missed its target. A couple had hit Knox, but they weren't powerful enough to really hurt him. Jonas, on the other hand, was weakening. Several patches of flesh were blackening and peeling from his body. The scents of blood and burning flesh pleased his demon immensely and—

Knox was standing in his Underground office. Another illusion, he knew. Recalling that pain had snapped him out of the last one, he dug his fingertips into a wound on his arm. The

world around him shifted back to normal . . . just in time for him
to see a long beam of fire soaring his way, aiming for his head.

Ducking, he let out a stream of hellfire from his palm as if it
were a flamethrower. Jonas's eyes widened—no doubt because
the stream had the head of a snake. It slithered toward him fast,
hissing loudly. Jonas tossed several balls of hellfire at it, but they
had no effect.

"You motherfucking bitch!"

The pain in his mate's voice snatched his attention. He
looked and saw her foot was caught in a fissure in the ground
and she was struggling to wrench it free. He used psychic hands
to pull her to safety and—

Knox staggered as blazing pain lanced through his shoulder
and skidded down his arm. Jonas, the bastard, had buried a fire
beam in his shoulder. Grinding his teeth, Knox slowly pulled out
the beam, hissing as it scraped against bone.

He slammed his gaze on Jonas, only then noticing that the
bastard's attention had moved to Harper. That was when Jonas
slung a ball of hellfire at her. Wicked fast, Knox threw one of his
own—the orb crashed into Jonas's, knocking it off-course. The
motherfucker had tried to hurt *Harper*. Now, his demon was no
longer amused. No, it was *pissed*. And it wanted to have some
fun of its own.

*

Icy psychic hands roughly snatched Harper's hips and dragged
her out of harm's way. But it was only mere seconds later that
the tentacle came at her again. Dizzy and uncoordinated, Harper
couldn't move fast enough to dodge the fucker. It wrapped
around her yet again, squeezing hard this time—hard enough to
cut off her breathing. And Harper decided she was done playing.
She grabbed the tentacle, releasing the protective power tingling

her fingertips—a power that rushed through Alethea all the way to her soul.

Alethea screamed, and the tentacles shrunk away, dumping Harper on the ground. Lifting her head and spitting out snow, Harper watched as a shaking Alethea dropped to her knees and then slumped to the ground, sobbing her little black heart out. Relishing the sight, Harper's demon bared its teeth in a blood-thirsty smile.

"Bitch." Splaying her fingers in the snow beneath her, Harper pushed to her feet and began tugging out more barbs—

"No! No! Stay the fuck away!"

Jonas's panicked words made Harper's attention snap to him. Blinking rapidly to clear her fuzzy vision, she saw that Knox was ... well, no longer Knox. In his place was a figure of raging flames. The archdemon was having its fun. And—like the fire-snake on the ground—it was stalking Jonas. Unsurprisingly, the Prime's eyes were wide with shock and horror. There was no mistaking what Knox was. Not now. And Jonas knew he didn't have even the slightest chance of winning a battle against an archdemon. He was *fucked*.

Breathing hard, Harper watched in grim satisfaction as Jonas backed away, hurling orbs of hellfire that had no effect whatsoever on the archdemon. The dumb bastard then tripped over his sister, who was too caught up in her own pain to even notice. On his ass, he scooted backwards, only stopping when he felt the heat of the tri-colored flames behind him.

"Alethea, get up, run!" warned Jonas. The fucker really did love his sister. But not enough to try dragging her to safety. No, he left her curled up like a fetus.

The archdemon stiffly halted in front of him. It was impossible to know what it was thinking. It had no facial features—not even eyes—though she knew it saw everything.

Staring up at it, Jonas shook his head. "Don't you—" His back bowed as he was wrenched from the floor by an unseen force and then slammed back on the ground hard enough to send a tremor through the earth. Then he was writhing. Thrashing. Face scrunched up in a terrible agony.

Crack.

A rib? His spine? She wasn't quite sure. It was doing *something* to his insides. Something that caused another sickening *crack*. And another. And another. Yep, probably his ribs.

His back arched again, and he coughed up blood. It splattered on his chest and dripped down his chin. Not a pretty sight. Then his hands slapped on his head and he fisted his hair as he roared in pain. A roar that rose in volume when his leg snapped at an unnatural angle. She winced, but she felt no sympathy for him.

He gurgled, eyes bulging, and his hands flew to his neck in a panic. The archdemon was choking him. And as Jonas's face turned crimson red and his eyes started to become bloodshot, she realized that—oh, fuck—it was going to kill him. Not part of the agenda.

Staggering toward the figure of flames, she said, "No. Drop him."

The archdemon's head slowly turned to face her, but he didn't release Jonas. Unable to sense its frame of mind, she touched its psyche. *Rage.* Well, that wasn't exactly surprising. "You can't kill him."

It just stared at her.

Her demon rolled its eyes and forced its way to the surface. "We want them to suffer," it reminded the entity. "There are far worse things than death."

Still, the archdemon didn't do anything. And now Jonas was turning blue.

Knowing that her demon wouldn't do much to calm the

entity, Harper resurfaced. "Asher's waiting for us. We need to get to our boy."

A flaming hand reached out and feathered its inferno-hot fingers down her wounded cheek. That gentleness said a lot. It was pissed that she was hurt, but it wasn't intoxicated on power or out of control—it could never have touched her like that if it was.

That was good. She could work with "pissed". Drunk on power? That was a whole other story.

"I'm okay," she told it. "I'll feel a fuck of a lot better when I know these two motherfuckers are shackled in the Chamber that Knox told me about. You remember your playroom, right?"

The crazy fucker still didn't respond.

"They need to suffer *big time* for what they would have done to Asher. So, let's make sure they do. Yeah?"

The archdemon's head stiffly turned back to face Jonas. And then the Prime sagged, hacking and heaving in air. The "snake" slithered around him, keeping him trapped.

The fire then began to peel away from Knox's head, gradually lowering, but his eyes were black. The demon hadn't retreated yet. It prowled toward her, face blank, taking stock of her wounds. "She will pay dearly for each bit of pain she inflicted on you," it promised in a chilling, disembodied voice.

"Damn fucking straight she will." Harper would see to that herself.

The demon stroked its fingertips down her throat. "I don't like the smell of your blood. She will—"

Something snapped tight around her ankle and yanked, making her hit the ground hard. *Tentacle*. Then she was skidding along the earth toward Alethea, who was still curled up on the floor but had managed to—

The archdemon pyroported to Alethea, long flames flickering

from its fingertips, and sliced out its hand. The flames cut right through the tentacle, hacking it clean off ... which meant half her arm went along with it. The bitch screamed. Really, it was a scream like nothing Harper had ever heard before in her life. An ear-ringing, bloodcurdling, stomach-churning sound that echoed all around them. And fuck if Harper gave a shit.

Standing, Harper glanced at Jonas. He seemed to be clamping his lips together, as if to stop himself from shouting out anything that would gain him the archdemon's attention.

Right then, said archdemon fisted his hand in Alethea's hair and yanked hard enough to pull her upper body off the floor. Obsidian eyes glittered at the she-demon, and Harper saw the lethal intent there. Honest to God, it was like dealing with a child with a one-track mind.

Harper rushed forward. "*Don't*. She *wants* you to kill her. Don't give her the easy death she's looking for."

Black eyes cut to Harper. "Nothing about her death will be easy."

"But death would be an escape from the pain, right? You want her to have an escape? Because I sure don't. Not for a long time. And think about it. What sounds scarier to the rest of the demon world—that we killed the people who targeted our son, or that we have them secured in your playroom where they're tortured for our amusement?" Personally, Harper thought it would add to the "targeting Asher would be a humungous mistake" message.

The demon stared at Harper, unblinking. Then it ceremoniously dumped Alethea on the floor, but not before doing something to her mind that made her pass out.

Harper let out a long breath. "Can we get back to Asher now? Speaking of Asher ... it would have been nice if you'd shared that he's an Anubis."

"If you had known the truth from the moment of his birth, you might have feared him. His demon would have sensed that fear and withdrawn from you. You needed to first see that he was primarily a child. A boy who also happened to be an Anubis."

While she got the entity's point ... "I would never have seen him as anything other than my son." But she couldn't really expect the demon to understand that—not when it couldn't experience love, let alone imagine the strength of parental love.

"His demon would never harm you," it assured her.

"Just as mine would never harm him."

The demon stroked its thumb along her jaw, and then it retreated. Knox gently pulled her to him and kissed her forehead. "The sight of you injured is pissing me off," he said, tone soft with menace.

She leaned into him. "I'll heal. First, we have to check on Asher, decide whether to let Drew live, and transfer Tweedle Dee and Tweedle Dum to the Chamber."

"Yes, we do." And Knox was looking forward to the latter. With a single thought, he made the flames of hell ease away. He'd stopped them from spreading beyond the circle, so their surroundings were still intact. Davis was standing with Noelle, who was holding Asher, while the sentinels guarded them.

Asher grinned at them, flashing his dimples and waving a hand that was holding Hound. "Ma!"

Crossing straight to him, Harper smiled and pulled him into her arms. "Hey, baby boy." He frowned at the sight of her injuries, but she distracted him by blowing raspberries on his palm.

Levi frowned. "What's with the snow?"

"We heard some kind of storm," began Tanner, back in his human form and wearing clothes that Knox knew he'd handed to Davis before he shifted shape. "But we couldn't see a thing

because the flames were too high. Speaking of flames ..."
Tanner gestured to the ones that were keeping Drew captive.

Knox turned to Harper. "Baby, any chance you can rein them
back in?" They were called by Harper, so they wouldn't answer
to him. She took a deep calming breath, and the flames eased.
Clarke had shifted back into his human form and was sitting on
the ground, pale and sweating.

"Levi, keep an eye on Jonas and Alethea, would you?" Knox
moved to stand in front of Clarke. The hellcat didn't stand—
possibly because he was naked, or possibly because he was too
drained from fighting off the incorporeal. Maybe it was a little
of both. "I don't suppose you'd care to explain why you were
working with Alethea and Jonas."

Clarke's jaw hardened. "It wasn't like that." His gaze slid to
Harper. "It wasn't."

"Then tell me what it *was* like," she said.

"*I can't.* I want to, but I can't. That fucking practitioner put me
under some kind of compulsion that binds me from being able to
tell anyone anything about him, Alethea, or Jonas."

Harper looked at Knox. "Is that true?"

"Let's find out." Knox plunged himself into Clarke's mind.
It took him only moments to confirm that ... "He's telling the
truth. I'm going to break the compulsion, Clarke. It's going to
hurt." To the hellcat's credit, he bore the mental pain in silence.
When it was over, he shuddered.

"Now tell us what you know," said Harper.

The hellcat looked up at her. "I never worked with them, I
swear. But I knew I'd fucked up and I needed to somehow make
up for it. Not just because you didn't deserve what I'd done,
but because I'd hurt my sister and left her torn. So, when I was
approached by a human without a scent who told me they could
help me get revenge on Knox, I figured it was the incorporeal

and I went along with it. The incorporeal led me to Charles, who insisted on the compulsion. I hadn't expected that, and I *really* hadn't expected to learn that Alethea was alive. I pretended to side with them."

"Why did they want *you*?" Harper asked.

"They somehow knew about my ability to detect what breed of demon a person is," replied Drew. "They thought I'd know what Thorne was. I lied and said he was a phoenix. Harper, I never intended to let them hurt you or your son. I figured I could help you somehow, and maybe redeem myself in the eyes of my sister."

"When did you go to the house where she'd been staying?"

"A few days ago. Alethea and the practitioner took me there. She wanted me to see the cage; wanted me to know her plans to put *you* in a cage like that. I think she was testing me to see if it would piss me off—she didn't quite trust that I'd let her kill you, even though I'd made out like I was more upset that you and I would never run Jolene's lair together than I was by you being with someone else.

"I wanted to go to another practitioner and have them undo the compulsion, but Jonas had taken my cell phone, and they watched me too carefully. I can hear thoughts directed at me, but I can't talk to someone telepathically. I had no way of asking for help or giving anyone a heads-up. I could only go along with their plan and hope I could step in to help you, which I did. I wasn't working with them, Harper. I swear to fucking God, I wasn't."

Knox tutted at him. "You're telling the truth, but not the entire truth. You'd wanted to redeem yourself, yes, but you'd also wanted to be Harper's hero; the one who saved the fucking day. That's why you didn't contact someone the moment the incorporeal approached you." Knowing that Knox had not only tortured him but robbed him of his memories had left Drew feeling weak and somewhat unmanned. This had been his attempt to prove to himself and others that he wasn't weak.

"If I'd thought they'd insist on a binding spell, I *would* have done," Drew insisted.

"Maybe, maybe not. I still very much doubt that Jolene will be happy with you. You broke her trust by staying instead of leaving for Cuba. But that's between you and her. Before I take you to her, I need to remove some of your memories." Clarke could *not* be allowed to remember that Asher was an Anubis or that Knox was an archdemon.

The hellcat ground his teeth. "Take the fucking memories. I owe it to Harper and Devon to fix my fuck-up."

"You need to take some memories from us, too," Davis guessed.

Knox looked at him. "I wish I didn't."

"Protecting Asher is important," said Noelle. "We would never betray you by sharing the knowledge, but that doesn't mean someone couldn't somehow access our memories. If we don't have the information, we can't be used against you."

"Thank you for understanding," Harper said. "Now let's get this done so we can get those two assholes to the Chamber."

Nodding, Knox turned to Clarke. "You first."

CHAPTER TWENTY

Two weeks later

Walking into the living room, Harper came to an abrupt halt. "What the fuck happened here?"

The four sentinels, looking varying degrees of frazzled, all sighed in relief as she entered. Cushions, books, DVDs, and Harper's knick-knacks were scattered around the room all over the hardwood floor. The lampshade was burned to a cinder, which explained the smell of smoke. Most notably, a ball of hellfire was hovering in midair.

Amidst all the chaos, Asher was sitting on the rug surrounded by his toys, Levi's cell phone, Tanner's car keys, Keenan's wallet, and Larkin's purse. He was also safely within his shield, *humming*.

Smoothing a hand down her raggedy jeans, Harper walked further into the room, high heels clicking on the floor—hobo or not, she was going to a party in heels. "I was gone, what, twenty minutes?"

"That's all your son needs to cause utter mayhem," said Tanner. "Basically, he decided it would be funny to pyroport stuff from the shelves into his little hands, and then he pyroported them in random places around the room. Once he got bored of that game, he started pyroporting our stuff right out of our pockets and adding them to his little collection over there on the rug."

"When I tried to get them back," Larkin cut in, "Asher playfully hurled a ball of hellfire at me. I dodged it, but it set the lampshade on fire. Of course, Asher thinks the whole thing is one big game, so he found it rather funny and saw no harm in throwing *more* balls of hellfire around the room. Levi's been catching them mid-air with his telekinesis and putting them out, which Asher also found funny."

Stifling a smile, Harper gave her son a stern look. "Asher."

He smiled. "Ma!" And then he was engulfed in flames that pyroported him right into her arms. She caught him with an *oof*. Since mastering that skill, he disappeared frequently—freaking her *the fuck* out—and then she'd have to run around the house searching for him, totally frantic. She often found him in the strangest places, including on top of the fridge. Her heart would be in her throat every time. Thankfully, he couldn't travel further than a few rooms away or he'd be off the estate every five minutes.

Harper gave the sentinels an apologetic look. "Sorry, guys, but it's hard to be mad at something this cute." Especially while he was wearing his little hobo suit, complete with the fake beard-scruff that Larkin had drawn on his chubby cheeks and chin.

Keenan inclined his head. "It *is* hard."

Harper was relieved that none of the sentinels were at all put-off by Asher being an Anubis. Agreeing with her that the sentinels would protect Asher best if they knew what he was,

Knox had chosen to let them keep their memory of it. Harper and Knox had also decided not to tell anyone else about Asher being an Anubis—not even Jolene or the girls, who they trusted to still accept him. The fewer people who knew, the better, since most people were no fonder of his kind than they were of archdemons.

Harper's only worry was that they couldn't count on Asher's demon to cloak itself at all times. Since the battle at the rainforest, the demon *had* occasionally dropped the cloak when Asher was at home—maybe because it trusted that its parents wouldn't reject it. As Asher's kind was so rare, it was unlikely that anyone would easily sense what he was even if they *were* exposed to his real psychic scent, so that was a little comforting.

Just then, Knox stalked into the room, fiddling with the collar of his deliberately haphazard suit. "You ready to leave, baby? You don't want to be late for Khloë's—what the fuck happened here?"

"I'll tell you in the car," said Harper, thinking it unfair that he looked just as sexy all rumpled as he did when stylishly suited.

Asher pyroported to the floor, toddled over to the rug, grabbed his Hound teddy, and then pyroported back to her.

"His balance is getting better," said Knox.

"I remember a time when he struggled to lift his head," said Harper. "Now he's walking. *Walking*. He'll be a whiny teenager before we know it."

Knox frowned. "No child of mine will be whiny."

"Think again."

Digging his flask out of his jacket, Keenan asked, "We going now?" He sounded about as excited as if she were taking him for a root canal.

"You don't have to come if you don't want to," Harper told him. "I know my cousin drives you crazy. Not that it's anything you should take personally. Khloë does it to everybody."

Grunting, Keenan took a long swig from his flask. "The

sooner she meets her anchor and has someone who can keep an eye on her and protect her from herself, the better." As Harper burst out laughing, the incubus frowned. "What's so funny?"

"It's just that she already met her anchor, and he's as unstable as she is."

Eyes flaring, Keenan turned rigid. "Who?"

"He'll be at the party—he'd never miss her birthday."

"Well, then, I'm definitely going." Keenan put his flask back in his pocket. "Someone needs to speak with him and make it clear that he's not protecting her as he should."

"Actually, Teague is a good anchor," said Harper. "You'd be surprised how much more shit she'd have gotten herself into over the years if it weren't for him. And he adores her."

"So, he's involved with her," Keenan assumed, voice flat.

"I didn't say that," said Harper.

Knox curled an arm around her shoulders. "Come on, let's go or we're going to be late."

They weren't late, but the party was in full swing when they arrived, which told Harper that her family had probably started it early just for themselves. People stood all around the extensive pretty garden, wearing old and raggedy clothes. The garden was amazingly vivid and serene with its colorful flowers, ice sculptures, rose bushes, lanterns hanging from the trees, and—at Khloë's request—the mermaid fountain.

But none of that was what made Tanner and Keenan skid to an abrupt halt in front of her, Knox, and Asher. No. Who *wouldn't* skid to a halt when a hellhorse was puffing and panting like a bull while playfully chasing little kids around the garden?

It was glorious. Elegant. Strongly muscled. Breathtaking with its large wide-set eyes, arched neck, long legs, inward-turning ear tips, and the onyx-black coat that had a metallic sheen. Its dark mane was as lush and luxurious as the high-carried tail that flowed down its back like a black river.

This particular hellhorse had a distinctive scar that slashed across its neck. The mark only added to its wild look. It also made the demon easily identifiable, especially if you were a fan of hellhorse racing. The sport often occurred in the stadium at the Underground.

Harper looked at Asher as his mind stroked hers in a "Wow, look, Mom!" way. She smiled. "I see it, baby." She moved further into the garden so that Asher could take a better look.

"Is that . . . ?" Keenan double-blinked. "Is that Teague Sullivan?"

"Yep," said Harper.

"His demon is probably the fastest hellhorse in existence."

Harper nodded. "Teague's also Khloë's anchor."

Keenan's mouth dropped open. "*He's* her anchor?"

"Uh-huh."

"You never mentioned it," said Knox, cupping Harper's hip.

Harper shrugged. "It never came up in conversation."

Khloë chose that moment to leap out of the bushes, wings extended, and land on the back of the hellhorse with a triumphant roar that had the kids laughing. It was well-known that you didn't climb onto the back of a hellhorse unless you were crazy . . . which said everything that needed to be said about Khloë really.

"Why would fate pair her with a demon who's no more stable than she is?" asked Keenan, baffled.

Harper shrugged. "Honestly, I don't think she'd have listened to anyone who couldn't relate to her on her level."

"You're here!" Devon dashed over and wrapped her arms around both Harper and Asher. "Oh, my God, how cute does he look with his fake beard?"

"Hey there, kitty cat," sang Tanner.

Devon scowled at him. "Stop sniffing me!" But he didn't. So she let out an honest-to-God hellcat hiss, which sounded like a mix of a lion's roar and a tiger's guttural hiss. And then she jerked away from Asher, eyes lit with amusement. "Harper, I'll swear he just cackled like Jolene."

"He did," said a voice behind them. "She's a bad influence on him."

With a sigh, Harper turned to Lou with a smile. Dressed in his usual scruffy manner, he fit right in. "I should have guessed you'd be here." Lou didn't require an invite—he went wherever the hell he liked.

Lou beamed at Asher. "Where's my favorite guy?"

"What time did you get here?" Knox asked him.

Lou pursed his lips. "I'm too stoned to be entirely sure, if I'm honest. And I'm rarely honest. But then, maybe that's a lie."

Knox sighed. "It was a simple question." But he wasn't surprised that he didn't get a straightforward answer. Lou went back to fussing over Asher, which made Knox frown. "You seem almost ... nice when you're with Asher. It's an odd thing to witness."

Head jerking back, Lou echoed, "Nice? I am not nice. Goodness and I got married *way* too young. The divorce was quick and painless." Glancing around, Lou rolled back his shoulders, seeming edgy. "The atmosphere is so ... relaxed. I don't like it."

"Everyone's feeling better now that the Horsemen are out of the picture," said Harper. Alethea and Jonas were tucked away in Knox's Chamber, and they had regular *visitors*. Their lair had already instated another Prime, who seemed much more suited to the position than Jonas had been. And no, Harper wasn't just saying that because she despised the asshole. "Thanks to us, the mystery has been unraveled."

Lou snickered. "Oh, *please*. That could have been done by a sedated amoeba. Come on, it was so obvious—" The cap on his head abruptly disappeared in a spurt of fire and then reappeared in Asher's hand, who then let out a fake laugh. Lou sighed. "If anyone does somehow manage to take this kid, they'll bring him back in a hurry. He's a handful."

Asher looked at Knox, demon rising to the fore. Knox's demon also surfaced, and the two entities stared at each other. It wasn't uncommon.

Harper sighed. "I hate it when they do that. It makes me nervous that Knox's demon has an invasive bond with Asher's demon. Even when Asher was in the womb, they seemed to communicate somehow. Obviously, not with words, but impressions and emotions."

Lou's eyes widened in delight. "Ooh, maybe they're plotting Earth domination."

Sighing again, Harper shook her head. "You're completely whacked."

"Why is he whacked?" asked Knox as his entity retreated. "Not that I disagree."

"Your son *is* capable of global domination, Harper."

She ground her teeth. "Lou—"

The devil slashed his hand through the air. "It is pure truth. There are no variables. If you can't handle that reality—" A sneer twisted his face. "Oh, not *her*."

Noticing that Jolene was slowly making her way toward them, Harper smiled and said quietly, "You know what, Lou? I think, in some weird morbid way, you actually like her."

His face scrunched up. "Your opinion has absolutely *no* practical basis." And that seemed to bother him more than the opinion itself.

Reaching them, Jolene doled out greetings and hugs before

sparing the devil a glance. "Well, hello, Lou," she said. "What are you doing over here?"

He gave her a brittle smile. "Oh, we're just chittin' the chat. You can go now."

Jolene tutted. "Really, Lou, must you be so rude?"

"Um, yes. Yes, I must."

"It won't make me march off in a huff. You know me."

"And I wish I didn't."

"Oh, how you lie. But you know, I genuinely respect just how fabulously honest you can look when you bullshit people."

He softened. "Really? Aw, thanks. You're a pretty good liar too." He moved a little closer to her. "You know, Harper has a theory."

"A theory?" Jolene echoed.

"Yes. A theory that . . . well, that I might actually like you."

"Hmm." Jolene's eyes warmed. "Maybe I actually like you. Perhaps I even *like* you like you."

"Perhaps I feel the same. Maybe we should even . . . *explore* that."

"Maybe we should."

And then the pair of them burst out laughing like they'd never heard anything more ridiculous in their entire lives.

Shaking her head, Harper turned just as Khloë, Raini, and Teague—who was no longer in his hellhorse form—headed their way. He was the definition of tall, dark, and handsome. And Harper didn't fail to notice the way Larkin ate him up with her eyes.

"Hey, Harper, how are you doing?" Teague asked.

"Good, thanks." She introduced him to Knox and then Asher, who burrowed into Harper, smiling shyly. As she then went on to introduce the sentinels, she smiled to herself when Teague gave Larkin one of his panty-dropping smiles.

He clicked his fingers as he looked at Tanner. "Wait, you're a hellhound. I saw you race a few times. You're good."

"Back atcha," said Tanner.

Devon leaned into Khloë. "Oh no, look, they're *bonding.* What do we do?"

Tanner gave her a gentle smile. "No need to be jealous, kitten."

As the others chatted, Harper touched Keenan's mind and said, *You don't need to keep glaring at Teague. He and Khloë aren't together. Don't tell me you wouldn't care if they were.*

It's none of my business. Keenan shrugged, nonchalant. *It just came as a surprise that she was anchored because, you know, she doesn't talk about him.*

Khloë's chatty, but she doesn't talk about herself much.

Knox lowered his mouth to Harper's ear. "Who are you talking to?"

"Keenan."

"Hmm." Knox pressed a kiss to her neck. *You're standing here wearing a scruffy checked shirt and holey jeans with your hair styled into a messy ponytail. And yet, I just want to ravish the shit out of you right here.*

She swallowed, feeling herself go damp. *Stop that or this will feel like a very long night.* But he didn't stop it. Of course he didn't stop it. He kept on teasing her with kisses to her neck, flicks of his tongue to her earlobe, and strokes of his hand over her ass.

By the time they were ready to leave the party, she was also ready to jump him. Asher fell asleep on the car ride home, so Harper tucked him into bed before joining Knox in the master bedroom ... which, for some reason, was in utter darkness.

Frowning, she reached for the light switch. Her hand was snatched from the air, and then she was spun around and caged against the wall with Knox's front plastered to her back, his hands pinning her wrists either side of her head.

Harper gasped. "Hey!" She struggled and squirmed, but he simply pressed her even closer to the wall, snuggling his hard cock against her ass.

"Shh," Knox said softly into her ear. "We need those jeans off." Using his psychic hands, he snapped open her fly and shoved down her jeans. "Better. Much better." He scraped his teeth over the crook of her neck, breathing her in. "I love your smell. Love it even more when you're wet for me." Transferring both her wrists to one hand, Knox slid the other hand down her side, fisted her long shirt, and bunched it up around her waist.

"Wait, let me turn—"

He roughly grabbed a fistful of her hair and snatched her head back. "When I want you to direct how things go, I'll tell you. But it won't be tonight. Not when my cock has been hard for you for hours. So here's what you're going to do—you're going to stay nice and still while I have my way with you. Don't fuck with me, Harper. Just take what I give you."

With his hold on her hair, Knox twisted her head and took her mouth. Her taste burst through him, so fucking sweet, so fucking addictive. Hungry and dominating, he ate at her mouth as he tore off her panties. He felt the tension in her, felt her defiant nature rising. Before it could surface, he cupped her hard with a psychic hand.

Harper inhaled sharply as two icy fingers plunged inside her. Her pussy clamped down on them, and he growled low in her ear; the sound made the little hairs on her nape rise. "Knox—"

"Don't come until I say."

Harper hissed in annoyance, which earned her thigh a sharp slap. "Ow!"

"Then behave." He ground his cock against her ass each time he thrust his icy fingers deep and hard, knowing the strange heat emanating from them would make her pussy spasm and blaze unbearably. He also knew she liked that he had her completely pinned. Liked that she couldn't move. Liked that she couldn't think about anything other than the release that was tumbling toward her.

Her pussy superheated around his fingers, and Knox knew she was close. He shoved a third psychic finger inside her and curved it just right. "Come, Harper, let me feel—Good girl." Her back arched as she came with a choked moan that was like a fist around his cock. "Now you get fucked."

Releasing her hands, Knox whipped off her shirt and bra and then tossed them aside. "Hands on the wall," he ordered. "That's it, just like that." Gripping her hips, he backed up a little, taking her with him, and then snapped open his fly. His cock sprang out, hot and hard and aching like a bitch. "Fuck, baby, this is gonna be rough." And fast.

"Rough is good."

Closing his hand around her breast, he nipped at her neck. "Yeah, rough is good." He sank his teeth in her shoulder and slammed his cock into her tight pussy, going balls-deep in one thrust. He groaned as her walls, hot and slick, contracted around him. "You can come when you're ready."

Harper's nails scraped the wall as he fucked in and out of her pussy, his balls slapping her with every savage thrust. He'd warned her that it would be rough, and he hadn't been kidding. But she loved it. Loved his grunts and groans and bite of his fingers on her hips. One little touch to her clit would set her off.

Almost as if he heard the thought, he used his psychic fingers to part her folds. But he didn't touch her clit. He let her feel the cool air, made her wait until it hurt. *Fuck this.* She went to take care of it herself, but a psychic hand slapped hers away. *Oh, the hell no.*

Knox tensed as the air chilled. Harper's head turned his way, but it wasn't her who glanced back at him. It was her demon. And then its hand reached back and grabbed his forearm. He hissed as the flesh beneath its grip began to burn. He'd felt that burn before. Knew the demon was branding him.

Fuck. Knox furiously powered into her. Brutal. Merciless. Out of control. Unable to hold on any longer, he bit out, "Come." Her pussy clamped around him as her head fell back and a scream tore out of her throat. Knox locked his teeth on her shoulder as he rammed his cock deep and exploded, shooting jet after jet of come inside her. Every ounce of strength seemed to then leave her, and she went limp in his arms.

Harper was in an awesome, post-orgasmic daze as he carried her to the bed. But she wasn't so dazed that she didn't watch and enjoy the show as he stripped off his clothes. And yeah, okay, she was a little nervous as he studied the new brand on his forearm. Like the others, it was all tribal solid lines and thick curves.

Turning, he asked, "Does it link to the brands on my nape and back?"

"Actually, yes, it does," she realized.

Facing her again, he arched an amused brow. "So, is your demon's plan to eventually have me wearing a full-body brand? Is it putting the brand together, little by little?"

She smiled. "Possibly."

Sliding into bed, Knox pulled her close. "I guess it's a good thing I like being marked by your demon." Splaying his hand around her throat, he kissed her, licking into her mouth. Pulling back, he watched the sea-blue shade of her eyes swirl and darken into an emerald green. Knox knew that he'd never get bored of watching her eyes do that. "Did you have a good time tonight?"

"I got to watch Lou climb a huge mermaid fountain while singing 'Under the Sea' in a very bad Caribbean accent. What's not to like?"

Knox grimaced. "It was hard to watch. Even harder than when Khloë sang 'Bed of Roses' into a non-existent microphone as she literally leaped into a rose bush."

Harper winced. "Yeah, that had to hurt. But she carried on singing. Didn't miss a note."

The imp also hadn't missed the tension between Keenan and Teague. Khloë's anchor had quickly sensed that Keenan had an interest in her and—as protective and meddling as anchors were prone to be—Teague had sent the incubus lots of *back off* looks. And, in typical Khloë fashion, the female imp dealt with it by saying to Teague, "If you guys are going to have a dick measuring contest, I think you just might lose because Keenan's is a *monster.*"

"Do you think you can let go of it yet?"

She blinked at Knox's question. "Let go of what?"

He curled her hair behind her ear. "The tension that's been your best friend since we discovered the Horsemen existed."

She sighed. "I really thought I'd be able to just relax now that they're no longer a threat. I'm relieved that it's all over, but I don't know if I properly *believe* it yet. It's weird not having danger hovering over our heads."

"There'll always be danger lurking, but I don't think it'll come too close to us. Not when I have a mate who can be absolutely terrifying when she chooses to be."

Harper's mouth curved. "So you fear me now. Good."

He hesitated. "I'm not saying *I* fear you. But I'm conceding that you can *be* scary."

She frowned, incredulous. "You still don't fear me?"

"Of course not."

"I sliced off that woman's toes with a flaming stiletto blade, one by one . . . and you don't find me scary?"

Fighting a smile, Knox rolled onto his back and draped her

over him. "It's hard to fear someone who once told me they loved me while bent over the toilet with vomit in their hair."

Harper cringed. "Stop. You fear me. You do. Accept it."

He skimmed his fingers through her hair, lips twitching. "You know, when you first told me you loved me, you shocked the absolute shit out of me."

The memory made her smile. "I know. Back then, I hadn't thought you'd ever feel the same, mostly because I hadn't thought that 'love' was anywhere on your emotional scale."

"It was on my scale a long, long time ago. But then that scale shrunk." He'd become someone hard. Cold. He couldn't say he was now either warm or cuddly, but he was no longer at risk of losing himself. And that was all because of the very person sprawled on top of him.

Knox caught her face between his hands. "I love you, baby. Always will."

She kissed him. "I love you right back, so I'd say all is good."

"Yeah?"

"Yeah. You love me, I love you, our son is safe, and you finally fear me. So all is definitely good."

"I wouldn't say that I f—"

"Just go with it, Thorne. Just go with it."

Acknowledgements

I have to start by saying a huge thank you to my husband for his ongoing support and patience, and for listening to me rant about characters who won't do as they're told.

Thanks so much to my kids—my ever-happy and even-tempered son, and my cheerful and incredibly mischievous daughter—because your combined natures helped create baby Asher.

Thanks to everyone at Piatkus for your support and insight, especially my very patient editor, Anna Boatman, and the greatest cover designer that ever existed, Ellen Rockell.

I also have to say a major thanks to my assistant, Melissa Rice, for being so amazing and for making sure I don't spend too long in the writing cave.

Last but certainly not least, thanks to every person who has taken the time to read the book. I hope you enjoyed Harper and Knox's story. Now onto the secondary characters . . .